REFLECTION

CAMILLE PETERS

To all those who fear they're never enough—
you are of great worth.

CHAPTER 1

C7/Y/L y hand shook where it hovered, poised to knock on the door of the study where my parents had asked me to meet them. The reason for the visit wasn't a mystery; I'd known for several months now that this day would come. Despite having had time to prepare myself, I still wasn't ready to hear the news that would change my life forever.

I took a wavering breath. *You can do this, Rhea. Be brave.* But despite being the eldest princess of Draceria, I didn't *feel* brave. I never did.

I took a deep breath and knocked before nodding to the footman standing outside the door, inviting him to open it. Mother and Father sat with their heads bent together, conversing quietly. They looked up at my entrance.

"There you are, Rhea." Mother stood to greet me with a hug while Father looked on with a proud smile, already pleased by the answer he knew I'd give in response to their news. He wasn't wrong; I knew my duty, although knowing it didn't make it any easier to fulfill.

He motioned to the settee. "Please have a seat, dear."

I perched on the edge, trying not to appear nervous. My parents took seats across from me with all the regal bearing expected of the king and queen.

"You wanted to see me?" I managed to keep my voice steady, a small victory.

Mother took my hand. "Your father and I have something to tell you."

I braced myself. Mother glanced at Father, allowing him the honor of sharing the dreaded words that would alter my life forever.

"We've been in contact with the Queen of Malvagaria, and all the arrangements are finally in place. We've invited her and her son for a visit so that you and Prince Briar can get to know one another before your betrothal."

I released a shaky breath. There it was. I wasn't surprised, as Mother and Father had told me a few months ago that during my brother's wedding reception, the Queen of Malvagaria had expressed interest in forging an alliance between our two kingdoms. The alliance made sense; not only was Draceria Malvagaria's only neighbor, but we were their primary trading partner.

What baffled me was why she was interested in having her son, the crown prince, marry *me*. I was an unremarkable princess, especially compared to my two superior younger sisters, both of whom were of age to wed. But I kept my confusion locked away, just as I kept every other emotion; it was safer that way.

Mother and Father were still awaiting an answer, so I forced a smile. "I'm pleased for the opportunity to get to know Prince Briar before our engagement." Especially considering I'd only met the crown prince a handful of times over the years; from what I remembered, he was a rather sullen man, even more so than my ex-fiancé, Crown Prince Deidric of Sortileya.

The familiar pain I fought to suppress returned to attack anew. I forced it away. Now wasn't the time to remember my broken engagement.

"That's what we were hoping, but"—Mother squeezed my hand—"please remember that your father and I would never force you into any arrangement that you're not comfortable with, especially after what happened with Liam…" She bit her lip guiltily.

Father rested his hand on her shoulder. "It's alright, darling. It all ended well for him."

She dabbed her eyes with a handkerchief. "I know, and I'm still so relieved. But I couldn't bear to watch another one of our children endure a situation similar to his. No political arrangement is worth the cost of our children's happiness."

"That's why we're arranging for Prince Briar to visit *before* signing any contracts." Father turned to me. "If you find you don't suit, please be open with us."

Even though I knew they were sincere in their willingness to put my wishes above the interests of our kingdom, I also understood that doing so would disappoint them, for it was their duty to see to the welfare of our subjects…a duty that was also mine. I'd known it my entire life and wouldn't falter.

"I understand." I took a steadying breath in an attempt to calm my nerves. "When are they to arrive?"

"At week's end."

My heart sank. *So soon?* But perhaps it was for the best so I wouldn't have time to get even more anxious than I already was. My chest tightened and my mind's familiar taunts returned before I had a chance to suppress them.

He'll hate you too, just like Deidric did.

I squeezed my eyes shut, willing the fearful words to leave me. They quieted but lingered, lying in wait to make another attack soon.

"Rhea, dear?"

Mother's face was twisted with worry. I forced a smile. "I have no doubt their visit will go well. Then we'll be aligned with a powerful kingdom."

Father frowned. "That's true...but Rhea, even though we'd be pleased with such an alliance, please know we're sincere in that we'd never force you to—"

"Liam's fell through with Lyceria, as did mine with Sortileya. This one has to go through."

My parents studied me closely, as if trying to pry off the rigid mask I wore in order to steal a glimpse of my true feelings. But they wouldn't succeed; I'd long since trained myself to keep my emotions hidden.

"There's no doubt this would be a wonderful alliance for us," Father said. "Not to mention I'd be pleased to have one of our daughters as the future queen of our primary neighbor, but this isn't the only potential alliance you can make. You could always marry Prince Briar's younger brother, or any of the four princes of Bytamia, or even Prince Nolan of Lyceria."

"Bytamia is too far away." Being aligned with a kingdom across the sea wouldn't be nearly as beneficial as being aligned with our neighbor. "Besides, their crown prince already has an arrangement with Princess Seren of Sortileya, and Crown Prince Nolan is likely not an option, considering our relations with Lyceria have been sour ever since Liam's betrothal with Lavena fell through. That leaves the three Bytamian princes, and none of them would provide the opportunity for me to become queen."

My stomach knotted at the thought. I didn't really want to be queen, but I knew Father desired it for me, which meant I should aspire to it, too.

"Indeed." Father was still perusing my expression. I fought to keep it neutral. He finally nodded, seeming satisfied. "Very well, I'm pleased you understand the situation. I hope you and Briar discover you're a good match, but if it doesn't work out, then we'll arrange a different marriage for you. All will be well." He patted my hand.

I nodded again. "It will be." But I didn't believe my own words, especially as my constant fear attacked anew.

What if you fail...again?

No, I couldn't. But how could I not when I still didn't understand what I'd done wrong the first time?

I SAT RIGIDLY in my seat, fighting the urgency to pace the parlor as my gaze repeatedly darted towards the window for any sign of the carriage bearing the Malvagarian royal crest.

Oblivious to my tension, Elodie wriggled excitedly beside me, her embroidery forgotten on her lap. "This is so exciting, Rhea. You're to marry the crown prince of such a wealthy kingdom, and Briar is so handsome."

My romantic younger sister thought *every* prince was handsome, even those whom she'd never met.

Elodie's embroidery slid to the floor as she swiveled in her seat to peek once more out the window with a disappointed frown. "The carriage still isn't here. I don't think I can bear to wait a moment longer."

I bent down to retrieve her embroidery. "Perhaps this will help you pass the time. Would you like some help?" I knew she'd been struggling with some of the more complicated stitches.

She wrinkled her nose at her unfinished pattern. "Who cares about embroidery when you're about to meet your future fiancé?" She pulled back the drapes to peer outside again with another sigh of longing. "They're taking a rather long time."

"It's a long journey, Elodie," Aveline said from her seat on the neighboring settee.

"How far, exactly?" Elodie asked.

Aveline didn't even look up from her needlework, nor did her perfect posture falter. "Three days, which you'd know if you ever paid attention in our studies."

Elodie rolled her eyes. "I do pay attention...to *interesting* subjects like music and dance, not dull facts such as how many days' journey it is between the five different kingdoms." She returned her gaze to the window for a minute more before swiveling to face me. "How can you sit so patiently when your future husband is on his way to the palace?"

Future husband...my stomach knotted. How could we marry when I knew almost nothing about him? I knew I should at least be grateful my parents cared enough for my welfare to allow me to get to know him before the wedding, but deep down I knew I really had no choice, despite the illusion I did. Which meant I'd have to learn to care for Briar.

Hopefully he wasn't as sullen as I remembered.

Elodie was looking at me expectantly, awaiting an answer.

"I'm pleased for the chance to renew our acquaintance." It was a diplomatic answer that didn't reveal my true feelings on the matter. "I'm sure he's amiable. I remember him being rather...proper."

Just like Aveline. My gaze darted towards her as she hovered over her embroidery. Why wasn't Briar pursuing *her*? The two would make a fine pair; their temperaments seemed better matched, not to mention she was more beautiful than I was.

Everyone is more beautiful than you are.

While my sisters were oblivious to my apprehension, it wasn't lost on my brother and his wife. Liam and Anwen had

6

been watching me carefully, Liam with protective worry, Anwen with compassion.

She leaned forward. "Are you alright, Rhea? You seem nervous."

I forced a tight smile. "I'm fine." *Liar*.

"Of course you're not," Liam said. "How can you be when you're expected to marry someone you hardly know? Having narrowly escaped a similar scenario myself, I greatly sympathize."

"We're not going to force a union between Rhea and Briar," Mother said.

He lifted his eyebrows. "So no contracts have been signed?"

"Not yet."

Liam relaxed back against his seat. "Lucky break, Rhea. In that case, there's still time to wriggle out of the arrangement. Do you need any tips? Because I have plenty. You'll certainly need them; Briar isn't exactly a basket of fun."

"Don't try to influence her." Aveline finally looked up from her embroidery to glare at him. "And don't encourage her to abandon her duty. She's not you."

He lifted his hands in defense. "I had a perfect excuse for my actions: I was engaged to *Princess Lavena*." His mouth twisted on her name. "Duty isn't strong enough to stomach *that* match."

"It all worked out," Aveline said.

"Only because a miracle occurred." He gave Anwen a snuggle and the two shared a smile.

My heart lurched at the sweet display, for it was a reminder that my dreams of someone falling in love with me would never occur. I'd always known a love match was impossible. Despite being a princess, I was entirely average, a fact that meant I would never secure any man's affections, let alone a crown prince's. We'd undoubtedly have a loveless union. The most I could hope for would be amiability between us, children to cherish, and the opportunity to make a difference for the Malvagarian people who'd soon become my subjects.

Some of the nerves I'd been attempting to mask must have shown on my face, for Elodie rested her hand over mine. "Don't worry, Rhea, I'm sure it'll be alright." She frowned. "Although as handsome as Briar is, there is a downside to your match, considering he's supposedly cursed."

"That's just a rumor, Elodie," Mother said. "Please assure me you have enough sense not to bring up such a thing when our guests are visiting."

"Of course I won't." But Elodie's smile was rather wicked. *Oh dear.*

Anwen tipped her head back to look at Liam. "I'm not aware of such a rumor."

Liam leaned closer and lowered his voice to a loud whisper. "It's said that all four Malvagarian royal children are cursed in some way. Nobody knows exactly what Prince Briar's curse is, but you can be sure I'll investigate during his visit in order to discover not only his, but the rest of—"

"Please, Liam." Mother's plea cut him off.

Liam winked at his wife. "I'll share the rest of the gossip later."

"I still don't understand how someone as odious as you ended up with the sweetest woman," Aveline said sourly.

Liam grinned. "It was undoubtedly due to my incredible charm. Isn't that right, darling?"

"You are rather charming," she said. He kissed the top of her head and she smiled up at him before turning back to me. "Please don't be nervous; I have no doubt Prince Briar will see all there is to admire in you. You're such a compassionate person."

"As always, my wife is right," Liam said. "Briar would be a

fool not to see what a wonderful woman you are; the trick will be getting *you* to fall in love with *him*." He wrinkled his nose. "Unfortunately it won't be difficult; you've always demonstrated kindness to all you meet—the servants, our grumpy old tutors, even rabbits."

Anwen furrowed her brow. "Rabbits?"

Liam chuckled and I fought my own smile. I knew which story he was about to tell; it was one he told often.

"Rhea and I spent most of our childhood frolicking in the orchard. One day we happened upon an injured rabbit. My taste buds immediately started to water as I imagined taking it to Cook so she could prepare rabbit stew."

Anwen covered her mouth to suppress her smile. "Oh Liam, you didn't."

Liam's grin was unrepentant. "Believe me, I *nearly* did, only Rhea refused to allow it. Instead she felt sorry for my supper and insisted on bringing it home in order to nurse it back to health. She kept it as a pet for years, and it lived to a ripe old age. If she feels sorry for injured rabbits, she'll undoubtedly feel sorry for a crown prince who lacks a personality and marry him out of pity."

"Really, Liam." Mother gave him a scolding look and he lowered his eyes in remorse. "You shouldn't—"

Elodie's excited squeal interrupted her. "The Malvagarian royal carriage just rolled through the gates. They're here!"

"Then you'd best not be seen gawking from the window," Aveline said wryly.

Elodie sighed but obediently settled beside me, poised like a proper princess, with no sign of her previous restlessness. Aveline set aside her embroidery and we all turned our attention to the door, waiting in silent anticipation for the footman to announce our guests.

I clenched and unclenched bunches of my skirt. *Perhaps*

he'll be better than you remember. Perhaps you two will be well matched after all. Perhaps—

The footman entered with a bow and my breath hitched. "Announcing Her Majesty the Queen of Malvagaria and her son, the Crown Prince Briar."

We all stood. I held my breath as the footman stepped aside and the queen swept into the room, followed by the most serious-looking man I'd ever seen.

The Queen of Malvagaria was striking in her beauty, with a youthful face despite her advancing years. She wore a crimson traveling gown that matched her lips, and her raven-black hair was adorned elegantly, making her look as if she were attending a ball rather than having just finished her third long day of travel.

I shifted my attention to Prince Briar, also dark-haired and dark-eyed, and wearing a blooming red rose pinned to his lapel. He stood with his hands clasped behind his back, his expression stoic as he listened to the exchange of pleasantries and inquires about their travels. I perused his face hungrily, trying to discern his personality, but the only thing that stood out were the dark circles beneath his eyes that made him appear exhausted.

In the first lull, I stepped forward for my own greeting. "It's a pleasure to welcome you. Thank you for traveling all this way for a visit. I hope your time here is pleasant." I curtsied.

The queen stared at me, and in my paranoia I was certain she was scrutinizing me for flaws. I shifted beneath her perusal.

Her expression quickly smoothed into a smile. "The pleasure is ours, dear. My, aren't you a darling little thing." Her smile widened, showing unnaturally straight and white teeth. The queen turned to Briar and tipped her head in my direction, beckoning him to step forward. "Isn't Princess Rheanna a charming girl?"

Prince Briar gave me a bored look but said nothing. My heart squeezed. We'd only just met and already he seemed unimpressed with me.

Are you really so surprised? You're entirely unremarkable.

It was one thing to believe that, but quite another to have my self-assessment confirmed, and by my *intended* at that.

The proper introductions made, Mother had a servant show our guests to their rooms, announcing that dinner would be in an hour's time after they'd had a chance to rest.

The queen gave a smile in return while Prince Briar looked entirely indifferent. The moment Prince Briar's back was turned, Liam raised his eyebrows at me with a look that clearly indicated he wasn't impressed, meaning his invitation to come up with an elaborate escape from the union was still open.

"He's rather...serious," Elodie whispered to me the moment the door closed behind the queen and Prince Briar. Dread pooled my stomach.

Perhaps he's simply tired. But I didn't believe my attempt to cheer myself up. The small bit of hope I'd been secretly clinging to faded. Had I really expected anything else?

I WISH this evening were over so I could escape.

But that wouldn't be the proper thing to do. No, instead I was expected to sit here and die a slow, torturous death. I was seated at the table next to Prince Briar and across from the Queen of Malvagaria, a seating arrangement that would allow me to begin getting to know my future family.

The problem was I didn't know how to begin such an overwhelming task. I frantically searched for something to say, but my shyness choked the words before they'd even formed, keeping me silent.

Around me, my family conversed with our guests with ease, asking for further details about their travels, the picturesque scenery that was a trademark of the long journey, and how things were faring in Malvagaria. I tried several times to join the conversation, but each time the words died in my throat.

Liam, who sat on my other side, patted my knee, his silent communication that he was aware of my struggles and his sweet encouragement not to allow them to overcome me. I gave him a small smile, which he returned with an understanding one of his own. I could always count on Liam.

Prince Briar didn't talk much until Elodie engaged him in a short conversation. I watched, envious of her ability to converse with charm and ease, just like Liam could. Surely she'd be a better match with Prince Briar than I would. Why then had *I* been chosen instead?

You can't just sit here mute, Rhea; say something. Heart beating wildly, I took a wavering breath and turned to our guests. "How were your travels?" My voice shook, betraying my nerves.

The Queen of Malvagaria's smile tightened. "As I said before, the journey was long but quite pleasant. Draceria's countryside is unparalleled."

My breath hitched. *As she'd said before?* Too late I remembered she'd already spoken of their trip. *Oh dear.* My cheeks warmed. I resisted the urge to bury my humiliation in my hands.

"Draceria is quite picturesque," I continued shakily. "From what I remember, Malvagaria is lovely as well."

The Queen of Malvagaria tilted her head, as if inviting me to say more, but I wasn't sure what else to add—my mind remained stubbornly blank. My indecision stretched on too long, making a belated reply almost more awkward than not continuing at all. I lowered my eyes to my lap. Once again, my attempts at a conversation had failed.

"Tell me, Rheanna, what are your hobbies?"

The queen again. I stole a peek up at her before glancing sideways at Prince Briar. Shouldn't *he* be the one asking me such questions? But he was still focused on his roast duck and parsnips.

I took a steadying breath. "I like—" I faltered. Most of the my pastimes were rather unexciting, but it would never do to admit such a thing. "I like to take long walks."

"How lovely." The queen replied smoothly. "Briar enjoys the outdoors as well. He spends most of his time in the gardens. Don't you, Briar?"

The prince looked up, his gaze meeting first his mother's, then mine. I searched his dark eyes for any sign of emotion, but his expression was flat, indifferent, and tired. "I find the outdoors quite pleasing. I hope you and I can spend some time exploring the gardens during my visit."

He returned to his food, finished with our conversation before it had even begun. Prince Briar was just like Deidric, who hadn't made much of an effort to converse with me either. Clearly I was a boring conversation partner. As if confirming my silent assessment, Prince Briar pressed his hand to his mouth, suppressing a yawn.

Liam squeezed my knee, a gesture that calmed me enough to make another attempt at conversation. I began speaking of the activities we had planned for their stay. My efforts felt forced, as if each word were being excavated. The queen's tight expression became more and more strained as I struggled. She obviously wasn't very impressed with me.

Stop jumping to conclusions.

But I couldn't help it, not when I felt like each passing moment in Her Majesty's presence was a test, one I was failing miserably. Why else would she be watching me so attentively? It wasn't just me who had captured her shrewd attention, but Liam as well. Surely she couldn't find any fault with him, not when he was so jovial and charming as he carried out his big-brother duty of trying to dispel the awkwardness I was silently suffering from. However, despite his friendliness and frequent jokes, Prince Briar never cracked a smile.

My brother frowned at him in disapproval before he leaned towards me. "The man is impossible," he murmured out of the corner of his mouth. "I've seen suits of armor make better conversation than him. Perhaps my favorite story will finally crack Prince Boring's hard shell." He winked at me as he straightened and lifted his goblet towards Prince Briar. "I see you've all been admiring my goblet." Liam slowly turned it in his hand so the candlelight glistened off the jewels.

Prince Briar glanced up with a raised eyebrow; he'd obviously taken no notice of Liam's goblet. He seemed to wrestle with himself before, like any proper prince, choosing the polite path. "Indeed. Is there a story behind it?"

Liam smirked, his eyes flashing in triumph that he'd gotten Prince Briar to ask. Beside him, Anwen smiled indulgently, knowing exactly what was coming next. For the first time all evening, I felt the beginnings of a smile on my own lips. This was one of Liam's favorite stories, and even though I'd heard it dozens of times over the years, I never tired of hearing him tell it.

"Funny you should ask, for there is. I've always been fascinated with the reigns of past kings. Years ago, I read an account of one of the ancient Dracerian kings who had the uncanny ability of making enemies wherever he went, which resulted in many attempts to poison him. Determined to thwart his would-be assassins, he sought the help of a renowned alchemist to create a place setting that would be immune to any poison. His request was granted, and for the remainder of his life, this king only ate from that place setting and enjoyed a long and healthy reign before dying of old age."

Liam paused with a look that invited questions. I fought my emerging grin. While Liam relished the opportunity of telling a good story, he loved an eager audience even more, one who asked follow-up questions that encouraged him to keep sharing.

Prince Briar said nothing for awhile, but then, as if realizing he was expected to, he asked dully, "What does such a fantastic story have to do with your goblet? Are you claiming this is one of the pieces made for the paranoid king?"

Liam's grin grew. "Indeed it is. The complete setting mysteriously disappeared after the king's death and hasn't been seen since, even though past kings searched for it for centuries. But my ancestors' failure was no deterrent for me. I spent years combing our palace's many passageways, several of which lead to ancient treasures hidden within the walls. I encountered many obstacles—fire-breathing dragons, weeks spent lost in the labyrinth of tunnels, decoding secret maps, battling assassins and fellow treasure hunters—"

From down the table, Aveline rolled her eyes, while Elodie whispered, "Ooh, this story gets better each time he tells it."

"It was a worthy quest that, after many years, finally paid off." He held the goblet up. It was solid gold and encrusted with jewels and intricately carved designs, far too elaborate for casual dining. "Do you know where I finally discovered it?"

He gave Prince Briar an expectant look, prompting him to speak. After a moment of clear reluctance, he humored him. "Do tell. Where?" he asked without any enthusiasm.

Ignoring his audience's blank stares, Liam leaned closer

and lowered his voice mysteriously. "Within one of the many labyrinths I discovered a hidden alcove, one which I must have passed dozens of times. Inside was a single bookshelf packed with dozens of books, likely hundreds of years old and shrouded in cobwebs. I investigated and found a secret panel, behind which I discovered an ancient map. Etched in fading ink was a message: *'The secret to a long and healthy life can be found hidden within a tomb.'*"

He wriggled his eyebrows and Elodie giggled. Prince Briar's expression remained impassive.

"I puzzled over the riddle for weeks before the answer came to me—*hidden within a tomb* was a play on words. I scoured the bookshelf and discovered the goblet within a hollowed-out *tome* entitled *Burials of Ancient King.*" Liam sat back in his seat with a pleased grin.

Prince Briar didn't respond. Liam frowned, for this was the first time his story hadn't received some reaction. At Liam's expectant look, Prince Briar quietly sighed, as if he found his duty to humor our crown prince wearying. "And you've been using it ever since?" he asked dully.

Liam grinned widely. "Indeed. This goblet is my lucky charm. Ever since I started using it, I've never even had a cold." The look he gave it was almost reverent. "No one ever drinks out of it except for me."

Prince Briar glanced at me with a raised brow, seeking validation for my brother's story. "It's true, Liam is never without his goblet—he uses it at every meal; no one else dares drink from it."

"Yes, that honor is strictly for the one who solved the centuries-old mystery." And he raised the goblet and took a long drink.

The Queen of Malvagaria smiled in amusement. "Indeed. What an interesting story. You have quite the imagination, Prince Liam."

Liam beamed. "I do what I can to make life exciting."

He glanced at Prince Briar for his reaction to the marvelous tale, but he looked almost bored as he returned to his food without further comment.

Liam frowned before leaning over to whisper in my ear. "That was one of my best stories and he didn't even crack a smile; I've gotten a better reaction out of a stone statue. Perhaps I should try a different tactic—regaling him with stories about *you*."

"Liam, there's no need—"

He ignored my pleas and enthusiastically shared some of the adventures from our childhood. Although most of the stories were quite humorous, Prince Briar's indifferent expression didn't change.

By the third story—an account of how he and I had frequently snuck out of bed after midnight to pilfer baked treats from the kitchens while trying to avoid the guards, who we pretended were enemy spies—he finally realized his rousing tales were falling on deaf ears. He waited for the conversation to shift before he heaved an exasperated sigh and leaned back towards my ear.

"Well, I'm out of ideas. If tales of his intended won't even stir his interest..." He shook his head as if Prince Briar were a lost cause. "You can't marry him, Rhea." His tone clearly stated: *case closed, you're free*. If only it were that easy.

Prince Briar suddenly stood up. "Forgive me, Your Majesties, Princess Rheanna, but it's been a long day and I'm rather exhausted. I'm going to retire for the night." Ignoring his mother's stern look, he bowed and left the dining hall.

I gaped after him, shocked and stung at his hasty departure. I glanced at Liam, who lifted his eyebrows in clear disapproval. I bit the inside of my lip and returned to my meal.

I spent the remainder of dinner ignoring the conversations around me and fighting to keep my burning tears at bay, all while longing to escape the table myself. Only a few hours into our courtship and it was already a disaster, just like I'd expected it'd be. I'd made so many mistakes—I was a shy, terrible, and inattentive conversationalist; Prince Briar, while handsome, was serious and clearly uninterested. Was it any wonder he behaved in such a way when he was expected to make a match with *me*?

Who'd ever be interested in you?

With each onslaught, the wall that normally kept my negative thoughts at bay crumbled. I couldn't silence them, nor could I control my anxious breaths. The moment dessert finished I stood, certain if I remained any longer my careful composure would crack, destroying any remaining hope of a union between me and Prince Briar.

Everyone looked at me, and Mother's brow furrowed in concern. "Are you alright, Rhea? You're a bit pale."

"Forgive me, but I feel unwell. I must retire for the evening."

Before Mother could even grant her permission, I hurried from the room.

CHAPTER 2

*R*ather than returning to my bedroom where I'd have no distraction from tonight's disaster, I wandered the shadowy corridors. Outside, a storm had begun and beat against the windowpanes in rhythm with my pounding heart. My mind swirled as fiercely as the wind. I frantically tried to calm it, but the stormy thoughts refused to leave.

You're a disaster of a princess.

I hurried through the hallways, my skirts swishing with my rapid footsteps, but no matter how quickly I walked, I couldn't outrun my thoughts. I turned another corner, then another, all the while fighting the tears burning my eyes. While I managed to keep them at bay, my attacking thoughts weren't quite as easy to suppress.

Once he realizes how incompetent you are, Prince Briar will reject you, just like Prince Deidric did.

I stumbled to a stop when I reached a decorative alcove. Dead end. I leaned against the marble wall, slid down to the floor, and finally allowed my tears to escape, all while fighting each painful breath as the war in my mind raged on

—the memories from the disastrous feast competing with the ridicule of my thoughts.

I couldn't do this. But I had no choice. I was expected to endure the duty I'd been born to fulfill: make an alliance. After my first alliance had fallen through, this might be my final opportunity to serve my kingdom. I could do this. I chanted this over and over in an attempt to dispel the sharp thoughts fighting to convince me otherwise. Slowly, ever so slowly, my thoughts stilled.

I took another wavering breath before standing and straightening my dress. A gilded mirror hung on the opposite wall, but I resisted the temptation to look at my reflection to see whether my eyes were puffy from my tears. I hated mirrors, and I surely didn't want to see myself right now; doing so would cause the attack from my mind to begin anew. I wiped my eyes and turned to begin the trek back to my bedroom.

I'd only taken a few steps when the strangest sensation washed over me, as if an invisible thread were tugging me. I paused and looked around. I was in a section of the palace that was rarely used, completely alone save for a row of locked rooms. And yet...I felt as if someone were calling me, despite there being no sound save for the howling storm.

Stop being ridiculous, Rhea; it's merely the wind.

My sharp scold put me in my place. I marched purposely down the corridor...until I felt the lure again, the soundless impression that compelled me to turn back around.

No one was there, but I experienced the odd impression that someone was close by. Against my better judgement I found myself walking back down the hallway, my ear cocked for that whisper caressing my senses.

It's just your imagination, Rhea.

Imagination or not, the lure beckoned me to pause outside the furthest door. I hesitated before an invisible urging compelled me to rest my hand on the brass knob, which was surprisingly warm. It turned easily, despite all the rooms in this section of the palace always remaining locked.

The door creaked open and I was greeted by a staircase twisting up into the darkness and the unknown. Instinctively, I withdrew back into the safe, cradling light of the corridor...until I sensed that seductive tugging again, urging me to climb the stairs.

That would be foolish.

But I couldn't resist the mystery: what was at the top of the staircase? Curiosity compelled me to take a cautious step closer and peer up. The darkness made it impossible to see where the staircase led, but from the stone walls, I guessed this was one of the unused turrets of the palace. I hesitated.

Don't investigate; you'll inevitably get lost in such an unfamiliar part of the palace.

The lure caressed my mind yet again, a silent invitation to explore. I found myself taking one of the flickering lanterns and slipping inside the tower, leaving the door open to allow more light from the hallway to dispel the shadows swallowing the base of the stairs.

With a wavering breath I ascended, the hesitance in each step quickly becoming eclipsed by my own curiosity—I needed to see what was at the top of this tower.

The staircase twisted upwards like a spiral. The higher I climbed, the thicker the darkness became. The hand holding my lantern shook, casting dancing patterns of light along the dank stone walls encompassing me. I rested my hand on the cool stone to steady myself as I continued to climb. Soon my legs were burning. Was I near the top?

A few steps later, I found myself within a circular room that was empty save for a rain-splattered window. I looked around, investigating every shadowy corner for anything of interest.

Nothing. The disappointment was crushing.

I told you, Rhea, that it was just your imagination. You need to get a hold of yourself.

I sighed and started to turn, but then—

The lure intensified, practically shoving me towards the window, where I crouched down, holding my lantern in front of me. Resting against the wall, its silver frame nearly blending in with the stone, was a large hand mirror. My brow furrowed as I stared at it. I could see only the back, which was carved with intricate patterns. I reached out to lightly trace one of the twisting vines—and yanked my hand away with a gasp. The mirror was warm.

*This is no ordinary mirror...*which meant I shouldn't touch it. But the urge compelled me to pick it up. I kept it on my lap facedown, admiring the patterns, puzzled by the warmth emanating from it. The lure returned, insisting I turn the mirror over. Did I dare?

My heartbeat escalated as I slowly flipped the mirror over. I didn't peek into the glass but instead admired the gems lining the frame, blending seamlessly with the pattern carved into the silver.

Look into the mirror.

With a wavering breath I slowly lifted it, keeping my eyes squeezed shut until the mirror was level with my gaze. Then I peeked one eye open.

In the mirror I saw...merely my own reflection. I sighed in disappointment. I wasn't sure what I'd expected to see. I squinted at my features: my red, puffy eyes were too close together, my forehead was too high, my lips too full. Surely I was the most unattractive princess who'd ever—

"How long are you going to stare at yourself? It's not a very interesting view...although admittedly it beats the wall."

I gasped and dropped the mirror, scrambling away until my back pressed against the stone wall, its coldness seeping through my gown to trickle down my spine. A *voice* had spoken from the mirror.

Impossible.

The mirror was now facedown on the stone floor. A moan emanated from it, followed by the same deep voice, snarky in his irritation. "What did you do that for? You could have broken me."

My heart beat wildly against my ribs as I gaped at the mirror. The voice had spoken again, which meant I hadn't imagined it the first time. Had it really come from the mirror? Was it enchanted?

Instinct told me I needed to leave this mirror, especially since it could very well be a cursed object. Curses were nasty things...not that I'd ever had any experience with one. Yet my curiosity had different ideas.

I've discovered an enchanted mirror. Nothing this unusual and exciting had ever happened to me before. Besides, if the mirror could talk, it likely had feelings, and it seemed rather rude to abandon it in this dank tower.

"Hello? Are you still there?" The voice from the mirror was hardening in his impatience. "I don't know about you, but I don't find staring at the ground particularly thrilling. I'd be much obliged if you could turn me back over."

His slightly repentant tone compelled me to bridge the distance between us and pick it up. With a steadying breath I flipped it over...and in my surprise nearly dropped the mirror again. Staring back at me this time wasn't my own reflection but a man...a scowling one.

I gaped at him, slowly taking in his features. He had dark hair, nearly black, and dark eyes, which were narrowed at me. He was admittedly very handsome, although his good looks were marred by the fierceness filling his expression.

I swallowed and pushed through the shyness that tormented me whenever I met strangers. I stood—taking the mirror with me—and curtsied. "Hello," I managed, shakily but politely. "My name is—"

He snorted. "There's no need to bother with formalities; I can't see that fancy curtsy of yours."

My cheeks flushed with heat but I pressed forward. "I'm Princess Rheanna of Draceria. I'm pleased to—"

"Oh, you're a *princess*." Most of the hardness left his expression. "Forgive me, I didn't realize my rescuer was someone so distinguished."

Hopefully he'd now be more polite out of deference to my title. "And what's your name?"

The man was silent a moment before he withdrew enough so that rather than just his head filling the glass, I could see his entire upper body. He wore a red velvet tunic, signifying he hailed from the upper class.

He rigidly crossed his arms. "Drake."

"Drake?" The name was familiar. I was certain I'd heard of a Drake before...but I couldn't remember where. "What's your surname? Your title?"

His eyebrow lifted in clear surprise. "You don't know?"

"No." There were so many Dracerian noblemen it was impossible to keep them all straight.

"Interesting," he said slowly. "Then simply *Drake* will suffice. And you're Rheanna." He smirked in a rather condescending way. "A princess. Do you expect me to bow?"

"It'd be proper," I managed.

"I'm sure it would." But he made no motion to do so. I bit the inside of my lip to keep from frowning. I wasn't sure I liked this man.

"Were you hurt when I dropped you?" I asked hesitantly. My princess lessons hadn't covered how to talk to a man within a mirror. I wasn't even sure whether he was part of the mirror itself or trapped inside.

"What do you think?" he asked. "If you were dropped, do you think it *wouldn't* hurt?"

"I imagine it would be quite painful," I said tightly, determined to remain polite, despite his own cold behavior; after all, it was my duty as a princess.

"Then why did you ask?"

I frowned. This man wasn't very pleasant. Did being trapped in a mirror do that to people?

His lips twitched into a smirk that seemed an almost permanent part of his features. "Forgive me, I'm behaving out of sorts. It would be in my best interest to be on my best behavior considering my fate lies in your hands—you can either leave me in this tower or help me."

I suppressed a sigh. So he needed my aid after all, which meant he was likely cursed. Cursed individuals usually had done something to deserve their fate. It would be in my best interest not to involve myself.

Despite the sensible discouragement from my inner voice, something stirred within me—a desire to be brave and do something daring and unexpected. Not to mention helping a cursed man would be a much-needed distraction from my dull life and unwanted courtship.

"So you're in need of my help?" I asked reluctantly.

He snorted again. "I would have thought that was obvious. If I could have gotten myself out before now, don't you think I would have?"

Yes, he was definitely cursed. Great. "I imagine it's extremely frustrating," I ventured. "Which explains your rather sharp tongue." I gave him an accusing look and he sighed.

"Then I must ask your forgiveness once more. I've been trapped so long that I'm afraid I've forgotten my social graces."

That was quite the understatement.

He grinned mischievously. "But even when I'm using my best manners, it's my nature to be upfront. Considering my circumstances, honesty seems my best course of action—after all, I'm trapped within a mirror, and very much want to be set free. And right now you're my only hope of escaping. So will you help me?"

I was tempted to decline, but I couldn't very well leave him stuck in this tower. Drake studied me as I deliberated, as if he felt it his duty to know the person whose reflection was supposed to be in the glass. He frowned. "Your eyes are puffy. You've been crying."

My cheeks burned. I looked so unbecoming with puffy eyes. I turned the mirror away so he wouldn't see.

He sighed. "Did I upset you? I didn't say anything rude; I merely made an observation. At least I kept my opinion that puffy eyes are rather unattractive to myself, despite being tempted otherwise."

"Your frankness isn't helping your cause. Perhaps you deserve to remain trapped in this mirror." I turned the mirror back over in time to see him flinch. Remorse filled me. *Far too harsh, Rhea.* "I'm sorry, no one deserves such a fate."

Drake's reflection zoomed closer, and the hardness filling his features softened into what almost looked like concern, as if he regretted his recent words. "I'm glad you think so, because I'd rather not be trapped in this mirror. It's a rather dull existence."

"How did this happen to you?"

"That's a story for another time," he said. "For now, I'd very much like to leave this tower; I could do with a change of scenery."

I looked out the window. The storm made it impossible to measure the hour, but considering it had been late when I'd escaped the feast, it was likely approaching midnight. I welcomed the chance to leave; the coldness of the room seeped over me, causing me to shiver, and the oil in my lantern was getting low.

"Very well, we'll leave, but I expect your full story tomorrow."

He grinned and a strange flutter filled my stomach. "So you're going to rescue me after all?"

I hesitated. "What exactly would rescuing you entail?"

He wrinkled his brow. "I don't actually know, so perhaps our first step would be to figure that out. So will you help me?" He widened his eyes imploringly.

"I'm considering it, but if I agree, I strongly suggest you tame your tongue, considering your fate lies in my hands." I startled at the comment the moment it left my mouth. Where had such feistiness come from?

He chuckled. "In that case, it appears I'll need to work on my charm." His humor left as quickly as it had come. "I'm glad you came. I was beginning to think no one ever would."

I startled as his words triggered a realization: the *mirror* had lured me to this tower. I wanted to examine this epiphany, but it was late, I was cold, and the exhaustion from my emotional day was beginning to press against my senses. I'd worry about this cursed mirror tomorrow.

I stood, brushed my now wrinkled skirts, and picked up my lantern before making my way to the stairs, my legs aching from having knelt on the stone floor for so long. "I'll want answers come morning." I wouldn't promise my help until I better understood the nature of this man's curse.

Halfway down the stairs, Drake spoke again. "Are you going to tell me why you were crying?"

"No." I didn't know much about this man, but I knew enough to confidently say he wasn't someone I'd ever confide in, especially my rather complicated insecurities.

He sighed. "It appears I have work to do in order to gain

your trust. But no matter; time is something I have an infinite amount of."

I frowned into the mirror, only to discover he'd vanished from the glass, leaving nothing more than my own reflection staring back at me.

CHAPTER 3

*T*he rumbling thunder woke me the following morning. I blinked drowsily at the rain-splattered window. Sleep hadn't been kind to me last night, both from the howling wind and the strange dreams about a snarky man trapped within a mirror. Thank goodness *that* had only been a dream; my life was complicated enough without having to deal with a cursed noble.

I groaned and rolled over, but thunder shook the sky, making drifting back to sleep impossible. I grumbled as I sat up and stretched.

"It's about time you woke up. Do princesses always sleep so late?"

I gave a squeaking scream at the snide voice. My gaze darted towards the vanity where, in my exhaustion, I'd foolishly left the mirror I'd discovered last night propped up. A man—Drake, I remembered—stared back at me from within the glass. I gasped and yanked the bedclothes up to cover my nightdress.

"You really are in the mirror." So it hadn't been a dream after all. Just great.

Drake rolled his eyes. "Didn't we already establish that fact last night?"

"I was hoping it had only been a dream."

He lifted his brow. "Do you often have trouble discerning between dreams and reality?"

"Only when confronted by rude men trapped within ordinary objects."

His lips twitched. "Does encountering such men happen often for you?"

"This would be the first time." And hopefully the last. The sooner I figured out the curse, the sooner I could be rid of him.

The problem was I wasn't even sure how to go about such a task. I'd never dealt with magic before; my life had been remarkably ordinary. But as strange as finding an enchanted mirror was, at least it promised an adventure.

"Can you turn around?" I asked. "I'm in my nightclothes."

He rolled his eyes but obeyed. I waited a moment to be sure he wouldn't peek before scrambling over and setting his mirror facedown on my vanity.

"What are you doing?" he exclaimed.

"There's no need to be cross; I'll prop you back up after I've finished changing."

He grumbled something indiscernible before ceasing his complaints. I didn't wait for the arrival of my maid before dressing as quickly as possible in one of my simplest dresses so I could do it up myself. With the alliance Mother and Father hoped to forge between Prince Briar and me, they wouldn't be pleased to see me in such simple attire for our guests, but I couldn't worry about that now.

"Are you almost finished?" Drake asked impatiently.

"Almost." I jerked a brush through my hair before checking my appearance in the vanity mirror. I frowned. Dark circles from my restless night were beneath my eyes, my hair hung limply, and the sunny-yellow gown I wore washed out my skin.

You're so plain, Rhea.

"I thought you said you were almost finished." Drake's voice tugged me from my thoughts before they could grow too sharp. I sighed as I picked up the mirror and turned it to face me. Drake's scowl stared back at me.

"Are you always so grumpy?"

"I'm not grumpy; I just speak my mind."

So I'd gathered. He wouldn't be fun company. "What can you tell me about your spell?"

"I'm not sure I want to divulge the details."

I bit the inside of my lip to suppress another sigh. "How am I to help you if I don't know what we're dealing with?"

He surveyed me for a moment, his dark eyes narrowed beneath his thick black brows. "First off, it's not a spell; it's a *curse*."

"Are they very different?"

He rolled his eyes. "Obviously."

My cheeks burned. "Of course." I hastily looked away as my mind flung insults at me for my ignorance.

Drake cleared his throat awkwardly, and when I peeked up at him, he looked almost remorseful. "I doubt spells and curses are part of a princess's training. You couldn't have known."

While it wasn't exactly an apology, it did quiet my thoughts and cause the familiar tension in my chest to slowly ease. "Will you tell me more about your curse?"

He frowned. "I wish I could, but unfortunately I don't know much about it."

"Then can you tell me how long you've been trapped?"

His forehead furrowed. "I'm not sure how long it's been. Time is different in here—on the one hand it feels like I've been in here forever, and on the other, it doesn't feel like it's been long at all. What month is it?"

"The second month of autumn."

"Then I've been trapped for at least a year, maybe longer. I'm not sure how many it's been." His entire manner drooped.

"That must be difficult," I said softly.

In an instant his vulnerability vanished, replaced with his usual scowl. "Obviously."

I flinched even as annoyance overcame me. "There's no need to be rude. I'm just trying to be empathetic."

The remorse I'd only caught a glimpse of earlier settled completely over him. He lowered his eyes. "I know. I'm sorry."

An actual apology? Unexpected. But it softened me. "It must be frustrating being trapped as you are."

"It is. I feel so…"

"Helpless?"

He sighed wearily. "Yes."

"I understand how that feels." It was an emotion I encountered every day as I did my best to try to fulfill my role, only to continuously feel like I wasn't measuring up. The frustration felt like a permanent weight pressing against my heart.

I carried the mirror to my window seat, where I pulled my knees up and rested it against my legs. "Are you comfortable?"

I expected another snarky response, but Drake merely nodded. "I'm well enough." He paused. "Thank you."

I nodded. Now that we were on amiable enough terms, it was time to do some digging. "Can you tell me more about yourself? Which part of Draceria do you fare from? Who is your family?"

But I'd no sooner made my inquiries than I remembered where I'd heard the name *Drake*.

"Wait, I think I know who you are. The Baron of Livre's eldest son is about your age and I'm fairly sure his name is Drake. From what I've heard, he's a rebellious wanderer who hasn't been seen in several years. His antics have caused his father much grief and, some say, declining health." I gave him an accusing look and he shifted guiltily.

"Not everyone is close to their family." His vague answer only confirmed my suspicions of his identity. Discovering it eased some of my lingering worries concerning him. He wasn't a villain, just a mischievous and defiant nobleman who'd gotten himself into quite the scrape as he'd spread his wings. I couldn't say I blamed him for wanting distance from his father, a man I'd met a handful of times and found quite disagreeable.

Still, no matter his sour temperament, he deserved to know the fate of his son. "I should write him and inform him I've found you." I began to stand to do just that.

"Don't be hasty," Drake said. "In case you haven't noticed, I'm still very much trapped in this mirror. Until you find a way to free me, I'd prefer if you kept your finding me quiet."

I furrowed my brow. "But he's sure to be worried."

"I doubt my family is worried about me in the least," he said. "So there's no need for *you* to start. I'm not sure how long I've been gone, but it's undoubtedly been a while. Informing my family I've been cursed would cause more alarm than simply leaving them wondering where I am."

I sighed and obediently sat back down, where I rested my forehead against the cool windowpane and peered out into the grey, dripping world outside. When I turned away, I found Drake looking towards the side of the mirror, as if trying to peer out of it. "Can you turn me towards the window? I haven't seen rain in a long time."

I tilted the mirror. His eyes widened in wonder, an emotion that softened the lines of his usual hardened expression. He stared, transfixed, for an entire minute, not speaking. I looked back out the window, trying to imagine what it'd be like to see rain for the first time after who knew how many years. I noticed things I hadn't before—the lovely shades of grey swirling the sky, the patterns the raindrops created on the glass, how green and fresh everything looked when it rained.

He finally spoke. "I'd forgotten how it looks during a rainstorm."

Empathy filled my heart. It must be so difficult finding oneself cursed. "Can you tell me more about your curse? Who cursed you?"

He didn't look away from the window. "I can't tell you that."

Alright then. "Then can you tell me *why* you were cursed?"

"Not really."

I waited but he didn't elaborate. So far my inquiries were getting me nowhere. At this rate, how would we ever work together to break his curse?

I couldn't hold back my impatient sigh. "I'm not sure how I can assist you when your answers are so vague."

"I am being quite unhelpful, aren't I?" He finally returned his now-mischievous gaze to me. "I assure you it's not on purpose; I have no motive for being unhelpful, considering I really want to get out of this mirror." He fully faced me. "I can't tell you who cursed me for reasons I can't divulge, and I can't explain why I was cursed because I don't really know myself." He frowned. "It all happened so suddenly. The one who cursed me was striving to do another spell, but something went wrong and they accidentally cursed me instead. I don't believe it was on purpose...at least I *hope* it wasn't."

"Hmm." I considered all this. "It must be even more frustrating to find yourself in such a situation through no fault of your own. But if you know the person who inadvertently cursed you, does that mean you're acquainted with one who performs dark magic?" My stomach knotted with unease.

"Not exactly," he said slowly, as if afraid of revealing too much. Was he trying to protect whoever had landed him in this plight? "While it's true I know the one who cursed me, I don't think they performed dark magic on purpose." But he said the words uncertainly, as if doubting his own defense of his curser. "It only made it all the more surprising when the spell backfired and landed me in this predicament. It was a mistake, I'm sure of it." But by the way his frown deepened, I could tell part of him doubted that assessment.

Now we were getting somewhere. "Have they tried to reverse it?"

"This curse can't be broken by its caster. Hence I was placed in that tower in hopes of someone coming along who could help me."

Considering I'd found Drake in an *abandoned* tower—making my discovering him mere happenstance—I doubted the person who'd cursed him had a genuine desire to break it. "Your tower was too secluded for me to think they had your best interest in mind or even wanted you to be found."

"But *you* found me," he said.

I remembered the strange lure that had guided me to him, as if some invisible force had purposefully brought us together. But why? I had no ability to break curses.

"That's only because I was led to you."

His eyebrows rose. "You were?" He studied me for a moment before shrugging. "Very well, I suppose you'll do."

Annoyance flared in my breast. "Considering I'm your potential rescuer, I'd appreciate more gratitude."

"Believe me, if you manage to rescue me, you'll receive it.

Until then, forgive me for not groveling at your feet, Princess."

Before I could give him the set-down he thoroughly deserved, someone knocked on my door. I gasped and shoved Drake behind the window-seat pillow.

"Come in," I said shakily.

The door opened to reveal my maid. She curtsied. "Good morning, Your Highness. Her Majesty requests your presence at breakfast with Her Majesty the Queen of Malvagaria and His Highness Prince Briar.

So our courtship was to begin immediately. The exhaustion from my previous night pressed against my senses, making the task that lay before me feel even more daunting. But I was a princess. Thus I had a duty to perform.

"Very well."

I stood and my maid's eyes widened to see me already dressed. She pursed her lips at my simple gown and hairstyle but said nothing. It wasn't her place to scold, but Mother would surely see to it, and she had every right to.

You're not doing your part to make Prince Briar want you. But there was nothing I could do about it now. "Please inform Her Majesty I'll be down in a moment."

The maid hesitated. "May I help you with your hair?"

"No, thank you." I wanted to use the precious remaining moments before breakfast continuing my conversation with Drake.

The maid curtsied and left, and with a relieved sigh I retrieved the mirror and settled back against the pillows, only to find Drake's scowl more pronounced than usual.

"I didn't accidentally squish you, did I?" I asked.

He ignored my concern. "What's this I hear? A *prince* is visiting you?"

"Along with his mother, the Queen of Malvagaria."

His eyebrows lifted in surprise. "May I ask why?"

My cheeks warmed. I felt shy discussing this with him, especially as it made my situation all the more real. "We're to have an...arrangement."

"An *arrangement*? What kind?" By the disdain in his voice, he seemed to know exactly what kind I spoke of.

"A marriage alliance."

Drake's scowl deepened.

"It's not official," I said hastily. "But it's likely inevitable."

He was silent for a glowering moment. "And how do you feel about your impending betrothal to this prince?" he finally asked slowly.

I'd never allowed myself to express my true feelings on the matter, but considering Drake was stuck inside his mirror and couldn't share what I told him with anyone, he seemed a safe enough confidant. "Our arrangement is purely political."

"Making it one to be endured, as all such arrangements are."

"Not all are that way; my parents' arranged marriage is a happy one." And I'd always wanted such a marriage myself. I sighed and broke my careful posture to slump against the seat. "If they could make an arranged marriage work, we can choose to do the same, although the task feels daunting considering he doesn't seem to like me much."

"What makes you think the prince doesn't like you?" Drake asked.

How could I explain my ingrained fear that there was something wrong with me? I thought back to last night's dinner—the stilted conversation and Prince Briar's obvious lack of enthusiasm. "He just seemed so bored with me; he even left dinner early last night." Whatever Deidric's objections had been, it was clear Prince Briar shared them. Would he toss me aside, just like Deidric had?

My heart tightened. No, that couldn't happen. I couldn't

endure another rejection. "If he doesn't like me, what if he no longer wishes to marry me?" My fear pressed against my chest until I could scarcely breathe.

Drake frowned. "But you don't appear to want to marry *him*."

"I don't."

Perplexity filled his expression. "So...the problem is...?"

"He might not want me." The thought only increased my despair.

"Even though you don't want him?" Drake stared at me like I was a complicated puzzle before he rolled his eyes. "Women are so confusing."

"You don't understand." How could he? "I don't think I could bear if he rejected me, too." I took a wavering breath to calm myself. It didn't work.

He frowned. "You've been rejected before?"

This wasn't something I wanted to discuss with a mirror, especially an unsympathetic one. "It's none of your concern."

He furrowed his forehead, thinking hard. "Ah yes, Princess Rheanna of Draceria was engaged to Crown Prince Deidric of Sortileya, at least at the time I was cursed."

So he'd been cursed for at least two years.

"I take it you're no longer engaged to Deidric?"

"Obviously." I got a strange thrill retorting to him in the same manner he'd done to me earlier. Not only did he appear entirely unfazed, but his lips actually twitched, a sign of his amusement.

"So what happened?"

"Deidric married someone else."

"I figured as much. And this bothers you because you were in love with him?"

"I wasn't in love with him."

He looked even more confused. His perplexity made him rather...*cute*. "So why does it upset you?"

38

I wouldn't tell him or anybody else about my true feelings. I hadn't even confided in my family. From the moment my engagement with Deidric had broken, I'd determined to act as though nothing was wrong, not so much for others but for myself. But ignoring my emotions hadn't made them go away; I couldn't escape them, no matter how hard I tried.

"It doesn't matter." There was no point explaining; men never seemed to understand emotions, whether they were trapped in a mirror or not.

Drake sighed heavily. "Your impending arrangement with Prince Briar will make our situation quite complicated. I'm beginning to realize this was all a mistake."

"What do you mean?"

"Perhaps you should introduce me to one of your sisters instead."

Rejection pierced my heart. Hadn't he been listening when I'd told him my fears? I glared. "You can't dismiss me so easily. *I* was guided to the tower where I found you, not my sisters or anybody else; if it weren't for me, you'd still be up there. So you can choose to accept my assistance or I can put you right back where I found you."

Drake stared at me long and hard before grinning widely. "Very well then, I accept your help."

I released a breath of relief and glanced at the clock on the mantle. I'd dawdled too long. "I should go; I can't keep Prince Briar waiting any longer."

"So I'm just expected to wait for you?" he asked.

"It's not my duty to entertain you," I said. "I've agreed to try and help you, but that's all I can do for the moment." It felt we'd made little progress. We still hadn't discussed *how* to break the curse. I hoped I wasn't making a mistake entangling myself in such a mess.

He said nothing, only continued to glower. I sighed and

CAMILLE PETERS

propped him against my pillows in the window seat to keep him upright.

"There, now you can face the window so you can continue to watch the rain." I knew he'd like that, and sure enough he actually smiled. It was a rather strange smile, crooked though not in a charming sort of way, but I found it surprisingly endearing all the same.

"That would be most agreeable." He hesitated a moment. "Thank you, Rheanna."

I blinked at him. "You called me Rheanna."

"That's your name, isn't it? Or am I supposed to call you *Princess* Rheanna?"

My cheeks warmed. The formality didn't seem fitting. "Rheanna will be fine. After all, we're to be friends."

He gave me another of his crooked smiles. "What a relief, for friends help friends out of enchanted mirrors."

I lifted a challenging brow. "Even when that friend is rather obnoxious?"

He tipped his head back and laughed, a rather contagious sound. "You're far more spunky than I initially thought when we first met. An admirable trait."

The backhanded compliment softened the last of my resistances. "Is this your way of flattering me into helping you break the curse?"

He smiled again, causing my heart to give a strange flutter, a puzzling reaction. "Is it working?"

I fought my emerging smile. "Possibly."

"Then it appears you and I have a quest." And he winked.

Which was how I found myself embarking on a strange curse-breaking journey with a snarky man in a mirror.

CHAPTER 4

*H*aving an enchanted mirror in my possession was rather complicated, especially when Prince Briar and I were trying to court; our mothers threw us together at every opportunity, causing us to spend far more time together than I welcomed. I felt like I was serving two masters: forcing an arrangement that after three days I could already tell wasn't working, and trying to help an often disgruntled mirror.

I was finally able to sneak away to the library one afternoon in order to research Drake's curse. After a tedious hour of finding no information, I slid the disappointingly vague book on enchanted objects I'd been perusing back onto the shelf.

"I can't find any information that would help me break your curse. Do you have any ideas?"

I glanced into my open satchel, where Drake's mirror lay faceup. As usual, he looked grumpy. "I have a vague idea, but I can't tell you what it is. Otherwise it might not work."

I sighed. "That's not exactly helpful."

Drake shifted, as if the conversation made him nervous.

"It's not the most ideal way, so I'd prefer we find an alternative. Until we do, there's no harm in spending time together while we research. It can only help."

"In the meantime, I'll continue to do my best to find a solution." It was growing late; I needed to dress for another awkward dinner. I wove through the shelves towards the library exit.

Drake frowned. "Are you giving up already?"

"It's time for dinner."

"Can't you be late?"

His tone was pleading, almost causing me to relent. I gave him an apologetic look. "Prince Briar is expecting me." Whether he wanted to be or not.

Drake's expression twisted into a scowl. "Oh yes, *Prince Briar*. It's selfish of him to eclipse your attention; he's not the one trapped in a mirror."

"He's my intended. I likely should be spending more time with him and less with you." Although strangely, I found I enjoyed my time with Drake more; while he was snarky, he was at least interesting. Prince Briar was just so…dull.

"And how is your *courtship*?" Drake's tone was hardening. Why was he getting so irritable?

"Well enough. We played backgammon this afternoon." A rather silent game of backgammon. "It was fun." If awkwardness could be construed as such.

"You're a terrible liar, Rheanna."

Why did I lower my defenses around Drake? I readjusted the invisible mask I wore that hid my true emotions. "Regardless of how well my courtship is actually going, I need to do my part."

He sighed. "I suppose I can't fault you for that."

Sympathy filled me at the vulnerability filling his eyes. "What's it like being inside a mirror? Is it tight and confining?"

"Surprisingly not," he said. "It's like I'm standing in a really small room, enough to move around in, but not much."

"Are you ever hungry?"

"No, nor am I tired. The only ailment I suffer from is boredom."

"Do you still?" My insecurity flared again. I knew I wasn't very stimulating company.

"Not as much anymore; I enjoy talking with you."

I froze and gaped down at him in astonishment. "Do you mean that?" I whispered.

Earnestness filled his dark eyes. "I don't say things I don't mean."

My heart swelled. *Drake enjoys talking with me.* At least someone besides my family did.

I withdrew his mirror once we were safely back in my bedroom. "Where would you like me to set you?"

He frowned. "Are you really abandoning me so soon?"

"Don't complain; I just spent an hour trying to help you."

"Well, there's not much to show for it."

The joy from his recent compliment melted away, leaving me annoyed, as was common while in his company. "It's not my fault I have other duties. Now, would you like to perch at the window again?"

At his nod, I set him on the window seat, but despite the gesture, he still appeared grumpy. "Do you only consider me one of your duties?"

I frowned at his cold tone. "Only if you continue being difficult. Don't make me want to return you to that tower to wait for someone else to find and help you."

"You wouldn't do that; you're too soft." But his voice shook, revealing his worry. Good. Maybe now he'd actually behave.

I lifted my chin. "Try me."

He slowly grinned. "Feisty girl. You keep surprising me. I like it."

Another compliment? He couldn't possibly mean it; he was likely only trying to flatter me so I wouldn't act on my threat to abandon him.

A knock sounded on the door and my maid entered to help me prepare for dinner. I hastily covered Drake with a pillow, but it'd do little to muffle any commentary he felt inclined to give; hopefully he had the sense not to talk.

I frowned at my reflection after she'd finished. Although my pale blue dress was lovely and my blonde hair was expertly arranged, the elegance couldn't enhance my plain features.

"You look lovely, Rhea." Elodie glided into the room, all smiles, and appeared beside me in the mirror. She herself was beautiful, far more so than I was. I tried to suppress the jealousy tightening my heart; Elodie was too sweet to be the recipient of my ill feelings.

"At least the dress is pretty," I said.

She sighed. "I hate when you deflect compliments. Why are you under the false impression that you're not beautiful?"

She only thought I was lovely because she was my sister. "It's not a false impression, because I'm *not*—"

"You *are* beautiful, and that gown only enhances your appearance; it brings out the blueness of your eyes." She frowned. "Perhaps you should change so Prince Briar won't be tempted to marry you."

I raised my eyebrows. "Only a few days ago you were gushing about how handsome he is."

She wrinkled her nose. "He may be handsome, but I'm afraid he has nothing else to recommend him. He's emotionless, nothing more than a portrait of an actual man. And between his mysterious curse, his residence being in Malvagaria, and your future responsibilities as queen, there are practically no advantages to your match. You can do better."

I squeezed her hand. "I appreciate your concern, but you know I have to marry him."

Her mouth fell agape. "But *why*? Mother and Father won't force you, especially after what happened between Liam and Lavena. Just tell them you're uninterested."

For a moment I was sorely tempted. It'd be so easy to say the words that would rid me of both Prince Briar and the obligations and expectations that had smothered me my entire life, a burden that was becoming more difficult to carry with each passing day.

But I couldn't. I knew my role: to do my best for my king-dom. But buried beneath all that, I knew the true reason, one I didn't want to acknowledge to myself or anybody else: the deep-rooted fear that if I didn't marry Prince Briar, I wouldn't marry at all, for no one else would want me. Never marrying was a rejection far more painful than the thought of a loveless union, especially when that union would benefit my people. It was my duty to help them if it was within my power.

"I'm marrying him," I whispered. "I have to."

Elodie heaved an impatient sigh. "Fine, if you're not going to listen to me, then I'll get someone you can't ignore." She left, undoubtedly to send for Liam, the one who had a way of convincing me in a way no one else could. I braced myself for battle.

He arrived a few minutes later with a wide grin. "I heard you're in need of some big-brother advice, and I happen to be an exceptional big brother." He gently took my hand and led me to the settee at the foot of my bed before settling beside me.

"As much as I welcome your advice under normal circumstances, I just can't afford to do so now."

His grin faded. "Ah, this is about your betrothal to Prince Boring?"

My lips twitched but I fought to hide my smile, else it'd only encourage him. "That's rather harsh. True, Prince Briar is rather...uninteresting, and he always seems either bored or tired, but that's likely because I still don't know him well."

"Ever the diplomatic one," Liam said. "But even if Briar miraculously stops being so sullen, I still don't sense a connection between you two."

I leaned forward. "Please be honest: what do you really think of him?"

Liam frowned. "Hmm...well, he seems like a good man, but there's something off about him...he has no *life* about him."

Leave it to Liam to notice such a thing. "He's completely different from you, but that's not necessarily a flaw in his character."

"Isn't it?"

Liam gave me a cheeky wink, and despite our serious conversation, I couldn't help but giggle. Although Liam smiled in return, his expression sobered almost immediately.

"I admit I haven't been particularly impressed. Briar seems to be a man comprised solely of duty and lacking in emotion. At first I wondered whether he was simply shy like you and needed time to open up, but after several days I'm concluding he's simply..." He frowned. "I don't know how to describe him, only that he doesn't seem to be the man for you."

"But that doesn't change the fact that he *has* to be; I haven't any choice in the matter."

"Don't say that, Rhea." Liam took both my hands in his, his expression earnest. "I've walked the dutiful path and it was unbearable. I don't want that for you, nor do our parents. They're sincere in their wishes and would never trap you in an unwanted union."

"Our situations are different; Prince Briar isn't Lavena." At least he had *that* going for him.

"That may be true, but you don't love him. I know you desire a love match, and as a man who's been blessed with one, I want that for you, too. You deserve that."

"There is no love match for me," I stuttered. "Thus I'm determined to do the right thing—our people will benefit from my marriage, even if I don't."

He sighed. "I respect your decision to do the right thing; it's why I initially married Lavena. I felt it was my duty as the crown prince to create an alliance that would benefit our kingdom."

"But lucky for you, your wife turned out to be an imposter. Are you suggesting my story will have a similar ending? Does Prince Briar have a lookalike servant, too?"

Liam's smile didn't reach his eyes. "Duty is an honorable trait that comes in many forms, but you're only focusing on your duty to our people and completely forgetting your duty to yourself. I now realize that if I'd actually married Lavena, she'd have slowly destroyed me by making me doubt myself and sucking all the enthusiasm and joy from my life, which would have made me an ineffective crown prince and future king. In contrast, Anwen makes me a better man. Duty to my heart allows me to be the ruler our people need. If you want to be loyal to this alliance, you must first decide whether the cost is too great—which it will be if it causes you to lose yourself, an outcome that will undoubtedly affect how you reign over the Malvagarian people when you become their queen."

Fear clenched my heart. *Queen*...how could I fulfill such an overwhelming role when I wasn't a good enough princess now?

Liam squeezed my hands. "I have no doubt you'll fulfill whatever role you're expected to with grace and compassion. You're a remarkable woman, never forget that. If Briar can't see that, then he doesn't deserve you."

It was a kinder way of saying Prince Briar wasn't interested in me. Even though Liam meant well—he always did—his words still hurt all the same. He didn't understand; I was in no position to wait to find someone who *deserved* me, not when I wasn't prize material. One broken engagement had been bad enough; breaking my relationship off with Prince Briar before it was even official would be just as humiliating. Then no one would ever want me.

But I forced a smile for Liam, unable to do anything else in the face of the sincerity filling his protective-big-brother expression.

"Will you think about what I've said?" he asked. I nodded. He gave my hands another reassuring squeeze and glanced at the clock. "We should go; we wouldn't want to be late for dinner."

The old Liam wouldn't have cared for such a thing. "Ever since your marriage, you've grown into a wonderful crown prince."

Liam helped me to my feet and looped my arm through his. "All Anwen's doing. Marriage is about finding a partner who can see the best in you and in turn makes you a better person. You shouldn't settle for anything less."

As Liam escorted me from my room, I glanced back to where Drake's mirror still hid beneath the pillow for a silent goodbye. During our walk to the dining room, Liam chatted about inconsequential topics, but as we neared the doors, he pulled me aside, his expression serious.

"One more thing: I want you to know that even though I want you to make a love match, I'll respect whatever choice you make. If you're determined to go through with your union with Briar, then I'll keep an eye on him to ensure he's worthy of you."

Warmth filled me. "Thank you, Liam."

Mischief filled his eyes. "But until it's official, don't expect me not to meddle." He kissed my cheek before leaving me to go embrace his waiting wife with all the enthusiasm of a man in love. "Would you like to join me in some sleuthing, darling? It'll be like a game."

Anwen smiled. "Is that the newest adventure up your sleeve?"

He chuckled. "It is, but I assure you I have plenty more."

He dipped down to lightly kiss her brow. My heart ached at the display of what I couldn't have, for I'd made my decision. Resigned, I searched the room for Prince Briar so he could escort me into dinner. As if on cue, Prince Briar appeared at my elbow and offered his arm with a flat expression. "May I escort you, Rheanna?"

"You may." I took his arm and waited expectantly. Elodie had said I looked lovely. Would Prince Briar acknowledge my appearance? Even if he didn't offer a compliment, surely he'd say *something*; even small talk about the weather would be welcome. But, as always, he remained silent.

I suppressed a sigh and allowed him to escort me into the dining room. As if sensing my hurt, Liam glanced over his shoulder to give Prince Briar a frown of disapproval and me a knowing look, another reminder that he thought I deserved better.

He was wrong, although I desperately yearned to believe otherwise.

CHAPTER 5

I needed to escape, just for a few hours, before I drowned. The moment I returned to my bedroom following breakfast several days later, I strode purposefully to my wardrobe for my shawl without even glancing at the windowsill where Drake was propped up.

"Where are you going in such a hurry?" he asked.

"What a greeting," I said. "A gentleman would first inquire after a lady's wellbeing." I wasn't sure why I was riling him. We'd gotten in a mini squabble the evening before, and between that and my current stress, I was feeling less than cheerful.

"Who can behave like a gentleman when trapped inside a mirror?" he grumbled. "I feel less like myself with each passing day."

Sympathy pierced my bad mood. "I'm sorry, I shouldn't be so grumpy with you. It's not your fault I'm feeling frazzled."

He was silent a moment. "You have no need to apologize; I'm merely making excuses for my poor behavior. Now let me try this again: how was your morning?"

I released a wearied breath. "Stressful. I'm desperate for an escape, however brief." Breakfast had been rather trying. While Briar had perked up and been a little more talkative, despite my attempts to engage him, he'd mostly conversed with my siblings. His disinterest had left me feeling so...hopeless.

I glanced longingly out the window. A few minutes in the crisp autumn air would undoubtedly do wonders for my spirits.

"You're going outside?" Hope filled Drake's voice. Even without his asking, I knew he wanted to accompany me. Normally I'd want to venture outdoors alone, but the more time I spent with Drake, the more I welcomed his presence, for he was quickly becoming more than a man in the mirror —he was becoming a friend.

Of course your friend is someone who's cursed and trapped. But the thought didn't feel as cynical as it normally would.

"Would you like to come with me?"

He brightened. "May I, Rhea?"

My heart gave an unexpected lift. "What did you just call me?"

Crimson filled his cheeks. He avoided my eyes. "That's what your family calls you, isn't it?"

It was, but it was a nickname that only my family ever used—Deidric hadn't even done so, despite our being engaged for several years. But despite that, it felt strangely...*right* for Drake to use it, and I couldn't explain why. The memory of him speaking it in his deep voice wrapped around my still-fluttering heart. I had the strangest urgency to hear him say it again.

"You may refer to me in such a way, if you wish."

He raised his gaze with a crooked grin. "Are you sure? It may not be proper with your being a princess, but then again, men trapped inside mirrors can get away with all sorts of things."

I giggled, and by his triumphant smile, it seemed he'd been wanting to make me laugh. "They certainly have up to this point. Is there a book outlining mirror etiquette?"

"I'm writing one myself. It's freeing to make up my own rules rather than being concerned with how others perceive me."

Such freedom seemed an impossible dream for me. But perhaps, just for today, I could have a taste of such a possibility. While I could never completely escape the thoughts invading my mind, perhaps my usual sanctuary would at least momentarily quiet them.

I carefully placed Drake in my satchel—with a promise to take him out when we reached our destination—before slipping from my room. From the slit in the opening, I could see his grin of anticipation.

"Where are we going?"

"You'll see. Is patience part of mirror etiquette?"

His grin widened, causing my heart to give another strange shudder, especially with the way his smile caused his eyes to crinkle at the edges. "It can be."

I reached the front doors and stepped outside. The moment I did so, my suffocating worries seemed to lift from my shoulders, finally allowing me to breathe again. I tipped my head back, soaking in the warm sunshine and the cool caressing breeze against my cheeks.

I didn't linger atop the front steps for long. As I descended, I stared in the direction of the woods, longing to do something daring and explore them. Instead, I walked through the gardens, heading for the orchard just beyond the manicured palace grounds. It was a long walk, but the moment I spotted the rows of apple-laden trees in the distance, my heart lifted. I'd missed my time within them;

returning was like visiting an old friend, a refuge that felt separate from the rest of the palace, allowing me to believe that at least while I was within its trees, I was free from my ever-present anxieties.

I pulled Drake from my satchel and tipped his mirror at an angle that allowed him a good view of the scenery as we walked. "Isn't it beautiful?" I breathed.

His eyes actually widened in wonder. "It's quite spectacular. I've never been inside an orchard before."

I shook my head. "I can't even fathom that. You're in for a treat, for this isn't just any orchard but an enchanted one; the fruit grows all year long and in different colors." I began walking with Drake through the trees. "This was my favorite place growing up, my own private hideout. I spent hours here. See the trees' vibrant colors?" Ruby and gold filled the branches. "They're even lovelier in the spring when they're filled with pink apple blossoms, although autumn is lovely, too." I breathed in the crisp and fruity air. "Don't the apples smell divine?"

Drake's expression—which had softened during my recitation—faltered, his sobering answer. Sympathy filled my heart.

"One day you will, and then we'll return to the orchard." If I hadn't already married Prince Briar and moved to Malvagaria by then. The thought caused my anxieties to flare again, but I pushed them away. I wouldn't dwell on my unromantic future now.

"I'd like that," Drake said quietly. "If you'd welcome my company. I feel bad invading your sanctuary. I can see how special it is to you."

"It is. I need to come here more often." Especially since there'd be few opportunities left before my marriage and subsequent move to Malvagaria.

I wove through the trees, caressing the trunks as I passed,

greeting each one before settling on the lawn beneath my favorite one—large, shady, and tucked away from the others. Carved into its trunk was a heart with my name inside. I lightly traced its outline with my fingertip.

Drake raised his eyebrow in a silent question, so I explained. "It was Elodie's idea. Years ago we each picked a tree to carve our names into." I pointed to a tree several yards away. "That one has Liam's and Anwen's names, and that one"—I pointed to another further away—"Kian's and Lavena's." Both couples had been a love match, representing the type of relationship I'd never have for myself.

Drake scrunched his forehead. "But I thought Prince Kian died before he could marry Princess Lavena."

"He did, and Lavena was never the same."

"Are you going to carve Prince Briar's name in your tree?" By his disgruntled frown, I could tell he hoped I'd say I no.

I swallowed the denial I ached to give. "Quite likely." Even though his name wouldn't fulfill the childhood dreams of romance I'd had for my future.

I propped Drake's mirror against the trunk so we were facing one another before leaning back on my elbows and tipping my head back, allowing the sunshine peeking through the canopy of branches to caress my cheeks.

At first Drake remained silent, as if he knew I needed a moment alone with the orchard, but eventually he broke the comfortable stillness. "The sunlight is dancing against your hair."

I straightened and peered over to find him blushing again; it deepened when our gazes met. He cleared his throat and hastily looked away.

"It's just an observation. It's been a while since I've seen the sun."

Once again, my heart reached out to him. "I haven't been able to spend much time outside lately either." I regretted the words almost the moment I spoke them. *How tactless, Rhea; your situation is drastically different than his.* "I'm sorry," I said hastily. "My experiences are nothing compared to yours."

"True, they're different, but they're more similar than you think. Aren't you also trapped, in a sense?" He leaned his torso against the mirror frame and gave me a rather penetrating look, as if he could see the secrets buried deep that no one was meant to discover.

"Trapped in my responsibilities, you mean?" I asked. He nodded. "It's not the same. At least I can come outside. I should do it more often before winter comes. I'll bring you with me."

"I'd like that."

I almost returned his smile before my usual negative thoughts returned, invaders ruining an otherwise sweet moment. *Don't get your hopes up; he simply wants to come outside, not to spend time with you.* I flinched.

"Is something wrong?" Drake was watching me rather attentively.

For a moment I almost told him so I wouldn't carry the heavy burden constantly weighing on my mind alone. But I couldn't. So I merely said, "It's difficult not to dwell on the duties I've left behind."

"Then perhaps a distraction is in order," he said. "I'd like to hear more about your time in the orchard. If the trees could speak, what memories would they share?"

Surely he couldn't possibly be interested in such a thing, could he? But his gaze was so earnest, inviting me to open myself up to him.

Once more I leaned on my elbows and tipped my head back. "During my childhood I spent many hours within these trees—exploring the orchard and eating the fresh fruit, picnicking on the lawn, or picking wildflowers for my hair.

Some of my favorite memories are the moments I spent with my siblings playing games."

"What kind of games?" he asked encouragingly. I searched his expression, and to my surprise, he looked like he genuinely wanted to know.

"Let's see…there was the one time my brothers pretended to be warlocks. Liam was naturally playing the evil one, whereas Kian"—I swallowed the sudden lump in my throat —"was the hero. Liam kidnapped us and was planning on cooking us in order to create an eternal youth potion. He put us in a cauldron he'd snagged from the kitchens and was filling it with all sorts of things from around the orchard— grass, wildflowers, apples, water from the stream—while we tried to appease him so he'd change his evil ways. Liam found it all good fun until Kian rescued us."

The lump in my throat returned, more pronounced than before. Thinking of Kian wrenched my heart, the wound his death had caused one that would never completely heal.

"There was another time when Liam was convinced all the trees led to different worlds," I continued. "He wanted to climb each and see if he could get high enough to discover one. I used to relish his stories about what he thought each world was like."

I smiled at the memory. Most of my childhood stories revolved around Liam. We were only a year and a half apart in age, making him the sibling I was closest to, my best friend and primary childhood playmate.

Drake was silent a moment. "I wish I had such fantastic memories with my own siblings." His expression was wistful.

"What was your childhood like?" I asked.

"Nothing like yours." He looked away to stare out across the orchard. "I often wonder if my family even cares I'm trapped inside this mirror. I doubt they even miss me." He sighed and returned his gaze to me. "I've never really gotten along with my own brother, and I never spent much time with my sisters, especially since the youngest is quite sickly. My relationship with my mother is…complicated. I'm closest to my father, but he's been ill for several years…at least, I *think* he's still ill; I haven't seen him since becoming trapped. What if he's died while I've been stuck in here and I don't even realize it?" He looked almost frightened.

"Would you like me to make inquires on your behalf?" I asked gently. "If you told me more about your family, I could—"

"*No!*" Drake's melancholy vanished in an instant, replaced with an almost panicked look. "Please don't. I don't want you to look into my family."

I frowned. "Why not?"

He hesitated. "Curses are tricky things and can be quite dangerous. It'd be better not to involve my family."

"Very well, I'll respect your wishes." Even though his cryptic comments only made me *more* curious. "And don't worry, I'll find a way to break your curse; then you can be reunited with your family."

To my surprise, he frowned at that, but before I could ask him what was wrong, he changed the subject, as if he didn't want to talk about his curse, which was strange considering he'd never turned down an opportunity to do so before now. "Tell me more orchard stories."

So I did, telling him about the various imaginative games my siblings and I had played together within these trees. It was strange how easy it was to open up to Drake—my usual shyness felt entirely absent, leaving nothing but our conversation, flowing easily between us as if we'd known one another our entire lives. It was a strange sensation, but one I welcomed. While my conversations with Prince Briar had gradually begun to improve, they were nothing like this.

I kept stealing tentative glances at Drake, monitoring his

expression to see whether or not he was bored, for surely he'd grow tired of listening to my ramblings. But as always, he never seemed restless. Instead, he actually seemed...*interested*. No man outside my father and brothers had ever seemed truly interested in me. Not Deidric and certainly not Prince Briar.

"Don't stop there," Drake said. "What happened after Liam tied you and your sisters to a tree?"

"He went off to retrieve Kian so he could rescue us, only to become distracted with another adventure and forget all about us. We were tied up for several hours before one of the orchard workers found us. Liam got in loads of trouble."

Drake chuckled. "Poor Liam. How long did it take before you forgave him for his negligence?"

"Not long," I said. "He was so penitent and gave us his desserts for an entire week to earn his way back into our good graces. He's impossible to stay upset with, considering his intentions are never malicious. He's incredibly kind and charming, and of course always fun."

As I thought of another adventure to share, I raked my fingers through the grass, quickly becoming distracted by the attentive way Drake watched my movements.

"I've almost forgotten what grass feels like," he murmured.

"How about leaves?" I picked up a discarded leaf and crawled closer to stroke it around the mirror's rim and across the smooth glass. His eyes fluttered shut and his lips twitched into a smile.

"I can almost feel that."

"One day you'll feel it for real." I dropped the leaf and he opened his eyes. "What are you looking forward to the most after you're free?"

"Hmm, that's an interesting question. There are so many possibilities." He considered for a moment before mischief filled his eyes. He looked up, as if trying to peer out of the mirror in order to see the tops of the trees. "I think the first thing I'll do is climb a tree."

I lifted a skeptical brow. "Climb a tree?"

"Yes, in this very orchard, in fact. Hearing about Liam's tree-climbing adventures has inspired me. I used to climb trees all the time."

"So did I. I often climbed them with Liam when I was little. He was always the captain of our treetop adventures and I was his loyal first mate."

His eyes widened exaggeratedly. "*You*, a princess, climbing trees? The scandal."

I yanked up a handful of grass and tossed it at him. He chuckled.

"Seriously, I don't believe you. I think a demonstration is in order."

"You'll get no such thing," I said.

"Then it must have been merely a made-up story on your part. Such a shame."

I glared. "Are you accusing me of telling a falsehood?"

His grin widened. "Then prove it."

My cheeks burned. "I can't *prove it*. It's not ladylike. Besides, I'm in a dress. It wouldn't be modest—"

"I'm trapped in a mirror. Just shove me in your satchel and I won't be able to see anything."

That was beside the point.

"I so happen to be an excellent tree climber," he said.

"Then prove it," I quipped.

He laughed, such a deep, warm sound. "I like it when you're feisty, Rhea."

He needed to stop calling me that. It made me want to give him his way far too easily. I glared at him, but judging by the wicked grin that spread across his face, the gesture had little effect.

I pressed my hands to my hips. "I haven't climbed trees in years, and never without Liam's help. I'm not sure I could do it anymore. What if I slip?"

"Not to worry, I'll catch you if you fall."

I rolled my eyes. "An excellent idea. I'll be sure to land right on top of you and crack your mirror. As such, it'd be in your best interest to climb the tree on your own." I stood on tiptoe and carefully rested his mirror on the first branch.

His entire expression brightened as he looked around from his new vantage point. His growing grin lit up his dark eyes, which were a lovely shade of chocolate brown. A strange flutter filled my stomach at the observation, and it only intensified when he turned his crooked grin on me.

"See, climbing this tree wasn't so hard. You should join me."

I worried my lip. "I can't. I told you: princesses don't climb trees."

Drake frowned. "But I can see that you want to."

He was right—I wanted nothing more than to just ignore my skirts and self-imposed rules and simply climb to the highest perch I could, without worrying about falling.

I sighed and wrapped my hands around the lowest branch above my head. "Maybe one day I'll be brave enough to climb a tree again. It'd be easier if you really could catch me should I fall."

"Then the moment I get out of this mirror, we'll do it." He glanced around his perch at the boughs surrounding him, laden with rose-tinted apples. "And then we'll pick apples and eat them until we're sick."

Longing, warm and powerful, filled my breast. I ached for that day to come. If Drake were out of the mirror, I was certain that somehow I'd be able to release my self-imposed expectations for myself. It was already becoming easier the more our friendship deepened.

It was almost a frightening thought, for if I allowed myself to be friends with Drake, what if he eventually discovered whatever lack others saw in me? The thought of enjoying his friendship only to lose it was far too painful.

Perhaps it had been a mistake to bring him to my orchard after all.

CHAPTER 6

*J*fidgeted in my seat beneath the Queen of
Malvagaria's attentive gaze, which made enduring
another awkward breakfast with Briar all the more difficult.
We'd already cycled through our usual small talk and now ate
in uncomfortable silence. By his typical stoic expression and
the attentive way he ate his food, I didn't think he was bothered by this, nor was I…but his mother clearly had different
ideas. How could I even try to get to know him with the
queen hovering in the background, scrutinizing our every
move, just as she'd done for every outing of ours since their
arrival? She certainly seemed determined to make our match
work.

I tried to ignore her as I conversed with my sisters, eating
as quickly as I dared without forgoing my manners before
rising from the table as soon as I thought I could get away
with it. I expected my parents' disapproval, but to my
surprise Mother smiled with understanding.

"Finished already, Rhea?"

"Yes. I think I'll take a walk through the gardens."

Mother nodded her permission, and I sighed in relief.

The Queen of Malvagaria frowned at me before giving Briar a pointed look, one that took him a moment to notice. His brow furrowed quizzically when he finally glanced up from his food. She tipped her head towards me.

Oh no, she was going to cajole him into another outing. I turned and hastened my retreat, hoping to escape before Briar's impending invitation.

His sigh brought me to a halt. "Wait, Rheanna. I was hoping we could spend the morning together."

No, that was his *mother's* wish. I was nothing more than a duty for him to accomplish on his daily checklist of tasks. We'd spent every day this week fulfilling our duty in the most menial of ways. Couldn't I have at least one morning free?

I schooled my expression before I turned back around to face him. "Were you?" I fought to keep my emotion at bay but my voice shook, betraying me.

"Yes. It would be my pleasure to join you in the gardens."

Liar. I forced a tight smile. "It's a lovely day, perfect for a stroll."

Briar glanced towards the window with an almost puzzled look, as if only just noticing how sunny it was, nevermind we'd discussed the pleasantness of the weather in our strained small talk mere moments ago. He'd clearly paid little attention to our awkward conversation.

Can you blame him? You're not a particularly interesting conversation partner. Although Drake never gave me that impression.

I forced another strained smile. "I'd enjoy your company."

The words burned on my tongue. I hated pretending, but it was even more unbearable doing it with a man who'd likely become my husband. But wasn't this the way of most arranged marriages—a performance where the two players spent a lifetime merely going through the motions? I'd never wanted such a marriage, but unfortunately I had no choice—for in my need to protect myself from the lonely future I feared, I'd decided this was my only option.

"How wonderful." The queen's bright smile seemed a bit forced. "This will be another lovely opportunity for you two to get to know one another better." She turned back to Briar. "Perhaps you can arrange for a picnic after your stroll."

Briar narrowed his eyes at her before his gaze slid to mine, resigned. "Does a picnic sound agreeable to you, Rheanna?"

"I love picnics."

He nodded and another awkward silence settled over us. I shifted from foot to foot, trying not to notice the concerned glances of Liam and my parents or Elodie's attempts to stifle her giggle. How humiliating my loved ones had watched my intended's mother orchestrating our courtship. If only Briar would seek out my company because he liked me.

I suppressed a sigh and squared my shoulders. I'd maintain my poise, even though I wanted nothing more than to hide in my room and cry. "I'll retrieve my wrap and meet you in the entrance hall."

"I look forward to it," he said hollowly before returning his attention to his breakfast, signaling an end to our strained conversation. *Finally.*

I escaped the dining room before slowly walking to my room. The clear blue skies and glistening sunshine greeted me from the windows I passed, but I no longer looked forward to spending what had initially promised to be a lovely morning outside, considering I'd be enduring another forced courtship outing with Briar. Too soon I entered my room, where I went to my wardrobe to retrieve my wrap.

"Are you going outside?" Drake sounded uncannily cheerful. I turned towards where I'd propped him at the window and almost cringed at the hope in his eyes. I was about to ruin his morning, too.

I sighed. "Yes."

He lifted an eyebrow. "Why do you sound so unenthusiastic? I thought you loved the outdoors."

"I do. It's just that…" I stared out my window, where the leaves of the distant orchard were tinged with autumn and golden sunlight spilled into my room. It truly was a beautiful day. What a shame it wouldn't be one for much longer. "Briar is being cajoled into taking me on a stroll and then later a picnic."

Drake's expression hardened. He tightened his jaw. "Do you fancy him?"

I collapsed backwards onto the bed. I knew I was being rude causing Briar to wait, but I wanted to delay our outing just a bit longer; he'd surely welcome the reprieve as much as I did. "I told you before that I don't."

"But I wasn't sure whether over the course of his visit your feelings had changed."

"They haven't." That was the problem.

His expression softened, but only just. "Then why are you still courting him?"

"Because it's what's expected. Our alliance will be quite beneficial. Besides, I could never disappoint my family by refusing it. It must go through, whether I want it to or not." My stomach knotted.

Drake's scowl deepened. "You shouldn't force it, especially considering from what I've heard about the prince, you two don't seem at all suited."

My agreement burned on my tongue, but I refrained from admitting it. I glanced at the clock on the mantle. "I should go; I've kept Briar waiting too long."

"Take me with you." Against my wishes, Drake's earnest plea tugged at my heart.

I snorted. "You want me to take you on an outing with my intended?"

"Yes." His tone left no room for argument, even though he had no ability to tag along unless I brought him with me.

"Don't be ridiculous." I strode for the door.

"Please let me come, Rhea. It's been days since I've been outside and I'll go crazy stuck up here waiting for you, wondering..." He trailed off, his cheeks ruddy once more. What had gotten into him?

"Why do you want to come?"

"I know you're not looking forward to your time with dull Prince Briar. Surely you'll feel better having me there so you don't have to endure his company alone?"

I froze with my hand on the door knob. He was right, I *wanted* him to come. The mere thought of having Drake with me, even when he'd be forced to remain silent and out of sight, lessened my pressing anxiety. I slowly turned around. He smirked triumphantly, already guessing my acceptance.

That changed my mind immediately. I lifted my chin. "I'm not having you tag along on my courtship outing." As if it wouldn't already be awkward enough.

"Think of me as a chaperone."

I rolled my eyes but couldn't dismiss the welcome thought of his presence. "Admittedly, I'm not looking forward to spending the entire morning with only Briar for company."

"Then let me come and you won't have to."

His imploring expression softened me further. I nibbled my lip, deliberating, before I relented with a sigh and walked over to pick him up.

He grinned broadly. "I knew I could charm you."

"Careful, I could still change my mind."

"But you won't." He sounded ridiculously confident. Curse him for knowing me so well. I gave him a stern look before carefully placing him in my satchel; it took some finagling to fit him inside without a portion of his mirror's handle sticking out.

"Not a word from you."

"Not a word. After all, my primary mission is to eavesdrop."

The thought of Drake witnessing my strained courtship outing with Briar caused whatever ease I'd felt at the thought of his presence to vanish. Nerves knotted my stomach.

Perhaps this wasn't such a good idea.

BRIAR MET me in the entrance hall, where he offered his arm and escorted me outside. The weather was perfect: sunny mingled with the slight chill of autumn. I ached to tip my head back and soak in the sun, and I would have if I were either alone or in Drake's company. But unfortunately it was Briar's arm I held.

"Do you have a particular destination in mind?" he asked.

"Would you like to see the orchard?"

At his nod, I pointed him to the path that led to the apple trees. As we took it, we walked by the Queen of Malvagaria sitting on a bench, watching us with a rather calculating smile that made me uncomfortable.

Briar cast his mother a wary glance as we passed before returning his attention to me with an almost apologetic look. "Are you warm enough?"

I tugged my wrap more firmly around my shoulders and nodded. He fell silent now that his dutiful inquiry had been performed. Even though his behavior was familiar, my heart still wrenched. *Is it wrong to want to be more than a man's duty?*

I felt the queen's sharp gaze follow us as we disappeared into the next garden. I couldn't help but glance back, hoping the meddling woman wouldn't follow us in order to monitor our outing. Luckily, she remained behind. I released a whooshing breath of relief. The sound drew Briar's puzzled attention.

"Your mother—" I began in explanation before snapping my mouth shut. He released his own sigh and glanced back at her.

"Yes, my mother. I hope she's not making you too uncomfortable. She's a rather determined sort."

That was an understatement if I ever heard one. "Doesn't she take into consideration what *you* want?"

Briar shrugged. "She cares little for others' opinions. I'm more a pawn than a son." He looked out over the manicured palace grounds, aglow in golden light, and took a long, deep breath. "It's nice being out in the gardens. Even though I was cajoled into this outing, please be assured I'm not opposed to spending time with you."

He couldn't possibly mean that. After all, he'd shown no interest in me before now. I searched his expression, trying to gauge his sincerity. Exhaustion filled his features, which I now realized could easily be mistaken for boredom, and his hand still cradled the rose he always wore on his lapel, almost as if he needed to touch it; even over a week into his visit, it was still in full bloom.

We continued our walk, during which Briar conversed more easily than he had in our previous outings, as if the outdoors had rejuvenated him. I was almost starting to actually enjoy myself when my bag jiggled against my thigh. *Drake.*

My surprise at his ability to move the mirror was quickly eclipsed by annoyance at his ill-timed interruption. I glared down at my satchel, needing to send him my disapproval even though he wouldn't be able to see it. He'd better behave.

What had I been thinking bringing a snarky cursed mirror with me?

The more freely Briar and I conversed—he was quite knowledgeable about the surrounding plants—the more my bag jiggled, as if Drake were growing restless. I subtly whacked the side of my bag to encourage him to remain still, but it had little effect. I had no choice but to try to ignore him and hope that Briar wouldn't notice. But the task quickly proved impossible when the bag jiggled again more forcefully. Obnoxious mirror.

I kept my arm loosely looped through Briar's as he led me into the orchard, where the boughs were laden with fruit and the air filled with the scent of fresh apples, which were a lovely shade of lilac today. Being back within these trees helped quiet my annoyance. Briar and I settled into a comfortable, companionable silence as we strolled deeper into the shady trees whose limbs created a leafy canopy above us. It was so peaceful...

Until that mirror had to ruin the moment. *"You two sure are talkative."* Drake's snarky tone drifted from my satchel, quiet but not quiet enough. Briar glanced over at me, his brows furrowed.

"Pardon?"

My cheeks warmed. "I didn't say anything." I whacked my bag again to urge Drake to be quiet, but I should have known him better than that.

"This outing is so dull."

Drake again. Briar didn't look over, but his eyebrows rose in surprise and his lips twitched, whether from annoyance or amusement I wasn't sure. Could he hear Drake? His silence led me to hope he hadn't.

As if determined to continue sharing his annoyance, Drake jiggled again. I tugged us to a stop and smiled sweetly at Briar. "Would it be alright if we rested a moment? This is a lovely spot."

He nodded and began to settle on the lawn. His brow furrowed when I wriggled my arm away. "Don't you want to sit down with me?"

"In a moment." I clutched my satchel close to my chest, earning a soft "*Oof*" from the mischievous mirror. "Will you excuse me? I'll return shortly."

I walked deeper into the trees before he could even respond. The moment I was out of sight, I yanked Drake from my satchel. He stared back at me, arms folded and glowering, even though the only one in this situation who had the right to be annoyed was me.

"You're supposed to stay silent," I hissed. "If you don't, I'll leave you in the orchard all by yourself."

"I am; I've only made two comments. You have no idea how many I refrained from making."

"I'm sure Briar heard you. Do you want to be discovered?"

"It's a risk I'll gladly take if it means making this outing something more than a snooze fest. That prince should be ensuring you're having a good time. He's failing miserably. He either walks in stoney silence or discusses the dullest things. *Plants*? Really? The man has no imagination."

"What's it to you?" I wasn't sure whether to be flattered that he was concerned or annoyed at his meddling.

Drake scoffed. "He's not even trying to get to know you."

"How well we know one another matters little in our world. The arrangement will go through regardless." My heart sank at my inevitable future.

Drake's scowl deepened. "Do you really expect so little for yourself? I know you, Rhea. Deep down you want more than just to make a match—you want to at least be friends with your husband."

"It doesn't do any good to dwell on impossible things."

Sadness filled his eyes at my statement. Why was he so concerned? Could it be... "Are you...*worried* for me?" My heart lifted at the thought.

"No," Drake said hastily, his cheeks growing pink, as if embarrassed. "Why would I be worried for you?"

The warm feeling that had been slowly seeping over me vanished in an instant. *He has no reason to worry for you. You're not worth worrying about.*

My dark feelings must have shown in my expression, for Drake's countenance immediately softened. "I'm sorry, Rhea, I didn't mean it like *that*. It's just—it's none of my business whom you marry." But that didn't change the fact that he seemed to want to *make* it his business.

"Thank you for caring," I said.

He merely grunted in a way that made it unclear whether he was agreeing with or denying my assessment. "If you're done scolding me, I suppose you should return to your beau."

He was right; I'd been gone too long to avoid Briar's suspicion. But I wasn't quite ready to return Drake to the bag. "Do you promise to be a *silent* chaperone this time?"

Drake's grin became wicked. "I make no such promises. After all, I consider it my duty to keep an eye on your scoundrel."

"He's behaving quite the gentleman."

Drake rolled his eyes before his attention was captured by something behind me. "Oh look, he's coming this way. Excellent. I have a few choice words to exchange with him—"

I gasped and shoved the mirror back into my satchel before dropping it on the ground, a gesture which earned me a muffled but disgruntled grunt from Drake.

"Is everything alright, Rheanna?" Briar's suspicious gaze flickered between me and the satchel.

"Everything is fine. I was just wondering if this would be the perfect tree to rest beneath." I'd no sooner made the

71

excuse for my lingering too long than I realized it'd be more prudent for us to settle as far away from Drake and his unwanted commentary as possible.

But it was too late; Briar was already settling in the grass, and the part of me that yearned to remain near Drake—for reasons I couldn't even begin to understand—compelled me to sit beside him.

I just don't want to cause Briar any more reason to be suspicious; that's why I'm not coming up with an excuse to move away from Drake. I almost believed my own reasoning.

More silence settled over us, which earlier had been comfortable but now seemed unbearable. I kept casting Briar anxious glances. He sat rather stiffly, his entire posture rigid. The more I watched him, the more I began to wonder if perhaps it wasn't my presence that was distressing him. Briar's fingers were burrowed in the grass, his knuckles white, as if he were trying to clutch the earth. But his expression was more relaxed than it normally was, a contrast to his rigid posture.

"Are you alright, Briar?" I asked quietly.

He gave a stiff nod before burrowing his fingers deeper in the ground. "It feels good to be outside again."

He spread his fingers through the grass with another slow, deep breath, almost as if he drew some sort of solace from touching the ground, stirring only to lightly touch the rose he wore.

Our peaceful stillness was soon broken by Drake, who'd apparently deemed he'd had a long enough break from creating trouble. The sound of a rather exaggerated yawn drifted from the bag.

Briar slowly opened his eyes and glanced warily at my satchel but said nothing. Instead, he gave me a small smile. "Forgive me. I'm not meaning to ignore you."

"It's no problem."

"*Liar,*" Drake muttered. Briar's jaw tightened. Had he heard Drake?

My cheeks warmed and I hastily attempted to smooth over Drake's interjection. "I'd welcome conversing with you, but only if you'd find such a thing agreeable."

"I find you very pleasant company, Rheanna, even though it might not appear that I do." He leaned back against the trunk of a tree and breathed in deeply before fixing his attention on me. "Do you like this orchard?"

"I do, very much. I've spent a lot of time here over the years."

When I didn't elaborate, Briar gave me an expectant look, as if encouraging me to keep speaking. I didn't at first, my shyness discouraging me from continuing.

Tell him stories about the orchard. You shared them with Drake. But Drake hadn't been so intimidating compared to this formidable prince. But I knew I was being unfair to him. Despite his indifference, he'd never given me reason to completely dislike him. If I wanted to make something more of our relationship, I needed to stop hiding behind my insecurities and make an effort.

Briar was waiting patiently, his expression rather sweet. It was enough encouragement for me to speak. I took a wavering breath. "My siblings and I used to play all sorts of games here—"

Wait, that had been the wrong thing to say; I was trying to convince Briar I was a suitable candidate for his queen, and a future queen didn't spend her childhood galavanting through orchards like a common peasant...did she?

But Briar didn't seem put off by my comment. The faint smile teasing at his lips grew. "I can't blame you. This orchard seems a fine place to have grown up. I myself spend an inordinate amount of time exploring the grounds at home." His hand went to his rose again, as if to assure himself it was still there.

I latched on to this topic eagerly. "My orchard was more than a place to play; I often came here to be alone. There's something comforting about the apple trees' branches; they encircle one like a cocoon. That is—" I lowered my gaze to my lap, my cheeks burning.

Briar gently hooked his fingers beneath my chin to lift my gaze, his expression kind. "I understand what you mean. I have a similar place. There are many gardens at my castle"—his lips twitched—"rather *mischievous* gardens."

"How can gardens be mischievous?" I'd never heard gardens described in such a way.

"The grounds of my castle are alive," he said. "Or perhaps a better description is that they're *enchanted*. They're quite spectacular. I'll be happy to show them to you when—" He cleared his throat awkwardly. "That is, if you should make Malvagaria your home, we can spend time there together."

"Wow, wooing you over his gardens. The man is quite the romantic." Drake's sarcastic tone drifted from my satchel. Briar's gaze snapped to it, his eyes narrowed. He'd definitely heard *that* comment.

"Is that—"

"Nothing," I said airily. "Absolutely nothing."

Briar frowned but said nothing as he glared at my bag with a darkening expression. There could be no more doubt; Briar knew that *something* was inside my bag. But why wasn't he saying anything?

My heartbeat escalated. "I need another moment alone," I stammered.

"I'm sure you do." He didn't look up, but kept his gaze locked onto my satchel. "When you return, I'd love to continue our interesting conversation. I find your companionship quite enjoyable. Perhaps we can take a stroll through the trees and, with your permission, I can hold your hand."

My cheeks burned and it wasn't lost on me how Briar seemed to be directing the comment towards my now squirming *bag*...or rather Drake *inside* it.

"We'll see." I snatched my satchel and scampered deeper into the orchard, where we could be relatively secluded. There I yanked the mirror out and met Drake's glower with a glare of my own. "I told you to keep quiet. You're ruining everything."

"Are you going to let him hold your hand?"

"I—it's none of your business whether I do or not."

"Of course it is. I'm your *chaperone*." He spat the word out as if he found it distasteful.

"No, it's not. Our being friends doesn't give you the right to stick your nose into affairs that don't concern you."

Drake's jaw tightened but he said nothing. A strange feeling of defiance swelled within me. I lifted my chin.

"And just so you know, I *am* going to allow him to hold my hand. It seems appropriate, considering we're to be married."

Drake's eyebrow twitched. "Why would you marry *him*? I'm practically falling asleep with how uninteresting your conversations are. You're not even being yourself. You haven't told him about all your memories you built in this orchard, that you enjoy climbing trees, why this place is special to you..."

"I—I find it difficult to share parts of myself with people."

"You shared them with me."

"Yes, but you're a mirror."

It was the wrong thing to say. His cheeks darkened with emotion. "I'm not a *mirror*, I'm a man *within* a mirror. I thought you, at least, knew the difference."

75

"Of course I do, Drake." Remorse squeezed my heart. I lowered my eyes. "I didn't mean it that way."

He was silent a moment before he sighed. "How about a truce: I'll stop interrupting your outing with my comments, and you make it your goal to share at least three stories about this orchard with Briar."

"*Three?*" I squeaked.

"Too many? Then how about at least one."

I bit my lip. "But what if he thinks them silly?"

Drake's expression softened. "You're a wonderful woman, Rhea. There's no need for you to hide yourself. Besides, I found your stories interesting…I find *you* interesting."

His sweet comment caused my heart to swell. "Really?"

He finally smiled, and not only was it welcome after the contention that had festered between us, but it caused my heart to give another strange flutter. "Really. You have nothing to worry about. If you've resigned yourself to marrying Prince Briar, you need to open yourself up to him so that he knows how wonderful you are."

The warmth within my chest expanded. "Thank you."

Drake released a long breath. "The prince is waiting. Even though I can't bear not knowing how it's going, it'd be best if I remained behind. Just promise me you'll ensure he treats you right." His look became almost desperate. "Are you really going to let him hold your hand?"

"Yes," I said. "We're to be married, after all."

His frown deepened and something flashed in his eyes, an emotion too brief for me to discern what it was. "I'm grateful I won't have to witness that." And before I could respond, his image faded from the glass, leaving only my own reflection staring back at me.

It took me a moment to carefully place Drake back in the satchel, which I left beneath the tree before I returned to

Briar, who stood waiting for me with a solemn and almost weary look, as if the entire outing was exhausting him.

His expression softened when he noticed I'd left my bag behind. "Is it just us then?"

He knows. But how was that possible? Had he stumbled upon me talking to Drake during one of our excursions to the library? And if he knew about the mirror, why wasn't he asking about him? Perhaps nothing surprised a man from a cursed family.

Even in my unease I forced a smile. "It is."

Briar nodded and extended his hand, inviting me to take it. I nervously placed my hand—sweaty with nerves—in his, which was just as clammy as mine. Would I feel anything from holding his hand?

Nothing. I peeked up at him to discern his own reaction. He was frowning at our connected hands with a look of frustration, which cleared the moment he noticed me watching him. He forced a smile. "Shall we, Rheanna?"

We walked through the trees, and while the conversation we shared was pleasant enough, for some reason I couldn't stop thinking about Drake, all while I tried to ignore the emptiness I felt holding Briar's hand.

CHAPTER 7

I nibbled my lip as I scanned the titles of the books on forbidden magic I'd stumbled upon in a tucked-away section of the library. After an hour's perusal, my initial hopes that I'd finally found the information that would help Drake had been dashed, leaving me lost once more. I sighed.

"I don't like the sound of that sigh," Drake said from his usual place within my satchel.

"I'm quite discouraged. It's been over a week and I'm no closer to figuring out how to break your curse than when we started. I feel like I've searched every book in the library, to no avail. "

"Don't be disheartened," Drake said. "At least we now know multiple ways that *won't* work. I'm sure there's an approach we haven't yet tried."

How could he remain optimistic when my failure kept him trapped in his confining prison indefinitely? "There just has to be something we haven't attempted." I crouched on my heels to once again study the bottom shelf.

Drake was quiet a moment. "No one has ever expended so much effort on me before."

I reached inside my satchel to pat the handle of his mirror, warm with his emotion, before resuming my search with renewed vigor. I hadn't been combing the shelves for long when a voice tore me from my concentration.

"Searching for a hidden panel?"

I spun around to find Liam leaning against the shelf with his usual boyish grin. I pressed my hand to my heart. "You startled me."

He tried to look contrite...an effort which failed miserably, for his wide grin couldn't be suppressed for long. "My apologies, dear sister." He glanced between me and the books he'd caught me perusing before plucking the nearest volume off the shelf. His brow wrinkled at the title. "*A History of the Forbidden Arts*? Quite suspicious. Are you concocting a devious plan to rid yourself of your unwanted engagement? If so, count me in."

The way he quirked his eyebrow made it clear he was eager to embark on such an adventure. I took the incriminating book and replaced it on the shelf. "I'm simply browsing."

Liam tilted his head to study me with a skeptical look. I shifted guiltily beneath his perusal. His grin returned, wider than ever. "My big-brother senses tell me you're lying, which means you're up to the mischief I've just accused you of." He sounded delighted.

I should have known I couldn't get away with telling tales to the *King of Tall Tales* himself. I chewed on my lip, deliberating. Liam would undoubtedly not rest until he'd extracted my reason for being in such an unconventional section of the library, which meant my wisest course of action would be to persuade him to keep it to himself; Liam was easily bribed.

Or...an idea illuminated my mind. Of course. *Liam*, my

mischievous, fun-loving brother, who had a knack for mysterious dilemmas. Why hadn't I considered him before? I seized his wrist and dragged him deeper into the library.

"Now that I've discovered your shady secrets, are you luring me to my death in order to silence me forever?" He sounded far too cheerful by the possibility.

"I have something to tell you. A secret."

My bag jiggled in warning, but I ignored Drake's subtle protests. Surely he realized he needed more help than I could give him, and Liam was the perfect choice.

Liam looked like his birthday had come early. "A secret? Really? This visit is taking an unexpected turn. Excellent." I paused to give him an inquiring look. He answered my unspoken question. "I initially sought you out so I could ask about your lackluster courtship and try to persuade you that you deserve better than Prince Boring's dismal wooing attempts, but this is a much more entertaining direction."

I bit my lip. "Do you really think it's going that badly?" For after yesterday's outing in the orchard, I'd begun to be more optimistic that Briar hadn't been as indifferent as I'd imagined him to be and we could at least learn to be friends.

Liam wagged his finger scoldingly. "Not so fast. I must use my opinion as a bartering tool to extract this secret of yours."

I sighed. Typical Liam. I led him to a tucked-away alcove deep enough into the library that I had no fears of our being disturbed. There we settled in neighboring armchairs. Liam propped his arms behind his head and leaned back with an expectant look.

I hesitated. Was I doing the right thing in confiding in Liam? He was the sole option, for he was the only member of my family who'd look at my possession of a cursed object as a grand adventure rather than something to be anxious over.

I took a wavering breath. "Do you remember the day Briar and Her Majesty arrived?"

"How could I forget? Prince Boring didn't appreciate any of my incredible stories." Liam shook his head with a *tsk*. "That was when I realized my favorite sister couldn't shackle herself to such a man. I would have sent him packing that very night if Anwen hadn't persuaded me to give him time to prove himself."

"Be serious," I said.

All humor left his expression. "I am, Rhea."

My heart swelled at his sweet protection. I rested my hand over his. His soberness melted into another of his easy grins.

"Is my big-brother caring cajoling you into sharing your juicy secret?" He gave me an expectant look.

I took another steadying breath. "As you know, that night I left the welcome feast early. But rather than return to my room, I wandered the palace, where in the west wing I sensed something."

Liam's eyes brightened. "Ghosts?"

I rolled my eyes. "Not ghosts, but rather…a strange lure, which led me to an enchanted mirror."

Liam's grin grew. I knew he'd love this story. He glanced at my satchel, where the handle of Drake's mirror stuck out. "An enchanted mirror? Intriguing. Share every detail."

"It'd be easier to simply show you." I reached into my bag to pull Drake out, but the moment I withdrew him, a flash of hot pain burned my hand. I gasped and dropped the mirror facedown onto the seat between us. "What did you do that for?" I asked Drake. He didn't respond.

Liam held up his hands. "I didn't do anything."

"Not you. *Him*." I pointed to the mirror.

Liam's eyebrows rose. "The mirror is a *him*?"

"Yes, a rather snarky and mischievous him."

I glared at Drake even though in his position he couldn't see it. I wanted to flip the mirror over and give him a piece of my mind, but my hand still throbbed from the pain of his anger, and I wasn't too keen on having him burn me again.

Oblivious to the danger, Liam picked up the mirror and turned it faceup. I watched his reaction with bated breath. Liam's expression remained impassive, showing no signs of the mirror burning him or any surprise at seeing a man *inside* it.

He slowly looked up at me, his brow furrowed. "I admit to being somewhat disappointed. I'd expected an enchanted mirror to be a bit...*more*. Or must its secrets be discovered?" Anticipation lit his previous disappointment as he eagerly scanned the mirror.

"There's a man trapped inside it. Can't you see him?" I leaned forward and peered into the glass. It was empty. "Where is he?"

"Maybe he's shy," Liam offered.

I snorted. "*Shy* is the last word I'd use to describe him." He was undoubtedly choosing not to show himself on purpose. My annoyance sharpened.

I snatched the mirror back. Only my reflection stared back at me, but I'd no sooner tipped the mirror away from Liam's view than Drake briefly appeared with a sharp glare and a firm shake of his head before disappearing again. I tightened my jaw. Stubborn mirror.

Liam's own grinning reflection appeared in the glass as he peered inside. "Ah, there *is* a man in the mirror, and a rather handsome one." He chuckled but stopped when he caught sight of my expression. "I take it I'm not the man you're referring to."

"No." I tightened my hold on the mirror's handle, the perfect outlet to let Drake know how displeased I was with him. A flare of heat pulsed against my palm, a sign of his own annoyance.

Liam tapped the mirror's glass with his finger. "Perhaps there's a riddle we must solve in order to see this mysterious man? Or are we required to do something a bit more sinister, considering anyone trapped in such an object is the victim of a curse? Regardless, it makes an excellent story, one I'll happily embellish and add to my collection to share at dull events." He winked.

His wink said it all: while he happily played along, he thought I was making everything up. I bristled. "Just because *you* make up stories doesn't mean I do. There really is a man trapped inside this mirror, and since I know little of curses, I wanted your help in freeing him. Clearly, my confidence was misplaced."

His humor vanished in an instant. He sobered. "Of course you wouldn't tell tales. I'm sorry." He glanced down at the mirror resting on my lap, its reflection still empty. "There's really a man inside this?"

"Yes, and a stubborn one at that, as he's choosing not to reveal himself now. While I can only see his reflection, we converse as normal people."

Liam picked up the mirror and examined it from all angles, his expression concentrated. His study didn't yield much information and he lowered it with a sigh. "A tricky puzzle, but one undoubtedly far more exciting for you than courting Prince Boring. We must figure out how to perform this elaborate rescue of your friend."

"Therein lies the problem—after over a week I'm no closer to finding a solution than when I started."

Liam stroked his chin thoughtfully. "Despite years seeking adventures, I have very little experience with curses —unless you count Rosalina's love spell or Anwen's enchanted ring. Admittedly, Anwen wasn't so much cursed as she was bound by a magical contract, but it trapped her in a way that seems similar to the situation your mysterious mirror man finds himself in. I don't know many details, but I do remember that one of the stipulations for her curse was that only the one who bound her could free her."

My heart lurched. What if Drake's curse was similar? But it couldn't be; he'd told me that the one who'd cursed him had done it by accident, which meant they'd undoubtedly already tried—and failed—to free him.

"I don't think that's the nature of this curse." Which meant there had to be another way.

"Then perhaps there's a requirement that must be met?"

I frowned. Drake had never mentioned such a thing, which meant he was just as ignorant as to *what* such a requirement would be as I was. I stared out at the vast and daunting sea of shelves. "Where should I look? I've already searched the library thoroughly."

Liam considered the puzzle. "Somewhere unexpected. Unconventional things—such as dark magic—likely require unconventional solutions, so perhaps you need to approach the problem in a different way." He leaned closer and lowered his voice to a conspiratorial whisper. "Perhaps instead of studying facts in books about spells and curses, you should instead study folktales and stories. After all, truth can always be found in stories. I'm sure if you look hard enough, you'll discover the solution hidden in plain sight."

It was an approach I hadn't considered. If nothing else, I was certain studying stories would trigger an idea for a path I hadn't yet tried. The mirror shifted slightly in my lap, Drake's own approval of Liam's suggestion.

"That's a wonderful idea. Thank you, Liam."

"I'm happy to help. You're rather fortunate to have such a brilliant brother."

My smile was accompanied by a piercing look. "Am I also

fortunate enough to have a brother who's good with secrets?"

"Perhaps you do…that is, for a small fee. How about tonight's dessert? I hear it's apple tarts." He wriggled his eyebrows and grinned when I nodded. "Excellent. Then you have my word that I'll keep your cursed mirror a secret. It's likely for the best—Mother and Father are rather superstitious about these sorts of things, Aveline would do nothing but scold, and everybody knows Elodie can't keep a secret. Anwen would definitely keep your confidence, but as much as I hate keeping secrets from my wife, I won't tell her if you don't wish it."

"Keeping secrets, Liam?" Anwen had arrived, looking curious. She pressed her hands on her hips and gave her husband a teasing scolding look. "When you told me to come find you after my nap, I didn't realize we'd literally be playing a game of hide-and-seek."

"Everything is always a game with me. I'm glad you won this round, as I missed you." Liam scooted over on his chair and patted the spot next to him, inviting her to sit down. He took her hands after she'd curled up beside him and held them comfortably in his. "How was your nap, sweetheart?"

"It was lovely. I needed the rest."

"Are you feeling better?"

I frowned. Anwen wasn't feeling well? I studied her. She looked quite healthy. She met my concerned gaze with an assuring smile. "I'm feeling fine. I just needed to lie down." She turned to Liam. "But now I'm ready for whichever adventure you have planned for us."

Mischief filled his eyes. "I thought we could do a little espionage: I want to find out more about Prince Boring, see if I can discover his mysterious curse and ascertain whether or not he'll be a good husband for Rhea. So far I'm not impressed—he'll undoubtedly put her in an early grave by boring her to death."

She gasped. "*Liam!*"

He blinked rather innocently. "You know I'm right. If you want to prove otherwise, then join me in my spying. It'll be a wonderful way to pass the afternoon until our meeting."

She laughed lightly as she looped her arm through his and tugged him to his feet. "You always find a way to wrangle me into your mischief—making paper boats out of important documents, searching for haunted settees, training my geese to take military orders…"

Liam grinned widely. "Ah yes, that has been quite the project, but you must admit it'll be most impressive once we succeed. Can't you just see General Hornet on the front lines instilling fear into our enemies? We'll certainly have the element of surprise, especially since no one will suspect the future king and queen of Draceria has a secret army of geese. I promised a fun and adventurous marriage, and I'm a man of my word."

Liam kissed her cheek before lacing his hand through hers and glancing at me.

"I'm off to be the best husband in the kingdom. Good luck with your own quest. We'll reconvene for a secret strategy meeting so we can share our findings about *you know*"—he wriggled his eyebrows mischievously—"as well as my newest discoveries about Prince Boring. I'm determined to do my part to convince you not to marry him."

He and Anwen left. I listened to their retreating footsteps, waiting impatiently for them to leave so I could confront Drake. The footsteps paused and Liam spoke.

"Good afternoon, Your Majesty."

My heart leapt. I peeked around the bookshelf to find the Queen of Malvagaria standing nearby, seemingly absorbed in browsing the shelves. How long had she been standing there, and how much of our conversation had she overheard? She'd likely missed my telling Liam about the cursed mirror, but by her cold expression, I didn't doubt she'd heard Liam's parting jab about his intentions to thwart my engagement with Briar.

The disapproving look vanished in an instant, replaced by a polite smile. "Good afternoon, Prince Liam and Princess Anwen."

Liam bowed, looking unruffled by the likelihood that my intended's mother had overheard his scheme to thwart the union. He scampered off with Anwen as if they were outrunning Cook after having nicked sweets from the palace kitchen.

The queen watched them go before glancing at me. While her expression remained friendly, her smile faltered. "It's lovely to see you, Rheanna dear. I've been looking for you. Briar is seeking your company...which will undoubtedly disappoint Prince Liam." Her smile tightened.

My heart sank. *She'd heard.* "Liam likes a good tease," I said in his defense. "While he often says the wrong thing, his intentions are good."

"I'm glad to hear it." Although the queen was still smiling, her gaze hardened.

"Please excuse me; I must find Briar."

I curtsied and quickly left the library, but I didn't seek out Briar...at least not yet. First I had a mirror to scold. The moment I was safely in my bedroom, I yanked Drake out and met his scowling reflection.

"Why didn't you appear for Liam? Thanks to you, I almost didn't receive his help." It was a good thing Liam was the type of man to believe a fantastic story even without a shred of evidence.

He crossed his arms with a glare. "Why did you tell him about *my* curse without consulting me?"

"He won't tell anyone. He's a man of his word."

"I wish I could say the same for you. It wasn't your secret to tell."

I flinched. "You never told me I *couldn't* tell anyone about the curse—"

"It was clearly implied."

Guilt prickled my heart. I lowered my eyes. "I'm sorry. I just felt bad I haven't been able to be much help. I thought if anyone could aid me, it'd be Liam."

Drake released a long sigh and to my fierce relief his face relaxed. "You *are* helping," he said gently. "Your efforts and persistence undoubtedly count for something."

"I want to do more than *try*; I want to succeed. That's the only reason I asked for Liam's assistance, and as I'd hoped, he had a new approach. What do you think of his idea?"

He was silent a moment. "It's something to consider. Be that as it may…please don't talk to him about the curse anymore."

I wrinkled my forehead. "But he already knows."

"I'd still prefer you didn't talk to him—or *anyone*—about it. At least you had the sense not to share my name."

"Would that have been bad?"

"Quite likely." He hesitated, as if debating whether to say more. "Many curses become permanent from even such a simple thing."

Just from sharing his name? It seemed a rather strict stipulation, but despite my own misgivings, I'd honor Drake's wishes; his becoming trapped permanently due to my own follies was the last thing I wanted.

"I promise not to speak of it to anyone else again." It was a promise I fully intended to keep. The more I came to know Drake, the more desperate I was to free him. If he thought my silence was the best way to do so, then I'd give that to him.

But that left me once more to my own devices, which had so far yielded no results. I prayed I had enough fortitude to break it on my own.

CHAPTER 8

*B*riar informed me the next morning that he'd requested his mother take breakfast with my parents so he could dine with me and my sisters on his own. I was relieved not to have the queen's watchful eye constantly upon me when her son and I were together, and perhaps Briar was too, for he paid more attention to me at breakfast than he ever had before. Almost every time I glanced at him I found him staring at me. This went on for several minutes until he seemed to summon enough courage to breach the silence.

"Did you sleep well?" He kept his voice lowered, as if he didn't want to alert the others at the table he was speaking to me. But Elodie perked up, her eyes wide and bright at this sudden turn of events.

I tried to ignore her as I turned my attention to Briar. "I slept well, thank you." In truth, I hadn't gotten much sleep. Drake and I had stayed up late first skimming a stack of folktales we'd acquired from the library in order to research more about Drake's curse before becoming engrossed in a mystery novel, which had led to a heated debate about potential suspects and solutions long past midnight. It had made for an exhausting but wonderful evening.

Briar was studying my expression carefully, as if trying to read the thoughts I wouldn't share. His eyes narrowed, filled with suspicion, as if he sensed I'd been thinking about Drake.

He knows. It wasn't the first time in the days following our outing to the orchard I'd suspected he was aware I possessed Drake's mirror, even though I had no idea how he could have come to that knowledge. How would he even know about Drake? If the rumors about the Baron of Livre's son were true, then perhaps Drake had traveled to Malvagaria and encountered the prince...but that wouldn't explain how Briar knew about Drake's curse, unless Drake had been cursed while over there.

Briar said nothing more until I finished my last bite of food. Before the servants could stir, he reached for my plate. "Would you like seconds?"

I nodded, ignoring Elodie's pleased eyebrow lift from her seat across from me. I watched him scoop up more eggs and bacon. *Why is Briar being so attentive?* His mother wasn't at the table giving him encouraging glares, so what could his reason possibly be? For surely he had some sort of motive... unless he was simply nicer than I'd given him credit for.

Briar placed my now-full plate in front of me. "Do you have any duties to attend to today?"

I slowly shook my head. I had no *royal* duties, at least, but I'd promised Drake we could finish our book today.

"In that case, will you do me the great pleasure of spending the day with me in the gardens...*alone*?" He added the last part sternly. My cheeks warmed.

Yes, he definitely knows. The question that still remained was: *how?*

I expected Briar's attention to falter now that he'd dutifully secured another courtship outing, but to my surprise, he continued conversing with me throughout the meal, a gesture that had Elodie repeatedly wriggling her eyebrows at me whenever she met my eyes, as if she'd come to her own conclusions as to why Briar was now being attentive. She was very much a romantic at heart...in this instance, too much so.

Don't get your hopes up; his attentions won't last.

But they miraculously did. Strange. What could possibly account for Briar's sudden change of heart? Could he perhaps now enjoy my company?

Briar finished breakfast first. "Thank you for spending this pleasant meal with me. I'll meet you in the entrance hall after you've finished eating." He rose from the table. "Might I suggest bringing a wrap? It's a blustery morning and I'd hate for you to catch a chill."

Elodie grinned widely as she caught my eye and mouthed, *Thoughtful and considerate.* Briar bowed to me before excusing himself, leaving only my sisters and me at the table.

The moment the door closed behind him, Elodie leaned forward eagerly. "Well, this is an interesting development."

"Whatever do you mean?" I stammered.

She rolled her eyes. "Don't pretend you don't know what I'm talking about—Briar is starting to realize you're his soulmate. His attentions make him all the more handsome." She pressed a hand to her heart with a wistful sigh.

I fiddled with my napkin. "You're being a bit too hasty in your assumptions, Elodie."

"Not in the least," she said. "He not only conversed with you the entire meal, but this is the second outing in a row he's invited you on. He finally seems eager to court you, and this time without encouragement from his mother. You must be leaving quite the impression on him."

"Perhaps Prince Briar is simply making the best of his duty," Aveline said.

Elodie waved that thought away. "Nonsense; he's starting to fall in love with her."

I wouldn't go *that* far. "Things are admittedly going better," I said tentatively. "But that doesn't mean—"

"I should say they are: you've even progressed to holding hands."

I startled, jolting the table with my knee. "How did you—you were spying again, weren't you?"

"Of course I was," she said, as usual unabashed. "It's my sisterly duty to ensure that your romance goes well."

Was it going well? Even without the Queen of Malvagaria's shadow hovering over us, Briar now paid more attention to me than he had when he first arrived in Draceria. But despite this change, the wariness guarding my heart remained unconvinced this relationship wouldn't end the same way my arrangement with Deidric had.

It took several attempts to shake off Elodie's nosy questions in order to meet Briar in the entrance hall. He greeted me with an uncertain smile, which I hesitantly returned. I sent a servant for my shawl so I wouldn't have to face Drake's disappointment that I was canceling our reading date. Once the servant returned, Briar carefully wrapped it around my shoulders.

"No satchel today?" His tone was a bit too innocent and knowing.

"Not today," I said.

Clearly relieved, Briar offered his arm and led me into the brisk outdoors. The biting wind nipped at my cheeks and quickly ruined my updo. Briar tucked a loose strand behind my ear. I stiffened as his fingers grazed my cheek and he hastily yanked his hand away.

He bit his lip. "Perhaps this isn't the best morning for a stroll." Despite his words, he looked out over the grounds with a look akin to longing, his free hand hovering over the rose he wore.

"I don't mind a bit of wind."

He sighed in relief. "Thank you. We'll only stay out for a short while. Let me know if you grow too cold."

We took a path that led through a garden whose hedges had lost most of their leaves. His expression was somber as he glanced around.

"I hate how the gardens here die when winter comes."

"Do your gardens never die?"

"Magic has a life of its own." He paused beside a rosebush whose flowers were nearly all shriveled; soon the gardeners would trim them back for winter. He stroked one of the rose's wilting petals and sighed. "It's not the same," he murmured.

A strange possibility occurred to me as I watched him, both with the dead rose bush and the anxious way he fiddled with the blooming one he wore on his lapel.

I studied it more carefully. Not only was it not wilted, but it hadn't lost any petals; it was still in perfect bloom, unchanged from the day he'd arrived. In the light, the petals almost glistened, as if shrouded in magic.

Is it the same rose? "I'm surprised your rose hasn't begun to die," I said slowly. "Is it because it's from your enchanted garden?"

Briar smiled as his gaze flickered to me. "You're a clever girl. Yes, it is."

Interesting. "You're always touching it. Is there a reason for that?"

"There is. I suspected you'd soon inquire about my rose." He led me to a bench between two hedges and we sat. "The rose connects me to the gardens at home."

I waited for him to elaborate. He didn't. "And you wear it because you miss them?"

He smiled wryly. "Something like that." He looked out over the grounds again, exhaustion filling his strained expression. "I've never been away from the gardens for so long."

My suspicion only grew. "Is it true that your entire family is cursed?"

He actually laughed, a rather forced sound. "That's the second question I've been waiting for you to ask ever since our courtship started. It took you longer than I expected."

He was evading the question. "You don't *appear* cursed."

He was silent a moment, as if debating how much to share with me. "Neither does my younger sister, Reve. Our curses are harder to discern compared to those trapping our other two siblings." He cast me a sidelong glance before forcing a smile that didn't reach his weary dark eyes. "But not to worry. Whatever afflicts me won't impede our match."

That wasn't exactly encouraging.

Briar stood and offered his arm once more so we could resume strolling the garden. "Despite the cold, I'm enjoying this walk more than our last one," Briar said. "Especially considering today I have your exclusive attention." He gave me a knowing look. My heart flared to life.

No doubt about it, he definitely knows. Then why wasn't he confronting me? "I'm sorry," I whispered.

"I'm sorry as well, Rheanna. I—" He took a deep breath before stepping closer. "I'm sorry I haven't been more attentive. I know it's no excuse, but I've been struggling ever since leaving Malvagaria."

"Because of our arrangement?"

"No, because...I'm away from home." He was fiddling with his rose again. "It's been more difficult than I antici-pated, and I'm afraid it's made me not quite myself. I apologize."

I furrowed my brow. Did it have anything to do with his

curse, or was he merely a man who was only comfortable within the walls of his own home? Either way, should we marry, I'd likely rarely have the opportunity to leave Malvagaria in order to visit my family.

"Thank you for explaining," I said. "I'm relieved that my assumptions about your lack of interest turned out to be unfounded."

"You believed I was uninterested?" He frowned. "There's some truth to that, I suppose."

My heart sank. I hastily blinked my burning tears away. "Is there?"

"What I mean is I wouldn't have sought a match with you myself, but while I didn't choose it, I'm not opposed to it either. I'm assuming you feel similarly?"

I did, but that didn't make the sting that *he* thought such a thing any less piercing. But I tried to push aside my feelings and focus on our conversation, which, once it resumed, ranged from small talk to deeper and more pleasant topics.

When it grew more chilly, we returned inside. I hoped I'd finally be able to return to Drake's company, but Briar surprised me by asking to accompany me to the library, where he continued monopolizing my attention, exploring the shelves with me and asking after books I'd read. From there, he invited me to take lunch with him, after which we played a game of draughts.

And so the endless day continued. It was pleasant enough but exhausting. And throughout it, I watched Briar carefully, wondering if Elodie's earlier suspicions had any merit: *was* Briar spending time with me because his feelings were changing? He didn't try to hold my hand again, which seemed telling, not to mention he wore a strange look— despite his friendliness, his dark eyes contained an almost competitive glimmer, as if I were a prize he'd do all he could to claim, even if it wasn't one he necessarily wanted to win.

~

LONG AFTER MY time with Briar concluded, my mind lingered over our day together, analyzing it from every angle. Surprisingly, the longer we'd been together, the more at ease I'd begun to feel in his presence, but it still didn't dissipate the forced feeling that filled each of our interactions; being with him was incredibly exhausting.

I stared gauntly at my reflection as my maid prepared me for bed. I'd never been more eager for a day to end, but what if tomorrow was also dedicated completely to Briar, and the day after that? As much as I was growing to like him as a friend, the thought of a future filled with more days like this felt entirely overwhelming.

"Are you alright, Your Highness?" my maid asked.

I blinked rapidly, tugging myself away from my thoughts. "I'm fine." But long after she'd left for the evening, I remained in front of the mirror, my confusing emotions pressing against me; I felt as if I'd slipped below the water and could barely keep my head above it. It was a suffocating feeling, made more so when I realized Briar's motive for seeking me out:

He's forcing himself to like you. Why else would he be pursuing you so intently?

"Is it finally safe to talk?"

Drake's sour voice tore me from my stupor. I glanced over to where he faced the wall, the usual position I put him in when I was dressing. I retrieved the mirror and flipped it over, only to find that his expression matched the grumpiness filling his tone.

"What's the matter with you?" I asked.

"It's been a boring day. And you broke your promise—we were going to finish the mystery book."

"I know." Guilt tightened my chest. "It's not my fault. Briar—"

"Don't tell me you spent the day with *him*."

His hardened tone rankled me. I wasn't in the mood for him to revert back to his usual snarky attitude; today had been exhausting enough. "Fine, then I won't tell you about it. Now, where would you like me to put you tonight?"

He scowled. If I didn't know any better, he actually looked hurt. "That's it? You broke your promise and left me bored all day, and now you don't even want to talk with me?"

"Your sulky attitude is making me less than eager to humor you." I stomped towards the desk where I'd left our mystery book, plopped him in front of it, and turned the page. "You can spend the night reading these two pages and coming up with theories on who the murderer is."

His frown only deepened. "But we were reading it together."

"I'm too tired to read tonight." I turned away.

"Forget the book, Rhea. Just please talk to me for a few minutes." His tone was so imploring that I felt myself gradually softening against my will. But I was tired of being a pushover. First Briar had cajoled me into spending the entire day with him, now Drake wanted my evening. Although I usually welcomed his company, tonight I just needed some time to myself.

"If you're going to continue whining, then I'll put you in my wardrobe so you can spend the entire night surrounded by my gowns and petticoats."

He looked truly horrified by the possibility. "This curse just keeps getting worse and worse. As if my day wasn't bad enough. It's been endlessly dull, and now I'm forced to deal with the wrath of an emotional woman. What did I do to deserve such a fate?"

I pressed my hands to my hips and glared at him. He lowered his eyes, contrite.

"Right, wrong thing to say. I'm sorry, Rhea." After a moment he looked up hopefully. "Did my heartfelt apology work? Will you spend time with me after all?"

My lips twitched against my will, but I forced myself to keep my expression stern. "Unfortunately not. I still want to retire early."

"But Rhea—"

My temper and impatience flared further. "Fine, if you don't want to read the book without me, you can spend the night staring at wood." I slammed his mirror facedown on my nightstand and crawled into bed.

He groaned. "Please don't leave me like this. It's not exactly comfortable." His voice was muffled.

I ignored him, fluffing my pillows.

"I'll talk all night and keep you awake."

"Oh, so you do want to spend the night in my wardrobe?"

"*No*! Listen, I'm sorry. I know you're in a bad mood, but it's not my fault. Don't take it out on me."

I stilled. He was right. I was allowing my confusion over Briar's actions and my own insecurities to cause me to be rude to my friend. Why was I doing that? Perhaps it was the uncertainty and fear of my imminent future with Briar; it pressed against my chest, making it difficult to breathe, let alone be cheerful.

I tentatively picked up Drake's mirror and flipped it back over. At seeing me, he immediately brightened. "Did I soften you with my apology after all? I thought it was a good one— one of my best, I should say."

My lips ached to smile. "It had the desired effect. I'm appeased."

"Thank goodness." He rubbed his head and winced.

The remainder of my annoyance faded away. "Did I hurt you when I slammed you down?"

"It didn't exactly feel good."

"I'm sorry."

He released a long sigh. "So am I. I shouldn't have goaded you into spending time with me when I could clearly see you're...*unhappy*. You'd think after spending an entire lifetime dealing with my two younger sisters that I'd know better." His expression became somber.

"Do you miss them?" I asked.

"I actually do. I used to tease them mercilessly, of course, and they often annoyed me. But..." His forehead furrowed. "I'm worried for them. When I became trapped, their circumstances weren't...particularly ideal."

Sympathy filled my heart, melting away the last of my annoyance. I settled in bed and propped Drake's mirror on my knees as I leaned against the pillows. "Tell me more about your sisters."

"They're stubborn, mischievous, and rather annoying, but adorable. I can tell you that because I trust you'll never tell them I have a soft spot for them." He sighed. "I doubt they miss me at all. As far as I know, none of my family has made any effort to discover what happened to me, not even my father."

"I'm sure that's not true."

"I know them, and I'm afraid it likely is." He released another weary sigh. "But it doesn't matter. Won't you tell me what's bothering you?"

"Nothing is."

He gave me a skeptical look. "We both know that isn't true. Do you want to talk about it?" But his offer was clearly a reluctant one.

"If you're hoping I'll refuse your offer, why did you extend it?"

"Because you're looking so gloomy. Besides, 'talking about it' always helps my sisters. I don't understand why; it's not as if words can make a bad memory go away. But if it helps them, I thought it might help you, too. You're a girl, after all." He shrugged.

I wanted to take advantage of the rare moment the elusive Drake was opening up about his mysterious past. "And where are your sisters now?"

"Since they're not with me in the mirror, I obviously have no idea."

This fact slowly settled in. "Do they know what's happened to you?"

"I'm sure they've *noticed;* whether or not they care is a different matter entirely." Vulnerability filled his eyes. He sounded so...*defeated*, unlike the snarky man I was accustomed to. Perhaps this was the real Drake, and his usual attitude was merely a mask, similar to the one I wore that allowed me to put on a brave face when inside me was a swell of insecurities, carefully hidden from not just the world, but also those closest to me, at times even myself.

Or perhaps until now, Drake's time in the mirror had merely hardened him. Not that I blamed him; if I found myself trapped behind glass, it'd be harder for me to be my best self. It was difficult to do on most days, even outside a mirror.

"I'm sure your sisters care that you're trapped," I said gently, hoping to reassure him.

He was silent a moment. "Thanks, Rhea. Now, won't you tell me what's upsetting you?"

"You really want to listen?"

"What else do I have to do?" But despite his snarky words, his eyes told a different story: he genuinely wanted to know what was bothering me.

My heart warmed at his concern, dispelling the tension

that had previously pressed against it. I'd spent years bottling all my emotions, as if by locking my hurt away I could pretend it didn't exist. But I was tired of pretending. For once, I wanted the mask to come off…at least with Drake.

"Have you ever been in love?" I asked.

The shock that filled his face might have been humorous if I hadn't been so desperate for his response. "*In love?*" He wrinkled his nose. "No, I haven't."

I found that hard to believe. "You mean to tell me that a handsome man such as yourself has never felt anything towards a beautiful girl?"

He grinned. "You think I'm handsome?" He chuckled at the blush burning my cheeks. "I can't deny I've had plenty of interest from women, and admittedly I think my fair share of girls are pretty." My stomach knotted at his admission that he considered other girls attractive, especially since I was likely not one of them.

"So you've liked several girls."

His cheeks darkened as he stared at me before he hastily yanked his gaze away. "But I've never loved any of them. Is there a reason for your curiosity?"

I bit my lip, almost afraid to continue questioning him. "I want to know how to tell when a man is falling in love…or at least has genuine interest in a girl. Does he frequently think about her? Want to be near her?"

Drake shrugged. "I'm not exactly sure. Like I said, I've never been in love. But I imagine a man would frequently think about a girl, want to spend time with her, and find many things to admire about her." He stared into my eyes with a look like he was searching for something…before he blushed and quickly looked away again. "Is there a reason for your questions?"

"I have no idea how to measure how well it's going with Briar. He did want to spend the entire day with me and he was unusually attentive, so I want to believe it's progressing, but—"

Drake stiffened. "Was he now? Do I need to fear that this recitation is going to be mushy?"

"Of course not. Briar isn't a mushy sort of man. Up until now, he's mostly been cool towards me, paying me attention only at the cajoling of his mother, who for some reason seems set on the match. So I was surprised he initiated an outing today, seemingly of his own accord."

Drake's jaw tightened but he remained silent.

"But on the outing…" I frowned, trying to find the words to describe the uneasiness I'd been feeling. "He—"

"Did he hurt you?" Drake's expression was fierce, almost…*protective*. Fire filled his eyes, as if he was determined to break out of the mirror and track Briar down right then and there.

I raised an eyebrow. "No, nothing like that."

"Did he make you uncomfortable in any way?" Drake's hands were now balled into fists.

I managed a smile. "Are you going to confront him?"

"If we ever break this blasted curse, I fully intend to."

My smile grew. No man outside my family had ever been so protective of me before.

"So enlighten me: did he make you uncomfortable?" His tone was fierce.

"No, he didn't."

He released a whooshing breath but didn't relax his stance. "Then why are you so melancholy? The scoundrel must have done *something*."

"He didn't. It's just that…" How could I explain when the words I needed were the very ones that would unlock the pain I'd kept buried for years, ever since Deidric's rejection?

"What is it, Rhea?" Drake's manner had softened.

I sighed. "He seemed determined to win my favor, but not

out of genuine interest. It's almost if he's competing for a prize merely for the sake of winning rather than because he values me. I'm not sure whether he cares for me." How could he?

Drake was silent a moment. "I don't understand, Rhea. Why does this upset you when you don't care for *him*...or have your feelings changed?" His question came out strangled. "And you must still care for Prince Deidric, because pain fills your eyes whenever he's mentioned, even though you claim you never loved him. You can't deny it; I've noticed."

Drake had the uncanny ability to see beyond the mask I was so determined to cling to. After all the years keeping my heartache a secret, I knew now was the time to share it; it was too heavy a burden to carry on my own any longer.

I turned the lamp down and snuggled deeper into my blankets before propping Drake up against the pillow so we faced one another. The moonlight illuminated not just his concern, but likely the tears already filling my eyes.

"Rhea?" Drake's voice was soft and still, just like the surrounding night.

"Deidric and I became engaged years ago," I began. "Even though it was a political arrangement, I was determined to try to love him. Despite my best intentions, the feelings just...wouldn't come. Our arrangement was made more difficult when from the moment Deidric and I met, I could tell he had no interest in me; he merely accepted our engagement as his duty."

My tears escaped and fell silently down my cheeks. Drake's breath hitched as he reached out, as if to wipe them away. But he couldn't.

I took a wavering breath and continued. "He avoided me whenever one of us visited the other, choosing instead to spend his time with Kian and Liam. He was more interested in pursuing a friendship with his future brothers-in-law than his future wife. This went on for years…until one day I got a letter."

"What did it say?" Drake asked quietly.

I wiped my wet cheeks. "It was very brief. Deidric broke off our engagement suddenly and without any explanation. My parents asked if I wanted to fight it—our contract could only be broken if both kingdoms were in agreement—but his rejection made me want little to do with him. At first I thought his spurning was the worst of it, but I was mistaken."

The sorrow filling Drake's expression deepened. "What happened, Rhea?"

The sharp, gnawing pain I'd spent so long fighting to ignore seeped out of its locked-away place in my heart. I squeezed my eyes shut.

"Deidric invited my sisters and me to Sortileya for a competition he was hosting to see who was the most worthy princess to be his queen. I hadn't been good enough for him, so he had to find a replacement. I'd always known he didn't love me, but I'd foolishly believed I was at least worthy enough to stand by his side. But I clearly wasn't. Protocol demanded I attend the competition and act as if nothing were wrong, when in reality I was utterly humiliated and breaking inside. I was forced to watch as he chose another woman. And do you know who he picked?" More tears escaped. "A *common girl*, Drake. A common girl was more worthy of being his queen than I was."

I pressed my hands to my eyes so hard I could see spots, an attempt to suppress my tears, but they slipped through my fingers, all while my dark thoughts returned to attack me.

You're worthless, Rhea. Deidric thought so and now Briar does, too.

"Prince Deidric is an idiot." Drake practically growled the words.

I gave a half laugh, half sob. "No, he's quite intelligent." Which had made his rejection even more stinging.

Drake snorted. "Forgive me, but I disagree; the prince is a fool. And he's not the only one—Prince Briar appears to be as well. You find yourself surrounded by blind men who fail to appreciate you. Idiots, the lot of them."

"It's not just them. I'm certain every man thinks as they do." My deep-rooted fear escaped, unable to be trapped in its prison any longer. "Is there something wrong with me?"

"No, of course not." Drake was all gentleness.

"Then why—"

"I don't know why Prince Deidric broke off his engagement with you," Drake said. "But you shouldn't let that single event define your self worth."

"How can I not?" I demanded. "It merely confirmed what I've always feared—that I'm not *enough*. There has to be something wrong with me." My lip quivered. "I have no interest in Briar, but I'm terrified of losing him all the same. I couldn't bear it if another engagement fell through; I can't experience such pain again." A wave of terror washed over me at the thought.

"Prince Briar won't reject you," Drake said.

"Maybe not like Deidric did, but even if our engagement goes through, his indifference will be a continuous rejection, and for good reason—I'm entirely unremarkable."

Drake sighed. "It appears you're rather blind as well, but I, for one, am not. You're a sweet and lovely woman, Rhea, not to mention quite clever and..." He trailed off, his cheeks reddening again. He cleared his throat. "But what I say doesn't matter if you don't believe me and see these traits within yourself."

I propped up on my elbow and fully faced him, where I became overwhelmed with the intensity of his tender gaze. "Do you really think I'm all those things?"

"Do you?"

"I'm not sure." I severed my gaze and looked out the window, where the stars glistened in the cold night.

He sighed. "I'm not particularly good at advice, but might I suggest something? You can't continue to let your past shape how you see yourself now, and you shouldn't keep bottling up your feelings. You need to share your burden so you don't carry it alone. Only then can you begin to heal."

I returned my gaze to Drake's and once more got lost in his eyes, so dark and tender. I slowly reached out to touch the glass and he lifted his hand too so that our fingertips grazed one another's. Despite him being trapped within the mirror, it almost felt...real, as if we were really touching. Maybe it felt real because now that I'd shared the deepest secret of my heart with him, I felt closer to him.

"Thank you," I whispered as another tear trickled down my cheek. Drake watched it with a broken look. He reached out again to try and dry my tears, only for his fingers to once more hit the glass. He was trapped, just like I was.

But even if I couldn't free myself, in that moment I became more determined to free him, so that the next time our fingers touched, it'd be real.

CHAPTER 9

"I'm afraid that despite my best efforts, I have yet to find anything condemning about Briar. But I'm still determined to make my case."

Liam's timing couldn't have been worse—pulling me aside mere minutes before Briar himself was to escort me into dinner.

I glanced around the crowded parlor to ensure our conversation wasn't being overheard before glaring at him. "Are you still so determined to thwart my engagement?"

He lifted his eyebrows in surprise at my snappy tone. "Certainly, until the moment I can tell you're genuinely pleased about the match." His knowing look told me he didn't believe that day was forthcoming.

I sighed. It made it so much more difficult to do the right thing when Liam was continuously trying to persuade me otherwise. "I know you feel it's your brotherly duty to meddle, but in this instance I'd prefer you leave me be."

"Your resistance only makes me more determined; you know I never back down from a challenge."

I rolled my eyes, but despite my annoyance, I couldn't

help but smile, not when his mischievous grin was rather contagious. "It's a good thing I love you so fiercely and know you're solely motivated by your good intentions, else I'd be quite upset with you."

"They're more than good intentions." He stepped closer and lowered his voice. "I'm genuinely concerned for you, Rhea, and not just because you're courting a sleeping draft; there's also the matter of the entire Malvagarian family being cursed. No matter how much I investigate, I can't figure out what curse ails Prince Boring. I don't want you involved with him."

Liam's sober expression melted away the last of my annoyance. I rested my hand on his arm. "While Briar hasn't given me details about his curse, he's assured me it won't affect me."

Liam rolled his eyes. "Of course he'd say that."

I sensed several impending arguments I didn't have the strength to endure. "Please don't try to dissuade me; I've made up my mind."

By Liam's fierce expression, I knew I hadn't heard the last of his protests, and the next topic he chose to discuss proved just as undesirable. He leaned in close. "Any success with your cursed mirror?"

Oh no, he wanted to talk about the mirror, and I'd promised Drake I wouldn't discuss his curse with anyone else. I was frantically trying to come up with a way to dissuade Liam's interest when I received an unexpected rescue: Briar suddenly appeared at my elbow.

I sighed with relief at his impeccable timing while Liam scowled. "An unfortunate setback. Not to worry, we'll reconvene later." He brushed a kiss on my cheek before leaving to greet Anwen. Briar raised his eyebrows at his retreating back.

"What was that about?"

"Liam is stubbornly pursuing a quest I'd rather he didn't."

"Unsurprising; he does seem a determined sort." Thankfully he let the matter drop and offered his arm to escort me into the dining room.

Dinners were no longer as torturous as they'd been when Briar and the queen had first arrived. Although I found it much easier to talk with Drake, Briar had been making more of an effort to converse with me, and many of our conversations were even pleasant.

Still, despite our progress, I couldn't help but be distracted by the conversations around me; it was impossible for Briar to compete with Liam whenever he dove into one of his entertaining stories, tonight's being an exaggerated account of his and Anwen's adventures during their morning trip to help build a school in a neighboring village.

Halfway through our third course, Liam's conversation began to wane, and after a few minutes he ended the story abruptly and fell into uncanny silence.

Anwen leaned towards him. "Are you alright, dear?"

He offered her a weary smile as he took her hand beneath the table. "I'm simply tired. It was quite a physical day today working in the village."

I wanted to make my own inquiries, but my attention was tugged away by Elodie, who began telling me about her recent interaction with a particularly dashing nobleman. I wasn't a particularly attentive sister as my mind repeatedly wandered to our brother sitting beside me.

I glanced at him; he remained subdued, his attention riveted on building a fortress with his mashed potatoes around his peas, as if they were his subjects in need of protection. Liam hadn't played with his food since his marriage, and even then he'd never done it without his usual animation.

Anwen rested her hand on his knee. "Are you sure you're alright, Liam?"

He sighed before forcing a smile that looked a bit strained. "I'm fine. Really." As if determined to prove her worries unfounded, he turned to talk to Father, but it was without his usual enthusiasm, tiredness filling his eyes.

Anwen watched with a frown before leaning around Liam's chair. "Has Liam ever acted like this before?" she asked me in a whisper.

"Only when he's not feeling well." But it had been a long time since he'd been sick.

She brushed his arm. "Are you feeling unwell, dear?"

He hesitated. "I'm fine. Please don't concern yourself."

Another course went by, during which Liam didn't even touch his food, let alone play with it. A few minutes later, he slumped in his seat and rested his forehead in his hands.

Anwen's eyes widened in concern. "What is it, Liam?"

"I...don't feel good."

Anwen stroked his hair back to feel his forehead. "No fever. What are your symptoms?"

Liam straightened. "I simply feel...out of sorts. But I'm sure I'll be fine."

Anwen clearly wasn't convinced. She asked for further details, and even though they were only whispering, they still drew the attention of the rest of the table.

Mother leaned closer, eyes lined with concern. "You really don't look well, Liam."

"I'm not sick," he said defensively, as if determined to believe his own words. "I never get sick. It's just been a long day."

"You're only human, dear." Mother stroked his hair. "Perhaps you should go rest. If you're ill, pretending otherwise won't help you."

Liam groaned. "But being ill is *boring*." It really was a horrible sentence for an active man like him.

Determined to prove he was indeed fine, he stubbornly remained at the table for the final course, but he didn't converse with anyone. Instead, he leaned on his elbow and poked at his slice of apple pie with his fork.

Anwen pushed her own untouched slice of pie away and stood. "Come, dear, you need to rest." When Liam didn't answer, Anwen looped her arm through his, encouraging him to stand. "Will you be convinced to retire if I tell you I'm in need of a rest as well?"

Liam hesitated only briefly before his resistance softened. "I'll be happy to escort you back to our room so that you can lie down."

Anwen smirked in triumph, but her victory melted away the moment Liam took a wobbling step and nearly stumbled. He closed his eyes, his pale expression twisted, as if he were in pain.

She wound a supporting arm around his waist. He slumped against her with a resigned sigh. "Very well, I'll stop being stubborn and submit to your nursing." He took her hand and turned to us. "Forgive us, but we're going to retire for the evening. Not to worry, I'll be as good as new after a night's rest."

The moment the doors closed behind them, Mother sighed. "Poor Liam. He hasn't been ill in years, but I should have known such a feat wouldn't last forever, no matter how invincible the dear boy thinks he is." She looked sternly at my sisters and me. "Take care not to fall ill yourselves."

I almost startled when Briar suddenly leaned towards me. "I certainly hope you don't also fall ill; I'd hate for you to be unwell."

My heart swelled at his unexpected but sweet comment.

"I'll be fine, as will Liam. I'm sure his illness is nothing to be concerned over."

"I hope he feels better soon."

I searched his eyes and glimpsed true concern there before he turned away once more. Despite his quick dismissal I felt a glimmer of hope. Perhaps Briar was a good man after all but merely hid his traits beneath a protective mask…just like I did.

"I hope the crown prince feels better soon," the Queen of Malvagaria said. "He's made us feel so welcome. I'd hate to miss out on his company."

Mother and Father nodded their gratitude. "Liam is a healthy man," Father said. "He'll recover soon; nothing keeps my son down for long."

We all chuckled and returned to our meal, which, between Briar's renewed attentions and my thoughts revisiting his sweet comment about my wellbeing, passed very pleasantly.

∼

I FOLLOWED *Mother as she led me down the corridor towards Kian's bedroom. We paused just outside the door, where Mother leaned down to look into my eyes, her own puffy and bloodshot.*

"Are you ready, dear?"

My heart constricted as I frantically shook my head. I wasn't. I never would be.

"You must be brave, sweetheart," Mother murmured.

No amount of bravery would make it any easier to tell Kian goodbye. My suppressed sob escaped. "I can't."

"I know, dear." Mother choked back her own tears. "But you must. You need to be strong…for him."

With a shaking hand, she opened the door and I peered into the room. Kian lay pale and motionless, his eyes closed and his breathing rattly. At first I didn't move; I simply stared, trying to memorize my brother's face so that I'd never forget it.

Mother squeezed my shoulder encouragingly, and with a wavering breath I tiptoed inside. Sickness filled the musty air, choking me so that I could barely breathe.

Kian stirred as I slowly approached the bed. His eyes fluttered open and he turned a weak smile towards me. "Hi, my little Rhea. I'm glad you came to see me." He weakly lifted his hand and I rested mine in his; it was cold and clammy.

My grief pressed against my chest. "Please don't go; I don't want to say goodbye."

"I'm sorry, Rhea. I wish more than anything I could stay and watch you grow up."

My heart wrenched at his words and I lost the battle against my burning tears. They escaped to trickle down my cheeks.

"Can I have one last kiss before I go?" he asked weakly.

I leaned down to kiss his cold cheek, but when I pulled back to stare into my dear brother's face one final time—

I gasped, for it wasn't Kian looking back at me...but Liam.

"No!" I jolted up in bed, my heart pounding and a cold sweat coating my skin.

"What is it?" Drake asked frantically. "What's wrong?"

I struggled to catch my breath as the images from my nightmare lingered, twisting my thoughts. "A nightmare," I gasped. "I dreamt of the day Kian died seven and a half years ago. But in the dream, it wasn't him, but—" Tears stung my eyes at the reminder of seeing Liam lying so pale and lifeless. I squeezed them shut in an attempt to suppress the image, but it remained, taunting me.

"It was just a dream, Rhea." Drake's tone was reassuring. "Liam is simply ill, but with how robust and energetic he is, he'll get well soon."

His assurances did little to abate my worry or the terror

squeezing my heart, both remnants from the nightmare. "But it seemed so real—"

I knew I'd have no hope of quieting my fears or even attempting sleep until I saw Liam for myself. I passed the remainder of the night at the window, where I watched as dawn greeted the horizon before going to visit him.

I knocked at his door and restlessly shifted my weight from foot to foot as I waited. I'd begun to wonder whether he and Anwen were still resting when she opened the door with a weary, "Good morning, Rhea." Her eyes were bloodshot and her expression haggard, but she still managed a small smile.

"How is Liam?" I asked as I accepted her silent invitation and entered their sitting room. She glanced towards the door that led to their bedroom. It was open, allowing me to see Liam still asleep; it was strange for him to linger in bed so long after dawn.

"He had a long night," she said. "There's been no improvement. In fact, I think he's a bit worse. At least he's finally accepted defeat and admits he's unwell, and is determined to make the speediest recovery."

"Has the physician determined his exact illness?"

"Not yet. Apparently, Liam's symptoms are from a variety of different ailments." Anwen gnawed her lip before managing another smile. "But I'm sure he'll discover it soon, and then he can better prescribe a more specific treatment. In the meantime, Liam is the most dutiful patient; he's getting plenty of rest and drinking every drop of the herbal remedy the physician has prescribed."

"I'm glad." I studied the weariness filling her expression. "Were you up all night as well?"

As if on cue, she yawned. "Liam slept restlessly. His tossing and turning woke me up several times."

"Now that Liam is resting, you should try to get some sleep. I'll have your breakfast brought up to you."

She managed a weary smile. "Thank you. I am quite hungry."

My gaze returned to Liam lying on his bed. Although he was pale, he didn't look at all like he had in my nightmare. Some of the worry pressing against my chest eased. "I don't want to disturb him, but do tell him I stopped by."

I took one final lingering look at my brother before tiptoeing from the room, scolding myself for my earlier worry. He'd be fine.

CHAPTER 10

*F*ather passed me in the corridor on my way back
to my bedroom. "Good morning, Rhea. Is everything alright?" Although he smiled, worry crinkled his eyes.
"When I didn't see you at breakfast I'd wondered if you'd
fallen ill as well."

"I'm fine. I simply wasn't in the mood to socialize this
morning." It was an excuse I used often, one my family
accepted readily, knowing how reserved I could be. This
time, however, Father frowned.

"I know it's hard, but you really need to try to spend as
much time with Briar as possible in order to determine
whether or not to accept his suit."

After such a long night, I hadn't felt up to spending the
morning with Briar. "I'm sorry, I didn't sleep well."

He rested a comforting hand on my shoulder before
glancing down the corridor behind me. "I was about to meet
your mother so we could check on Liam. Have you seen him
this morning?"

"I just came from his room; he's still sleeping. Anwen says

116

he's disgruntled he didn't experience a miraculous healing overnight."

Father chuckled. "He really hates being ill, doesn't he?"

I managed a smile.

"I expected he'd still be unwell, so I'm requesting your presence at a meeting he was due to attend this morning."

My stomach sank. "A meeting?" I squeaked.

"Nothing too serious, just our weekly meeting with our advisors. There's no need to worry; you've been trained to handle such matters."

I had, as had both of my sisters, but I'd never been required to put this training into action. I'd been born third in line, and even after Kian's death made me second in line to the Dracerian throne, Liam's vibrancy had spared me from ever having to take his place. He'd only been absent during his honeymoons, but I'd thankfully fallen ill the first time and been busy assisting with one of Mother's charities the second time, leaving Liam's duties to the more capable Aveline. If only I could have such a reprieve now.

I took a steadying breath. *Stay in control.* "But I'm unprepared for today's meeting. Can't Anwen attend?" My heart tightened with guilt the moment I made the suggestion. Anwen was tired and had enough to worry about in caring for Liam.

Father frowned. "You know this is a duty you must see to. Besides, this will be a wonderful experience for you. If all goes well between you and Prince Briar, you'll be the Crown Princess of Malvagaria, and with the King of Malvagaria's rapidly declining health, it won't be long before you're Malvagaria's queen."

My nerves escalated, pressing against my chest until I could barely breath. But I fought to hide my rising panic. "It'll be an honor to attend the meeting in Liam's place." If only my words were actually true.

"I knew I could rely on you." Father handed me a stack of documents. "Read over these so that you're prepared. The meeting is in an hour." He started down the hall but paused to glance back at me. "When they learned of your involvement, the Queen of Malvagaria and Prince Briar requested to attend as well. It'll be the perfect opportunity for you to showcase your skills as a leader."

My panic escalated into full-blown terror. The queen and Briar were going to be there? As if I weren't already frightened enough. "They want to *observe* me?" My incompetence would make quite the show.

"Naturally. You're their kingdom's future queen."

My stomach churned, my previous attempts to be brave and dutiful crumbling. "Father, I can't—"

"Yes you can, Rhea." He returned to my side and once more rested his hand on my shoulder. "You need to stop believing you can't do things. You *can*. You have trained for this your entire life. I believe in you."

He patted my shoulder before taking his leave with a fatherly smile, leaving me staring after him, paralyzed as my fear slowly crept over me and knotted my stomach. I eventually managed to stir and trudge back to my room. Once inside, I leaned against the door and took several steadying breaths in an attempt to quell the panic. It didn't work.

"What happened? Are you alright?"

For the second time today, Drake sounded concerned. It took me a moment to find my voice in order to answer. "I'm fine."

I fought to ignore the attack on my mind reminding me of all my failings and glanced down at the overwhelming stack of documents Father had given me. How could I adequately prepare for the meeting in less than an hour?

"I may be in a mirror, but I'm not blind; you're clearly *not* fine."

"You're right, I'm not, but I will be." I *had* to be.

I wandered towards the window where Drake's mirror still resided. I'd used a pillow to prop open one of the books of folklore we'd been studying so he could peruse the two pages while I went to check on Liam. I moved it so I could settle beside him. It was strange how natural the gesture felt, even though Drake had only been in my life for a while.

"Do you need to talk about it?" When I didn't answer, he asked, "Is it Liam? Is he any better this morning?"

"He's still unwell, but I'm not worried about him making a full recovery. No, it's something else that's bothering me."

His eyebrow quirked up. "You mean there's more to your melancholy morning? Do share."

I picked Drake up and rested him on my knees. A strange sense of calm dispelled my anxieties merely from touching him.

"Because Liam is ill, I have to temporarily take over his duties, beginning with attending a meeting." I held up the documents. "I'm expected to become well-versed in all of this. How can I accomplish such a task in a mere hour?"

"It does seem quite daunting."

I glared at him and he held up his hands defensively.

"What do you expect me to say? Do you want me to assure you that an hour is adequate enough time for you to become completely informed and perform your duties flawlessly? That would be a lie. No one could do that, even if they had more time than you've been allotted."

"That doesn't change the fact that I'm still *expected* to perform flawlessly." The anxiety was rising, tightening my chest with its icy fingers.

Drake sighed. "I doubt anyone expects that…except you. I thought we'd talked about this. Why do you always hold such unrealistic expectations for yourself? It's only making you miserable."

My glare sharpened. "Pointing out my flaws isn't helping."

He rubbed his temples, as if dealing with me was creating a headache. "Right, wrong thing to say. I take it you don't want me to be frank right now."

"This isn't the best time."

"Fine, I'll try a different tactic." He propped his hand beneath his chin and considered. "How about an observation: no ruler can perform flawlessly, not even one thoroughly prepared. All that can be expected is to do one's best." His tone gentled. "So you only have an hour?"

"Less than that." I thumbed through the daunting stack of documents. Drake eyed them too and, to my surprise, he smiled.

"That stack isn't so big. Perhaps I can help. Read the reports out loud and I can either offer my insights, provide witty commentary, or help you not to fall asleep."

His offer partially lifted my overwhelming burden. "You really want to help?"

"Certainly, just as soon as I clear my to-do list." He winked.

We spent the next forty-five minutes poring over the reports. Although they were overwhelming and often confusing, going over them with Drake made me feel like I was at least keeping my head above water rather than drowning. We finished going over the final one just as the clock struck quarter to the hour—it was time for the meeting.

I sighed. "I suppose I should go." But I didn't want to; I wanted to stay curled up in the window seat with Drake. By his expression, he looked as if he didn't want me to leave either.

"Are you still nervous? I can come with you, if that'll help."

My heart lifted. "Would you?"

"Of course. I can whisper suggestions and make fun of the advisors." His look became wicked.

"If you come I'll be keeping you in my bag, and for goodness' sake you better keep your voice down; I don't want a repeat of what happened in the orchard with Briar."

"I give you my word." He grinned, a smile both crooked and encouraging, and my heart gave a strange flutter. He was turning into a true friend. Knowing Drake would be with me gave me an unexpected confidence I rarely felt.

Perhaps I could do this after all.

UNFORTUNATELY, my doubts were relentless and proved too strong to be so easily quenched. Mere minutes into the meeting and I already found myself overwhelmed as Father and the advisors discussed topics that my careful study hadn't prepared me for, most from past meetings I hadn't attended.

I fought to keep the sharp attack of my thoughts at bay in order to focus on the discussion, but the longer it went on, the more lost I became. I felt adrift in an ocean of information, expected to swim but too ill-equipped to come up with anything to contribute.

All the while, the Queen of Malvagaria studied me with a disapproving frown, paralyzing me from sharing even an occasional insight. It was probably for the best; Father and the advisors seemed to be doing fine without me.

I wasn't needed. So I stayed silent.

As the meeting progressed, I found myself repeatedly reaching into my satchel, where Drake remained hidden. At first I merely brushed against the mirror's handle, but soon I found myself clutching it, its warmth reassuring me in the way only Drake could.

"What do you think, Rheanna?" Father turned to me, the encouragement in his eyes inviting me to participate. I startled. I'd let my mind wander too long. What was the current discussion about?

"Um…" I frantically scrambled for something to say. Sensing my predicament, Drake stirred from within my bag; I felt the subtle movement against my hand that still held his mirror.

"They're discussing trade," he whispered. "I have no idea on the specifics, only that it's rather tedious. If I could sleep within this mirror, I assure you I'd be snoozing right now."

All eyes were on me. *Focus, Rhea.* I recalled the information I'd studied before the meeting—trade was currently strained due to a shortage of our kingdom's resources, making it difficult for us to get the supplies we needed for the approaching winter.

Father waited patiently, but the Queen of Malvagaria watched with a rather nasty smirk as I shakily searched the documents for something to contribute. I finally found something.

"We've had an overabundance of wool this year," I managed, internally flinching at the obvious observation. "Perhaps doubling that export will allow us to import more of the goods we lack." It was such a ridiculous suggestion; the only nods it earned were likely given out of pity, not approval. I tentatively peeked at Father, expecting his displeasure, but he merely appeared thoughtful.

"An excellent suggestion, Rheanna." A new discussion started concerning my idea and which kingdoms would benefit enough to take advantage of it.

I attempted to contribute to the discussion, but every comment became more difficult to make than the last, especially when the Queen of Malvagaria's expression hardened with each one, as if she found fault with everything I said. It was clear she thought I'd make an unfit queen for her kingdom. Her disapproval caused my anxiety to flare once more and close off my throat. My hold around Drake's mirror tightened.

"Ow," he muttered. I forced myself to loosen my grip, but nothing would compel me to speak up again. What if I said something else wrong, made a mistake, and the queen—who was watching me closely—became dissuaded from an alliance?

The meeting finally concluded and everyone stood. Father waited until everyone had left the room before turning to me, his expression both kind and clearly disappointed; my heart sank.

"What happened, Rheanna?" he asked quietly. "You were doing so well until you gave up halfway through."

Instinctively, I reached in and gripped Drake's mirror, as if the gesture would allow me to find my voice. "I didn't think anything I said mattered."

"Of course it matters," Father said. "Your comment regarding the wool trade was admirable."

"It was a suggestion that lacked insight."

"It was just fine. *You* were fine…until you gave up. You can do better than that, Rheanna." He sighed, patted me on the shoulder, and left. As soon as the door closed behind him, I sank back in my seat and stared unseeing down at the circular table.

"Rhea, are you—" Drake's inquiry was cut short by the sound of the door opening. My head jerked up to see that the Queen of Malvagaria and Briar had returned. Briar looked impassive, as always, but a shiver crept up my spine at the cold look filling the queen's eyes.

"What an interesting display that was," she said. "And quite insightful. Tell me, Rheanna, is that how you usually perform all your royal duties?"

Her blatant inquiry startled me. My face burned. "I did my best," I offered quietly. "This was my first meeting, and I had short notice—"

"I'm not interested in your excuses. A future queen must always be prepared, no matter how daunting the task." Both her tone and her expression were sour. "I want to know if your performance today was an accurate example of how you conduct yourself, because if it is, I may need to seriously reconsider a union between you and my son."

I felt the blood drain from my face. "I—" The words stuck in my throat. I had no explanation, because both she and Father were right: I'd performed poorly and given up too quickly. I was unfit for my royal responsibilities.

But hearing her say so was the last thing I needed. I ached to escape this confrontation, but unfortunately, the queen wasn't finished. "For your sake, Rheanna, I hope that today's display never happens again."

I wasn't sure I could do better in the future, but I forced myself to answer, "It won't." Tears burned my eyes; I bit the inside of my lip to keep them at bay. I couldn't cry; it'd only make me appear even weaker.

From within my bag, I could have sworn I felt Drake stiffen; not only that, but the handle of his mirror began to heat; I could almost sense his emotions seeping out from behind the glass: annoyance, anger, and a strange yet fierce flare of protectiveness that momentarily left me speechless.

"She was just fine, Mother. I was no better when I first started attending meetings in Father's place after he fell ill."

My head whipped around and I gaped at Briar, whose usual stoic expression had cracked; he was actually *glaring* at the queen.

She returned it with a steely glare of her own. "I have more experience in this area. Please allow me to handle this, dear."

"I have enough experience to judge Rheanna's performance," Briar said stiffly. "She contributed adequately. Her observation about the wool was—"

"Too simple," the queen finished. "Any advisor could have easily made such a point." She gave me a long, penetrating look before she sighed. "I'm sure it's not entirely your fault, dear. Your past royal duties obviously haven't prepared you for being queen." She patted my hand, her touch as icy as her voice. "Considering your union with my son will give you such important responsibilities, you can understand why I'm disappointed in your performance today. Make sure you do better in the future so I'm not forced to change my mind about uniting our kingdoms. Draceria needs what Malvagaria has to offer. You'd be wise to remember that."

And with that last biting comment, she turned and exited the room. Briar, however, lingered. "Pay her no mind; you were fine today, Rheanna." He bowed and followed his mother out of the room.

I sat frozen. A few seconds passed before Drake spoke. "Are you alone now?"

"Yes." I could barely say the word.

"Finally." And what followed was a bitter swear word that caused my cheeks to warm.

"Drake! That was uncalled for."

"It was exactly what that fiasco called for," he muttered. "I have plenty more, but I shall refrain from speaking them—I am in the presence of a lady, after all—but not from *thinking* them."

Such a strong reaction from him could only mean one thing: I truly had been a failure. I felt like swearing myself, an impulse I'd never really had before now. The tumult of my emotions overpowered me as the sob I'd been trying to suppress finally escaped.

"Was I really so terrible?" I asked.

"I wasn't swearing about the meeting. You were just fine, Rhea. A bit unpolished, but that was to be expected. After all, this was your first official meeting."

I pulled his mirror from my bag so I could see his expression and discern his sincerity. His eyes were filled with undeniable concern…or perhaps pity. "Then what were you swearing about?"

"The encounter afterwards. Does the Queen of Malvagaria always treat you in such a way?"

"She's never been so overt in her displeasure, but ever since her arrival, she's been disapproving, like I'm not measuring up."

Because you're not.

"Does Prince Briar always stand by and allow you to be treated in such a way?"

"Of course not. He defended—"

Drake scoffed. "Do you call what he did *defense*? That was weak and pathetic."

"It was a lot, coming from him. He actually glared at her."

Drake snorted. "A mere *glare* isn't enough. If you're his intended, he should have grown a backbone and defended you more." He balled his hands into fists. "If I weren't trapped in this mirror, I wouldn't have let her speak to you in such a way. You deserve better."

If I'd figured out how to break Drake's curse before now, he could have had his wish in acting as a shield from the queen's toxic attack. I needed to free him, but how? We hadn't yet looked through enough books of folklore in order to find anything useful. A trip to the library was in order.

I shoved Drake into my satchel and hurried through the corridors, wanting to put as much distance between myself and the meeting room, as if I could outrun my memory of what had just transpired there. I took each turn sharply, nearly tripping over my skirts in my haste to descend the stairs to the grand floor where the library was located.

A disgruntled *"Oof"* emanated from my satchel. "What's the rush? Need I remind you I'm not the only occupant of your bag?"

I glanced down and noticed my books knocking against the mirror, crushing him in a way that didn't look at all comfortable.

"Sorry." I adjusted my bag but didn't slow.

"You're still thinking about that meeting, aren't you?" he asked knowingly. I pursed my lips and didn't answer, which was clearly all the answer he needed. "As I suspected. If you're anything like my sisters, you'll need to 'talk it out.'" He made quote marks with his fingers. "I'm a good listener. Terrible at advice, but…" He shrugged. "I'll do my best."

"I don't need to talk about it."

Drake didn't look convinced, but thankfully he didn't press me.

We soon reached the library, where I began to comb the shelves of one of the few remaining sections I hadn't yet searched. I tried to concentrate on each of the titles I perused, but my thoughts kept returning to the toxic confrontation with the queen. Her words were like poison, seeping into my mind, enhancing the insecurities already residing there.

I didn't realize I'd paused in my searching until Drake spoke. "Why have you stopped? You aren't still thinking about the meeting, are you?" At my nod, he continued in a soft tone, "Are you sure you don't want to talk about it?"

"No, it's fine." I tried to refocus on the task at hand, but instead I stared unseeing at the bookshelf until all the volumes blurred together. "It was such a disaster." The build-up of tears finally escaped and I buried my face in my hands.

He released a long breath. "I thought we weren't going to talk about it?"

I ignored him. "I can't possibly be queen, but if Briar doesn't marry me…" My heart felt on the brink of breaking at the very thought. I couldn't possibly survive another rejection.

"So we're going to talk about it? Alright then." He seemed to brace himself, as if preparing for battle. "Well, should the worst happen and Prince Briar doesn't marry you, then you can just marry someone else."

"That's your advice?" I glared down at him. "Don't you understand? That would be *two* men who have rejected me, two *princes* no less. Do you really think I'll have suitors flocking to me?" I snapped my mouth shut. I'd said too much.

"Rhea, you don't know that no other man wouldn't want you."

"Yes, I do, because if Briar—"

He rolled his eyes. "Why would Prince Briar's opinion of you determine what anyone else thinks?"

"Because it's what *everyone* thinks." Deidric's rejection had only confirmed my own fears that something was wrong with me. "I'm plain, my knowledge and accomplishments are inadequate, I lack the grace and refinement expected of me. In short, I'm a terrible princess. So if Briar and his mother also reject me, I'll be doomed to a lonely future, which I couldn't possibly bear."

Drake frowned as he stared at me, almost as if he were trying to match my words with what he saw. Finally he shook his head. "You're wrong, you know. Even if you think everyone views you the way you view yourself, *I* certainly don't."

Hope fluttered in my heart before I forced myself to squelch it. "You're lying," I whispered.

"Am I?" He folded his arms and leaned against his mirror frame, his grin almost challenging. "Prove it."

I certainly couldn't, and by his triumphant gleam, I could tell he knew it.

"But what I think doesn't matter," he continued. "Despite plenty of evidence to the contrary, you've already convinced yourself that your perception is the only accurate one. Perhaps the challenge you should accept is not to prove yourself right, but to prove yourself wrong."

"What do you mean?" I asked, but he'd already faded from the glass, leaving me more confused than ever.

Life certainly had become more complicated since I'd met Drake. Who knew a man within a mirror could create such upheaval?

CHAPTER 11

*L*iam was awake when I stopped by his room several days later. He offered me a weak smile. "It's about time you visited your favorite brother."

"Finally you're awake; I was beginning to suspect you were feigning sleep every time I came by as an effort to avoid me."

"I was." He chuckled at my resulting glare. "Forgive me for teasing you. Anwen has told me of your faithful visits. I'm grateful I'm awake today in order to enjoy one." He motioned to the empty seat beside his wife.

"If you didn't tease me, I'd expect an imposter." I sat and took the opportunity to examine him more closely—pasty skin, gaunt expression, and weariness in his bloodshot eyes… he didn't look well at all. My heart sank.

"How are you feeling?" I asked hesitantly.

He managed a smile that looked more like his usual wide grin than his initial greeting had, as if he were determined to make an effort on my behalf. "I've been better. Now, tell me about your latest adventures; I've been anxious for you."

Before I could begin, Anwen stood. "I'll give you two some time alone."

She started to leave but Liam seized her hand and gave her an imploring look. "Won't you stay? It's not as if Rhea and I will be exchanging state secrets."

He quirked an eyebrow up at me in a Liam-like way that clearly asked, *Or will we?* When I didn't answer, his lips twitched.

"Perhaps in the time I've been ill, Rhea has become more mischievous and has been engaging in espionage and needs our assistance. You must stay and join us; you make an excellent partner in crime, darling."

"We'll plan an elaborate adventure for the two of us when you're better. For now, you should enjoy your time with your sister; I can't be the only one spoiled with your attention." She leaned down and kissed him.

"Very well," he murmured when she pulled away. "Don't stay away long." After they'd exchanged a lingering look and squeezed one another's hands, Anwen left. Liam sighed and turned his attention towards me. "I don't envy you at the moment; considering how I treasure my wife's company, you have big shoes to fill."

"Luckily for me, I'm your favorite sister." His responding grin confirmed what I'd always suspected.

"I really am happy to see you. You can't imagine how boring it has been being cooped up here all day every day."

I scooted my chair closer and took his hand, alarmed by how clammy it was. "How are you doing?"

"I'd love to claim I'm feeling fine, but I've felt poorly too long to continue to believe that lie." He sighed wearily before managing a smile. "But enough about me. I've been torturing myself wondering how you're doing. Please give me the good news that you've sent Prince Boring packing."

I bit my lip. "Not exactly."

"What's the hold up? Don't tell me he's *grown on you*." He pulled a face. "They don't get much drier than Briar. I've seen enough of your interactions together to know it's not working. I want more for you."

"Admittedly, while things have gotten much better and we're starting to become friends, our relationship hasn't progressed as much as I'd hoped, but it's still too early to dismiss him entirely."

Liam scoffed. "*Too early*? Rhea, it's been two weeks. Even when I believed Anwen was the horrible Lavena whom I adamantly hated, it didn't take me that long to realize there was something between us, and I'm not exactly an expert in romance."

"But you spent more time with Anwen than Briar and I have."

Liam shook his head. "That's not true. We spent the first week ignoring one another, meaning it only took a week for things to begin to progress. Considering how stagnant your relationship is with Briar, I'm not hopeful much will change, even if you had all the time in the world."

"That's not exactly fair," I said. "He's been paying a bit more attention to me lately, and we spend time together at least once a day." Although I still wasn't sure whether these attentions were from a man starting to fall in love or from a man only determined to see his duty through. "Besides, Mother and Father needed more time than a few weeks, and look how wonderfully their relationship turned out."

Liam sobered at that argument, but in typical Liam fashion he refused to give up. "What about my earlier advice —just because a match isn't horrible doesn't mean it's the right one. Your happiness is too high a cost to force yourself into an unwanted union. If it's not working, it's not working."

"But my happiness isn't the only thing to consider," I said.

"I'll disappoint so many people if I'm selfish, and I will be able to help them if I perform the duty expected of me. And you know how important it is to me to help people."

Liam opened his mouth to argue but I talked over him.

"I truly haven't been fair to Briar. It's too premature to end it if I haven't given him a chance. I've decided I'm going to make more of an effort."

Liam sighed as he squeezed my hand. "You've always been far wiser than me. Very well, I'll save my arguments for after you've given your courtship more time. I wish I weren't ill so I could continue to observe it. I promised to keep an eye on Briar, and I'm now being a lousy brother by breaking that promise. Stupid illness." Remorse twisted his expression.

"It's not your fault," I said. "Besides, there's still time for you to keep your promise once you get better. Then you can continue your clandestine mission to discover Briar's true character and ascertain if he has a secret past identity."

"That sounds like excellent fun. It'll be a great game." He gave a raspy cough and leaned back against his pillows with a weary sigh. "If only *this* were a game."

And suddenly he looked quite tired. Worry pressed against my chest and must have shown on my expression, for he forced a smile.

"Let's talk of more pleasant things. Have you succeeded in breaking the curse on that mirror?"

I hesitated. I'd promised Drake I wouldn't talk about it, but the longer it took me to help him, the more concerned I grew, especially as he'd seemed more despondent this morning. "I'm doing what you suggested and have searched through every book of folklore I could find, but so far I haven't discovered an answer that doesn't involve magic and countercurses." Neither of which I could perform.

He frowned. "It's quite the puzzle. I'll continue to think on it and let you know if I come up with anything new." He glanced at the teapot on his nightstand. "Can I trouble you for more of that remedy?"

I helped him sit up before pouring some of his medicinal tea into his lucky goblet, which he'd specifically requested be brought to his room. I eyed the dark bits of herbs floating in the putrid green mixture and wrinkled my nose. "What's in this?"

"I don't want to know else I won't drink it."

I swirled the contents gently but it didn't make the green bits look any more appetizing. "Might I have a taste?"

Liam's eyebrows rose. "You're willing to subject yourself to such torture? Or do you just want to sip from my lucky goblet? Regardless, you're a brave girl. By all means." He waved his hand, his permission to proceed. "Just don't let Anwen know; she's rather insistent I drink every last drop myself."

I took a cautious sip…and gagged at the bitter taste. I jerked the cup away, nearly causing the remedy to spill over the sides. "That's vile."

"I can't argue with that. I take it you don't envy my drinking five goblets a day like a good patient." He reached for the cup and I happily relinquished it so I could pour myself a glass of water and guzzle it down. It did little for the lingering foul aftertaste.

I pulled a face. "Disgusting. How can you even drink that?"

"I want to get well, and it eases Anwen's heart when I do all I can to achieve that desire. Love makes you do all sorts of crazy things. You'll understand when you fall in love." He gave me a disapproving look, clearly not pleased I'd so easily given up on the future he wanted for me.

He lifted the goblet as if to make a toast before quickly drinking the tea, almost retching. He only managed half before his expression twisted. "*Disgusting* is right."

"Is it helping at all?"

"It's likely my imagination, but I almost feel *worse* after I drink it. But who wouldn't? It truly is nasty stuff. But I'll persevere; anything to get well and leave this prison. If it weren't for Anwen's constant presence, I'd have died from boredom long before now."

He drained his cup and shakily handed it to me. I frowned. He *did* look a bit more pale than before.

Liam and I conversed for a few more minutes, during which his strength visibly started to fade. It was time to take my leave. I started to stand but Liam grasped my hand.

"Will you come back soon?"

"I will."

"I'll do my best to be awake for you."

I started for the door, but Liam's grip on my hand tugged me to a stop.

"Wait, Rhea. I want you to remember that I'll support whatever you decide about your future."

I squeezed his hand. "Thank you, Liam."

He managed a wan smile before dropping my hand and closing his eyes. I stroked his damp hair off his forehead.

"Are you alright?"

"I feel so...*tired*." For a moment he didn't move, his breathing shallow, before he weakly opened his eyes. "Can you get Anwen? I want to see her before I fall asleep."

My heart tightened. "You *are* only falling asleep, aren't you?"

He gave a breathless chuckle that turned into another rasping cough. "You can't get rid of me that easily." His smile faltered and his eyes fluttered back shut. "Please get her?"

"Of course. I'll visit again soon."

He smiled weakly but didn't open his eyes. I kissed his forehead before hurrying into the corridor. I expected to have to track Anwen down, but to my surprise she sat just outside the door, sobbing into her pulled-up knees. I knelt beside her and embraced her. She immediately burrowed her tear-stained face against my shoulder.

"He's going to be alright, Anwen."

"I know," she whispered. "It's just seeing him so weak…I couldn't contain my emotions any longer. I don't want to cry in front of him; I need to be strong. But it's so hard, for he's not getting better. What kind of illness escalates so quickly except for a serious one? What if he—" Her words were swallowed by another sob.

I stroked her hair. "He'll be alright. This is *Liam*, after all; nothing can defeat him. He won't let it."

She didn't answer. Instead, she straightened with a jolt. "I must return to him."

"He was asking for you."

She was on her feet immediately. Without sparing me a glance, she slipped inside their room. I stared at the closed door before trudging down the hall, my heart heavy, for I secretly doubted my own assurances I'd given Anwen.

Halfway to my room, a sudden headache pierced my senses and nausea churned my stomach. I slumped against my doorframe and took several long, deep breaths.

What's happening to me?

The world swayed, but I managed to stumble into my room, where Drake's alarmed voice greeted me. I barely paid him any attention. I was suddenly so…tired. Perhaps I'd lie down, just for a moment…

CHAPTER 12

$\mathcal{J}$ woke up to late afternoon light spilling into the room, but even though I'd clearly slept for most of the day, exhaustion still pressed against my senses. I groaned and rolled over.

Drake spoke the moment I stirred. "Are you alright, Rhea? I've been so worried."

I analyzed how I felt after my long nap. I'd been startled by the suddenness and the severity of how unwell I'd felt, but now it seemed to have mostly dissipated. My stomach no longer churned, and save for a mild throbbing against my temples, my headache had disappeared.

I slowly sat up. The world spun and it took me a moment to focus my gaze on Drake, propped in the window seat where I'd left him and staring at me with an expression swirling with worry.

"I think I'm alright."

"You *think* you are?" He didn't look convinced.

"I'm fine," I hastily amended.

His frown only deepened. "I don't believe you. Come

closer so I can examine you more properly and assure myself you're fine."

His concern was rather sweet. My lips twitched, aching to smile…although at the moment it felt like too much effort. I swayed slightly as I stood and pattered to the window, where I sat down and picked up his mirror, holding it eye level as if I were looking at my own reflection so that he could examine my face thoroughly, as any proper mirror would do.

"So what's your diagnosis, Physician Drake?"

After a minute's perusal, Drake actually *blushed* and quickly looked away. "You do look like you're alright, although you seem tired. What happened?"

"It was the strangest thing, but I suddenly felt quite ill."

"Did you come from visiting Liam?"

"Yes, but if I caught his illness during my visit, it'd be too soon to notice any symptoms." I rubbed my temples, hoping the gesture would stave off the throbbing pain. It took several minutes for my head to clear and my grogginess to recede, allowing me to think better.

I thought back over my visit with Liam and suddenly remembered him mentioning feeling worse after drinking his herbal remedy…the very remedy I'd taken a sip from before feeling ill myself. I gasped. "The remedy."

"What about the remedy?" Drake asked.

My heart pounded and my mind whirled. "Liam complained that his remedy makes him feel more tired, and I took a sip of it…there must be something wrong with it. I need to talk to my parents." Before Drake could object, I hurried from the room as quickly as my weakened state allowed.

I found them in Father's study, going over reports. Their eyes widened at my frantic entrance. "Rhea, what on earth—"

"The remedy," I panted before breathlessly recounting my

visit with Liam and my sudden illness that followed. "It has to be the remedy; something's wrong with it. I'm sure of it."

Mother pressed her hands to her mouth to suppress a sob while Father, grim-faced, turned to the attending footman. "Send for the physician immediately." The footman promptly bowed and left to carry out his orders.

We waited in anxious silence. Father stroked Mother's hand as she took several calming breaths. A knock interrupted the tense silence and the physician entered.

"How may I be of assistance, Your Majesties?"

Father looked at me expectantly and I shakily repeated my story. The physician listened gravely, asking several questions about the symptoms I'd experienced.

He stroked his chin thoughtfully. "His Highness has complained about acute exhaustion and exaggerated symptoms, but I'd assumed they were merely results of his illness. However, considering Her Highness's similar reaction, I need to reexamine the herbs. Certain combinations have been known to cause headaches and nausea. I will consult with my associates and come up with an improved remedy that will hopefully alleviate His Highness's discomfort during his recovery."

"Thank you," Father said. "You've served our family well over the years. I have no doubt you'll do your best to ensure that Prince Liam has the best possible care."

"You can be assured, Your Majesties, that the health of the crown prince is our highest priority." The physician bowed and exited the room. As the door closed behind him, Father turned to me.

"Thank you for your astuteness in bringing this to our attention. You are a bright, capable woman, Rheanna, and will make Malvagaria a fine queen."

"Thank you, Father." If only I could believe him.

I returned to my room to a frantic Drake. "There you are. Why did you run off like that without saying a word? I'm worried about you enough as it is. When you didn't return, I feared you'd fainted."

"For a mirror, you sure are a worrier." I curled up beside him on the windowsill. "I needed to talk to my parents about Liam. I'm so concerned about him; it was startling how sickly he looked. It reminded me of how Kian looked before he—" My heart squeezed as a terrifying possibility occurred to me. "You don't think Liam—" I couldn't even finish.

"There's nothing to worry about," Drake said. "Liam is healthy and vibrant; he'll beat this. It's *you* I'm concerned about. As such, I don't want you doing anything strenuous for the remainder of the day."

This time my lips twitched into an actual smile. "So are you experienced with the healing arts, Physician Drake?"

"No, but—"

"Then I don't have to listen to you." I rested his mirror on my propped-up knees, finding strange amusement in his disgruntled look. "While I'll agree not to go over the reports for tomorrow's meeting, I refuse to stay cooped up in my room. Perhaps we can visit the orchard."

"Absolutely not," he said. "It's too cold to go outside; I've spent most of the day watching the sky and I don't like the look of those storm clouds."

My heart warmed. His concern really was rather sweet. "Then do you have another activity in mind?"

He considered before brightening. "I know the perfect place we can go. Have you been to the Hall of Mirrors?"

"I used to go there all the time before..." I frowned, studying him suspiciously. "Wait, how did you know about the Hall of Mirrors?"

He shifted, almost guiltily. "I visited the Dracerian palace several years ago."

"You've been to the palace before?" Not that a visit would have been unusual if he was a member of the Dracerian nobility, but how could I not remember him visiting? He only looked to be a few years older than me. If he'd been old enough to remember his time in the Hall of Mirrors, surely I would have been old enough to remember him.

"It was a long time ago."

"Which means you're a member of the Court." I furrowed my brow at his nod. "If that's true, then why haven't I met you before now?"

"My family is rather elusive." But by the way he wouldn't meet my eyes, I sensed there was more to it than he was sharing. "Would you like to visit the Hall of Mirrors or not?"

I hesitated, both because I didn't want to drop my interrogation and because there was a reason I'd stayed away all these years. But Drake looked so hopeful, and with the approaching storm outside and the likelihood of encountering the Queen of Malvagaria or Briar while inside, it seemed the best option for a pleasant afternoon.

"I'd love to go there." I gave him a teasing smile. "But aren't you tired of mirrors?"

"Only *this* mirror." He eyed me skeptically. "Are you certain you're up for an excursion? We can always go a different day."

"I'm sure." I picked Drake up and tucked him into my satchel before heading for the Hall of Mirrors, which was located at the far end of the palace.

My breath hooked the moment I slipped inside. I stared wide-eyed around the room, which was filled with hundreds of mirrors lining the walls from floor to ceiling, all of various shapes, sizes, and styles. I stood utterly transfixed; my fond memories of this room hadn't done it justice.

I retrieved Drake from my bag and slowly moved his mirror around so he could get a full view of the splendor of the room. He grinned. "Wow, it's just as fantastic as I remembered."

"No other palace in the four surrounding kingdoms has anything like this." I walked the circumference of the room so we could examine some of the mirrors more closely.

"Where did such a spectacular collection come from?" Drake asked.

"Liam could tell the story better than I can," I said. "But there was an ancient Dracerian Queen who was extremely vain. According to the legend, she was obsessed with mirrors and spent hours admiring her reflection. Her goal was to find the mirror that would show her at her greatest beauty. Hence this collection was born."

"So she's responsible for all of them?" he asked.

"No. After her death, it became tradition for the new queen to find an unusual mirror to add to it. Both my grandmother and my mother have made contributions." I pointed each of them out; their designs were more simple but just as elegant. "One day Anwen will add her mirror."

His forehead furrowed. "Who's Anwen?"

"Liam's wife."

"But I thought he was engaged to Princess Lavena of Lyceria?"

I laughed. "That's quite the story. When you get out of the mirror and Liam gets well, he'll have to share how he got out of that arrangement." I continued our walking tour past the mirrors. "Being here again brings back so many memories. When Kian was alive, he used to come up with riddles that would lead us to different mirrors in order to retrieve our next clue, just like a treasure hunt. It was always a competition between my siblings and me...except for the one he designed just for me for my birthday, which led to my favorite mirror."

I paused in front of it. The frame was cherry wood,

carved with an ornate design of an orchard, with miniature rubies embedded into the frame to represent the apples.

"The orchard?" Drake's tone was almost reverent.

"I often came here just to admire this mirror, especially on days when the rain forced me indoors and away from the real orchard. For years I've pleaded with my parents for it, and they've recently said they'll gift it to me at my wedding when I marry—"

I swallowed my words and, to my surprise, Drake's expression hardened.

"Do you have a favorite mirror?" I asked him hastily.

"I do." He turned around in the frame, as if to lead me to it, and sighed. "No matter how long I've been trapped here, I'm still not entirely used to it. I think the mirror is on the other side of the room."

I carried him to the opposite wall, full of dozens of mirrors which were quite ornate and rather masculine. "Which is it?"

His grin became mischievous. "Perhaps you can guess?"

"Challenge accepted."

I began examining each. There were so many varieties— round, square, rectangular; some with wooden frames and others made of bronze, silver, or even gold; some were decorated with carved patterns and others with jewels; some had frames that told a story while others were more simple in their designs. I slowly walked along the wall, admiring each while trying to avoid focusing on my reflection.

On my second pass through, I paused in front of a large circular mirror with a golden frame, where engraven dragons with glistening emerald eyes circled the glass. "This one."

Drake chuckled. "You really are quite clever. And here I thought my challenge would be a difficult one."

"For my prize, I want you to tell me the story behind why this is your favorite."

Drake's gaze took in the mirror. "I like dragons. They're rather formidable beasts, aren't they? Not to mention they're my namesake—*Drake* means *dragon*, you know."

"And like dragons, do you have a fiery temper as well?" I asked teasingly.

"I certainly hope not. Shall I tell you about the first time I saw this mirror?" Enthusiasm lit up his deep brown eyes, leaving me transfixed before he'd even begun sharing his story. "The first time I saw this mirror, I'd just finished reading an epic story involving dragons, kidnapped princesses, a stolen cursed treasure, and a dragon war, which I told Liam about in vivid detail."

My heart lurched, jerking me from his words. He had met Liam when he'd first visited the palace?

"Liam became really excited," Drake continued, so caught up in his tale that he remained oblivious to my reaction. "He showed me this mirror and I was immediately enamored with it. He teased me that I was obsessed with my own reflection." Drake rolled his eyes but he was still smiling.

What would it have been like to have met Drake *outside* the mirror and to see him as a little boy? "I can't believe you've visited the palace before and met my brother. Why didn't you say anything before now?"

Drake's smile faltered slightly and he hesitated. "I'm sorry, I thought you'd remember. But I'm not surprised you don't. I was just barely out of the nursery at the time, and considering I'm a few years older than you, you were likely still there, which explains why I met your brothers but not you."

Brothers? "You met Kian too?" I held my breath, awaiting his assessment. Drake's expression softened.

"I did. I remember him being kind but rather serious. He

got along quite well with my older brother, whereas I preferred Liam's company." He chuckled. "Liam told me the most outrageous story, claiming that if you arranged the mirrors in such a way—turning some sideways, others upside down, and removing others entirely—it'd open up a secret passageway that would lead to an actual dragon's lair. He was quite eager to find it so that we could be knights embarking on an adventure to claim the fiend's stolen treasure. As much as I wanted to see a real dragon, I was too frightened to actually manipulate the mirrors. What if I dropped one and broke it, cursing me with bad luck?" He sighed. "I suppose it doesn't matter I didn't play along, considering I'm now cursed anyway. What irony." He caught sight of my expression. "What is it?"

"Why didn't you tell me this story about my brothers before?" After all, I'd told him all about my siblings the day we'd spent in the orchard, and yet he'd kept all this to himself.

Guilt twisted his expression. "I don't know. You didn't seem to remember my visit to the palace, and I saw no reason to remind you." He lowered his eyes.

I took a steadying breath. "I suppose it doesn't matter. Can you tell me more about your time in the Hall of Mirrors?"

His penitence faded at my forgiveness and he grinned. "I dared Liam to try and find the dragon's lair, and he might have too if Kian hadn't stopped him." He frowned once more. "I was truly sorry to hear about Kian's death. All the kingdoms mourned for him."

My heart constricted but I managed a nod.

I settled on the floor with my back pressed against the wall and propped Drake up beside me. From this position, we had a clear view of almost every mirror in the room.

They glistened in the golden light tumbling in from the high windows. I tried to focus on the dancing patterns, but instead my mind swirled with thoughts of Liam, more acute after my recent visit with him.

"Liam and I spent more time here together than any of my other siblings. He was fascinated with looking into the mirrors at various angles to see a reflection within a reflection. He was convinced some could potentially reveal hidden messages. He had a story and a game for everything..."

My throat clogged with tears. I tried to swallow them away. "What if Liam has the same sickness that Kian died from?" I hadn't let myself wonder at the possibility before today, but now that I thought of it, I couldn't shake it. "You don't think he'll die, do you?"

"I'm sure he won't," Drake said, but his words sounded like an empty promise.

"But Kian did." My words came out choked. "Even though it's been years, it still hurts. I doubt it'll ever stop."

"I don't think it's meant to. It means you still love him." As if sensing I needed a distraction, Drake spoke again. "I enjoyed hearing about your childhood. You must finish your story. Did you and Liam ever find anything within any of the mirrors?"

I shook my head. "We never did. The older I grew, the less I believed such a thing was possible. It made it all the more startling when I discovered *you*." My gaze slowly took in each of the surrounding mirrors, all of which contained a memory. One in particular stood out amongst the rest. "The story Liam told you about rearranging the mirrors in a way that opened up a passageway to a hidden dragon lair is one he also told me. We spent many afternoons rearranging them in such a way that the sunlight bounced off the mirrors at various angles in hopes of finding the correct arrangement. We never could."

And if Liam didn't get better, we never would. My heart wrenched at the thought. I leaned my head back and took in the view of all the mirrors, lit with the light from the approaching dusk.

"I'd forgotten how much I love it here. It's been years since I've come here. I no longer like it—there are too many mirrors. I've avoided them ever since what happened with Deidric."

That was when seeing my reflection had become almost painful. A room like this with hundreds of mirrors represented hundreds of reminders that I didn't measure up. I half expected Drake to laugh. But he didn't; by the look in his eyes, he seemed to sense the words I hadn't said.

"I can understand that," he said. "When I first became trapped, I felt all I could see was my own reflection, revealing all my shortcomings, which made me believe I deserved my fate. There's nothing scarier than seeing exactly who you are. But I've come to discover that mirrors aren't completely accurate; they only show what one can see on the outside, not one's true worth hidden within each of us. Your best traits can't show up in a mirror." His gaze intensified. "You're a lovely person, Rhea. You're compassionate, intelligent, a good listener, and you go out of your way to do thoughtful gestures for cursed men trapped inside mirrors."

My heart warmed at his kind and surprisingly perceptive words. I stared at him, almost as if seeing him for the first time myself. On the outside he was snarky and often grumpy, but there was more to him than what I could see within the glass. Did that mean his words were true, that there was also more to *me*?

I didn't realize our eyes had been locked until Drake yanked his gaze away with a blush. As if seeking a distraction, he cast his eyes around the room. "I'm terrified that one day I'll end up here. What if my curse can't be broken?"

I stroked the rim of his mirror, a gesture I doubted he could feel, but by the way he shuddered in response, I thought perhaps he had. "I promise I won't let that happen."

It was a promise I'd do all I could to keep, especially for one who somehow truly saw me.

CHAPTER 13

I wandered the familiar library shelves, frowning at the titles, which after an hour of searching were beginning to blend together.

"Have you found anything yet?" Drake asked, his voice nearly drowned out by the rain pattering the windows and the fire crackling in the nearby hearth.

"Not yet." I was beginning to doubt I ever would, despite the vast number of books housed in the palace library. "I don't see many books on folklore, and I've already searched every book I could find on curses."

He sighed. "I suspect that the information needed to break my curse isn't found in any book." I glanced down at my satchel, open enough to give me a view of his crestfallen expression.

"I won't give up," I said fiercely. Although Drake depended on me, I didn't continue researching the curse solely for *his* sake—I wanted to break the curse for me, because even as a mirror, Drake was a wonderful companion. The thought of being with him as a real person rather than merely a reflection…of caressing his cheek, running my fingers through his hair, maybe even—

My cheeks heated and I hastily ended my thoughts there. *Drake is my friend.* Thinking of him in any other way was inappropriate, especially when I was nearly engaged to another man. I forced myself to shove those thoughts aside and focus on my search.

"I feel bad taking so much of your time with little to show for it," Drake said after several more unproductive minutes.

"Just because we haven't found something yet doesn't mean we never will." I rested my hand on his handle in hopes of reassuring him before I climbed up a ladder to reach the books on the upper shelves.

"It's not so much I doubt we'll find anything; I'm concerned I'm wasting your time." Drake's quiet comment pulled my attention from the shelf I was perusing.

"Of course you're not. Why would you think something so ridiculous?"

"Because you have better things to do than help a cursed man pathetic enough to find himself trapped in a mirror."

I lifted my eyebrows, both at his scowl and his un-Drake-like attitude. "There's no need to worry about that—I'm free from my duties for the day, I won't meet with Briar until later, and I find the thought of spending the afternoon in the library with my friend a lovely one." When he didn't respond, I descended the ladder so I could pull him from my satchel and raise him to eye level. "What's wrong, Drake? You're not being yourself."

It wasn't just today that he was behaving strangely. Ever since our conversation in the Hall of Mirrors, he'd become more withdrawn, which seemed strange considering I'd felt closer to him after our experience there together. But perhaps he didn't feel the same way.

Why would he?

He avoided my eyes for a moment before slowly meeting my gaze. "I'm wondering if my freedom is worth it...if it comes at too high of a cost."

I frowned as I studied his somber expression. "My time in exchange for your freedom is really a small price to pay, so please don't worry. I want to help you, and I will, whether you want me to or not." I carefully put him back into my satchel faceup and reascended the ladder.

"But what if it takes too long?"

"You're really not behaving like the snarky man trapped in an enchanted mirror I'm used to," I said. "Breaking your curse will take as much time as it needs to, and in the meantime, Liam always taught me to think of such things as an adventure."

Liam would know. His persistence had allowed him to win many prizes over the years—finding a loophole in his arranged engagement so he could marry Anwen, discovering his poison-resistant goblet...thus I'd take as long as I needed to help Drake.

"We'll find a way out of your mirror somehow. Now cheer up and let's keep looking." I ascended another step and began scanning the top shelf of books.

"I've been trapped so long that freedom seems impossible," Drake said gloomily. "What if there's no way to break the curse?"

"Every curse has a countercurse." There were no relevant books in this section; it was mostly comprised of dry political tomes. I descended the ladder and moved to another shelf. "Perhaps you should tell me about it again. You said the caster was trying to perform another spell and it backfired. Do you know which spell it was?"

He frowned. "I've been pondering about that lately and I'm actually beginning to wonder if the spell backfired at all."

"You mean you were put into the mirror *on purpose*?"

He sighed. "I'm beginning to wonder. I likely deserved it, somehow."

"Did you do something to warrant punishment?" My heart tightened as a possibility occurred to me. "Did you spurn a pretty girl?" *Please say that's not what happened.*

"In a sense…"

My heart squeezed tighter. My horror must have shown on my face, for Drake managed a humorless chuckle.

"Not to worry, the situation likely isn't what you're imagining. You see, before I was cursed, I wasn't exactly embracing the duty expected of me; in a sense I was running away from it."

Another horrific possibility occurred to me. "Are you betrothed?" *Please say no.*

"Thank goodness, no. That's the last thing I want…which is likely how I ended up inside this mirror." He sighed. "Perhaps the key to breaking the curse is I have to be willing to accept such a fate, which means I'll be trapped here forever."

"Does this mean you're creating your own prison?"

His frown deepened. "Perhaps I am." He shook his head. "But this conversation is getting us nowhere."

"Nor is this section of books." I wandered to another shelf in hopes that one would contain something more useful, but I'd barely started browsing when Drake spoke again, his tone more bitter than before.

"Speaking of betrothals, how is yours coming?"

We hadn't spoken of it since the night I'd confessed what had happened between Deidric and me. "There's no engagement contract signed yet, although Briar has still been more attentive…although not just to me." I frowned as a memory resurfaced, uninvited.

Drake's hardened expression softened. "What is it?"

"It's nothing really." I ran my fingers along the spines. "It's just that…Briar has a habit of noticing other women of the court, particularly my sisters. He's always staring at them. I can't help feeling he finds other women prettier than me."

Drake snorted. "Prince Briar is a fool. It's wrong of him to be unfaithful to your union."

To be fair, we weren't engaged yet. And wasn't I doing the same thing by spending all this time with Drake? I bit my lip. "Do you really think he finds other women more attractive?"

"Well…" Drake shifted uncomfortably. "It's well known that Prince Briar has a weakness for beautiful things."

My heart sank. Obviously, I wasn't pretty enough. It was a confirmation of what I'd always feared.

"I'm sure it's not that he doesn't find you pretty," Drake said hastily, his tone reassuring, as if he sensed the onslaught of negative thoughts already attacking my mind. "From what I hear, he simply likes to seek for and admire beauty wherever he finds it."

That still wasn't assuring, but before I could continue to discuss my intended's lack of interest in me, my attention was drawn to a book whose faded title was barely discernible: *Dangerous Plants*. I pulled it out.

"Did you find something?" Drake asked hopefully.

"Not about the curse." I opened the book and skimmed its contents. None of the plants listed were familiar, and scanning a few entries confirmed this volume detailed their more sinister uses. "All of these plants cause either illness or death to those who are exposed to them, either through touch or ingesting them." What was such a book doing in the palace library?

I'd only read a few pages when the sound of the library door opening caused me to slam it shut with a gasp. I shoved the book back in its place and tiptoed deeper into the shelves.

"Why are you hiding?" Drake asked quietly.

"I'm not sure…" I had no reason to, for I wasn't doing

anything wrong. But I couldn't shake the uneasy feeling knotting my stomach.

Footsteps approached the back shelves, coming nearer. They paused on the other side of the shelf I hid behind and fell silent. It didn't sound as if the intruder was searching the shelves. Were they waiting for someone? I crouched down and tried to peer to the other side, but the books blocked my view.

"I thought princesses didn't eavesdrop," Drake whispered.

"Be quiet if you want to overhear anything."

He obediently fell silent. After a minute of restless waiting, the door opened again, and the sound of the Queen of Malvagaria's approaching heels echoed against the marble floor. I crouched lower and pressed my finger to my lips, an admonition for Drake to remain silent. By his expression, he had no intention of giving us away.

"So you decided to meet with me after all." The queen's voice pierced the silence.

"I'm admittedly curious about your secrecy." I'd recognize that emotionless monotone anywhere. *Briar.*

"There's no secrecy, merely…discretion. I haven't had an opportunity to check in with you for several days. How is your courtship with Princess Rheanna going?"

My heart lurched. I instinctively reached for Drake's mirror, seeking his comfort.

"It's going better," Briar said. "We've spent time together every day this week. I find her quite pleasant company."

"The time you've spent with her is irrelevant," the queen said. "I want to know if you believe she'll accept the union."

"I don't see why she wouldn't, though it'd help if you weren't so hard on her."

"Never mind that. Your duty is to ensure that she accepts the union, no matter what it takes." The queen's voice was firm, business-like. My hand tightened around the mirror's handle.

Briar was silent a moment; I could almost sense his usual frown. "Might I ask why?"

"You know why," the queen said.

"Yes, but I don't understand your urgency."

"How can you not?" The queen's tone was hardening. "This union will be prosperous for Malvagaria. As the crown prince, you have a duty to better your kingdom, one you must take seriously, especially since your useless brother is failing to do his."

"It's not his fault," Briar said. "How can he when—"

"He has nobody to blame but himself," the queen said. "He dug his own grave and isn't doing anything to get himself out of his predicament. You'd think after three years he'd show some initiative, the useless fool."

"Why won't you help him?" Briar asked.

"Because he's weak, and weakness is something I will not tolerate. You're Malvagaria's future king. It's time you realize that our kingdom's future prosperity depends on a strong monarch willing to make difficult sacrifices."

"But—"

"Your brother is of no concern to you. Just focus on getting Rheanna to agree to the engagement. Her parents claim she's still hesitant."

Briar sighed. "Must it be forced? I don't think Rheanna will be happy with me."

"Happiness is not a factor in political arrangements. She should be grateful for the privilege of becoming the Crown Princess of Malvagaria. She'll not get a better offer; princes aren't exactly lining up for her hand, since her original fiancé wised up and left her."

I flinched, and the handle of the mirror vibrated against my palm, as if Drake was shaking with suppressed emotion.

"I don't want her to accept my hand for such a reason," Briar said. "Perhaps it'd be more prudent for me to pursue Princess Aveline—"

"No," the queen hissed. "You will marry Rheanna. It's been decided."

Briar sighed again, this one more resigned. "I'll do my best."

"Good. Now go find Rheanna and invite her on another outing."

"Yes, Mother." His agreement was followed by the sound of their retreating footsteps.

I waited for them to fade away before I straightened, but it took me a few moments to recover enough from the queen's verbal assaults to speak. "There's something more going on here," I whispered even though I was fairly certain we were alone. "She's plotting something and I seem to be at the heart of it. But why is she so invested in Briar's choice of a wife?"

"Her interest is natural, considering he's the future king."

"True, but she's made it no secret she dislikes me and doesn't believe I'll be a capable queen for Malvagaria," I said. "Hence you'd think she'd be trying to *dissuade* him from courting me, not pressuring him into it. What's more, if a political alliance between our two kingdoms was all she cared about, she could achieve that just as easily through Aveline, who is much better suited to Briar than I am. Something is going on, and I intend to find out what it is before entering any arrangement."

Drake hesitated before frowning. "I admit it does seem suspicious."

"It certainly does." I began walking briskly towards the library exit, my mind whirling with every step. "She must have a strong motive for Briar to marry me. What do you think it could be?"

Drake shifted nervously. "It seems a beneficial arrangement, considering Draceria and Malvagaria are neighbors."

"Yes, but she obviously sees our arrangement as something *more*." I paused in my musings when I noticed Drake's expression—pain filled his eyes, as if the conversation we'd overheard had hurt him on a deeper level. "Are you alright?"

"I'm fine." He sounded weary, enough so that I decided to drop this line of questioning...for now.

A few corridors away from the library, I turned a corner and nearly ran right into the Queen of Malvagaria herself.

Her dark eyes narrowed. "Watch where you're going, Rheanna. A future queen doesn't careen through the hallways like—" The words died in her throat as her gaze honed in on the handle of Drake's mirror poking out of my satchel. Her jaw tightened.

"Forgive me, I didn't mean to run into you." I hastily tried to smooth my skirts.

She continued glaring at the exposed mirror. My heart pounded. Did the queen know about the enchanted mirror? And if so, *what* did she know? I ached to hide Drake from view, but I didn't want to draw further attention to him.

The queen finally lifted her cold gaze and forced a smile. "Briar informed me he's eager to spend the afternoon with you. Why don't you seek him out? You two make the most charming couple."

Her cloak swirled as she turned and walked briskly down the hall. I waited for the clicking sound of her footsteps to fade away before slumping against the wall. I peeked into my satchel. Drake's countenance was hardened.

"Did she see the mirror?" he whispered.

"I believe so." I swallowed. "Is there any reason she'll suspect the mirror is enchanted?"

He didn't respond.

"Drake? Does she know about the mirror?"

He hesitated. "I was in Malvagaria at the time I was cursed, so it's highly likely she's at least *heard* about it."

I startled at this revelation. "You were in Malvagaria? What were you doing there?" And how had he ended up at the Dracerian palace?

His face paled and without another word he faded away, as if he thought that hiding now would revert the damage of the queen noticing him. I wanted to believe nothing would come from the encounter, but by the icy look that had filled her eyes, I doubted this was the end of it.

CHAPTER 14

I looked away from Liam's empty seat at the breakfast table and noticed Mother also staring at it, her expression strained. "Have you had a chance to visit Liam this morning?" I asked her.

"I did, but he was sleeping. He's been sleeping quite a bit." I didn't even need to ask her whether it was making a difference. I knew the answer to that, had seen the evidence myself —Liam's health was steadily declining.

"I do hope he makes a speedy recovery," the Queen of Malvagaria said, her expression somber. "It'd be tragic for your kingdom and your family to lose the crown prince."

I flinched. How dare she insinuate that Liam might die? Mother exchanged an anguished look with Father, a look I still remembered from when Kian had unexpectedly fallen ill and never recovered. The memories of our fear and uncertainty as we watched Kian's life slowly fade away still haunted our family, even seven and a half years later.

What if Liam dies, too? The memory of my nightmare taunted me. I struggled to push it away, even as I fought against the worry knotting my gut. I was being ridiculous.

Liam wouldn't die. He was far healthier than Kian had ever been.

Besides, he hasn't been ill for very long, I reminded myself. He'd be fine. I silently chanted this to myself over and over as I returned to my eggs and toast.

"Thank you for your concern, but he'll recover soon," Father said to the queen with far more confidence than filled Mother's expression. He turned to me. "Until then, I'm expecting you at tomorrow's meeting, Rheanna."

Anxiety flared in my heart at the thought of enduring another horrible meeting like the last one. Sensing my nerves, Father rested his hand over mine.

"You'll be just fine," he murmured. "Don't doubt yourself. Doubt is more harmful to us than our actual weaknesses, whereas confidence enhances our abilities and gives us strength."

I tried to embrace his words, but the doubts filling my mind wouldn't be silenced so easily.

Immediately following breakfast, I stopped by Liam's room so I could see for myself how he was faring. He was still asleep. Anwen sat at his bedside, holding his hand and reading an insect anthology. She looked up at my arrival and offered a tight smile that didn't reach her eyes.

"How is he?" I asked, though my inquiry was pointless considering I could see for myself that he was still unwell—pale, gaunt, and beginning to look quite sickly.

Anwen sighed. "His condition is the same, but he's a dutiful patient." She glanced at the pot of tea at his bedside. "He's due for more of his remedy."

"Is the new one helping at all?" I asked.

She sighed and shook her head. "The physician is already coming up with another. In the meantime, Liam continues to drink this one faithfully." She stroked his damp brow. "Perhaps I can let him rest a bit longer, for I hate to wake him.

Not only is the rest good for him, but I'm hoping the adventures in his dreams will help him better endure the restlessness during his waking hours. Being bedridden seems more difficult for him than not feeling well."

I managed a smile. "Liam has always been this way. When we were children, he broke his leg while climbing a tree in the orchard. He'd insisted on tackling the tallest one and fell quite a ways; he's lucky he didn't break his neck. Still, he behaved as if his fate of staying in bed for weeks was almost worse than death. His recovery took longer because he grew so bored that he kept sneaking out of bed and attempting to walk on it."

My story caused a glimmer of light to flicker in Anwen's worried countenance. "Why had he been climbing the tree?"

"He was pretending to be a pirate and wanted to use the tallest tree as a lookout for enemy ships."

She laughed lightly and gave Liam a tender look. "That sounds like my adventurous husband." She pressed a kiss on his hand before returning to her book.

As I quietly took my leave, my gaze lingered on the couple. I couldn't imagine either me or Briar constantly remaining at the other's bedside should one of us fall ill. Would I ever experience a love such as my brother and sister-in-law shared?

Worries about my courtship, Liam's illness, and tomorrow's meeting haunted me all the way back to my room, causing the palace walls to feel as if they were pressing in on me. I slowed when I heard voices coming from the partially open door to my parents' sitting room.

"I agree, the courtship isn't going as well as we'd hoped."

My heart flared to life. They were discussing Briar and me. Despite the tentative friendship we'd been forming since our walk in the orchard last week, our relationship still felt forced. While Liam and Elodie had been open about their agreement on that point, I hadn't had an opportunity to learn my parents' opinion.

I wasn't much of an eavesdropper—that was more Elodie's speciality—but I couldn't resist edging closer, ignoring the almost scolding look from the attending guard as I peered inside the room.

Mother sat with her skirts flowing elegantly around her while Father paced. My stomach sank; pacing wasn't a good sign. "It's not. It's been nearly two weeks and she still seems indifferent towards him."

"At least they're becoming better friends," Mother said. "Not to mention Rhea seems more at ease with him."

Father sighed. "While I'm pleased they get along, their relationship just doesn't seem strong enough for a union between our two kingdoms. They need a stronger foundation in order to best serve their subjects. How can we ask her to marry when the two are still practically strangers?"

His pacing quickened in his agitation. Mother watched, her expression full of a quiet fondness. "Give it time, dear. I have every confidence they'll grow together and learn to love each other. After all, we did, and we started our marriage after a much shorter acquaintanceship."

Father paused to turn to her, the affection in his eyes unmistakable. "We certainly did." He reached out a hand and Mother placed hers in his.

"I think she can learn to be happy with him," Mother said.

"I agree. He's a good man. I want nothing more than for it to work out between them. At the same time I don't want to pressure her, which is why I haven't mentioned to her just how invaluable this alliance would be. Not to mention it would be wonderful having our daughter on the Malvagarian throne."

Mother smiled. "I'd also love to see Rhea queen. She

would make a wonderful monarch to the Malvagarian people."

My heart dropped as any hopes I'd harbored of my parents not being upset if I chose not to marry Briar vanished. How could I disappoint their wishes for me and deny Draceria the great benefits my union would bring? Seeing my parents now only reminded me how beautiful an arranged relationship could become. I felt a renewed determination. If theirs could work out, then so could mine.

Mother and Father began discussing other things, and I took the opportunity to slowly back away from the door... where I bumped into someone. I spun around with a gasp and came face to face with Elodie and Aveline.

Aveline frowned in disapproval, but Elodie looked mischievous. "Eavesdropping?" she asked in a bright whisper.

My cheeks warmed. "I—I was simply passing by and couldn't help but overhear—" I swallowed the rest of my words. No excuse could adequately justify my behavior.

Elodie bounced lightly on the balls of her feet. "You don't need to defend yourself to me. You know how I feel about eavesdropping; it helps you learn such fascinating information you couldn't otherwise discover."

Aveline frowned at her. "That doesn't make it appropriate, especially when it's done on our *parents*."

The heat in my cheeks deepened. Chagrined, I lowered my eyes.

Elodie looped her arm through mine and tugged me away from our parents' still partially open door so we wouldn't be discovered, Aveline following closely behind.

When we were safely tucked away in Elodie's sitting room, she turned an expectant look towards me that pleaded for me to share everything I'd overheard. She pouted when I remained silent.

"Oh, you can't leave me in suspense. What were Mother

and Father discussing? It must have been quite interesting since you aren't one to eavesdrop." She leaned closer encouragingly.

Elodie was almost as persistent as Liam when it came to these types of things. This battle had been lost even before it had begun. I sighed. "They were discussing my courtship with Briar."

"I hope they were discussing breaking it off."

Aveline gave her a scolding look. "You're just as bad as Liam. You can't discourage Rhea from doing what's right."

Elodie frowned. "You can't really want Rhea to enter a loveless marriage, can you?"

Aveline straightened and clasped her hands primly in front of her. "I have every confidence that Rhea and Briar will learn to love one another. Rhea is too sensible to reject such a beneficial match."

She gave me a *look* that silently pleaded that her assessment of my character was deserved. I ached to disagree with her, but she was right.

"Overhearing them reminded me that while they want what's best for me, they undoubtedly desire this union and hope I choose it," I said.

"But—" Elodie protested.

Aveline cut her off. "There's more at stake than Rhea's happiness; she must consider the wellbeing of our kingdom. It's selfish to focus solely on our own wishes and desires when we've been born into a position that allows us to serve our people in whatever capacity may be required of us."

My heart sank further. She was right, I knew she was. But it didn't make her words any easier to hear.

Elodie glared at her. "It's easy for you to speak of duty when you're not the one forced to fulfill it."

"But that day will come," Aveline said. "And when it does, it'll be a pleasure to perform it."

Elodie frowned skeptically. "Are you really suggesting you'd *welcome* an arranged marriage?"

Aveline lifted her chin. "It would be an honor."

Elodie gaped at her in disbelief, and while I found my sister's words just as shocking, I couldn't help but silently admire her strength of will.

Elodie finally found her voice. "Well, *I* mind. I definitely don't want such a future, although I fear when the time comes, I won't be able to escape it." Sorrow filled her eyes. "Mother and Father told me just last week that the King and Queen of Bytamia have begun discussing a match between our two kingdoms."

"I was told the same," Aveline said.

"Then I pray it's *you* they're considering, because duty or not, I'm definitely not interested in any of the Bytamian princes." Elodie wrinkled her nose. "I want a love match like Liam and Anwen have."

"An arranged marriage wouldn't make such a wish impossible," Aveline said. "Love matches can be created through determination and nourishing a relationship."

Elodie pressed her hands on her hips. "I don't want to have to force myself to love my future husband. Is that so wrong?"

"Yes," Aveline said. "We're princesses. One day you'll have to accept all the responsibilities that come with our title. After all, there are still five eligible princes in the surrounding kingdoms who have yet to make a match—the three younger Bytamian princes, the Crown Prince of Lyceria, and the second prince of Malvagaria. Odds are you'll end up wed to one of them."

Elodie's eyes dimmed at the thought of her unfulfilled romantic dreams, and my heart ached for her even as her disappointment reminded me of my own secret hopes for a fairytale future. Elodie and I weren't so different in that regard; I'd simply given my dreams up long ago. It was easier that way.

Despite that, I couldn't escape the sadness tightening my chest, nor the sense of loss brought on by overhearing my parents and having Aveline put me in my place regarding my duty—a duty that seemed far more difficult now than it had when I'd accepted Deidric's proposal several years ago. What had changed?

My hand instinctively went to the mirror in my satchel, where I ran my thumb along the handle. The familiar touch both soothed me and caused a strange longing to fill my heart, causing me to want something *more* for my future, just like Elodie.

My movements attracted my sisters' notice. Elodie's brow furrowed as her gaze lowered to the mirror's handle poking slightly out of my satchel. "What's that?"

I didn't have a chance to react before, ever nosy, she withdrew the mirror, where Drake's reflection was briefly visible before promptly disappearing…but not before my sisters spotted him. Aveline's mouth fell open and Elodie's eyes widened. She blinked rapidly before looking inside the mirror again, but only her reflection stared back at her.

"What was that?"

"What was what?" I fought to steady my voice.

"Inside the mirror. I thought I saw…" She stared at the glass, which remained empty. She examined the mirror carefully before shaking her head, as if dismissing her suspicions.

She frowned. "There's nothing there. It must be a trick of the light. It's a lovely mirror. Wherever did you get it?"

"I've had it a long time." I plucked it from her grasp before she could question me further.

Aveline's eyes narrowed at my satchel as I hid Drake. "Why are you carrying a mirror around?"

I nervously wiped my sweaty palms against my skirts. "I—"

But I had no explanation, and nothing was coming to me. Aveline's gaze remained riveted to where I'd tucked the mirror away. My heart pounded anxiously. Aveline was quite clever...and prone to suspicion. Would she act on it and investigate the mirror further? I couldn't allow her to have that chance.

"If you'll excuse me, I'm scheduled to meet with Briar." I rose and exited the sitting room, forcing myself to walk at a normal pace, for any haste would only cause me to appear more suspicious.

Back in the refuge of my bedroom, I pressed my hand against the closed door and willed the nervous pattering of my heart to settle. Then I slowly withdrew Drake, whose own expression was laced with worry. "I'm sorry I didn't hide myself in time," he said.

"Why was your reflection in the glass at all when we weren't alone?" I didn't mean to sound accusing, but my question came out sharper than I'd intended.

"It takes more effort to remain hidden," he said. "Not to mention I can hear conversations better when I'm within the glass. Admittedly, I was just as curious about your parents' conversation as you were."

Despite my anxiety, I couldn't blame him.

He studied my expression. "Are you alright, Rhea?"

Weariness washed over me at the unwanted reminder of my duty to choose a loveless future. "I'm not sure." I collapsed in our usual window seat and rested Drake on my lap. "What did you think of their conversation? Is my future as set in stone as I fear?"

Drake frowned, his answer. I sighed.

"I suspected as much. Which means I'll have to try harder to make it work with Briar."

My stomach knotted at the thought, but what choice did I have? It was up to me to make the best of my situation.

So I locked away the foolish secret hopes that had recently begun prickling my heart. Dreams of love had no place for a princess. The sooner I realized that, the better.

CHAPTER 15

*D*rake was behaving strangely. While he used to frequently seek my company in order to stave off boredom or try to find a way to break the curse, he now seemed to be avoiding me, appearing less frequently in the mirror, some days not at all. The longer he stayed away, the more I wondered whether he was tiring of my company.

I had another scheduled courtship outing with Briar, but I didn't want to leave until I'd made another attempt to talk to Drake.

"Drake?"

No answer.

"Drake? I know you can hear me. Please come out."

I waited, passing the time by resting my head on the cool windowpane to stare out at the falling rain. When Drake still didn't appear after several minutes, I gave up.

I crawled off the window seat with a sigh. "Perhaps he doesn't want to be friends anymore." My heart tightened at the thought.

It's for the best. After all, my relationship with Drake was distracting me from Briar, the man I *should* be focusing on befriending...and who was waiting for me right now.

I'd no sooner set the mirror on my vanity than my name drifted from it. "Rhea?"

Drake appeared within the glass. I stared, waiting for him to disappear. When he didn't, I snatched him up. "Where have you been?"

He hesitated before smiling crookedly. "Where do you think? I'm in a mirror. It's not as if I have anywhere else to be."

"Then why haven't you been visiting me? I've missed you." My cheeks burned at the admission, and my blush only deepened at the tender way Drake looked at me.

"You missed me?"

"Of course. You're my friend." The truth of my words wrapped around my heart.

"I consider you a friend as well," Drake murmured. "That's why I've been staying away. It's for the best, for both of us."

I furrowed my brow. "I don't understand." But before I could inquire further, the clock on the mantle struck the hour. I gasped. "Oh dear, I'm late."

"Late for what?" But by Drake's darkened tone, I could tell he knew exactly the nature of the appointment I needed to keep.

"I'm meeting Briar for tea in the mauve sitting room."

Drake snorted. "You're meeting him for *tea*? That's the romantic outing the stuffy prince planned? He certainly knows how to woo a girl."

I glared. "Taking tea is a lovely way to spend an afternoon, especially as it provides the opportunity to converse and get to know one another better. We were going to go outside to the orchard, but..." I looked out the rain-splattered window.

"The weather is no excuse," Drake said. "Even if it's raining, there are more creative activities than *tea*." He rolled his eyes. "The man has no imagination."

"Don't be so hard on him. He's doing his best."

Drake lifted a surprised eyebrow. "You're *defending* him? This is new. What has he done to earn such an honor?"

My cheeks warmed. "Nothing. We're just...becoming better friends, that's all."

"I see." Drake's entire manner was hard and unreadable. I glanced at the clock again.

"I really should go. We can talk when I return...if you don't stay away again." I gave him an accusing look.

"Trust me, I'll be here when you return."

I smiled and carried him to his perch at the window before opening the book he'd been reading to its book-marked spot.

I left my room and hurried as gracefully as I could to the mauve sitting room, where Briar was waiting. He rose when I entered and even managed a smile that seemed genuine. "Good afternoon, Rheanna. It's a pleasure to see you."

"And you as well." For once the words didn't feel forced or insincere.

Briar helped me with my chair before taking the seat across from me. "I apologize for the rain."

I smiled teasingly. "Why? Do you control the elements?"

He blinked, confused, before grinning crookedly in return, similar to the way Drake did. I shook my head. I needed to stop thinking of him; I was in Briar's company right now.

"I wish I possessed such a fantastic ability," he said as he poured my tea. He added my usual dose of cream and two spoonfuls of sugar without my prompting before handing me the steaming cup. "Controlling the rain would be quite useful considering I spend most of my time in the gardens at home, although the gardens would continue to thrive without any interference on my part."

I blew on my tea before taking a dainty sip. "Do you merely spend time in the gardens, or do you tend them yourself?"

"I often get my hands dirty, although my help does little; the *garden* gardens itself."

I lifted my brow and he grinned.

"Intrigued?"

"Quite."

He chuckled. It was the first I'd ever heard him laugh. Thank goodness Briar had some personality buried beneath his stoic exterior. Liam would be thrilled to hear of this new development.

"You should be. The gardens are remarkable, unlike anything you've ever seen. I can't wait to show them to you; you'll love them." His cheeks darkened. "Forgive my presumption."

He lowered his eyes. His timidness was a new reaction, but it made him rather...endearing. I instinctively reached out to rest my hand over his. He jolted but didn't pull away. Instead he peeked up at me, his eyes shy.

Hmm...is the prince shy, even more so than me? That was an emotion I could understand. Perhaps he wasn't as indifferent as I'd initially supposed.

Hopefully I could put him at ease. "Can you tell me more about the gardens?"

"Don't you like surprises?"

I smiled coyly and leaned closer. "Couldn't you give me just a little hint?" I lightly caressed his elbow. His eyes widened and his blush deepened.

Goodness, am I flirting? But when he slowly grinned in response, I didn't regret the gesture. *This man is to be your husband. Choose to make this work.*

"Well, perhaps a small hint is harmless." He hesitated before shyly running his thumb along my hand. It felt nice, although not the stimulating response I'd always expected to receive from a man's touch. "The gardens are not only enchanted, but they also have a mind of their own, particularly the roses."

As he spoke, he caressed the flower that was always pinned to his lapel.

"Is that rose from your garden?"

"Yes. It's always in bloom because the plants in that garden never die."

Fascinating. "How many gardens are there at the Malvagarian palace?"

"Several, but in a way there are even more considering these gardens *change* depending on when you enter them… but I'll leave you to discover them for yourself."

It sounded magical. How thrilling it'd be to explore them. And for the first time, the thought of living in Malvagaria intrigued me. Perhaps I could be happy there. "I'll allow you to keep your gardens a secret, but at least tell me one thing: is there an orchard?"

"Not yet, but I know the perfect place we can plant one, if you'd like."

We…my stomach flipped. Strangely, *we* was a concept I was becoming more used to considering the inevitable conclusion to our courtship. "I'd love that. Will it be enchanted, too?"

"Everything growing in the gardens is enchanted."

I couldn't wait to see it. My heart tightened with guilt that I was more intrigued by my intended's home than in the man himself, but I'd do everything in my power to change that.

My neck suddenly prickled, as if a heated gaze were coming from behind me. I looked around the room. Save for the attending guards and servants—none of whom were looking at me—we were alone. Perhaps it had been my imagination. I faced Briar once more.

"Is something wrong?" he asked.

"No, I just…nevermind." I nibbled one of my tea sandwiches. "Please tell me about your favorite childhood memory you experienced in your gardens."

The conversation prompt got Briar talking, hesitantly at first, but he became more animated the more he spoke. I did my best to listen—for his story about the mischievous roses' teasing was quite intriguing—but the strange sensation had returned. Instinctively, I glanced at the mirror hanging on the wall behind me.

It was empty. Of course it was. *Don't be absurd, Rhea; no other mirror but Drake's houses cursed individuals.*

Even so, I couldn't shake the feeling someone was watching me from within the glass. I repeatedly glanced at the mirror, feeling drawn to it in a similar way I felt whenever I was near Drake. But that was a ridiculous thought…wasn't it?

Drake has made you obsessed with mirrors.

"Are you sure you're alright, Rheanna?" Briar asked.

I snapped my gaze back to him. "Yes, I'm fine. My apologies."

He nodded with a look like he didn't believe me. "It appears the rain has stopped. Would you like some fresh air? We can step onto the balcony." Briar stood and offered his hand, and I accepted it gratefully. I needed to get away from that mirror.

Briar looped my arm through his and escorted me onto the balcony, wet from the recent rain. My paranoia immediately melted away as I stepped into the brisk outdoors, the air full of mist and the smell of the recent storm.

I breathed in the brisk, rainy air as I leaned against the damp railing and looked out over the grounds, which were still fairly green despite the approaching winter. Briar mimicked my position and we stood side by side. After several minutes, I looked away from the grey sky and stole a peek at Briar, who was fiddling with his rose again.

"Does it help you to touch it?" I asked.

Briar startled and whirled around to face me, looking almost panicked. "What do you mean?"

I motioned towards the rose with my chin. "You're always touching it, especially when you're nervous. I wondered if it helps you think of home."

He released a whooshing breath. "Something like that." He leaned back against the railing, not looking at me. "You're rather observant, Rheanna. It's a trait to be admired, one of many admirable traits I've seen in you."

My cheeks warmed at the compliment. Perhaps Briar and I were making more progress than I'd initially believed.

Briar continued staring out over the grounds, his brow furrowed and his normally stoic expression somber. "It makes me sad to see the grounds in such a state, where everything is dying. I'm not used to being in a garden like this; gardens are meant to always be vibrant."

"Perhaps a long winter helps us better appreciate their return to life in the spring."

Briar's lips quirked up as he returned his attention to me. "You continually surprise me, Rheanna. But there's truth to your words. I believe we can apply them to our situation as well—I better appreciate your company now after our rough beginning." He fully faced me, hesitated, and shyly took one of my hands in his. "I must again apologize for the way I treated you when I first arrived. The more I dwell on it, the more I regret my behavior. I sincerely hope you didn't think me unenthusiastic for our union."

"Weren't you?" The accusing words escaped before I could stop them.

"In truth I wasn't particularly thrilled, but most of my behavior came from...adjusting." Once more, he cradled his rose. "It's wearying being away from home, especially for such a length of time. On top of that, you weren't what I expected."

I held my breath, waiting for him to elaborate on that particular point—afraid of what he could possibly say—and was relieved when he didn't.

"You weren't what I expected either," I said.

He actually chuckled. "Undoubtedly not." He searched my eyes, as if looking for something he needed to find. "It appears we're at a crossroads. Despite my mother's wishes, I don't want to force a union between us. Would you like to continue our courtship? Or is there...someone else?"

My heart leapt when Drake's face bombarded my mind, uninvited. I hastily shoved it away. "No, there's no one else." There *couldn't* be. I wouldn't be responsible for our kingdom losing another alliance. I liked Briar enough to make it work between us.

"Are you sure?" Briar's look became penetrating. My heartbeat escalated. *Does he suspect?*

I took a wavering breath. "I am."

He nodded and rested his hand over mine that clutched the railing. At his touch, I relaxed and loosened my hold. "Then I'm certain, too. I'll do my best to be a better suitor than I've been in the past. You deserve nothing less." He softly kissed my knuckles.

We exchanged smiles before turning back to look over the grounds. My attention was captured by the orchard in the distance, where autumn tinged its branches and the leaves were beginning to fall, while the fully ripened fruit lingered, ruby ornaments against the boughs.

Despite the approaching winter and the chill in the air, the moment was nice, one of the best I'd experienced with

Briar. I could enjoy our union if it was filled with more moments like this. Perhaps our arrangement would work after all.

Notwithstanding my resolution, I couldn't stop thinking of Drake, even though doing so now seemed even more inappropriate than it had before.

~

"How was your *tea*?"

Drake's disdainful tone pierced the contentment I'd carried back with me after my afternoon with Briar. Our time together had only improved after our conversation on the balcony—we'd talked with more ease, exchanged many smiles, and he'd even laughed several times. Then he'd kissed my hand again in departure after escorting me back to my room.

For the first time since his visit had started, it felt like we were actually courting. *Perhaps Briar is different than Deidric. Perhaps you're worth caring about after all.*

"Aren't you going to tell me?" Drake's grumpiness interrupted my thoughts. My smile faltered. Leave it to Drake to ruin the moment. Sometimes he could be sweet, and other times rather…annoying. Such as now.

"Goodness, you're sour today. Must you ruin my mood?"

He scowled. "So you're actually in a good mood after being with Prince Briar? That's a change."

"Yes, a welcome one." I frowned at his hardened expression. "Briar is my intended. After our relationship's rough beginning, it's a relief that things are finally going better. As my friend, shouldn't you be happy for me?"

"I'm simply concerned. Frankly, I'm surprised your opinion of him has changed so quickly."

I sighed and picked up Drake's mirror so we could settle

177

in our window seat. "It's not just today's outing; he's been more attentive for a while now. I'm simply being grateful for it as I make the best of our situation."

"No, you're denying the fact that you have a choice."

But I didn't. Either I could be a dutiful princess or a selfish one; no other choice lay between those two paths.

At my telling silence, Drake frowned. "So you've resigned yourself to your future? No amount of romantic garden tours and planting orchards together can make a poor match a happy one." His tone was bitter.

"If I didn't know any better, I'd say you were jealous. Just because you don't like the idea of gardens and orchards docsn't mean—" *Wait*...I narrowed my eyes suspiciously. "How did you know we spoke of planting an orchard together?"

He bit his lip before hastily smoothing his expression. "You told me."

"No, I didn't give you any details about what we spoke of. How could you have known then? You weren't there."

The guilt that filled his face confirmed my sinking suspicion. The only question that remained was *how*. It didn't take long for me to form a theory, one that, if true, meant I'd been looking at Drake's curse all wrong.

"Drake, can you enter mirrors other than your own?"

I saw the answer in his eyes before he hastily lowered them, as if his guilt prevented him from looking at me. I tightened my jaw.

"I see." Hurt prickled me. "This is yet another secret you've kept from me. How many more are there? Were you ever planning on telling me about your ability? As the only one helping to break your curse, it seems like something I should know."

Drake lowered his head. "I don't know why I didn't tell you. It's not something I do often."

"But you did it today—you were in the sitting room mirror." So I hadn't imagined the feeling of being watched throughout tea with Briar after all. "But how? I didn't see you within the glass."

He sighed, finally giving up the fight. "Just because you don't see me doesn't mean I can't see *you*. I can always see the outside world, even if I'm selective about when I reveal myself."

My stomach sank. "So you *were* in the mirror. What were you doing there?" His guilty silence confirmed my suspicions. I balled my hands into fists. "Were you *spying* on me?"

He hesitated. "I admit I was in the sitting room mirror, but I wasn't *spying*, per se..."

"Then what were you doing?"

"I was...chaperoning."

I folded my arms across my chest. "You'd best explain yourself."

He braced himself, as if he expected his explanation wouldn't go over well. "You always return from your outings with Briar pensive and somber, but you rarely give me any details. I figured if I had more information, I could better help you."

"Don't pretend your shady act was *noble*," I snapped. "You invaded my privacy. We're friends and yet you snooped on me behind my back?"

"If it makes you feel any better, I didn't do it for very long because I couldn't stomach your *flirting*."

My cheeks burned. "I wasn't *flirting*."

"You certainly were." Drake's expression twisted in disgust. "It was rather nauseating to witness—coy smiles, caressing his elbow, touching his hand...you even twirled your hair around your finger while *giggling*." He shuddered.

The heat filling my face deepened. I hadn't done all those things, had I?

179

"Not to mention, you got starry-eyed when he spoke of his *special gardens*." Drake rolled his eyes. "Who knew the way to your heart was through something so shallow?"

"Stop it, Drake," I hissed. "You're being cruel. Why can't you just be happy for me that things are finally going well between Briar and me? You know how difficult this arrangement has been for me."

"Trust me, the moment you're genuinely happy with Prince Briar, I'll be the first to congratulate you. Until then, forgive me for not expressing insincere joy on your behalf."

My anger only intensified. My fist clutching the handle of his mirror tightened.

He winced. "Ow, careful."

"If being inside this mirror is so unpleasant, perhaps you should just enter another one."

"It's not that easy; it's rather difficult and exhausting." Now that he mentioned it, weariness lined his eyes…a weariness I'd occasionally caught glimpses of over the past several weeks, meaning this wasn't the only time he'd done this.

"How many times have you used your ability to spy on me?" I asked curtly.

"This is the first time, I swear. *Ow*." He winced again and I realized I was still gripping his mirror handle. I forced myself to loosen my hold, even though I was tempted to hold him tighter. He visibly relaxed. "Thank you. Now, if I explain myself, will you stop being mad?"

"Not likely."

"Well, at least you didn't say *no*." He sighed. "I didn't realize I could enter another mirror until only a few months ago. Whenever I grew bored, I began to explore the small space within my mirror. There isn't much here, but occasionally I thought I caught glimpses of other rooms, like portions of paintings, which I now realize were the views from the other mirrors hanging on the walls of whatever building I'm in. When I focus on them hard enough, I enter them. I don't think I actually leave this mirror; rather, I temporarily change the glass I'm looking out through."

He paused with an expectant look, as if he wanted some sort of praise for such an interesting ability. But I was too annoyed to humor him.

"Fascinating," I said wryly.

He frowned. "Come on, Rhea, don't be like that."

"Oh, so I should be *flattered* you used your special abilities I had no knowledge of to *spy* on me after I trusted you?"

He bit his lip. "I just wanted to see how things were going between you and the prince. I now realize it wasn't my business, but I only did it because I was worried for you. Your concerns about doing your duty are making you rather blind."

"Blind to what?" I asked stiffly.

"What's best for you compared to what's best for your people."

My heart lurched. "I'm a princess and have duties to my kingdom. What would you know about royal responsibilities and what it means to have to sacrifice for the greater good?"

Drake's expression hardened. "I know what I did was wrong, but even so, I only had your best interests in mind. I'm sorry it was such a sneaky way of helping you, but in case you hadn't noticed, I'm inside a blasted mirror. How else could I have done it?"

"A less deceitful way, that's for sure."

Drake released an aggravated growl. "What do you want from me? An apology?"

"That would be nice, but it'll do little to mend the trust you've broken." The betrayal was worse coming from him considering I didn't open my heart easily.

Drake rolled his eyes. "Prince Briar sure has his hands full with you," he muttered darkly.

The anger festering inside me immediately vanished, replaced with stinging hurt. Drake's expression transformed in an instant.

"Wait, Rhea, I didn't mean it like that."

"What, then, did you mean? Do share how difficult you find me, because I'm always eager to hear more about my inadequacies." My tears escaped before I could stop them and Drake's expression crumpled.

"I'm sorry, Rhea." And although he looked like he meant it, I wasn't ready to forgive him just yet.

"You can't just smooth over you hurtful words so easily." I stood and stomped towards my desk.

His eyes widened. "What are you doing?"

"Getting some distance from you. If you grow bored or want help with your curse, go to another mirror and charm some other unsuspecting fool. I'm done." I shoved him into a drawer before slamming it shut.

CHAPTER 16

I couldn't stop thinking about my fight with Drake. It consumed my mind as I went about my duties. My biggest distraction came when I visited Liam; his health had shown no improvement, despite his taking a new remedy for the past several days. Even though the physician assured us it would likely take some time for the old remedy to leave his system, worry still knotted my gut.

What if Liam's illness isn't natural? The thought came out of nowhere and caused my heart to pound wildly in my chest. *Don't be ridiculous; he's simply ill.* All the same, I ached to confide this new fear to Drake, but we still weren't speaking.

As the next day wore on, my hurt and annoyance with his betrayal gradually faded. I missed him—our long conversations; his humorous commentary, crooked smile, and sweet words; even his snarkiness. I especially missed confiding in him and finally feeling, for the first time, that I had a true friend outside of my family.

The evening after our fight, I returned to my room after a rather stressful discussion with Father and several of our dignitaries. My mind was currently a battleground ripe for another onslaught of attacking thoughts. I needed my confidant more than ever.

My gaze immediately went to the desk drawer where I'd stashed Drake's mirror. Ever since our fight, the drawer had stayed resolutely shut and Drake hadn't made a peep, undoubtedly his way of paying penance.

Remorse softened my heart. No matter how annoyed I'd been, my friend deserved better than to be locked away in the dark. It was time to apologize. Besides, I really did miss him. A lot.

I trudged to the desk and opened the drawer. "I'm sorry, Drake. I'm being really stubborn—" My breath hooked.

The mirror wasn't there.

"Drake?"

No answer. My heart pounded.

"Drake? Aren't you here?" I knelt down and sorted through the drawer, even though I was certain I'd put him on top. "Drake? *Drake?*"

I yanked the drawer out and dumped its contents, fully expecting—and hoping—to hear Drake's pained *oof* from the landing, but he didn't make a sound. I scattered the contents of the drawer around, desperately searching, but it didn't take long to confirm my fear—Drake wasn't here. Where could he be?

Panic pressed against my chest. I took several steadying breaths. Maybe I'd put him somewhere else…or had moved him and forgotten. But I knew both scenarios were unlikely.

"Where are you, Drake?" I opened each desk drawer and looked through them, and when each search yielded no results, I sat back on my heels and frantically looked around the room for any possible places where he could be. "Drake?"

Still no response. I tore my room apart, searching every potential hiding place I could think of—inside my wardrobe, the drawer of my nightstand, beneath my bed. He was nowhere to be found.

"Drake..." But it was no use; he wasn't here. I collapsed on the settee and buried my face in my hands. *What kind of princess loses her best friend?*

I sat there for several miserable minutes, trying to think through my suffocating guilt. Where could Drake possibly be? If only I'd accepted his apology instead of losing my temper.

You're a terrible person.

I took a deep breath and pushed that dark thought away.

No, you're simply someone who made a mistake. Don't let it paralyze you. You need to find your friend. Now think.

Resolved, I stood and paced the room, frantically considering all the places Drake could possibly be. Drake was in a mirror and couldn't move on his own, which obviously meant...dread pooled my stomach—he must have been *taken*. There was no other possibility. But who could have done such a thing? Nobody even knew I had the mirror.

The answer came immediately. Nobody knew except my sisters, who had both caught a glimpse of Drake's reflection several days ago. My hope that neither had seen him had clearly been in vain.

Of the two, Aveline was likely the one who'd stolen the mirror; she was especially clever and must have deduced there was something special about it for me to be carrying it with me. If she investigated further and discovered it held a cursed man, would she inform our parents? If she did, they'd surely forbid me from handling a cursed object. If I couldn't break the curse, what would happen to Drake?

Calm down, Rhea. Drake is clever enough to not reveal himself to her. Aveline will just assume it's a normal mirror.

Still, I couldn't rest until I found my friend. I hurried to Aveline's bedroom next door and knocked, praying she wasn't there. When she didn't answer I knocked again before trying the knob. Unlocked. Perfect.

I opened the door only a few inches so I could peer inside. It was abandoned. I slipped inside and shut the door quietly behind me before glancing around. Everything was impeccably neat, leaving very few hiding places where Aveline could keep a stolen mirror.

I searched all her drawers, rummaged through her wardrobe, investigated the desk, and looked not only beneath her bed but underneath her mattress. There was no sign of an enchanted mirror.

"Drake?" I whisper-called as I walked the perimeter of the room again, looking for any places I might have missed. "Are you in here?"

No answer. My frustration mounted. Where was he? If Aveline hadn't taken Drake, that left only Elodie. The more I considered it, the more certain I was. Yes, it had to be Elodie. She was rather nosy and enjoyed poking herself into other people's business. After one final look around Aveline's bedroom, I went to the door and eased it open to peer into the hallway. Abandoned. I tiptoed towards Elodie's room next door, and after my knock went unanswered, I quietly entered.

I expected to have to begin a thorough search—for Elodie came up with the most elaborate hiding places for the most trivial of things—but to my surprise, I discovered Drake's mirror resting on the vanity, as if he'd been waiting for me to find him. So she'd taken him after all.

Fierce relief filled me. "Drake! I've been looking every-where for you." I'd no sooner grazed the mirror's handle than—

"Rhea?"

I froze at Elodie's voice drifting from the bed. I spun around—keeping Drake firmly behind me—to find her sitting up and rubbing the sleep from her eyes after a late afternoon nap.

Curses. I forced a smile. "Good afternoon, Elodie."

She blinked sleepily at me, as if she was trying to discern whether my presence were real or a figment of her tired imagination. "What are you doing in my room?"

I shifted uneasily from foot to foot. What could I tell her? "I'm just…" No lies were forthcoming.

Elodie's forehead furrowed. "Was there something you needed?"

Yes, *Drake.* But I couldn't very well tell her that she'd stolen my best friend when she'd snuck into my room and taken my mirror.

"The first step in getting out of a predicament such as the one you currently find yourself in is to come up with *something* rather than stay silent." Drake's whisper drifted from the mirror I held behind my back. Relief washed over me. It was wonderful hearing his voice again.

I stroked the rim of his mirror with my thumb, finding solace in the gesture. "I was just…looking for you," I told Elodie. "I finished my meeting and am in desperate need of a distraction. Would you like to go on a stroll through the garden?"

"A walk sounds lovely. We should enjoy the good weather before winter arrives in a few weeks." Elodie stretched before standing, but after taking a few steps towards me, she paused, frowning. "What are you doing with my mirror?"

My heart pounded. "What mirror?"

She grinned mischievously, which was a far better reaction than the condemning one I'd expect after being caught in the very act of snooping. "The one you're holding behind your back. I can see its reflection in my vanity mirror."

I glanced behind me. Sure enough, Drake's mirror was clearly visible. So much for escaping this situation without

Elodie noticing I'd stolen back my mirror. I sighed and withdrew it.

"I'm just taking back what's mine. Why do you have my mirror?"

"*Your* mirror? This mirror is mine."

She reached for it and tried to extract it from my hands, but my grip only tightened. She tried again, and after a moment's hesitation this time I let her take it, afraid that any struggle resulting from Elodie's stubbornness could cause us to drop it and hurt Drake.

She flipped it over and I tensed. To my relief Drake's image wasn't in the glass. Elodie smiled at her reflection before tracing her finger along the floral pattern engraven in the silver rim. I stiffened to see her touching Drake so familiarly.

"It really is a beautiful mirror," Elodie said. "It was such a sweet surprise when I discovered it on my vanity yesterday."

I wrinkled my brow. "You mean you didn't take it from my room?"

"Of course I didn't. You gave it to me, didn't you? It was so sweet of you after seeing me admiring it."

I frowned. None of this made any sense. Elodie's eyes were wide with innocence, compelling me to believe her. But if she hadn't taken the mirror, who had, and how had it ended up in her bedroom? If Liam weren't bedridden, I'd suspect his usual mischief.

But that was a puzzle for another day. For now, all I wanted was Drake safely back with me. "I'm sorry, Elodie. I didn't give you the mirror. The servants who clean our rooms must have simply misplaced it."

She sighed in disappointment. After another admiring look at the mirror, she handed it to me with a resigned sigh. Thank goodness for her trusting nature. If Aveline had ended up with the mirror, she wouldn't have relinquished it so easily without a lot of prying questions.

I cradled the mirror close. It was wonderful having it in my possession again, as if Drake was exactly where he belonged. I ached to see him again, to assure myself he was really here. I tipped the mirror so the glass only faced me. As if sensing my secret wish, Drake appeared briefly enough to wink before disappearing again.

I released the breath I'd been holding. "Thank you for returning it. I'll give you a similar mirror for your upcoming birthday. If you'll excuse me, I just remembered something I need to do; can we postpone our stroll for another time?"

"There goes my excuse to wriggle out of my piano practice." She followed me out of the room before we parted ways, her to the music room, me to my bedroom.

I flipped the mirror over the moment I stepped inside. "Drake?"

He appeared with my favorite crooked smile. "Hello, Rhea."

"Oh Drake, I'm so happy to see you." I actually hugged the mirror, earning a muffled *oof* from its occupant. Even though it wasn't exactly a real hug, I could have sworn I felt the shadow of his arms around me, embracing me in return.

"It's good to see you as well, Rhea. I was hoping you'd notice I was missing and come find me, but after two days I was beginning to worry." Hope filled his dark eyes. "Does this mean you're not upset with me anymore?"

"I'm not. I missed you."

"I'm glad." His smile faded. "I've spent the past several days coming up with a proper apology, but I'm not sure what else I can say other than, 'I'm sorry.'"

I gave him a teasing smile. "As lovely of an apology as that is, I'm curious what other proper apologies you came up with. Let's hear some of them."

"I admit most of them were more groveling than actual apologies, pleading for you to forgive me so that we might remain friends." His imploring expression said more than any words could. The rest of my anger softened.

"I forgive you." My look became stern. "Just don't do it again."

"I promise."

That settled, I skipped to the window seat so we could talk. "Now tell me what happened. How did you end up in Elodie's room?"

"Someone took me from your drawer. I instantly knew it wasn't you."

"How could you tell?"

His cheeks darkened. "I recognize your touch."

My heart gave a strange flutter. "Do you know who it was?"

"Yes, but don't worry, we only spoke for—" he snapped his mouth shut.

"You *spoke* with them? But I thought you were supposed to be a secret. Whom did you speak with?"

He lowered his gaze. "I can't tell you."

I sighed. "Drake, we just stopped fighting. I don't want any more secrets between us."

"I know, Rhea, I'm sorry." He peeked up at me with such a raw, vulnerable look that my annoyance immediately softened.

"Is there a reason you can't talk about it?" I asked.

He hesitated. "I'm afraid so. It wasn't exactly a pleasant conversation. But that's who put me in Elodie's room. It didn't take long for her to discover the mirror, but I didn't reveal myself. That privilege is reserved only for you." His half-crooked smile faltered. "I'm glad you found me. Even when you noticed I was missing, I wasn't sure whether you'd know where to look."

"After my sisters nearly discovered you the other day, I assumed one of them had taken you. Why didn't you tell me where you were? Couldn't you have shown up in my vanity mirror?"

"I tried, but I was unable to. While I can *see* through other mirrors, it's more difficult to appear or speak from any mirror other than my own. I don't often manage it."

I held him closer. "It doesn't matter now, I'm just relieved I was able to find you. Promise me you won't run off again."

"I promise." We exchanged smiles. Something passed between us in that moment, another thread connecting me to Drake in a way I couldn't explain, but one I desperately wanted to explore.

CHAPTER 17

I hastily shut the door and leaned against it, fighting the hyperventilating breaths struggling to escape.

"What is it, Rhea?" Drake's panicked voice came from his usual perch at the window. "Did something happen?"

"Deidric is coming! He and his wife. Oh, I can't bear to face him." I fought against the tears already burning my eyes.

"Prince Deidric? Your—"

"Ex-fiancé. Yes." I sank to the ground and buried my face in my knees. How could my parents not have warned me that Deidric and his wife were coming to visit Liam? I knew they were worried about how I'd handle his arrival due to our tumultuous history, but to have had *no* warning until the evening of his arrival…

"Please don't cry, Rhea." Drake's tone was both soothing and agonized. "Since I can't go to you, will you please come here?"

I did need to be closer to him, so I shakily stood and approached. A sliver of calm penetrated the panic clawing at my rapidly beating heart the moment I picked up the mirror and glimpsed his concerned expression.

"Deidric is coming here." My breathing escalated, each sharper than the last.

"Slow, deep breaths, Rhea."

Drake's tone was incredibly gentle. I closed my eyes and focused on steadying my breathing. Slowly, it calmed.

"There, that's better," Drake said. "Are you alright?"

"I think so." I opened my eyes to Drake's dark gaze, wide with worry. "I can't believe he's here and that I have to face him."

"Is this the first time you've seen him since…?"

I shook my head, trying to still my panicked thoughts. "I caught glimpses of him at his Princess Competition in Sorti-leya but managed to avoid a dance, both at that ball and the one we hosted several months later. He was at Liam's wedding, but I didn't have to speak with him. Considering tonight is a more intimate gathering, I don't think I can avoid him any longer. But I can't bear to face him after what he did. I never want to see him again, not when he tossed me aside." The anxiety was returning, squeezing my heart in a vise.

"But I thought you didn't love him?" Drake had never been so gentle.

"I told you before that I didn't, but his breaking our engagement still hurts because it meant I wasn't good enough." The painful memories of Deidric's agonizing rejection were escaping the prison where I'd kept them locked away so they couldn't hurt me anymore.

"Oh, Rhea." Drake's sympathy was so sweet. In those two words I knew he understood this portion of my heart I'd only tentatively shared with him.

"*Why* didn't he want me?" I asked. "What was wrong with me that caused him to reject me so cruelly?"

He was silent a moment, considering. "Well, did you want him?"

"No…but I pretended I did in hopes that doing so would make our arrangement more bearable." It was a relief to finally admit this.

"Was there something wrong with *him* that caused you to not want to marry him?"

"No, he's all that's proper in a prince, although he's rather formidable." And frightening, but admitting such a thing was one secret I was too embarrassed to share.

"Then why do you believe there's something wrong with *you?*"

My brow furrowed. "What do you mean?"

"If there's nothing wrong with Prince Deidric even though you didn't want to marry him," Drake said carefully, "then why do you assume there's something wrong with you because he didn't want to marry you?"

"Because—" I scrambled for a reason, for surely there had to be *something*. I'd spent two years believing I was at fault for what had happened, and questioning that assumption was almost frightening. "Because after he broke off our engagement, he arranged for a competition to find a proper princess. Our union would have brought many benefits to both our kingdoms. Why would he toss them all aside unless I wasn't good enough?"

Drake frowned. "I don't know Prince Deidric's motive for breaking off your engagement…except for the fact that he's an idiot. Don't let this incident, as painful as it has been for you, cause you to doubt yourself and sour your future. You've held on to this pain long enough; it's time to let it go and no longer let it define you."

My breath hitched. "How do I do that?"

But before Drake could elaborate, my maid arrived with a

curtsy to prepare me for dinner, and Drake faded from the mirror, leaving only my reflection.

≈

I LOOKED every bit a proper princess—dressed in my favorite lilac silk dress and my hair hanging down in loose ringlets— but I didn't *feel* like one, not when my insides were a tumult of emotion. My stomach twisted at the thought of seeing Deidric again. I hadn't spoken with him since receiving his letter. Now I was expected to face him as if nothing were wrong. I couldn't do this.

But I was expected to. With a steadying breath, I entered the parlor where our guests were assembled. Upon entering the room, my gaze immediately went to Prince Deidric, chatting with Father, with his wife, Princess Eileen, on his arm. I froze in the doorway, staring at him, all while the words from his letter repeated over and over in my mind: *I have determined that we're ill-matched and am releasing you from our engagement contract.*

My eyes burned at the memory, but I rapidly blinked away my invading tears before they could escape. I wouldn't cry. I wouldn't let him have the satisfaction of knowing how much he'd hurt me. I'd endure this visit by maintaining my poise and ignoring him as much as possible.

I'd no sooner decided this than he and Eileen caught sight of me. My stomach sank, and before I could decide how rude it'd be to pretend I hadn't noticed them, Deidric smiled politely and Eileen lit up, immediately breaking away from her husband to hurry over.

A curse I'd learned from Drake filled my mind, but unfortunately it was too late to escape now. "It's so good to see you again, Rhea," Eileen said the moment she arrived at my side. "How have you been?"

She embraced me. I stiffened and didn't hug her back. I felt bad resenting her—for we'd been friends until I learned that she was the reason for my broken engagement—but my bitterness kept the flames of my grudge burning brightly.

Eileen pulled away, her brow furrowed in puzzlement. I forced a polite smile. "I'm pleased to see you as well." My tone was cold, betraying me. Hopefully I could escape this conversation before I made a biting comment I'd inevitably regret. "I understand congratulations are in order for the new Prince of Sortileya."

Eileen brightened. "Yes, Deidric. He's seven months old now. He's already a bit mischievous like his father but is such a delight. We both adore him." She took my hands in hers and I fought the impulse to pull away. "I hear Prince Briar is courting you."

I nodded again but said nothing. Eileen waited expectantly.

"And how is your courtship going?" she prompted.

"Fine," I clipped. "I'm sure you'll have a chance to meet him." I searched and found him near the fireplace with the Queen of Malvagaria, deep in discussion with Mother.

"I'd love to meet him. I hope your match is a happy one. You're such a sweet person and deserve nothing less." She squeezed my hands.

The icy resentment I'd built as a protective wall around my heart softened against my will. Why did she have to be so *nice*?

It's not her fault she and Deidric met and fell in love; you can't hold it against her. My gaze flickered towards Deidric, watching us. *He* was the one who deserved my anger.

Too late I realized I'd failed to greet him. I gave the briefest curtsy and turned away before he could bow in return. I briefly caught sight of his bewildered expression before returning my attention to Eileen. "Tell me more about your son."

While Eileen was clearly at ease as our conversation continued, it was all I could do to maintain my façade of calm. When dinner was announced, I was relieved when Briar appeared at my elbow to escort me.

"Good evening, Rheanna," he said as he offered his arm with warmth filling both his eyes and soft smile. I smiled in return as I wove my arm through his and his hand curled over mine.

"Good evening, Briar. Have you had the pleasure of meeting Deidric's wife, Eileen?"

She was studying him with open curiosity and curtsied when Briar bowed to her without comment. The moment he looked away, she arched her eyebrows at me. I tried not to dwell on what such a look could possibly mean...but I did anyway. Did she think us a poor match? For I'd truly begun to feel things were going well between us.

I'd hoped to evade the couple at dinner, but to my horror I was seated right next to Deidric with Eileen on his other side. Now there would be no way to avoid a confrontation with my ex-fiancé, and when I was sitting beside Briar no less.

Please don't speak with me, please don't speak with me, please don't speak with me...

We'd no sooner been served our mushroom soup than my hopes were dashed. He turned to me with a surprisingly friendly smile. "It's a pleasure to see you again, Rheanna. How have you been?"

How could he ask such a ridiculous question? Didn't he realize that I'd been anything *but* fine since his letter? Or did he simply not care?

I lifted my chin. "Not particularly well, Deidric, but thank you for asking."

He raised his eyebrows at my straying from the script

protocol dictated we follow, and I felt a flare of pride for my defiance. "I'm sorry to hear that. What—"

"I'm sorry, but I'm in no mood for pleasantries with you at the moment." I kept my voice quiet so Briar wouldn't overhear. Luckily, he was deep in a discussion with Father and hadn't noticed the tension between the Crown Prince of Sortileya and myself.

Deidric gaped at me in a rather undignified manner, one I would have found amusing if not for the circumstances. He leaned closer. "Rheanna, what—"

"Perhaps I didn't make my point clear," I said stiffly. "I don't want to talk to you."

He blinked, his confusion evident. "Why not?"

I narrowed my eyes. "Do you really have no idea?"

"No. We haven't conversed in a long time, but the last time we did was amiable. What reason could you possibly have to—"

Did I really have to spell it out for him? "Need I remind you," I hissed quietly, "that since our last conversation, you broke off our engagement?"

At the word *engagement*, Eileen's head whipped towards us. She took in both our expressions—Deidric's bewilderment and my anger that was undoubtedly slipping out from beneath my proper mask of indifference.

Deidric leaned closer. "That was…what, nearly two years ago now? Why are you upset about it? I thought you didn't want to marry me."

I ached to unleash all the hurt and anger I'd kept locked inside ever since that fateful letter. It took every ounce of self control I had to keep all my resentment tucked away so our heated, whispered conversation wouldn't attract the attention of others at the table, specifically Briar.

I lifted my eyebrow. "So you finally want to discuss it?"

His bafflement only grew. "What is there to discuss?"

"Everything, considering we've *never* discussed what happened."

Eileen's eyes widened. "You mean you two never resolved your past engagement?"

"Of course we did," Deidric said, but at my glare his certainty faltered. "Didn't we?"

My grip tightened around my spoon. The man was unbelievably clueless. "No, we certainly did not."

Deidric's confusion only deepened. Eileen sighed and gave me an apologetic look on his behalf. "It appears you two are in need of a discussion. Not here, dear"—for Deidric had opened his mouth, as if to launch in immediately—"but a private one following the meal."

Yes, not *here*, with my family and guests surrounding us. I returned to my now-cold soup, signaling an end to our brief and unpleasant conversation, while beside me Deidric, still looking quite lost, leaned over to whisper in his wife's ear.

Dinner had never felt so long. I could scarcely taste my food, not with the way my stomach knotted in nerves. I was hyperaware of every movement Deidric made beside me, every puzzled glance he cast me midst his own polite princely pleasantries with my family.

When the meal finally concluded, Briar offered his arm to escort me to the parlor as was his duty, but Eileen was quicker. She looped an arm through mine and Deidric's before briskly leading us from the dining room. My heart beat wildly against my ribs with each step. Was I truly ready to confront Deidric after masking my pain and resentment for so long?

Eileen pulled us into an abandoned antechamber and shut the door before spinning on Deidric. "Is there anything unresolved from your engagement to Rheanna?"

"Of course not, darling," Deidric said, giving me another baffled look. "We broke it off and there's nothing more to it."

"No, *we* didn't break it off," I snapped. "*You* did."

"But you agreed to it. Your signature was on the contract I sent to you." His tone clearly stated he considered the matter settled, but Eileen looked unconvinced.

"Yes I agreed to it, but we never resolved it." My voice shook as the two years of bitterness began to overcome me. "You broke it off without any explanation, without even the courtesy of telling me about your change of heart yourself. You just *ended it.*"

"I sent a letter—" Deidric began, but he was cut off by Eileen's gasp.

"You *sent a letter*? Oh, Aiden." Eileen shook her head in disbelief before resting her hand on his arm. "Dear, that's not the way to handle these things. No wonder poor Rhea is upset."

"I don't see why," Deidric said. "We always communicated by letter."

"But to handle such a personal and sensitive matter via letter—" she began gently.

"Why not?" Deidric asked. "I've always conducted business with diplomats in such a fashion."

"I'm not a diplomat!" I said. "I was your *fiancée.*"

Deidric's brow furrowed. "But it was my understanding that neither of us wanted the match. I thought you'd be pleased to get out of it. So why did my letter upset you?"

Eileen exchanged an exasperated look with me, and in that look I felt a kinship with her. Perhaps after this was over, we could return to being friends.

"Why wouldn't it upset me? We were engaged for five years before you suddenly, without warning, ended it via a *letter*. The least you could have done was have the decency to tell me yourself...*in person*, not in the detached and formal manner you did, as if you were dealing with another royal duty rather than my heart. And then, to make matters worse, you had the gall to invite me to your humiliating competition so I could watch you choose another wife, reminding me that you found me inferior and unsuitable."

"I never found you unsuitable," he said. "That's why we were engaged in the first place."

"If that's the case, then why did you no longer want to marry me?" I snapped.

He dug his fingers in his hair with a weary sigh. "I'm... confused. I thought it was understood that neither of us wanted to marry the other. Our arrangement was merely a dutiful one that would have benefited both of our kingdoms. Did you expect something more from me?"

"I wanted to feel like I was good enough." My voice wavered, betraying the emotions I could no longer suppress. "I wanted to be a good wife for you and a capable queen for your people. Throughout our engagement, we frequently discussed how our union was beneficial to both of our kingdoms. I suppose I can understand why you felt falling in love with Eileen was a good enough reason to break it off, but then you had to prove to everyone through your Princess Competition that your new choice of wife was better suited to being queen than I was. You rejected and humiliated me."

Deidric stared blankly at me, but sympathy and understanding filled Eileen's expression. She pulled me into a hug. "Oh, Rhea, I'm so sorry for all of this."

My fragile hold on my emotions snapped, causing my tears to escape. "Why wasn't I good enough?" I stuttered.

And finally, Deidric's confusion melted away, replaced with remorse. "I never found you lacking, Rheanna. If the match had gone through, you would have been a fine queen."

"Obviously not," I said. "Because the moment our arrangement ended, you hosted a competition to find one more suitable. It was mortifying."

Deidric bit his lip. "I thought inviting you would be a

kind gesture to show there was no animosity between us; I didn't consider how it would make you feel."

I stared at him in disbelief. Sensing my disapproval, Deidric turned to his wife, as if appealing to her, but she simply shook her head. "I'm sorry, dear, but I'm on Rhea's side in this matter. I can see why she's hurt."

"I never meant to hurt you, Rheanna. Please believe that." Deidric bridged the distance between us and took my hands. "It was through no fault of your own that I didn't want to marry you; it was because I'd fallen in love with Eileen. But due to her station, I needed to convince my father she'd make a suitable queen. That Princess Competition was my father's idea. I agreed to it for one purpose only: to appease him so I'd be allowed to marry the woman of my choosing, not to find someone more worthy of being queen than you. I should have realized…" He sighed, looking truly remorseful. "But I didn't. I'm truly sorry, Rheanna."

I searched his expression to gauge his sincerity, and when I found it, the hurt and tension that had felt like a permanent weight on my chest for so long slowly began to ease. "You didn't reject *me?*" I whispered.

He shook his head. "No, I simply chose Eileen. I love her. You and I never loved one another." He said it like a question, as if suddenly fearing I'd been in love with him. I managed a small smile.

"No, we didn't."

He released a whooshing breath of relief.

I wiped away the tears streaking my cheeks. "I wish you'd simply told me why you didn't want to marry me. You only sent a letter. I felt dismissed, unworthy."

Regret twisted his expression. "I'm sorry. I now realize I went about breaking our engagement in the wrong way. At the time, I was just so desperate to be with Eileen, but it was inappropriate for us to be together when I was still formally attached to you. A letter seemed the fastest and cleanest way to get what I wanted sooner. Please forgive me."

And to my astonishment I realized I did. The feeling was warm and relieving, as if a heavy burden had been lifted from my shoulders, leaving me lighter and freer than I'd felt in a long time.

"I forgive you," I said. "Will you forgive me for resenting you these past two years?"

"Of course." He gave my hands a squeeze before dropping them and looping his arm around Eileen's waist. I tilted my head and studied the sweet way they nestled together. Because I'd been blinded by my anger, I'd never noticed until now how suited they seemed for one another.

I smiled. "You two belong together."

Deidric gave Eileen a snuggle as he grinned down at her; she looked up at him with a tender look in return. "I'm so grateful for your grace in stepping aside so I could marry her. Thank you, Rheanna."

I smiled. "Thank you for talking with me."

"I clearly should have done it two years ago," he said. "I know I have no right to ask, but might we be friends?"

"I'd like that." And to my surprise, I meant it. "In that case, please call me Rhea."

He grinned. "I'd be honored to. I only allow my close friends to call me by my middle name, so I'd be pleased if you'd call me Aiden in return." At my nod, he held out his hand and I placed mine in his. He lifted it and lightly kissed my knuckles. "Thank you."

He dropped my hand and wove his through Eileen's. Although I was now happy for them, a new pang pierced my heart—I wondered if Briar and I would ever look at one another in such a way.

Deidric—no, *Aiden* I hastily corrected myself—gave me an admiring smile. "I had no idea how much you resented coming to my ridiculous competition. You were so poised. It was very brave of you."

"I didn't go for you; I had something to prove to myself." But I hadn't proven anything. Instead, I'd lost my sense of worth. "I'm still trying to prove things to myself."

"For what it's worth, I believe you'll make a fine queen of Malvagaria. I have complete faith in you."

His words healed the remaining broken parts of my heart that he'd caused. Perhaps in time, I could root out the remainder of the doubts that had been engrained in me for so long and be free from them forever.

I followed Aiden and Eileen from the room with a much lighter heart than I'd entered it with. Halfway to the parlor, Aiden paused, deep concern etched in his expression. "I've been waiting all evening to ask you about Liam; he's the reason Eileen and I made this visit. Rumor is he's at death's door. How's he doing?"

The lightness I'd just been experiencing quickly vanished as my heart grew heavy. "While he's not faring as badly as you've heard, he is quite ill and hasn't been improving like we hoped. We've been trying to keep his condition quiet." I struggled to hold back the sob that always ached to emerge whenever I spoke of my dear brother.

Eileen leaned around her husband, her eyes glassy. "Is it serious?"

"We think so." My tears returned, blurring their worried expressions. "The royal physician has tried two different remedies, but nothing is helping. "We're beginning to fear… that we'll lose him." I'd never voiced it out loud, for it would make it all the more true.

They gaped at me in disbelief. "But—" Aiden had no words. In all the time I'd known him, I'd never seen him rendered speechless.

"That can't be true," Eileen breathed. "Liam has always been so healthy."

Fear crushed my heart. I took a shaky breath. "It happened so suddenly. We're at a loss as to why his health has taken such a drastic turn. It's Kian all over again."

Aiden's jaw set in determination. "Liam won't die like Kian did. There's more to be done. I'll send my own royal physician at once, whose skills are unparalleled. Working with your own healers, I'm sure they can find a cure. We'll visit him this evening. For now, we should rejoin the others in the parlor."

He looped his arm through Eileen's, but we'd only gone a few steps when Aiden suddenly stopped as we caught sight of the Queen of Malvagaria, standing in a nearby alcove, watching us through narrowed eyes.

My heart lurched. Had she been spying on us? A chill rippled over me at the coldness filling her expression. Her blood-red lips quirked into a smirk before she turned and walked down the corridor, her heels clicking against the marble floor.

"Hmm, that was interesting."

I glanced at Aiden, who was frowning at the queen's retreating back. "What is it?" I asked.

He hesitated. "How long has the Malvagarian Queen been visiting?"

"Nearly a month," I said. "She's accompanying Prince Briar." And dictating our courtship behind the scenes.

"And when did Liam fall ill?"

I was so startled by his question that a bubble of laughter escaped, even though the situation wasn't at all amusing. "What are you suggesting?"

Aiden hesitated. "Nothing. Forgive me." But his eyes were still narrowed at where the queen had disappeared. He shook his head, as if to dispel an unpleasant thought. "It's just...

there are a lot of rumors, but it's inappropriate for me to put any weight on them without evidence."

"Perhaps there's a shred of truth to be found in rumors," Eileen said. "After all, the rumor concerning Liam's failing health turned out to be true."

Aiden frowned. "We should go to a more private place to discuss this." He led the way back to the antechamber we'd just abandoned and turned to me the moment the door clicked shut. "I'm sure you're aware that there are many whispers surrounding the Malvagarian Royal Family. Not only are all the princes and princesses said to be cursed, but the king's health is slowly deteriorating. Some are questioning whether his illness is due to natural causes. It made me wonder whether Liam's illness might also not be natural."

My heart pounded wildly. "But no one would want to harm Liam; he has no enemies." But despite my protests, I couldn't shake the foreboding feeling that had been nagging at me, one which I'd refused to vocalize. If his illness wasn't natural… "What possible motive could there be?"

"Liam *is* the future King of Draceria," Aiden said. "With that kind of power comes great danger. It's something to consider."

For a brief moment I did…before I shook my head, dismissing the possibility. Liam was simply ill; he *had* to be.

Aiden hesitated, as if debating whether or not he should continue. "There's another thing—if you're planning on uniting with the Malvagarian Royal Family, I'm concerned about the curses each member is supposedly under."

My chest constricted while Eileen frowned at her husband. "You don't think Rhea will become cursed merely from joining them through marriage, do you?"

Aiden shrugged. "Curses are strange things. I don't pretend to know much about them. In any case, she should at least be aware of Briar's, considering he's to be her husband. Do you know anything about his curse, Rhea?"

I frowned, remembering that awkward conversation. "I've brought up the rumors about his cursed family to him, and while he didn't shed any light on them, he shared enough to confirm he's under one himself."

Eileen looked back and forth between Aiden and me. "But surely they're not *really* cursed...are they?"

Aiden leaned against the wall, arms folded. "It's speculated that all four Malvagarian royal children are indeed afflicted in some way. The two princess's curses have been confirmed, giving me no reason to doubt that the princes suffer from them as well, even if the nature of theirs remains a mystery."

"What are the two princesses' curses?" Eileen asked. "Is Princess Gemma really trapped in a tower?"

Aiden nodded. "Although no one knows *where* this tower is or *why* she's trapped, let alone how to free her."

"What of the other princess, Princess..." I scrunched my brow, trying to remember her name.

"Princess Reve," Aiden supplied. "It's said hers affects her mind, some sort of sleeping curse from what I've heard, but again, no one knows any details."

"So then how is Prince Briar cursed?" Eileen asked. "He seems perfectly fine." She turned to me, as if she thought I could supply further details, but I simply shrugged.

"Like I mentioned, he hasn't shared any details with me." But despite his elusiveness, I felt I was beginning to pick up clues here and there to form some sort of picture, although an incomplete one.

"Have you noticed anything unusual about him?" Aiden asked.

"He always wears a rose from his enchanted garden that remains in perfect bloom," I said. "He touches it frequently. It seems to give him some sort of comfort. And he's always so weary."

Aiden's brow furrowed. "I noticed that, too. When I visited him in Malvagaria a few years ago, he wasn't so subdued. There's definitely been a change in him. I'll look more into it and see if I can gather any information; you deserve to know what afflicts him before marrying him." He paused. "And then there's Prince Drake."

I startled. "Did you say *Prince* Drake?"

"Yes, Prince Drake of Malvagaria."

I stared at him in disbelief. Surely I'd misheard. I *must* have. It would be too much of a coincidence if the Drake in the mirror shared a name with the prince of Malvagaria; it wasn't as if Drake was a common name. Did that mean that Prince Drake and the Drake in the mirror were one and the same? But they *couldn't* be...could they? And if so, why hadn't Drake told me his identity?

Eileen lightly grazed my elbow. "Are you alright, Rhea? You're awfully pale."

I took a steadying breath. "I'm fine." But it was a lie. I felt as if my world had been tipped upside down. My heart pounded painfully. "What of Prince Drake?"

Aiden's frown deepened. "He's been missing for several years. No one knows what happened to him."

My heartbeat escalated. Missing for several years...*trapped inside a mirror*, perhaps? I swallowed, hoping the gesture would calm me. It didn't. "Perhaps he's trapped somewhere, like Princess Gemma."

Aiden merely shrugged. "Perhaps. No one really knows for sure."

But I was; it hadn't been a coincidence I'd found him the same day Briar and the Queen of Malvagaria arrived. But while my heart confirmed it, my mind couldn't even begin to make sense of this revelation. It was all I could do to focus on Aiden as he continued speaking.

"While the Queen of Malvagaria has no curse as far as anyone can tell, there are certain concerns surrounding her. Have you seen anything during her visit that could warrant suspicion?"

"In the library a week ago," I said in a rush. "I overheard a conversation between her and Briar. It sounded as if..." I hesitated. Could I accuse a monarch without a shred of evidence? But the gentle prodding of Aiden's gaze gave me the courage I needed. "I fear she may be plotting something."

I expected Aiden to scoff, but instead he became pensive. "What did they talk about?"

"She was quite urgent about having Briar and me make a match, as if there's something more she desires than an alliance."

"There may be some truth to that," Aiden said. "I haven't had many dealings with the Queen of Malvagaria, but I cannot deny that I've had my own suspicions. I advise you to keep on your guard while I do some digging of my own." His dark eyes met mine, filled with concern, and in that moment I realized that our past truly was behind us—and we were now allies, *friends*. "Please be careful, Rhea."

We parted ways, but I didn't return to the parlor; it would be impossible to follow the polite conversations following my interaction with Aiden and Eileen, not when my mind was still whirling from my recent discovery. Instead I returned to my bedroom, where I paused outside the door with my hand on the knob, hesitating. Drake was waiting for me...*Prince* Drake. I wasn't sure I was ready to face him after learning the startling truth about who he really was.

But I'd have to face him sooner or later. I took a deep breath and pushed the door open. I was immediately greeted by Drake's voice. "Finally you're back. I've been practically overcome with curiosity wondering how your visit with Prince Deidric was going. Tell me everything."

My gaze immediately found Drake's mirror where I'd left him half-facing the window, now overlooking the velvety night.

Drake is really a Prince of Malvagaria. While I had no proof that he and the missing prince were one and the same, my heart confirmed the truth I didn't want to acknowledge.

For a minute I couldn't help but stare at him, as if seeing him for the first time. I noticed similarities between him and Briar that I'd been so blind to before—the same dark brown eyes and black hair, the same strong jaw, and a similar facial structure. There was no doubt they were brothers.

As I noticed these resemblances, other pieces suddenly fit together in my mind: how Briar hadn't been surprised when he'd heard Drake's voice from my satchel, how the Queen of Malvagaria had seemed to recognize the mirror when she saw it...how could I not have realized the truth before now? Perhaps I'd been so certain he was the son of the Baron of Livre that I'd never considered any other possibility.

I slowly closed the door behind me and settled in the seat beside him, although I made no motion to pick him up. His concerned gaze searched mine. "I can't take the suspense any longer. How did it go with Prince Deidric? Are you alright? Because if he hurt you again, I'll break out of this mirror and hunt that rotter down." He balled his hands into fists.

Oh, yes. I'd forgotten that the last time Drake—*Prince Drake*, I reminded myself—had seen me, I'd been anxious at the thought of seeing Aiden again. It was incredible how much had changed in only a few short hours.

Drake was searching my expression frantically, as if he could discern my confrontation with Aiden through perusal alone. "Things went well with Aiden," I finally managed.

While he didn't loosen his fists, Drake's eyebrows rose,

and I couldn't help but notice how thick and dark they were, just like Briar's. "*Aiden? Who's Aiden?*"

"That's Deidric's middle name. He allows his friends to call him that."

His eyebrows rose further. "So you two are friends now?"

"Yes. We talked and worked things out. I feel so much better." It was an understatement; I felt not only that a huge burden had been lifted from my shoulders, but as if the wound Aiden had inflicted on my heart had finally been stitched up.

"I'm glad." He sighed in relief and unclenched his fists, but continued his searching stare; I shifted restlessly beneath his perusal. "There's something else, but I can't quite...did something happen?"

I not only learned that you're Prince Drake of Malvagaria, but I learned all about your cursed family...and the possibility that there's a reason the Queen of Malvagaria desires a union between Briar and me.

My stomach knotted. Not only did my impending engagement to Briar now seem more dangerous, but the discovery that Drake was his younger brother complicated things even more. Why had he kept such a secret from me, and what was I to do with this knowledge?

CHAPTER 18

I slammed the door, a much-needed outlet for my raging emotions. I fought to contain them, but the bars of their prison were weakening, causing them to escape.

"Are you alright, Rhea?"

I kept my hand pressed against the door, taking several deep breaths, each sharper than the last.

"Rhea?" Worry laced Drake's tone. I managed to straighten and warily turn towards his concerned expression. His eyes widened as he took in my expression. "Something's happened," he stated.

I was about to nod but hesitated. Everything felt different now that I knew who he truly was. He could no longer be my best friend and confidant, not when he was to be my *brother-in-law*. It would be best to keep him at arm's length.

Tell him you know who he is. Ask him why he kept such a secret. But just like the past several days, the words wouldn't come. There had to be a reason he was keeping his identity a secret.

"Rhea? Please talk to me."

The tender way he looked at me weakened the defenses

I'd built around my emotions. No matter who he was, I didn't want to lose him. He wasn't my brother-in-law yet.

"I've just encountered the Queen of Malvagaria." I began to pace, hoping the movement would calm the storm inside me as my emotions bombarded me.

"What happened?" Drake asked.

I briefly hesitated, uncertain how I should behave around Drake now that I knew who he truly was. But I ignored my misgivings and stomped over to collapse in the window seat beside him. "That *queen* is the most—" I swallowed the tumult of curses fighting to escape, remembering just in time that any insults I flung at that horrible woman would be given to Drake's *mother*.

I still couldn't believe this entire time he'd been the Malvagarian prince.

Drake's entire manner hardened. "What did she say?" he asked darkly. I eyed the way his eyebrow twitched, as if he could barely contain his own emotions.

I silently spouted the venom I was aching to release before softening it for Drake's sake. "She's always pointing out my failings, but with false sweetness that disguises the fact she's attacking me." But I knew she meant every word; she couldn't mask the disdain that filled each look she gave me.

"She does have a cloak-and-dagger way about her, doesn't she?" The bitterness in his tone was unmistakable.

Despite the hurt festering from the queen's latest attack, my heart softened for Drake. My interactions with Her Majesty were minimal compared to what he must have experienced from her his entire life. At least being trapped inside a mirror was a temporary refuge for him.

"What did she say to you?" Drake asked.

The words returned full force—venom spoken in the Queen of Malvagaria's sugary tone, her lips curled in a smirk: *I must admit to being very disappointed in you. I expect the woman who eventually follows me as queen to at least be half the monarch I am, but I'm quickly realizing such hopes are futile.*

Her words had unlocked my own insecurities, always waiting in the wings to attack. I squeezed my eyes shut in hopes of staving off the onslaught before it began anew. "I don't want to repeat them."

Drake cursed bitterly, using a word that was quite disrespectful to use in reference to one's mother. "I'll confront her. No one deserves to speak to you the way she undoubtedly did, not even"—he swallowed —"the queen."

"You can't talk to her; you're trapped in a mirror." Did the queen realize he was trapped? Surely she did, which explained her reaction when she'd spotted him inside my satchel. But then why hadn't she done anything to help him? Had she even tried?

"Being trapped in a mirror can't stop me."

Warmth blossomed in my heart at the protective way he balled his fists. "Thank you for caring, but it's alright."

But my assurances were a lie. Her hurtful words returned again, attacking my mind over and over like poisonous darts. Her doubts—compounded with Liam's illness, the news that my dearest friend would soon become my brother-in-law, and my newfound fears regarding my impending engagement—overwhelmed me. Panic quickly set in.

"Rhea?"

The anxiety in my chest tightened, making it difficult to breathe, and the walls of the palace—a place that represented my inadequacies—suddenly felt too confining. I needed to escape.

Abruptly I stood. "I'm going outside." I went to the wardrobe for my cloak and wrapped it around my shoulders.

"You're going outside? *Now*? But it'll be dark soon, not to mention it's about to rain. You'll catch a chill."

"I won't be out long, just enough to clear my mind."

He released a long breath before glancing back out the window. "I suppose if you're only going to the orchard—"

"I'm not going to the orchard, but the woods." I headed for the door.

Drake gasped. "The *woods*?"

"They're not far; they're on the east side of the palace, directly beyond the gate."

"I know where they are," Drake snapped. "I've been inside them; they're large with no well-marked paths. You could get lost."

"I'm not going to get lost." When did he become such a mother hen?

"You are, but you're too stubborn to admit it." He sighed. "You're going regardless of my arguments, aren't you?"

"I'll only be gone for a little bit."

Drake's jaw set in determination. "Then take me with you."

I paused, my hand on the knob. "Why would I do that?"

"Because I refuse to allow you to enter the woods alone. If you don't take me, I'll enter your parents' mirror and tell them everything that's been happening these past—"

"You said you couldn't appear in other mirrors," I interrupted.

"I said it was *difficult*, not that it was *impossible*."

"For goodness' sake." I stomped to the window seat and picked him up.

He smirked. "I win."

"Making threats to a princess isn't a very gentlemanly thing to do."

"It is when it's for a good cause—you're not going into the woods alone."

I wanted to point out that there would be little he could do should I get lost, but I bit my tongue; it was flattering he

cared so much. Besides, I secretly welcomed his company...
not that I'd ever admit it.

"Odious man," I grumbled. He only chuckled.

I opened the door and peered into the corridor. It was
abandoned. I crept quietly towards the back entrance of the
family's private quarters that the servants used; the stairwell
was also empty. Good.

"Why the secrecy?" Drake whispered.

"I can't allow the guards to see me."

He frowned. "Shouldn't you let the guards know where
you're going just in case you—"

"Would you stop clucking? I'm not going to get lost." Did
he really think me so incapable? "Stop mothering me and be
quiet, or I'll shove you into a drawer."

"A drawer won't limit my ability to appear in your
parents' mirror." He sounded smug. I gritted my teeth and
muttered an unsavory word that only caused him to laugh.
"Oh dear, I'm a bad influence on you."

"Shh, be quiet."

To my surprise, he obediently fell silent. I sidled along the
wall towards the back entrance, peering around corners and
waiting until the coast was clear. While I frequently saw
servants, there were very few guards in this section of the
palace...until I reached the door that led to the gardens,
which was flanked by two guards. I nibbled my lip. How
would I sneak past them?

As if he heard my silent question, Drake said quietly, "Not
that I want to encourage tonight's outing, but if you're at a
loss as to how to get past those guards, might I make a
suggestion?"

I peered down at him. "If it's a *helpful* one."

"When are my suggestions ever not helpful?" His cheeky
grin faltered at my glare. "Right, now is not the time for

games. You're a princess, aren't you? Just walk with confidence and the guards will likely not question you."

It almost seemed too simple, but it was worth a try. "Promise me you won't gloat if this works."

"I promise I won't gloat...*much*."

I rolled my eyes. It would have to do. I tucked Drake close to my body and wrapped my cloak around the mirror to hide him from view. Then I lifted my chin and walked confidently into view.

The bustling servants barely tore their attention from their work to spare me a glance other than to curtsy as I passed before returning to their duties. While the guards' looks lingered, they didn't question me as they stepped aside to let me through.

I slipped outside into the brisk evening air. The sun hung low in the sky, casting the grounds in golden light. I shivered and tucked my cloak more tightly around me.

Considering I still held him close, Drake felt my shiver. "You're going to catch a chill," he said disapprovingly.

"Thank you, Mother." I took him out from beneath my cloak and strolled towards the east gate. Drake twisted around in his mirror, trying to stare towards the path that led to the orchard.

"Are you certain that the orchard isn't the more sensible destination?"

I didn't answer as I walked purposefully to the gate. I hid Drake once more as I went by the guards; although they looked baffled, they didn't stop me, just as Drake had predicted. There would be no living with him now.

Peace enveloped me the moment I stepped within the trees and was cocooned within their autumn-laden branches, their fallen leaves coating the forest floor in a ruby-and-orange carpet that muffled my footsteps.

I sighed contentedly as I tipped my head back. The nearly bare branches allowed the fading sunlight to tumble across the woodland floor and warm my cheeks. The trees were thick and wild undergrowth obscured the paths. Being here was like being part of a world entirely separate from the palace.

"You look peaceful," Drake murmured.

How could I not be? There was something so tranquil about the woods. "I'm already feeling better."

I began walking, being sure to keep the palace, which loomed over the trees, within sight so I'd be able to find my way back. The deeper into the woods I ventured, the further behind the palace and all it represented—the queen, my imminent engagement, Drake's surprising identity, and Liam's illness—became. The only sound was the whooshing of branches above and the crunch of leaves beneath my feet. With each moment within the trees, my swirling thoughts began to quiet one by one.

"Do you have a specific destination in mind?" Drake asked after several peaceful moments.

"No. I don't know the woods particularly well."

"Which makes this excursion even more foolhardy."

"I can see the turrets of the castle; I won't get lost. Now please be quiet; I'm here for a reprieve, so your skeptical commentary isn't welcome." I ducked beneath a low-hanging branch and wove through some evergreens, whose needles filled the brisk air with the scent of pine.

"Whether you admit it or not, I know you secretly enjoy my company." He sounded ridiculously confident. Unfortunately, he was right—his presence was quite soothing—but I refused to admit it; there was no need to stroke his ego any further.

I glanced down at him; his look was prodding. I sighed. "Fine, your company isn't entirely unwelcome."

He grinned widely, triumphant. I rolled my eyes but couldn't resist smiling in return.

I lifted my skirt to step over a fallen moss-covered log and walked deeper within the trees, which were growing thicker. "You mentioned you've been in these woods before."

"Only once. Liam took my brother and me."

Who I now knew was Briar. It seemed so obvious that Drake was a Prince of Malvagaria. "Did Kian come?"

Drake shook his head. "No, he wanted to stay behind and study. Liam tried to convince him to come by telling us a story about how the woods are the home to the spirits of dead royals who cause the pathways to shift."

"Only the Forest in Sortileya has shifting pathways."

Drake shrugged. "Liam thought otherwise. He was determined to have them lead us on an adventure. But we didn't get far before we discovered the pathways of these woods are always still. Our excursion was discovered shortly after and we were brought back to the palace. Liam was less bothered by our punishment than by the fact that the woods weren't magical."

That was so like Liam. My heart ached. I missed him fiercely and he wasn't even gone yet. I drew in a startled breath. *No*, Liam wouldn't die. I wouldn't allow myself to believe he would, not when there was a chance he could still get better.

We ventured deeper. The longer we walked, the more agitated Drake became; he began to shift restlessly, eying each of the passing trees with growing anxiousness.

"How far are you planning on going?" he finally asked.

"You don't really want us to go back yet, do you?" I asked. "It's not even dark, not to mention it's so peaceful here."

"Forgive me for disagreeing with you, but from my vantage point, I can see the sky better than you can and must say that you're wrong."

I tipped my head back. He was right—the sun had nearly set; the daylight had faded so gradually I hadn't noticed.

"And I hate to be *mothering*," he continued, "but I think it's going to rain."

I bit my lip. Thick storm clouds now masked the settling dusk. The light was quickly fading and the approaching darkness created long shadows, making the woods appear less tranquil and more...spooky.

Apprehension knotted my gut. "We should go back."

"An excellent suggestion. If only I'd thought of something so clever."

I turned around to walk back the way we'd come...but paused after only a few steps. My breath hitched as I looked around. The palace in the distance was no longer in sight, having been swallowed up by fog. Without it and with the bare-branched trees stretching in every direction, it was impossible to orient myself. Which was the right way?

"Why have you stopped?" Drake asked, his tone knowing.

"Just...getting my bearings." *Be confident.* I lifted my chin and picked what I thought to be the most likely direction, but after only a few minutes of walking, I paused. The trees didn't look familiar, which meant this was the wrong way. I looked around again and picked another way, my steps slow and hesitant.

Drake groaned. "We're lost, aren't we?"

"Of course we're not." But my voice shook, betraying my growing fear. "I'm just...having a difficult time remembering the way we came, that's all, but I'm sure I'll find the right course soon."

"I'm sure you will," he said wryly. "And I'm just as sure that we'll stumble upon a random cottage to take shelter in, or perhaps we'll meet some helpful dwarves who'll volunteer to serve as our personal guides, or maybe—"

"Your cynicism isn't helping," I snapped.

"Forgive me." He didn't sound sorry at all. "Allow me to take charge now. I figured you'd find yourself in this predicament, so I made sure to pay attention to our path and—wait, stop."

I did with a sigh. He surveyed the trees he could see from his vantage point.

"Can you turn the mirror around so I can see the entire area?"

I did. His brow furrowed in concentration as he studied the woodland surroundings. He nodded to himself.

"I'm pretty sure we passed these trees only a few minutes ago. Go the other way."

"No, that'll take us deeper into the woods."

"No, it won't. You obviously don't know where you're going. It's my turn to lead."

"How can you lead when you've only gotten a few glimpses of the woods from within your mirror?" I asked. "I'm the one who's more qualified."

"More qualified to get us lost, you mean."

We continued bickering back and forth but stopped when thunder rumbled. Drake lifted his brow in a clear *I-told-you-it-was-going-to-rain* look. "Maybe we'll find our way out before the storm hits," I said shakily.

"Perhaps." But he sounded doubtful. I picked another direction and increased my pace, my hem catching on the undergrowth and branches scratching my arms as I pushed through the trees. No matter which direction I walked, my surroundings looked entirely foreign, with no sign of the edge of the woods or the palace in the background.

What was I thinking? That was my problem, I *hadn't* been thinking. I should have listened to Drake. Instead, I'd allowed my insecurities and worries to cause me to behave recklessly.

My white-knuckled grip tightened around the mirror as I increased my pace. I kept Drake tilted at an angle so he could see the path ahead. "Does anything look familiar yet?"

"I'm afraid not."

Don't panic. But despite my firm command, panic rose in my chest anyway, squeezing my insides with its icy fingers.

A few more minutes passed. "How about now?"

He bit his lip and studied the nearby trees carefully. "No."

The sky rumbled again before releasing the first drops of rain, pattering on my hair. My tears were building, burning my eyes. "We're lost, Drake."

"Stay calm. It'll be alright. I have an idea. I'll try to appear in your parents' mirror to tell them you're lost in the woods so they can send help."

The fear which had been slowly rising stilled. "But I thought you didn't want others to know about your curse?"

His eyes blazed. "My curse doesn't matter right now. The only thing I care about is making sure you're safe."

Warmth seeped over me, dissipating some of the chill.

He disappeared immediately, and I leaned wearily against a tree to wait. It felt like he'd been gone a long time before he finally reappeared.

I straightened. "Did you—"

He slowly shook his head. "I'm so sorry, Rhea. I tried repeatedly to appear in different mirrors, but we're too far away from the palace."

The hopelessness filling his eyes caused my taut emotions to unravel. "Then we're never getting out. We're lost in the woods because I'm a fool." The storm of my thoughts gladly repeated that assessment over and over, each escalating my panic.

Drake's attention snapped away from his careful study of the surrounding trees. "Don't say that. You can't think that."

"But we're lost in the woods...because of me." That fact alone contradicted his assurances.

"Yes, we are, but that doesn't make you a fool." His lips curved up slightly. "Now, I won't deny that you made a foolish decision, but that's not the same thing. Not at all."

His words softened my thoughts. Yes, this was why I needed him—he was my voice of reason. Not to mention his presence was comforting; being lost in the woods would be much more terrifying if I'd been alone.

I took a steadying breath and tightened my cloak around me. Now was not the time to allow my emotions to overcome me. *It'll be alright. Stay calm. Just keep going.*

Darkness settled around us, more potent with the dense clouds smothering the moon and stars. The biting wind stung and the rain fell in sheets, masking the trees in front of us and quickly soaking me and making the ground muddy.

Rain splattered the glass of Drake's mirror. I feebly tried to shelter him with my cloak but it did little good. He gave me a soft look. "Don't worry about me." His anxious gaze took in my soaking hair and chattering teeth. "Just focus on getting out of the storm before you catch a chill."

"We're never getting out," I stuttered as I slowly trudged forward, silently cursing my stupidity with each slogging step. "It's too dark. How will we find the way?"

"Don't give up, Rhea. We'll be alright."

It was becoming harder to have faith in Drake's words the colder and darker it became. "Do you regret accompanying me?" I asked.

He jerked his gaze away from the passing trees. "Not at all, Rhea. I'd rather be lost in the woods with you than have you lost in the woods alone. I mean that. We'll get out of here."

Warmth filled my breast, the only respite from the coldness washing over me in shivering waves the more soaked I became.

"Thank you, Drake. You're so—"

My words were swallowed up by a startled gasp as I suddenly tripped over a large log. The mirror flew out of my hand; I scraped my palms and soaked my front with mud as I braced my fall.

I moaned in pain as I struggled to my knees. "Drake?"

He didn't answer. I looked wildly through the sheets of rain and cloaking darkness for any sign of him. My panic rose when I couldn't see him.

"Drake? Where are you? Answer me."

No response. I crawled through the mud, combing my hands across the woodland floor, searching, searching...

My touch finally grazed the cold, smooth metal of the mirror's back. "Thank goodness. Why didn't you answer me when I called—"

My breath hooked as I turned the mirror over. The waning moonlight glistened off the glass, revealing a long crack across the mirror.

Drake's reflection had vanished.

CHAPTER 19

*H*orror squeezed my heart as I gaped at the jagged crack marring the surface of Drake's mirror like a gash. "Drake?" I stuttered.

He didn't answer. I raised a shaking hand and lightly ran my fingertip along the crack, wincing at the biting pain as the broken glass cut my finger, causing blood to pool at the tip.

"Drake? *Drake?*" My tears joined the rain falling down my wet cheeks. "Answer me, Drake."

He didn't. My panic rose, clawing at my heart. Why wasn't he answering? He couldn't be—

"No, no, no, *no*. Drake. *Drake!*"

Lightning flashed, illuminating the mirror's broken surface. I cradled it in my arms and bent over it to shield it from the raging storm as my sobs escaped.

Numbness filled my limbs, both from the cold and the horror over what I'd done. Because of my foolishness in entering the woods so close to dark, I'd *dropped* Drake, and now he was possibly trapped in his mirror forever. Guilt squeezed my heart, cracking it in two.

"Please be alright, Drake." I caressed his frame, as if to soothe away any pain he might be feeling. "I'm so sorry."

I knew I couldn't kneel in the mud forever. Drake would want me to try and find my way out of the woods. But how could I when I was hopelessly lost?

I took in the surrounding trees, whose dark outlines were almost completely swallowed up by the stormy night. There was just enough light peeking through the clouds to make out a moss-covered log. I squinted. Could it possibly be the same one I'd passed when I'd first entered the woods? If it was, that meant I was close to the edge.

I scrambled to my feet and began walking, each step a struggle in my soaked skirts. I wasn't sure how long I traipsed through the woods. I focused on each heavy step, each shiver that raked over me, the hot tears that mingled with the icy rain, and the coldness and exhaustion pressing against my senses, all while I held Drake close.

"We're going to get out of here," I told him through my chattering teeth. "And then I'm going to fix you. Somehow." I gave his mirror a comforting squeeze, wanting to reassure him, desperately hoping that he was alright so that he *could* be assured. Though the mirror remained cold and silent, keeping it in my arms gave me comfort.

I can do this.

I paused when, through the sound of the howling wind and rain, I heard my name drifting from the distance. "Princess Rheanna!"

Relief surged through me. "Someone is coming!" I told Drake, stroking the back of his mirror reassuringly. "Everything will be alright. I'll fix you the moment we return to the palace. I won't let you leave me."

"Princess Rheanna!" My name sounded closer, and through the darkness I saw the flicker of a lantern. We were saved. My arms tightened protectively around Drake as I headed for the light.

"I'm here," I squeaked, but my voice was swallowed by the howling storm. I tried again. "I'm here!"

The sounds of shouting, running footsteps, and crashing branches approached me. A group of guards appeared, the orange glow of their lantern light washing over my drenched and shivering frame. Their eyes widened before they surrounded me.

"Princess, are you hurt?"

"What are you doing in the woods at night, and during such a storm?"

"Come, let's get you back to the palace." One draped a thick blanket around me before taking my arm and guiding me through the trees. I'd only gone a few steps before I tripped over my wet skirts and stumbled, shielding Drake with my body before I landed.

The guard immediately scooped me up to carry me, his strides long and brisk. He searched my face, trying to discern my wellbeing. "Are you well, Your Highness?"

I managed a nod before allowing my eyes to droop shut. He quickened his pace, and soon I heard the sounds of others up ahead.

"Your Majesty, we've found her."

I heard Father crash through the trees before I felt his familiar caress on my cheek. "Rhea…" Relief enfolded my name. He scooped me from the guard's hold. "Are you alright, Rhea?"

My eyes fluttered open to meet his concerned gaze. "I got lost. I'm sorry."

He released a whooshing breath of relief before cradling me close and stroking my dripping hair.

Someone else hurried over. "Are you alright, Rheanna? I've been so worried."

Briar? What was he doing here? I managed to wearily glance over. His wet dark hair was sprawled across his forehead, dripping rain into his worry-filled eyes. In that moment, he looked more like Drake than I'd ever noticed before.

My arms tightened around the mirror as my frozen fingers managed to caress its frame, an assurance that all would be well for both of us now that we were found. "I'm fine," I said weakly. "Thank you for coming to look for me."

"Of course, Rheanna. When the guards said they spotted you going into the woods…"

He shook his head, his expression indicating he found me foolish, but neither he nor Father reprimanded me. And even though Briar's dark gaze flickered once to the mirror cradled in my arms, he didn't look disapproving, only concerned. I was relieved he didn't ask questions about Drake; I couldn't bear to tell him I'd *dropped* his brother.

"I'm so glad you're alright, Rheanna." Briar lightly brushed my cheek once before withdrawing his hand. I stiffened at his touch, not because it was unpleasant, but because it was unexpected…and had come from the wrong brother. What would it feel like to have Drake touch me instead?

I held him closer. "Briar just brushed my cheek," I whispered. It might have been my imagination, but it felt as if the mirror warmed, as it usually did whenever Drake was annoyed. It gave me hope that even though his image had vanished from the glass, he was alright. But if I didn't somehow fix the crack, would I ever see him again?

"Let's get you back to the palace." Father followed the guards as they led the way through the thick woods. Soon the trees began to thin, and then the lights of the palace appeared in the distance, glowing in the night. Assurance washed over me at seeing them, allowing me to close my eyes and snuggle against Father's chest. Warmth bathed me the moment he carried me inside, although it did little to quell my shivers.

"Rhea!"

Mother was at my side immediately. She stroked my face, compelling me to open my eyes to assure her I was awake and well. Tears streaked her cheeks, as well as Elodie's, who stood behind her. Aveline hovered a few feet away, her own eyes glassy with worry.

"Are you alright, dear?" Mother's touch went to my wet hair.

I managed a weak smile. "I behaved rather foolishly."

She released a shaky breath. "Oh Rhea, what were you thinking? Do you have any idea how worried I've been?" Mother walked alongside Father as he carried me up the grand staircase, not ceasing to stroke my hair. We passed the Queen of Malvagaria standing at the top of the stairs, her eyes cold and her expression disapproving.

"She'll be alright, darling," Father murmured to Mother.

She didn't look convinced as she continued to fuss over me as we walked the halls, leaving a trail of water after us. She only paused long enough to speak with a passing footman. "Please inform Prince Liam and Princess Anwen that Princess Rheanna has been found." After he bowed and left, Mother turned her anxious attention back to me. "They've both been worried sick. Liam even tried to get out of bed to join the search party."

Guilt gnawed at my heart at the heartache my ridiculous actions had caused, especially to my parents, whose emotions were already taut with Liam so ill. "I'm sorry."

Mother gave a tight smile as she cradled my cheek. "Don't worry about it, dear. I'm relieved you're alright." She said it like a command, as if she willed it to be so, even as her lip trembled.

We arrived at my bedroom, where Father carefully laid

me on the settee while Mother ordered a bath to be drawn. When it was ready, Father left and Mother gently removed my soaked cloak. She paused when she noticed the mirror I held tightly against my front.

Her brow furrowed. "What's that, dear?"

"I broke my mirror," I sobbed in explanation. I'd broken *Drake*. Mother looked like she wanted to question why I'd taken a mirror into the woods, but instead she gently extracted it from my hold. I tried to take it back, but my fingers barely grazed the handle. "No, give it back."

"I will after you've bathed." Mother's tone was patient as she set the mirror faceup on the vanity.

"Can you put it facedown?" I wasn't sure whether Drake could see out of it when it was cracked, but if I was going to take a bath, I didn't want to take any chances. "Set it down gently."

Mother humored me before leaving me to the ministrations of my maids, who stripped me out of my sopping clothes and helped me into the bath. I sighed contentedly as the warm water instantly soothed my cold, aching body and washed away the memories of my ordeal...save for one. *Drake broke*. While I wanted nothing more than to linger in the bath, my anxiety compelled me to finish quickly so I could check on him sooner.

When my bath ended, my maids helped me dress in my nightgown before wrapping me in a warm blanket. Mother brought me a cup of hot tea and sat me in front of the hearth, settling behind me to gently brush my hair in the way she hadn't done since I was a little girl.

I closed my eyes and leaned against her soft, loving touch. It had been so long since we'd shared such a moment, and even longer since I'd felt so cherished in the way she made me feel. It wasn't until experiencing it now that I realized how much I'd missed it.

Mother broke the peaceful stillness to begin the inevitable discussion. "What were you thinking, Rhea?"

"I'm so sorry," I whispered. "Today was difficult. I had to get away from the palace"—from *myself*—"just for a little while."

"And you chose the *woods*? Without guards and with night approaching?"

"I'm sorry," I said again. There was nothing more to say for my foolishness, especially when I had no explanation myself.

Mother sighed. "It doesn't matter anymore. You're safe. Just please don't ever do it again."

If only I could reverse tonight's foolhardy actions. I knew after a warm bath and a good night's sleep I'd be as good as new, but Drake…I craned my neck to try to see him on my vanity, but he was too far away. I was anxious to check on him; perhaps he wasn't as broken as I believed.

I turned back to Mother, whose cheeks were now streaked with tears. "Please don't cry. I'm alright."

She wiped her cheeks and forced a smile. "I know. My emotions are just so raw. What with Liam's health, then your going missing…and then there's Kian."

My breath hooked. "Kian?"

"I can't stop thinking about him lately," she whispered. "Ever since he"—she swallowed, seeming unable to say the word *died*—"he's always been here." She pointed to her heart. "Kian has always been in the back of my mind, but with Liam's illness not improving, I can think of little else than how losing my eldest son nearly destroyed me…and will completely break me if it happens again."

I remembered that time well. When Kian died nearly eight years ago, Mother had been inconsolable. For several months she remained locked in her room and neglected all her royal duties, and even after she finally emerged she seemed to be sleepwalking. It had taken a long time for her to emerge from her grief enough to return to us as more than a shadow of her former self.

"Kian's death was impossible to endure," Mother said. "I can't experience that again. So with Liam continuing to fade and losing you in the storm tonight..." She covered her mouth to suppress a sob.

Remorse knotted my gut. "I'm truly sorry." But I knew my apology couldn't take away her pain, both from Liam's condition and my own foolishness. And she wasn't the only one I'd hurt. I glanced towards the mirror, aching to check on Drake.

"Briar was worried for you tonight," Mother said suddenly. "He'll be a good husband for you, should you choose to marry him." She gently turned my head to give me a searching look.

I understood her silent question. "Yes, I think we'll marry." For I now knew enough about him to know I'd be content in our arrangement. But if we married...my heart wrenched as my gaze darted back to Drake's mirror, still facedown on the vanity. My heart filled with a yearning I couldn't put into words, one not for Briar, but for his brother...a brother I was anxious to check on.

"Do you *want* to marry him, Rhea?" Mother asked as she resumed her brushing.

I considered my answer carefully. "Enough. Your arrangement with Father gives me hope of what my own marriage can be." I was silent a moment. "I know he's willing, but do you think he genuinely wants to marry *me*?"

"Why wouldn't he, dear?"

I hesitated. "Because I'm broken."

Mother froze. "Why do you feel like you're broken?"

"Because I'm not fit to be a princess, let alone a queen." Even though I now knew the truth about why Aiden hadn't wanted me, I could still see the evidence of my shortcomings: my difficulty in performing Liam's duties in addition to my own, Briar's kindness but continued lack of enthusiasm, the frequent condescending comments from the Queen of Malvagaria. "I don't measure up."

Mother cupped my chin, turning me to face her. "You're not broken, darling. You're doing so well. You need to stop being so hard on yourself. You're only focusing on your perceived weaknesses and not noticing your many strengths. You're a strong woman, Rhea, one who is kind, loyal, and endures difficult things well. I wish you could see yourself as I see you." Mother lightly kissed my brow. "I know this courtship has been difficult for you. I'm sorry I haven't been there for you since Liam fell ill. I promise to start helping you more—"

"It's alright," I said hastily. "Liam needs you, as does Anwen. They have to be your priority right now."

Mother nodded, her eyes glassy with unshed tears. "Please remember that having weaknesses doesn't make you broken, and even if you feel that way, know that anything broken can be repaired."

Hope filled my heart, but it wasn't myself I was thinking of. My gaze darted once more to where Drake rested. Could he be fixed as well? I was eager to check on him, and as much as I enjoyed my time with Mother, I was more than a little relieved when she finally tucked me into bed and bid me good night.

The moment the door clicked shut behind her, I scampered from bed and seized Drake's mirror from the vanity, flipping it over.

"Drake?" While my heart sank at the jagged crack, I could have sworn it almost seemed...*smaller*, no longer stretching as a diagonal zigzag from the top of the glass to the bottom. The parts around the rim seemed to have smoothed over, almost as if the mirror had begun to repair itself—

"I'm wondering if perhaps I didn't properly explain the help I need from you: I need you to break the *curse*, not *me*."

I nearly startled at Drake's deep, wonderfully snarky voice. I pressed the mirror so close my nose grazed the glass. "Drake?"

He flickered into view for an instant...only to vanish again. Panic eclipsed my hope.

"*Drake!*"

"It's alright, Rhea. Just give me a moment."

I watched with bated breath as he flickered in and out of the glass before managing to remain. He released a whooshing breath.

"That was exhausting." He flashed a boyish grin. "Good evening. I see you've managed to find your way out of the woods."

I gaped at him before my tears returned. "*Drake!*" I hugged him tightly. He gave a soft *oof* before mumbling something, his voice muffled. I pulled back. "What was that?"

"I said, 'I take it you're happy to see me?'"

"You have no idea. Oh Drake, I'm so sorry I dropped you."

"It's alright. I doubt anyone could have held on to me after tripping in such a storm." His eyes softened. "How are you?"

"I'm fine."

Clearly unconvinced, he scanned me from head to toe, as if to discern my wellbeing, and frowned when I shivered. "Go sit by the fire."

This time, his mothering didn't bother me. I happily took a blanket and settled cross-legged back in front of the hearth, keeping Drake in my lap. There I examined him thoroughly from front to back in order to assess the damage I'd caused. He appeared intact...except for that hideous crack.

Guilt tightened my heart once more. "Are you sure you're alright?"

"I'm completely fine." His tone was gentle and reassuring. "It hurt when I fell, and I suffered one injury, but otherwise there's no harm done."

My fading panic flared to life again. "What injury?"

He pointed to a long cut across the side of his face, one that looked to still be bleeding.

"*Oh no.*"

"Not to worry, it's already fading. See?" He zoomed in closer and turned his cheek towards me so I could better see. It looked worse close up. "It's shrinking."

"Like the mirror's crack." Were the two connected?

I lightly ran my fingertip along his cheek. His eyes fluttered closed, as if he could feel my touch. I thought that perhaps I could feel his skin too; *something* was warm and not quite smooth, as if I were running my finger along a cheek covered in a thin layer of stubble rather than the glass. I ached to touch his face properly, run my fingers through his rumpled hair...

Drake's eyes fluttered open in time to see another tear trickle down my cheek. "What is it, sweet Rhea?" he whispered.

"I was so worried," I stuttered. "I thought I'd hurt you...or worse."

His entire manner softened. "I'm sorry I worried you. I tried desperately to tell you I was alright, but the crack prevented me from showing myself to you. But I heard you crying."

His expression twisted at the memory. He reached out, as if to wipe away the tears staining my cheeks, but as before his fingers hit the glass. He dropped his hand with a frustrated sigh.

"I couldn't help but overhear your conversation with your

mother." His gaze become penetrating. "You're not broken, Rhea. You're the most remarkable woman I know."

My heart swelled. "And you are as well."

His lips quirked up. "I'm the most remarkable woman?"

I laughed and his grin became triumphant, as if he was pleased he'd cheered me up. "You're ridiculous. And annoying."

"But you like me anyway," he said smugly.

"You're my best friend," I whispered. "Truly."

His expression softened. "And you're mine."

Warmth seeped over me—from his words, his gentle tone, and the tender look in his eyes. *He cares about me*. And tonight had made me realize that I cared for him more than I ever thought possible. Aching to express this feeling, I leaned down and lightly pressed my lips against the glass, directly on his cheek. I could have sworn I felt him stiffen and then relax against my kiss.

"I'm so glad you're alright," I whispered. My cheeks were warm when I pulled away. For a long, wonderful moment, we didn't sever our gazes. So many beautiful emotions stirred within my heart as I looked into his dark eyes.

I wish you were out of the mirror, I ached to say. *Then we could*…what? It didn't matter how I felt about him; my future was set. I was still expected to court his brother, for a union with him would give our kingdom the strongest alliance and put me in line for the Malvagarian crown, which I knew was what my parents wanted for me…even though what I wanted was something—or rather *someone*—else.

But I couldn't be with him. I was now motivated by more than duty—Briar's evident concern tonight when I'd been found in the woods made me realize how much he'd grown to care for me. If I rejected him now, I'd be doing the same thing Aiden had done to me. No one, especially not a man who'd become a dear friend, deserved that kind of pain.

Drake cleared his throat and tore his gaze away first, his cheeks crimson. "You should be getting to bed. You need a good night's sleep after our adventure in the woods."

I didn't want to end this perfect moment, but I was too tired to protest. I slowly stood, and after carefully setting him on my nightstand, I snuggled beneath the covers and turned down the lantern. But the darkness did little to quiet my thoughts, or to make me less aware of Drake's presence, so close to me I felt I could reach out and touch him—the *real* him, not the man in the mirror. It felt so *right* to have him so near.

But I knew I shouldn't feel this way. I had a duty to my kingdom and to Briar. Thus I couldn't involve myself with Drake beyond breaking his curse. As painful as distancing myself would be, I knew I could do hard things.

"Drake?" I whispered in the darkness as sleep began to claim me. "Thank you for going into the woods with me."

"I'll always be there for you, Rhea," he whispered back. "Always."

And with his sweet promise enveloping me, I fell asleep.

CHAPTER 20

J woke up the morning after my misadventures in the woods with a cold that forced me to remain in bed. My weak protests against this arrangement were immediately silenced by Mother, who fought to mask her worry as she settled on the edge of the bed and took my hand.

"I know it's likely just a cold," she said as she stroked my hair. "But I can't bear the thought of you exerting yourself and growing worse, what with Liam still ill—" She choked back a sob.

"How is he today?" My sore throat made each word painful.

"Not well, I'm afraid." Fear filled her glassy eyes. "I just came from visiting him. He continues to grow worse with each passing day." Just as he'd done the past several weeks.

"And the latest remedy isn't helping?"

Mother sighed and shook her head. "The physicians have tried different combinations of herbs, but none are making a difference. They're growing concerned that Liam won't recover."

Her words only confirmed the thought that had begun

niggling the back of my mind since talking to Aiden. "Are we sure Liam's illness is natural?" I asked tentatively. "We've been assuming that he has what took Kian, but what if it's something different?"

Mother's brow furrowed. "What do you mean?"

"I mean..." What *did* I mean? Just because the remedies weren't helping my brother didn't mean there was foul play involved. And yet...I nibbled my lip. "It was just so sudden and so intense, not to mention he's getting worse despite treatment. Liam is normally very healthy. I just wondered if there was another explanation."

The bafflement filling Mother's expression made me wish I'd kept my mouth shut rather than voice such a ridiculous thought. My cheeks burned as I lowered my eyes.

"I appreciate your voicing your thoughts, dear," Mother said slowly. "But I don't believe there's anything unusual about Liam's illness, not when it so closely resembles Kian's —although I pray his doesn't end the same way." She wiped away the tears already staining her cheeks before taking my hands. "I worry your own illness will grow worse if you're not cautious, so please stay in bed. For me."

"But I have a meeting—"

"Aveline has agreed to go in your place."

I slumped against the pillows, secretly relieved that at least for today I could be free of my wearying duties. "Then I'll heed your wishes. But try not to worry; it's just a cold. I'm sorry last night's actions are now causing you unnecessary distress."

She cradled my cheek. "I know. Now get well. I'll come check on you soon." She pressed a soft kiss on my brow and left.

As soon as the door clicked shut, I seized Drake from my bedside table. "Can you believe I have to stay in bed all day?"

"After being caught after dark in the rain so close to

winter, you're fortunate you're only suffering from a mild cold."

His wide grin softened his gentle admonition and caused my stomach to flip. For some reason I couldn't help but notice how endearing his smile was, or the way his hair fell across his forehead. My cheeks warmed. "And how are you feeling?" I ran my fingertip along the large crack still marring the mirror's surface. Although it was still large and jarring, it had at least shrunk slightly in the night.

"Well enough, although it's more difficult to appear in the mirror; it took me several tries when you were talking with your mother." Even as he spoke, his image flickered a few times before settling.

Panic clenched my stomach. "Drake?"

"Don't worry, Rhea, I'm not going anywhere. I promise."

Relief washed over me…along with something else. The feelings from last night not only lingered but were magnified this morning, causing me to be more aware of them—such as the way Drake's crooked smile lit up his dark eyes and caused them to crinkle around the edges. The heat in my cheeks deepened.

Drake's smile vanished immediately. "You're flushed. Do you have a fever?" He reached out, as if to rest his hand on my brow and muttered a curse when, as always, his hand hit the glass of the mirror.

I giggled. "Cursing in a sick lady's presence? However will I get well now?"

"You better get well," he muttered. "I'll pester you incessantly until you do. I mean it, Rhea." Blazing determination filled his eyes. My stomach gave another flip, but I refused to acknowledge what such a reaction meant.

I knew that maintaining distance from him was prudent, but the idea of Drake being so concerned thrilled me. I could always start doing so *after* I got well, I rationalized…but my promise was half-hearted.

True to his word, Drake kept me company throughout my day in bed and proved to be the most attentive nurse. He watched as I drank my herbal remedy and my broth to ensure I had every last drop, and he would fade from the mirror whenever he thought I needed a nap. Otherwise we spent hours conversing, interrupted only by the physician or visits from my family…as well as an unexpected visitor in the late afternoon.

Drake's animated childhood story about hiding from his tutor only to get locked in a broom cupboard was interrupted by a knock on the door. I quickly set him aside. "Come in."

A maid entered. "His Highness Prince Briar requests to see you."

Briar was visiting me? I flattened my rumpled hair. "Thank you. You may show him in."

She curtsied and left, and in the few seconds before Briar entered, Drake seemed determined to cause mischief. "*Prince Briar?*" He sounded disgusted.

"Shh, be quiet while he's here." The last thing I wanted was a confrontation between two brothers who I had the impression were not particularly close.

Drake muttered something indiscernible before obediently falling silent, and not a moment too soon. Briar entered carrying a bouquet of small white, purple, and yellow flowers. He blushed the moment he spotted me and lowered his eyes to the bouquet. "Are you well, Rheanna?"

I smiled. "Well enough. It's just a cold. Won't you sit down?"

Briar hesitated before slowly approaching and settling in the chair at my bedside. After another moment of silence, he handed me the flowers. "I picked these from your garden. I was pleased to find any when it's so cold, but I knew I could find crocuses, which often bloom even throughout winter. They—" He abruptly snapped his mouth shut, as if he feared he was boring me.

I smiled encouragingly and burrowed my nose in the blossoms, whose sweet perfume was unfortunately masked by my stuffy nose. "They're lovely flowers. Won't you tell me more about them?"

Briar launched in immediately, looking and sounding more animated than I'd ever seen him. I listened attentively, holding the lovely bouquet beneath my nose so I was enveloped in the soft feel of the blossoms' petals.

He only stopped when a loud yawn emanated from Drake's mirror. Briar immediately glared at it, obviously knowing the source of such a rude sound.

Of course he knows his brother is in the mirror. I wondered why he isn't saying anything about it. I glared at the mirror, too. "Will you excuse me for a moment?" I asked Briar sweetly.

At his nod, I picked up the mirror—whose handle was hot with Drake's annoyance—and shoved it into my nightstand drawer, slamming it shut with more force than necessary. Briar guffawed but tried to disguise it with a cough.

I smiled. "Forgive me. Please continue."

"I've already spoken too long on such a trivial topic." He lowered his eyes self-consciously.

"Not at all. I enjoy learning about plants. Perhaps you can teach me how to garden and we can do it together after we —" My face enveloped in heat at the implication but I didn't avert my gaze.

He hesitated before smiling, and although it seemed sincere enough, it didn't quite reach his eyes. "Are you sure you want to marry me, Rheanna?" His gaze darted towards the nightstand where I'd shoved Drake. My heart lurched. Just what was he suggesting?

"I—of course. Why wouldn't I—"

He didn't look at me as he leaned over to fluff my pillow. "I just wondered if there was…someone else."

Did he mean *Drake*? Before last night, I might have dismissed the possibility entirely, but now I couldn't, despite wanting to. If Drake ever got out of the mirror, would such a future with him be possible?

When I didn't answer, Briar smiled wistfully. "Not to worry. I'm fine with whatever you decide."

"But—" There had never been a decision for me to make. From the moment I learned of Malvagaria's interest in an alliance, I'd accepted my fate without question. I couldn't fail my duty to my kingdom or my people.

But Drake is a Malvagarian Prince who would also bring an alliance. Hope lifted my heart before I could squelch it. No, making a match with Drake was impossible. The conversation I'd overheard from my parents had made it very clear that it wasn't simply an alliance they sought; they hoped I'd become queen. How could I disappoint them? I couldn't, which meant I needed to guard my heart…although I feared it was too late.

After a brief but pleasant visit, Briar took his leave, and after schooling my rebellious heart I retrieved Drake from the drawer. I expected him to be scowling, but to my surprise, he looked quite cheerful. "Prince Briar gave you an out. Are you going to take it?"

"I'm not sure." Until his visit, I'd never allowed myself to entertain a possibility of not marrying Briar, let alone choosing someone else. I searched Drake's dark eyes before hastily looking away with a heated blush. "I need to think about things."

When I dared look at him again, his gaze became smoldering. "Please do, and take all the time you need. I'm not going anywhere."

My thinking wouldn't take long if Drake didn't feel anything for me beyond friendship. Then there was the matter of him still being trapped in a *mirror*, which definitely complicated things. Still, the hope didn't go away, but instead planted itself firmly in my heart. The question that remained was: would this new seed bloom or die?

Drake kept me company for the remainder of the day. Soon dusk settled, causing the light to fade in my room. I was growing tired but I didn't want to go to sleep for the night. I wanted to continue talking to Drake, for with each word, I tentatively began to explore a possibility I'd never previously considered, one I still was almost afraid to hope for.

Drake's image flickered within the mirror, like it'd been doing for most of the day. I took a deep breath to soften the tightening worry whenever this occurred.

After a moment his image steadied. He eyed my expression. "Still worried?"

"Of course." I caressed the mirror's frame. He leaned against my touch, his eyes half closed...before he suddenly jerked away from my caressing fingers.

Cheeks crimson, he cleared his throat. "You're not the only one who's worried—it's time for you to rest again. Physician's orders."

I sighed. "You're a rather strict physician."

"I'm a man of many talents."

I snorted but couldn't help smiling. "I suppose you're right; I am quite tired. I really enjoyed spending the day with you." Who knew being ill could be so...*wonderful*? But as lovely as our time together had been, I was still ready for it to end. I needed to think, although I wasn't sure whether I could examine my emotions and potential future with my stuffy head.

"Drake? *Drake?*"

Finally a flicker, and he appeared, his brow furrowed. "Why do you sound so panicked?"

Relief rushed over me. "I kept calling for you and you didn't come."

"My apologizes. I was simply…delayed."

I slumped against the pillows. "Don't *do* that to me. After what happened after I first broke you…are you trying to abuse my heart?"

"I'm sorry," he said.

I took a steadying breath and tried to school my rapid pulse. "What was the cause of your delay? Was it because of the crack?" I eyed it, still far too large for my liking.

"No, I'm able to appear just fine. I was just…" He trailed off, looking guilty.

"Were you somewhere else?" Considering he was trapped, he had nowhere else to go, except… "Were you in another mirror?"

He bit his lip, his answer, and I frowned.

"What were you doing?" He hadn't been *talking* to some-one, had he? But no matter how many times I pressed, he didn't divulge any information, and soon he faded altogether.

I stared at the empty mirror, suspicion tightening my chest. Something was going on. What reason did Drake have for going to another mirror, and why wouldn't he tell me about it? What new secret was he hiding from me?

THE NEXT MORNING didn't bring any answers to my ques-tions, for although Drake appeared when I called, he remained stubbornly uncooperative and somewhat distant. I finally gave up on trying to extract any kind of information and stomped off, fuming. Thank goodness I had my duties to distract me.

I still had a mild headache and a stuffy nose, but otherwise I was able to perform the tasks expected of me—spending the morning with Liam, going over reports with Father, attending a tedious two-hour meeting, and taking a very pleasant lunch with Briar, which was definitely the highlight of the day considering we were becoming increasingly more comfortable around each other. When we parted ways, I went to the library, where I researched not only Drake's curse, but the symptoms of Liam's illness, unable to shake the nagging feeling that something was unnatural about it. As usual, I didn't find any answers.

When I entered the parlor after dinner to spend the evening with my family and our guests, a footman handed me a letter. I immediately recognized Aiden's handwriting from the years we'd corresponded. Heart hammering, I settled away from the conversation and tore it open.

Dear Rhea,

As promised, I've looked more into my suspicions regarding the Queen of Malvagaria—as well as the curses that surround her family—and I'm afraid the news isn't reassuring. While my findings aren't conclusive, I have managed to learn that the Malvagarian palace gardens grow unusual enchanted plants, which, according to my reports, the queen seems obsessed with. While this information may be irrelevant, there are whispers that many of those plants have unusual effects, and while it's unclear if any are fatal, the fact that His Majesty and all four of the royal children are trapped in a curse while she remains unaffected leads one to wonder...

Rhea, if there's any truth to this information, then connecting yourself to that family will be detrimental. I urge you to take caution. No alliance is worth your wellbeing. I'll continue to research—as I promised both you and Liam—and will write you with any further developments.

Take care,
Aiden

MY HANDS SHOOK as I reread the letter twice before folding it and tucking it away. His insinuations left my mind spinning. I ached to take a moment to ponder them and perhaps even return to the library to track down the book I'd discovered about dangerous plants, but my family was waiting, so I rejoined them and picked up my embroidery, promptly tuning out the conversation swirling around me as well as the piano music Elodie was playing rather poorly.

I needed to ask Briar more about his palace's enchanted gardens, but even if I did, would he know the specific uses of his plants? It seemed doubtful he'd know about all of them. After all, he was trapped in one of the curses that might have been caused by them. Perhaps I could ask Drake…

"How are you feeling, Rheanna?"

I jolted and nearly pricked myself with my needle. I'd recognize that sugary voice anywhere. *Oh no, what does she want now?* I forced a tight smile and looked up to see the Queen of Malvagaria's own sickly sweet smile directed towards me.

"I'm feeling much better, thank you. I'm only suffering from a few lingering symptoms but should be completely well soon."

Her expression tightened. "What a relief. I'd hate to have you be as ill as poor Liam. Such a loss that would be." She shook her head.

I narrowed my eyes. Despite her somber expression, an almost *gleeful* look filled her dark eyes. My hand tightened over my embroidery needle. I must have imagined it; Aiden's letter had undoubtedly made me paranoid.

The queen took a sip of tea through her pursed red lips. "I had the pleasure of sitting in on yesterday's meeting where Aveline took your place. She did exceptionally well. I was extremely impressed." She gave me a subtle smirk that clearly said, *she did much better than you ever could hope for*.

My heart tightened at the subtle insult. *A cloak-and-dagger approach, just as Drake said.*

To my surprise, Briar spoke suddenly from beside me. "Aveline did well, but Rheanna never fails to give a wonderful performance. She's poised, well spoken, and always prepared." He gave the queen an almost defiant look and my heart warmed at his defense.

The queen frowned at him before forcing another smile. "It pleases me to hear you think so highly of your intended's accomplishments. I want nothing more than for you two to be happy together. It appears you already are. Perhaps the time has come for us to draw up the betrothal contracts."

Both he and I stiffened.

"Please, there's really no rush," Father said, eying my reaction with concern. "After what happened with Liam's arrangement with Lyceria, we hesitate to move forward until we're certain Rhea is ready."

"I'd appreciate a bit more time." My comment caused the queen to narrow her eyes almost dangerously and for Briar to visibly relax beside me, but for once his disinterested gesture didn't bother me...especially considering my heart quite likely lay with another prince.

"Of course," the queen said sweetly. "I only have your best interests in mind."

Liar. I responded with my own fake smile before returning to my embroidery...and my thoughts to Aiden's letter. He was right to warn me. The queen was a snake. Caution was undoubtedly wise.

I didn't remain in the parlor for long before using the lingering effects of my cold as a much-desired excuse to retire early. I'd no sooner escaped into the corridors and heaved a sigh of relief than the familiar clicking of the queen's heels sounded behind me.

I groaned quietly. *What now?* I slowly turned but didn't even bother pretending to be pleased to see her. "Is there something I can help you with?" I asked stiffly.

Her own usual polite mask was missing, but her frown was more welcoming than her insincere smiles. "A word, Rheanna?" She motioned to a nearby antechamber, which she followed me into.

My thoughts frantically tried to come up with a reason for what would surely be a *delightful* conversation. *Surely she can't tell me anything that she hasn't already said.* I raised my defenses in preparation for battle.

"What is it?" I asked the moment the door clicked shut behind her. My heart pounded wildly as I eyed it, too late remembering Aiden's letter. Being alone in a closed room with someone who was likely responsible for the curses haunting her family was not the wisest course of action.

She gave a long-suffering sigh. "I must admit I'm rather displeased with you, Rheanna."

I stiffened. *Here it comes…*

"Your parents and I only want what's best for our children, yet how can we give that to you or Briar when you're being stubbornly resistant?"

"Forgive me for my caution, but considering I'm the one who will have to live with the union, I believe I have every right to take all the time I need to make sure I'm making the right decision. My parents will fully support me, regardless of what I decide."

She raised an eyebrow. "Goodness, you've become more bold."

I merely lifted my chin and said nothing.

She smirked. "How interesting. Well, this is an unexpected development...assuming it lasts, which I doubt. But is this new attitude of yours boldness...or selfishness?" She continued studying me with her usual critical air. "Hmm, selfishness, I think. The benefits of your kingdom aligning with one as great as Malvagaria are many, both to your monarchy and to your people. But you don't seem to care about those benefits, a vice almost as bad as the foolishness you exhibited the other night when you recklessly went off into the woods alone. I confess, after that display, I almost changed my mind about uniting you with my son. One more stunt like that, and I'll have no choice but to...*end things*, and trust me, that's an outcome you won't like."

A chill rippled up my spine. "Shouldn't *Briar* have a say in whether or not our marriage goes through?" I tried to sound brave, but my heart pounded painfully against my ribs.

"Like you, Briar is a fool and doesn't know what's best for him. I'm cursed with weak children." She sighed and shook her head.

My fear from her earlier threat was already fading, replaced with annoyance. I almost rolled my eyes, but I managed to quell that impulse and merely raise my eyebrow instead. "Briar is your kingdom's future king. It doesn't bode well if you doubt his abilities."

"It's not *his* abilities I'm doubting."

Despite the shield I'd put up against the imminent verbal onslaught, I still flinched at the attack. The queen's next smile was triumphant.

"I may seem harsh," she continued. "But trust me, my honesty is for your own good."

"If you insist on being honest, then why do you pretend

you're interested in a union between Briar and me at all?" I asked. "Why bother when you've made it clear you don't find me good enough to be queen? Aveline seems much better suited for both Briar and Malvagaria. "

"I have my reasons." She studied me with a chillingly calculating look. "I've spent years researching royal history. It's quite fascinating studying the strengths and weaknesses of past kings and queens; my favorite accounts are of those who valued cunning over might. True achievement comes through strategy, not bloodshed. Thus any queen who rules Malvagaria should possess the abilities needed to accept a mantle with such a history of greatness."

Trepidation filled my stomach at the sinister glint filling the queen's eyes. She took a step forward.

"I've undoubtedly made the past queens proud with my own cunning," she continued. "In fact, I've surpassed them all. Whereas you, Rheanna, will likely only bring shame without my help. You know this, don't you? The thought of anyone discovering your shortcomings terrifies you...but not as much as you fear being rejected."

My breath caught. How could she possibly know that? I hadn't told anyone, except...my heart lurched before I immediately dismissed the possibility. Drake would never tell his mother my secrets. We were friends...perhaps even *more* than friends.

"I don't know what you mean," I finally said, fighting to keep my voice steady.

"Don't you?" The queen seemed on the brink of laughter. "Then you're a bigger fool than I initially thought if you're so keen on lying to yourself. I know how horrible Prince Deidric's rejection was for you. I can't say his action was a surprise. I see what he saw—that you weren't worthy of ruling at his side."

I clenched my fists in an attempt to fight against the

anguish the memory of Aiden's rejection caused. *Don't listen to her*. She couldn't use that attack on me any more, not after I'd talked to Aiden and finally knew what had really transpired between us. But the words still hurt, for they played off my fears, ones that still hadn't completely gone away, no matter how much I fought them.

"Keep in mind that I control whether Briar chooses you or not," the queen said. "Aveline could just as easily give our kingdom the alliance it seeks, which means I must warn you —you're *very* close to your greatest fear, that of another broken engagement. I'd be very careful if I were you."

My breaths were coming up short, and the thoughts that hadn't visited me in a while returned. *No one wants you.*

I struggled to push them away before they could take root. I needed to get away from her. "Forgive me, but I'm feeling poorly and need to retire." I turned to leave before she could say another word, but even after I left her behind, her poisonous comments lingered.

I hurried through the corridors, my heart pounding and my eyes burning. By the time I arrived at my room, my tears had escaped. I seized the mirror. "Drake!"

He appeared immediately, his expression anxious, his previous avoidance of me seemingly forgotten. "What is it? What happened?"

"The queen! She…she…" My sobs made it impossible to speak.

His expression twisted. "The Queen of Malvagaria? Did she say something that hurt you?"

I could barely nod. *Your mother is venomous and vile*, I ached to say. "She—" My sobs choked my voice again, keeping me from speaking.

"Deep breaths, Rhea. Please tell me what she said."

Through my tears, I somehow managed to tell him everything. His entire manner hardened with each word…and his expression crumpled when I told him she threatened to call off the betrothal.

"She used your fears against you?" he whispered.

"Yes." The pain was just as sharp now as it'd been when she'd first confronted me, and whatever bravery and display of confidence I'd managed to maintain with her faded. "She's not right, is she? I couldn't bear to face another rejection." I buried my face in my knees.

"Oh Rhea, I'm so incredibly sorry." His apology was heartfelt, despite his having nothing to do with his horrible mother's cruel actions.

"It's not your fault," I murmured, but by the anguished look he gave me, he seemed to blame himself all the same. He opened his mouth a few times, as if there was more he wanted to say, before closing it with a sigh.

"I'm so proud of you for standing up for yourself. I knew you were strong."

"I don't feel strong, nor brave. I feel…defeated." I sighed as I leaned my head against the cool window and stared out across the velvety night full of stars. "Is it wrong for me to want to marry Briar because I'm afraid of dealing with the emotions *not* marrying him would cause? He and I are getting closer, but I'm not convinced we're a good match. Forcing him into it for my sake…" I shook my head. "Perhaps I am selfish, just as the queen said."

"Even if you have an occasional selfish desire, you're the opposite of selfish," Drake said gently. "I wish you could see yourself clearly; you're strong, compassionate, and good. If your engagement does fall through, it won't change who you are…unless you let it."

I'd allowed Aiden's rejection to break me before, but I couldn't let that happen gain. "Do you think my arrangement with Briar will fall through?" I wasn't even sure I still wanted it, although I was admittedly too afraid to let it go myself.

"If it does, I know you'll get through it. You overcame your first broken betrothal and you can do it again because this time you're much stronger."

Warmth seeped over me at his words. *You need to believe how he sees you.* "Thank you, Drake." My feelings for him only deepened with his sweet comfort. What was I to do with these new emotions?

Part of me yearned to act on them, while the other part of me was just as afraid to choose Drake as it was to choose Briar, especially if my motives for doing so were selfish. Was I wanting Drake because of *him*, or because he was the safer choice where I could escape the duties of being queen while still acquiring the alliance with Malvagaria? Until I knew the answer to that question, I couldn't make an informed decision.

But by the way my heart swelled as I looked into the mirror, I feared it had different ideas.

CHAPTER 21

*T*he orchard trees were nearly barren, their fallen leaves a ruby-and-gold carpet that covered the ground. The crisp scent of autumn mingling with the apple's fruity smell filled the air. I sat beneath my favorite tree and propped Drake's mirror on my legs. It had been a while since we'd spoken, for he'd taken to appearing only occasionally. The longer his absence, the more I missed him…and the more I understood my feelings for him.

The emotions bloomed inside me like apple blossoms in spring, warm and tender. It was similar to how I felt towards my family but deeper, for Drake had become more than my friend and confidant.

I love him.

I'd kept this realization locked away for several days, for I wasn't sure which path to take now that I realized the truth of my feelings. And things were complicated considering I was nearly engaged to his brother, not to mention the object of my affections was currently trapped in a mirror, a curse I was no closer to breaking than when I'd first met him. Part of me still feared I loved him because he was the safer path.

But despite that, I did love him. After pondering my dilemma, I knew I needed to be true to my heart. If Drake felt similarly about me, choosing him would still benefit my kingdom with a coveted alliance, not to mention it would make me happy.

So I would confess to Drake in the orchard that had become our special place. I gripped the mirror tightly as I stared at my nervous reflection, trying to gather the courage to call his name.

You can do this. After all, this is Drake, the man you care for deeply. I took a wavering breath. "Drake?"

My heart hammered as I waited, an anticipation that turned to fear when he didn't appear, even though the crack in the mirror had long since mended.

"Drake?" My voice shook, betraying my anxiety. At the sound, he appeared almost immediately, his dark eyes soft with concern.

"Are you alright, Rhea?"

Warm relief washed over me. "You didn't come when I called." It had been a recent habit of his, one that made me worry that despite my deepening feelings, the relationship we'd forged was crumbling.

"I'm sorry, Rhea. I—" He looked like he wanted to say more before he closed his mouth with a sigh. "Was there something you needed?"

"You." My cheeks warmed but I refused to allow my insecurity to prevent me from doing what I had to do. *He has to know how you feel...as does Briar. You can no longer continue courting him when your heart belongs to another.* But instead of saying all of this, I simply whispered, "I missed you."

Drake was silent a long moment, a tumult of emotions raging in his eyes, the primary one being *pain*. "Rhea." His voice was agonized.

"What is it?" I stroked the rim of the mirror, a poor

substitute when I really wanted to stroke his hair. As he usually did, he leaned against my touch, as if he could feel it. Perhaps he could.

"I've been doing a lot of thinking and I—" He lowered his eyes, as if he couldn't bear to see my reaction to his next words. "We can't see one another anymore."

I nearly dropped the mirror in my shock. This was not how I'd expected my confession to begin. Despite his words, my hold on the mirror tightened in my desperation to keep him close. "Why? I don't understand. I thought we were friends."

"We *are* friends, Rhea." His voice was so gentle. "That's why I can't see you anymore. I shouldn't have allowed this to go on for as long as I did. I'm sorry."

"But—" My mind was swirling, and it was a struggle to keep back the tears already burning my eyes. *This always happens to you, Rhea. When will you realize that nobody likes you?*

No, that wasn't true. *Drake* liked me. This knowledge burned in my heart, almost as brightly as my own feelings for him—I loved him. Thus I had to help him, even if I couldn't keep him.

I set my expression and lifted my chin. "If you think I'm going to abandon you and leave you trapped in that mirror, then you're mistaken. I'm going to continue helping you whether you want me to or not."

His expression crumpled at my promise. "Oh, Rhea... you're so sweet. But it's wrong of me to involve you. I can't do this to you anymore." He took a deep breath before his gaze met mine, piercing with intensity. "I don't want you to break my curse."

I gaped at him. "You want to remain trapped in that mirror? We've spent weeks working together to try and break the curse, and you expect me to believe you've suddenly changed your mind?"

The look he gave me was caressing. "Some things are more important than my freedom."

I shook my head. "Not to me."

"Rhea—"

"I'm going to help you," I said fiercely. "No matter what you say."

"But you can't. *Please.*" He looked almost desperate. "You could get hurt. I could never…" He reached out and pressed his fingers to the glass and I rested mine over his, and for a startling moment, I could have sworn I felt his touch.

What would it feel like to really touch him? I ached to experience that. "I wish you were free." My voice choked on my suppressed sob. "Then perhaps we could be together."

"Rhea…" Sadness filled his eyes and his voice. I pressed my palm against the glass and he began to stroke it on the other side with his fingers. Soft tingles spread up my arm, almost as if we were actually touching. How I wished we really were.

"Briar doesn't love me," I whispered. "And I don't love him." *I love you.* "I'm bound by duty, you're bound by your curse. But there has to be a way."

"Rhea…" Drake looked as if his heart were breaking. "Please. I could never hurt you."

"Then stay with me."

I wasn't sure what made me do it, but the deep feelings of my heart guided me. I bent down, and as if he felt the same urge he came closer too, leaning up until he was right against the glass. I pressed my lips against the glass, directly on his. I saw his reflection respond before my eyes fluttered close.

Despite kissing nothing more than a mirror, I felt as if I were kissing him—a shadow of the real thing, but a kiss nonetheless. I thought I felt his lips move against mine, and the breeze caressed my hair, as if he were urging his fingers through it. My arms tightened around the mirror in an embrace, bringing it—bringing *him*—closer.

It was amazing how real this felt. Sensations coursed over me, the magic of experiencing one's first kiss, despite my lips merely being on glass rather than his. But I was still kissing Drake. It was enough.

Even though the kiss was short, I felt as if I'd experienced something life changing. Cheeks warm, I pulled away, leaving a mark on the mirror, which gradually faded. Drake stared up at me, his dark eyes blazing with an emotion I couldn't decipher.

"Rhea…" He said my name like a caress, and it was the key to unlocking the feelings I'd kept cradled close.

"Drake…" I curled my hand around the frame of the mirror, as close as I could be to stroking his cheek. "I love you."

His eyes widened and his expression lit up…before sadness overcame him. "Oh, Rhea." And then he disappeared.

I gaped at his missing reflection, my own staring back at me, stunned and confused. "Drake?"

Suddenly the mirror began to heat and glow. It slipped from my fingers, but instead of falling, it floated in the air, encircled by a golden halo, which grew brighter and brighter. I twisted away and covered my eyes.

I heard a loud *thump* as something landed in the grass beside me. I peeked my eyes open and gasped. The mirror lay on the lawn, and next to it, *Drake* was sprawled in the grass. I watched in disbelief as he sat up and slowly looked around, his expression dazed. He examined his hands, wriggling his fingers, before tipping his head back to blink up at the sky.

His gaze slowly met mine and my favorite crooked smile filled his face. "I'm out of the mirror."

My brain finally registered the miracle I was seeing. Joy melted away my surprise. "Drake!"

I pounced on him, knocking him backwards onto the grass. His arms immediately tightened around me, holding me close, and I marveled at the sensation. Drake was a real man. I could touch him, feel his warmth, and be held in his arms. I nestled against his firm chest and burrowed my nose against his throat with an ecstatic grin. He smelled like apples.

He sat us up and helped me to my feet. He ran a hesitant hand through my hair and I tipped my head back to stare at him. His handsome face looked almost strange to no longer be a two-dimensional image trapped behind the glass... strange but *wonderful*. My hand, shy and hesitant, went to his face, and finally I acted on the desire that had ached within me from the first moment he entered my heart: I stroked his cheek and smiled when he leaned against my fingertips.

"Rhea..." His hand went to my own face, his fingers light and caressing. His touch caused delightful sensations to ripple over me; it was my turn to lean against his touch, so soft and inviting. He grinned. "I can't tell you how long I've wanted to do that."

"I can't believe you're free," I whispered. "How did I break the curse?"

He pressed his forehead against mine. "Because...you love me?" His tone was filled with hope.

My cheeks warmed and my smile became shy. "Yes. I love you, Drake."

Grinning widely, he pulled me closer and kissed me, a real kiss. Whatever sensations I'd thought I'd experienced through the mirror were nothing compared to what I felt now. His lips were both soft and warm, fierce and passionate, yet incredibly gentle. I wrapped my arms around his neck and curled my fingers through his thick hair.

This is what it feels like to be loved.

Our kiss ended far too soon. Drake's gaze was smoldering

as he smiled down at me. "Yes, that was much better. I've wanted to do that for so long." He kissed me again, one that was both heated and incredibly tender. "You smell like irises," he managed to murmur against my lips. "I've spent far too many hours wondering what you smell like, wondering if your skin and hair are as soft as they look. You're so beautiful." As he spoke, his fingers cradled my face and he softly brushed his thumb against my cheek. "This is everything I imagined and more. This is real."

I rested my hand against his pulsing heart, relishing its beating against my palm. "This is real," I murmured. The moment was perfect. I loved Drake, and by the soft way he looked at me, he clearly felt the same for me. *You're worth caring about.* It was a beautiful thought, one I wanted to keep forever.

"Rheanna?" My name drifted through the orchard, spoken by a familiar voice.

Briar...

I gasped and tried to jerk away from Drake's embrace, but he held me securely. My gaze frantically searched for Briar through the trees. I couldn't see him, but I heard him once more call my name. He was looking for me, and he was about to discover not only me but his curse-free brother as well.

Guilt squeezed my heart. I looked at Drake, whose eyes were narrowed in the direction from which Briar's voice had drifted.

"I shouldn't have—" I'd done this in the wrong order. I should have broken off my courtship with Briar *before* confessing my love for Drake and kissing him. But I hadn't, and my intended was about to find me in the arms of another man, and not just any man...

My cheeks burned at the thought and I immediately wanted to hide. I tried to wriggle away, but Drake's hold tightened desperately, keeping me pressed cozily against his chest. "Please, Rhea. I've waited too long to hold you for you to escape now."

"But your brother—" Once again I tried to pull away, and this time I succeeded, for at my words, his arms slackened as his eyes widened.

"My *brother*? You mean you knew that he and I—"

Now was not the time for this conversation. "Of course I knew, and he's about to see us *together*."

"Excellent. I can finally stake my claim." As he spoke, he pulled me back against him. "He'll find out eventually. After all, you love me, right?"

"Yes, but he shouldn't find out like *this*. It isn't proper." I tried again to extract myself from his arms, and to my surprise, he let me. I took his hand and tried to tug him deeper into the trees. "We need to hide."

He lifted his eyebrows but didn't budge. "We shouldn't, Rhea. We need to tell him now."

Was he crazy? We couldn't do it *now*. My pulse pattered wildly at the very thought.

"Rheanna?" Briar was coming closer. Soon he'd be upon us. I gave Drake a pleading look. I wasn't ready for this. He and I needed to talk, make plans, and *then* approach Briar and my parents. Having Briar discover us now was completely the wrong way to go about it.

When I saw that Drake wouldn't budge, fear compelled me to yank my hand out of his and duck behind a clump of shrubs that masked me from view but allowed me to still see Drake through the leaves. He stared at where I'd hidden with a look like he was going to come after me.

"Rhea—" He took a step closer.

At that moment, Briar emerged from behind an apple-laden tree and came into view, freezing when he spotted his brother. For a moment he merely gaped at him. "*Drake?*"

Drake winced and slowly turned to face him. "Hello, Briar."

Briar continued to stare before he grinned, the most animated look I'd ever seen from the prince. "Are you finally free?" He stooped down to pick up the mirror.

"No, I'm not free," Drake said drily as he used Briar's distraction to cast another lingering gaze towards my hiding place. "I'm still trapped in that blasted mirror."

Briar chuckled. "Believe it or not, I've missed your sarcasm." He turned the mirror around in his hands, examining every surface. "It's hard to believe you were trapped inside this. How did you break the curse?"

Drake hesitated and said nothing. I prayed he'd remain silent on that matter.

Briar's forehead furrowed. "Mother said it'd only break if you got a princess to fall in love with you. But last I saw, Rheanna had your mirror—" His entire expression darkened and I winced. *He's just put it together.* "Rheanna?"

Drake groaned and nodded. Briar's jaw clenched as he took a foreboding step closer.

"You chose *Rheanna*? Why her? You know she and I are going to make a match. She has two other sisters, Drake."

"I—" Drake looked like he wanted the ground to swallow him whole, and I felt guilty leaving him to Briar's wrath alone. I was just about to emerge from my hiding place and join him when Briar's next words caused me to still.

"I never agreed with your plan of tricking one of the princesses into falling in love with you so you could be free," Briar said coldly. "But I thoroughly disagree with your choosing my intended for your scheme. How could you do that to her?"

My heart lurched and my breath caught. *No*...he couldn't really be saying...I must have misheard him. Drake wasn't like that. He wouldn't—

Unbidden, the voice I'd struggled to keep at bay returned, sharp and poisonous. *You know it's true. Drake could never care for you. He was trapped in a mirror and would have done* anything *to escape. You're merely a means to an end.*

The dark thoughts slithered deeper into the recesses of my mind, whispering their taunts. Their words mingled with the fruity scent of apples filling the orchard, churning my stomach. I ached to escape, but I was rooted to this spot.

"I couldn't help it; she's the one who found the mirror." Drake said as he cast another frantic look towards my hiding place, looking thoroughly miserable. "But I tried to stop her. I didn't want—" He said nothing more.

"Don't lie. You manipulated her for your own ends and will now toss her aside, just as you always planned to do."

"No, I—"

"You disgust me." Briar clenched his fists. "Does Rheanna know?" Before Drake could even answer, Briar was already leaving the orchard, his strides long. "I need to find her. I'm sure she's utterly distraught." He disappeared into the trees.

A horrible stillness settled over the orchard following his departure. Drake stared after his brother before spinning towards the bush where I hid, his expression desperate. "Rhea?"

I didn't answer. Instead I pulled my legs to my chest and buried my face in my knees. My breath was coming too rapidly, too sharply, even as the implications from the conversation I'd just overheard squeezed my chest so tightly I could scarcely breathe.

Drake used me to get out of the mirror. Even after overhearing the truth, I still didn't want to believe it.

"Rhea?" I heard him approach until he was beside me. I stiffened but I didn't look up. He crouched down and hesitantly caught an end of my hair. "Rhea? I—"

I jerked away and glared at him, but the effect was likely

marred from my red eyes and tear-streaked face. Guilt twisted his expression when he saw it.

"I know this looks bad, but—"

"You—*you!*" I was so angry I could scarcely think, but my anger was nothing compared to the cold despair slowly seeping over me. I pressed my hand to my heart, as if the pressure could keep its shattering pieces together.

"Please, Rhea, just let me explain." He reached for me again but I scrambled away.

"Explain what? Is there any truth to Briar's words?"

Drake looked like he ached to deny it, but he didn't. Instead, he slumped before nodding. "But I swear I didn't mean for this to happen."

"Didn't you?" My thoughts were swirling, trying to hold on to the facts I'd been presented with in such a cruel manner. "This entire time the key to breaking your curse was getting someone to fall in love with you?"

Drake hesitated before nodding again. "A princess," he clarified.

I winced. So my *royal title* had been all that was required, not me as a person. Any princess would have sufficed. I just happened to be the unlucky one who'd found the mirror. "And you knew that all along?"

Drake eyed my agonized expression with growing alarm. "It doesn't matter how the curse was to be broken; what matters is that it brought us together." He reached for my hand but I yanked it away.

"You never cared for me at all," I hissed. "I'm just a gullible princess you used to get out of the mirror."

He frantically shook his head. "That's not true. I admit it may have started out that way, but that was before—"

The words were a punch in the gut, confirming my darkest fears. I stared at him in horror.

It was all a lie. Every word, every affection—he'd *used* me.

267

How could I have deluded myself into believing he was different than Aiden, than Briar, than anyone? I'd *kissed* him. I'd given him my heart, only for him to carve it out for his own selfish purposes, leaving me hollow.

Who knew love hurt so much?

He reached out and gently wiped my tears away. For the briefest moment I let him—marveling at the sensations filling me from his touch, reminding me he was out of the mirror like I'd always wanted—before it became unbearable.

I jerked away. "Don't touch me."

Remorse filled his eyes. "Please Rhea, I didn't—"

I tried to stand, desperate to escape. He helped me up but let me go when I glared at him. "I *trusted* you," I whispered. "You knew my pain of being used, rejected, and yet—" I squeezed my eyes shut and allowed my tears to escape. "How could you do this to me?"

"I didn't mean for this to happen. Please, Rhea, you have to believe me." I sensed him step closer. His warmth enveloped me, tempting me to lean against him and let him hold me. I resisted the impulse. "I tried to stop you from falling in love with me."

Only after it had been too late. "But you can't deny that before that, you tried to get me to fall for you to achieve your own selfish ends. I shared everything with you—" My heart twisted. I'd been such a fool. "Thank goodness Briar didn't see us together. Not only would I have not learned the truth about you, but I'd have ruined things with him."

After losing everything else, I couldn't bear to lose Briar, too. He was the steady path; a life with him would be safe, which was so much better than blindly giving my heart away only to have it trampled on.

Drake's expression twisted. "You can't marry him, Rhea. You deserve better than to—"

"—than to be used to break your curse?"

He groaned and buried his face in his hands. "Please Rhea, just let me explain. I can't lose you, especially not to him. He wouldn't care for you the way I—"

"You don't care for me at all. If you did, you wouldn't have tricked me." Saying the words shattered my heart further, confirming my painful decision. He took another step closer, but I picked up a fallen apple and threw it at him, square in the chest. "Leave me alone. I never want to see you ever—"

"Rheanna?"

I stilled at Briar's voice before spinning around to face him. He looked frantic and his breaths were heavy, signs of his desperate search for me. I didn't hesitate—I ran into his arms and broke into sobs. He immediately embraced me, rubbing my back soothingly, all while expressing some very colorful thoughts to Drake before gently winding his arm around me.

"Rhea, wait—"

"Leave her alone," Briar snarled. "Haven't you hurt her enough?"

That silenced Drake. He made no other attempt to come after me as Briar led me from the orchard. I didn't look back at him, still too shattered after what I'd discovered: my heart was worthless to him, nothing more than a plaything.

How did you ever expect anything else?

CHAPTER 22

$\mathcal{I}$ stared unseeing up at my canopy, clutching my pillow to my chest as if it could shield me from the pain squeezing my heart. After a long, restless night, the pain hadn't dissipated—it'd only grown worse, especially as my raging thoughts forced me to relive the horrible memories in vivid detail.

I pressed my hand to my heart, a feeble attempt to keep its broken pieces together. I'd thought the pain of Aiden's broken engagement had been bad, but this…this was pain of an entirely different sort. I'd finally become brave enough to give my protected heart away, only for Drake to abuse it. The shadow of his kiss still lingered on my lips, but the memory was tainted by the fact that he hadn't meant it, nor had he meant his friendship or any of the sweet words he'd shared with me.

No one will ever love you. You're unlovable.

The familiar words that I'd previously fought so hard not to believe were strangely soothing, like old friends. It was easier not to fight these thoughts; then I wouldn't be disappointed when they continued to repeatedly come true.

A knock sounded on the door, tearing me from my poisonous thoughts. "Rhea dear? Are you alright?"

Mother. I was tempted to ignore her, but I knew doing so would only cause her to worry. I sighed. "Come in."

She entered, her concern-filled eyes immediately going to my motionless form on the bed. "Rhea?" She closed the door behind her and hurried over to kneel beside me. "Are you ill?"

I shook my head and tore my gaze away from hers to stare miserably back up at my canopy. She released a sigh of relief as she squeezed my hand.

"Thank goodness. If you'd caught Liam's illness—" She released a choked sob and pressed her forehead against my hand. "The physicians from Draceria and Sortileya have been working together and have tried every herbal remedy they can come up with, but no treatment seems to be making any difference. I think…we're going to lose him."

My breath caught and suddenly my own problems seemed inconsequential. Liam *couldn't* die. He was so fun, vibrant, and full of life, not to mention the future king. Our people needed him; *I* needed him. I'd already endured the pain of losing my oldest brother, but to now lose my best friend…

My tears escaped as I embraced her and she melted against me. Comforting her helped alleviate some of my own pain, if only a little.

After a moment, she sat up and wiped her eyes as she pulled away, her expression shrouded in worry. "It's unlike you to lock yourself in your room. Did something happen?"

What could I possibly tell her when I'd kept my relationship with Drake a secret? When I remained silent, Mother cupped my chin, the concern in her eyes deepening.

"What is it, darling? Please tell me."

271

I shook my head. Telling her wouldn't mend the broken pieces of my heart. Only one man could do that.

"Please, Rhea." Mother took my hand and held it between hers, her gaze imploring. "I can't do anything for Liam but watch helplessly as his life slips away and his wife grieves. So if there's anything I can do for you, I must. What's troubling you?"

Her earnest plea cracked my resistance. My lip trembled. "I fell in love and he doesn't love me in return, even though I thought he did." It made his rejection all the worse.

Her brow furrowed. "Briar?"

I slowly shook my head and burrowed myself against her shoulder. She tenderly wrapped her arms around me.

"I see." She nestled against my hair. "Then who is it?"

I shook my head again. I couldn't tell her now, not when the wound was still so raw. Sensing this, Mother didn't pry for his identity any further.

"Is that why you've been resisting a union with Briar, because of this other man?"

I nodded. "I know it was wrong of me to fall in love with another man. I didn't mean for it to happen; it just did." And if I'd known it'd hurt this much, I'd have done everything in my power to safeguard my heart. I took a shuddering breath and looked up at Mother. "But I'm done with him now. Do you think it can still work with Briar? I want us to love each other, like you and Father do."

Mother's expression gentled as she took out her handkerchief and carefully dried my tears, just as Briar had done yesterday after he'd led me away from Drake. "I believe it can."

"Then I want to marry him." After Briar's sweet comfort last evening where he'd simply held me while I'd cried, I realized his steadiness and friendship were what I needed. I trusted him, for unlike Drake, he hadn't hurt me. Choosing him felt safe; I couldn't risk my heart again.

Mother stroked my hair, her touch soothing. "Are you sure, sweetheart?"

I merely nodded.

"Very well. I'll talk to your father, but since the deadline is still a week away, I think it's wise to wait a little longer. The time to make an important decision isn't so soon after a broken heart."

She was likely right, but I was desperate to do *something*, anything to escape the pain Drake had caused me. But escape likely wouldn't be forthcoming anytime soon, for now that Drake was out of the mirror…

I took a wavering breath, dreading the inevitable answer to my question. "Has anything interesting happened while I've been hiding in my room?"

She nodded. "That's one of the reasons I came to see you. We have a new guest, one who arrived rather unexpectedly."

My pulse pounded frantically. *Him…*

"It's Prince Drake, Briar's younger brother. I don't know why he didn't arrive with his family earlier."

My heart constricted to hear his name.

"He's eager to meet you and has requested an introduction."

*No…*I squeezed my eyes shut. I couldn't face him. I never wanted to see him again. And yet, despite my determination, my heart had different ideas. My gaze drifted to his now-empty mirror resting facedown on the nightstand, kept nearby so part of me could believe I hadn't lost anything, when in reality I'd lost *everything*.

If only I could stop caring. It'd make it so much easier to face him.

"Are you up for that, dear?" Mother asked gently. "It

would be good for you to meet him considering he's your future brother-in-law."

Dread knotted my stomach, but I knew I couldn't hide away forever, despite wanting nothing more. I was a princess and thus I had a duty to my future husband to be courteous to his family, whether or not they deserved it.

∾

EVERYONE AWAITED us in the amber sitting room, the Queen of Malvagaria with a dark glower, which she directed towards me the moment I entered. I ignored her, my gaze immediately drawn to Drake sitting beside Briar, having what appeared to be a silent stare-down. They both looked up at my entrance and Drake immediately leapt to his feet, his expression calm but his eyes frantic. I couldn't help but hungrily look at him, taking in his features that had been previously hidden by the mirror—he was taller than Briar, quite a bit so.

Mother led me towards him. "Darling, I'd like you to meet Prince Drake, who arrived last evening."

He bowed. "It's a pleasure, Princess Rheanna." He reached for my hand to kiss it, but despite having spent hours longing for his touch, I couldn't bear it now. I yanked my hand away.

"Rheanna!" Mother looked scandalized by my rudeness, but despite her look that admonished me to behave properly, I kept my hand firmly behind my back. When it was clear I wasn't going to apologize, Mother turned towards Drake. "Forgive her, she's…had a difficult day."

Drake's eyes met mine, which were undoubtedly still puffy from all the hours I'd spent crying. "It's quite alright. I hope you feel better soon, Rhea."

I flinched at my nickname. I glared at him before looking

away, seeking…ah, there he was. Briar, watching the exchange attentively, leapt to my side and looped his arm around my waist. He'd never done such a thing before, but there was something soothing about the contact. It wasn't intimate, nor did it cause my heart to flutter, but it made me feel…safe. From the corner of my eye, I caught the queen's smirk.

Drake scowled at Briar's hand resting on my waist. Triumph and guilt warred within me. Triumph won. "What brings you to Draceria, Prince Drake?" I asked sweetly. "Are you here for the wedding?"

He stiffened. "No, I—" He sighed and stepped closer, dropping our façade of indifference. "Rhea, I was hoping you and I could—"

"It's Rheanna," I said coolly. "If you'll excuse me."

He looked like he wanted to say more, but I didn't want to hear it; being close to him was too agonizing, the force of his dark gaze magnifying my pain.

I gently pulled out of Briar's embrace and silently retreated to stare unseeing out the window, my folded arms pressed against my chest in a vain attempt to contain the sharp pang. Too late I realized this window overlooked the apple orchard, a place now full of poisonous memories.

I started to turn away but froze when I noticed Drake hovering only a few feet away, his expression twisted in what appeared to be remorse, but which was undoubtedly another ploy. Behind him my parents conversed with the queen while Briar watched us attentively, his stance protective. I took solace in his presence before I tightened my jaw and defiantly lifted my chin, swiveling back around so my back faced Drake. I'd rather look out at the orchard than at *him*.

"Rhea?"

My heart fluttered to life at the way he whispered my

name. I cursed my body's reaction but refused to acknowledge him.

"Please, Rhea." He brushed my hand and I jolted at the contact.

"Don't touch me," I snapped. "And don't use my name so familiarly."

"Please, Rhea, don't be that way. After everything—"

"Everything was a lie," I said, still refusing to look at him. "Thus I want nothing to do with you."

Ironically, those words—which burned my tongue to speak—were also lie. I didn't want to lose Drake, but I also didn't want to experience the fierce, unrelenting heartache his betrayal had caused.

He was silent so long I wondered if he'd left. But then he spoke, his voice wavering. "It wasn't a lie. I admit there were lies in the beginning, but everything we developed was real."

"If it was real, you would have told me the truth."

More silence stretched between us, along with something else—despair, not just mine, but his, rolling off him in waves, pleading for me to give him another chance…

No, Rhea. This time you've learned your lesson. Don't risk your heart again.

"I've been so worried for you," he said. "I know you locked yourself in your room because of me. Please believe me that I never meant for this to happen, for I knew if you broke the curse, I'd inadvertently hurt you. And I have." He sounded so broken. The part of me that still cared for him yearned to reach out to him.

No, I couldn't give in. I refused to let him hurt me again. "At least you understand your offense," I said.

He released a long sigh. "I do, and it pains me to no end."

His pain was nowhere near mine. Thus I refused to turn around.

"Just let me talk to you and explain."

"I don't want to hear it. I can't bear any more lies."

"They wouldn't be lies, I promise, so please—"

"Rheanna?" Briar's arrival at my side compelled me to finally turn back around. I caught sight of the tumult of emotions raging in Drake's eyes before I hastily looked away and faced Briar, who frowned at his brother before his gaze flicked back to mine.

"Is everything alright?"

"Yes, Drake is simply trying to get reacquainted, even though I've made it clear our relationship is one I have no desire to pursue."

Briar frowned at his brother. "Is he getting the message, or do I need to intervene and emphasize your wishes?"

"That won't be necessary." I gave Drake a cold look before I looped my arm through Briar's. "I'm in need of some fresh air. Might I trouble you for a stroll?"

The look Briar gave Drake was almost triumphant before it softened as he took in my puffy eyes. "Of course, my dear. Where would you like to go?"

"Anywhere except the orchard."

"Then we'll spend the afternoon in the gardens. Hopefully that will help you forget my scoundrel of a brother." He gave Drake a parting look of warning before he led me away.

I left the last piece of my heart behind, and despite the pain Drake had caused me, I still felt a twinge of regret.

THE NEXT SEVERAL days were agonizing to endure. Each time I saw Drake, the wound he'd inflicted ripped open anew, making it impossible to heal, especially when I quickly realized that despite his betrayal, I foolishly still loved him, even now. But loving him didn't mean I had to relinquish my heart to be abused again.

Briar became a much-needed distraction, but even his steadiness and kindness couldn't dissipate the pain, which was like poison, searing and relentless, made all the more unbearable when Drake refused to leave me in peace. He repeatedly tried to talk with me at every opportunity, but I ignored him...or I *tried* to, but the task was a difficult one when my heart had different ideas.

I missed him. I missed our friendship, his sweet assurances, and the long hours we'd spent together conversing, reading, and exploring the orchard. What had once been our special place was now tainted by the memory of Drake's betrayal. I avoided it—for the crisp, fruity scent of the apples now made me nauseous—though I longed for the endless hours where I used to find solace cradled within the branches of the trees.

I ached to escape into the orchard now. I pressed my forehead against the cool windowpane and looked out at the rain that kept me cooped indoors. It didn't look like it'd relent any time soon. I sighed and turned away to stare at the library. Despite the room's memories of the cozy afternoons with Drake, the familiar shelves were almost as comforting as the trees. I couldn't imagine spending a rainy day anywhere else.

As if sympathetic to my heartache, the shelves seemed to embrace me as I roamed them. My fingers trailed along the spines of the books I passed until I paused to pull one out at random. I curled up with it in my favorite armchair, the one near the window overlooking the orchard and tucked away from prying eyes.

The words of my book quickly blurred together, making reading impossible. I kept it open in my lap and rested my chin on my hand as I watched the raindrops form patterns on the windowpane, their gentle patters strangely soothing. Although my heart still ached, for a small moment I felt a brief respite, one I accepted gratefully.

"Rhea?"

Him...

My rare peaceful moment shattered. I stiffened, even as my heart flared, both with nerves and, annoyingly, excitement.

I didn't even warrant him a glance. "What do you want?"

There was a pause before he responded, his voice thick with emotion. "You."

My heart ached at his sincerity. I heard him approach and crouch beside the armchair. His nearness taunted me, compelling me to look at him. I didn't, instead hastily building up walls to protect my fragile heart; I refused to allow him to claim it again.

"I've been trying to talk with you for days, but you're rather good at evading me."

"Now that I've broken your curse, I have no reason to be around you any longer. Leave me alone."

He sighed. "I deserve that. You're normally so kind and forgiving, which means I hurt you deeply, just as I feared."

I wasn't ready for this conversation. "Please go away. I'm reading." I opened my book at random and buried myself behind it.

"Please, Rhea, don't do that. Please let me talk to you and try to explain."

I lifted the book higher, my shield against looking at him, for I was certain one glimpse into his eyes would cause me to open my heart to him once more and allow him to tell me all sorts of things I wanted to believe—pretty excuses and apologies that would lure me into another trap. But I'd learned from my mistakes and wouldn't be so easily fooled again.

"Rhea..." He tried to pull the book away from my face but

I slammed it shut on his fingers. He swore and yanked his hand away, but to my surprise he grinned crookedly, effectively disarming me. "I deserved that."

"You deserve a lot more."

"I know." Remorse filled his expression as he reached for the book and this time successfully tugged it from my hands, forcing me to give him my attention. "I need to talk to you."

"Why? So you can spin a tale that will compel me to forgive you so that you can hurt me all over again?"

"No, to explain."

"What is there to explain?" I demanded. "You *used* me, even after everything…"

He didn't deny it. Instead he gave me a rather heartbreaking look as he reached for my hand, sighing when I yanked it away. "Please, Rhea, there's more to the story. Just let me explain. Please."

I folded my arms across my vulnerable heart, a shield for his upcoming words. "Make it quick, and I want the whole truth. As I see things, you betrayed me, even after knowing how crushing my past rejections had been for me. I shared that part of myself with you, only for you to use it against me."

He settled cross-legged at my feet on the floor and leaned towards me, so close I could feel his warmth, a warmth I yearned to scoot closer to. Despite my anger, I couldn't help but hungrily watch his movements, fascinated. How strange it was to see my Drake as a real person.

"I won't deny that I initially set out to use you. Years trapped in a mirror made me bitter and I was willing to employ any means necessary in order to escape. You were insecure and gullible. I thought it'd be easy to sweet talk myself into your good graces."

I flinched, for once his usual frankness unwelcome. I took a steadying breath. "So the nature of your curse was you were supposed to get a princess to fall in love with you, and when we first met, I seemed an easy target?"

He grimaced and nodded. I tightened my jaw.

"So despite my having dedicated hours to trying to find a solution to your curse, you knew how to break it the entire time and simply chose not to tell me?"

He bit his lip. "I didn't tell you at first because I didn't think it would work if you knew, but my reasons soon changed—I was hoping there'd be another way, one that wouldn't use you."

I raised my eyebrows skeptically. "If that was your new plan, it certainly failed."

"I know how this looks," he said, his tone desperate. "But I swear I didn't mean to hurt you, especially after we became friends."

Yes, we had been friends. That's what made everything worse. It took me a moment to find my voice.

"I can't believe you used me so selfishly. I've never been in love before. It was supposed to be special." My heart constricted. I fought to keep my burning tears at bay. Crying in front of the man who'd broken my heart would only make me look more a fool.

"I can't tell you how truly sorry I am, Rhea."

I lowered my eyes, unable to look at him, certain I'd lose this precarious battle with my emotions if I did. "How can you be truly sorry when using me freed you from your curse?"

"I'd rather be trapped in that mirror for eternity than hurt you like I have."

My gaze snapped up to meet his dark eyes. Did he mean that? He *seemed* sincere, but could I trust him again after everything?

No Rhea, don't fall for his deceit again. You're stronger than that.

But I *wanted* him to be sincere. Couldn't I take a risk and trust him, one last time? Yet fear kept me back, just as it always did.

"Do you regret freeing me?" He asked quietly, almost as if he was afraid to hear my answer.

No. Even though it had all been a trick, I couldn't regret that. "I guess I can't blame you," I said hollowly. "I know how desperate you were. I was an easy target, so desperate for someone to love me that I gave away my heart too easily." And I would never make such a foolish mistake again.

"Oh Rhea, please don't think that." He rested his hand over mine and I startled at his touch, so warm and assuring; despite my reservations I didn't pull away. "Being out of the mirror has been torture, for it's marred by knowing that you falsely believe that just because everything started out as a façade, it ended in one as well."

"But it did." Hadn't it?

He shook his head. "As soon as I came to know you, everything changed." He began to rub circles across the back of my hand with his thumb, a gesture that sent a ripple up my arm and straight into my wounded heart.

"What changed?" I whispered breathlessly.

He scooted closer, his eyes wide and urgent. "Our friendship became real, only to deepen until I fell in love with you."

His beautiful words caused my heart to swell, threatening to put the broken pieces back together. I wanted so desperately to believe him, but I was terrified of allowing myself to. *Don't let him hurt you again.*

I shook my head. "You don't love me."

"I do. So much." He cradled my face, and against my better judgement, I leaned against his hand. How I wanted this.

"I still love you," I whispered. "Despite the way you hurt

me, the feelings won't go away. But I can't risk my heart again; it's too painful."

"I promise I'll never betray you again," he whispered. "Please give me another chance. Allow me to prove myself— that I love *you*, not Princess Rheanna, but my best friend Rhea."

I shook my head. "It's too late," I whispered.

"It's not. It can't be. Please." His gaze was imploring.

"Even if you're sincere, it's inappropriate for us to create a romantic relationship—I'm about to become engaged to your brother."

His entire manner hardened before softening into resolve. "I've been watching him obsessively ever since my freedom and I do believe he'll treat you well. And after what I did to you, I don't deserve you, even if I selfishly want you all the same."

"Why do you want me?"

He pressed my hands against his chest, holding them close. "Because I care for you, and I need to heal the heart you entrusted to me. Even if I'm not the man meant to cherish it, I want to return it to you whole. Please let me at least do that for you."

I searched his tender gaze. I ached for his words to be real, even as I also dreaded the possibility, for learning he loved me in the same way I loved him would make it all the more unbearable to let him go. And yet I had to. Somehow.

He hesitated before caressing my cheek, but despite having yearned for this moment when he was still trapped, my heart couldn't handle his touches anymore. I crawled off the armchair, forcing him to drop his hand. He stared up at me with a rather vulnerable, heartbreaking look.

"Thank you for your apology," I said hollowly. "But I need time." Although with my betrothal deadline only a few days away, time was a luxury I didn't have. "If you truly care for me at all, you'll give it to me. Please."

I left the library without looking back. Our conversation had wrought a subtle change in me—a sliver of hope had wriggled past my protective walls. Only time would tell if this hope would blossom or die.

CHAPTER 23

*O*ver the next several days, Drake took his quest to heart. While he respected my desire for distance, he bestowed countless subtle but caring gestures: friendly looks, encouraging smiles, rapt attention whenever I spoke, sincere compliments that extended beyond the expected polite pleasantries, and frequent concerned glances to ensure I was well.

Try as I might, I failed to ignore Drake as I knew I should. I told myself it was too late for him to earn my trust—but my heart had different ideas, for each sweet gesture slowly healed the pain he'd caused me, one broken piece at a time, causing me to hope that what had existed between us had been more real than I'd thought. But I was still afraid of allowing myself to forgive him, convinced that doing so would only set me up for more pain should he betray me again.

But as time went by, the wound he'd inflicted began to more fully heal. The softer my heart became, the harder it was to resist him. He seemed to be struggling too, resulting in many stolen glances between us, each accompanied by a soft look or a warm smile.

I took to avoiding him as often as possible, but that didn't prevent me from noticing him. His gaze was the first I sought whenever I entered a room, his voice the one I picked out from any conversation, and he was the person I thought about whenever he wasn't around. I spent hours holding his mirror when I was alone, stroking its frame.

I missed him. And despite my hurt, I still loved him, a fact which made it that much harder to resist him. It was torturous having him constantly near but for things to be so different between us. And if I did marry Briar, this would be the way things always were—where the few conversations we engaged in were overly polite and impersonal. But as much as I hated it, I knew it was necessary. In time, I was sure the pain would lessen.

Briar watched us closely, ensuring Drake didn't do anything to hurt me, and he wasn't the only one who paid careful attention—the Queen of Malvagaria did as well, the look in her dark eyes cold and conniving, as if she not only disapproved of our knowing one another, but would do everything in her power to keep us apart.

But what was the cause of her resentment? Didn't she realize I was the one who'd broken her son's curse and finally freed him? Or was it because she understood the curse's stipulations and feared my union with Briar was in jeopardy? But why would it matter which Malvagarian prince I married? Either union would forge an alliance between our two kingdoms. Something more was going on, and somehow I was at the center of it.

I wasn't the only one who received the queen's disapproval; she scolded Drake whenever he was overly familiar with me. I frequently caught them in whispered but heated discussions, which always ended the moment I entered a room, leaving little doubt that I was the subject of their arguments.

Tonight Drake was being extra attentive. I tried to ignore him and focus on my conversation with my sisters, but while my body was present in the parlor, my mind was elsewhere: on Liam's continual decline, on today's meeting with the advisors that hadn't gone well, and on my interactions with Briar which, while pleasant, had felt more forced today than usual.

Halfway through dinner I'd begun to feel the beginnings of a headache, and now it was a throbbing pain against my temples. Briar had made his concerned inquiries when I'd told him I wasn't feeling well, but since there was little he could do about it, his attention quickly became diverted.

But not Drake's. I once again sensed his gaze, and when I risked looking up, it was riveted to me, his dark eyes warm with concern. I stared for a long moment, basking in his sweet attention, before I remembered myself and hastily looked away, only to notice the queen watching us through narrowed eyes, her blood-red lips pursed in a thin, disapproving line. She turned her glare onto her son, but Drake's attention was still captured by me and he failed to notice it.

When she finally looked away, my eyes were drawn back to his of their own accord. He seemed to have been waiting for me to look at him again, for the moment I did so, he subtly tapped the side of his head, a question in his gaze.

Despite knowing the danger of such an action, my heart warmed. Briar had known about my headache only because I'd told him; Drake had known simply by watching me. This, almost more than anything else, caused me to believe his assurances that he truly did care and that he deserved my trust and forgiveness after all.

He tilted his head, awaiting an answer about my wellbeing. I nodded and his expression twisted in sympathy before it became slightly mischievous. He motioned towards the door with his chin then made a shooing motion, his silent order for me to leave.

I gave him a look that said, *you know I'm expected to stay*. He rolled his eyes and tilted his head back towards the door.

Go rest, he mouthed with a rather fierce look that clearly meant his words weren't a suggestion but an order.

I hesitated and glanced around the room. Everyone was involved in their own conversations, including Briar, giving me no motivation to stay. I finally summoned enough courage to stand. The conversations paused as everyone glanced at me.

"I'm feeling rather tired and am going to retire for the evening. Good night."

My family bid their goodnights and Briar stood to escort me, but I shook my head. He frowned and leaned closer. "Are you sure? I know you have a headache."

"I'll be fine."

He didn't look convinced, so I offered him a reassuring smile.

"I appreciate the gesture, but you don't need to trouble yourself."

He finally nodded and, after a moment's hesitation, leaned over to kiss my cheek. "Sleep well." He squeezed my hand and sat back down, and I left.

Instead of going to my room, I ventured outside. Sunset shrouded the sky, casting the dying grounds in a sheen of golden light. Although it was cold, the brisk air was soothing for my pulsing head. I wrapped my arms around myself and walked alongside the hedgerows, no particular destination in mind.

I hadn't been walking long when I heard footsteps behind me. I turned to find Drake approaching. Despite my firm warning to remain unaffected, my heart lifted anyway.

After a moment's hesitation he tentatively stepped closer, and when I made no move to pull away, he closed the distance between us.

"I wasn't going to follow you," he said. "But I was worried about you. I know you likely still need some time...unless you've had enough distance?" His look was so hopeful.

I hesitated before all my missing him and longing for him overcame my good sense. "Will you walk with me?"

He brightened and was immediately at my side, offering his arm, which I shakily took. The moment I did so, calm washed over me. Unlike all the times Briar had escorted me, it felt *right* being with Drake. Guilt prickled my heart at my forbidden feelings, but I felt them all the same.

Drake started walking, but he wasn't looking ahead, but at me, his eyes soft with worry. "I wasn't sure you would want to talk to me, but I had to ask how you're feeling. You're quite pale. Is your headache quite painful?" He looked so worried that despite my efforts, the walls I'd rebuilt around my heart cracked; it wouldn't take Drake much more to cause them to crumble completely.

I managed a small smile. "You've been paying quite a bit of attention."

"Of course. While you need distance, there's nothing I need less." He gave me a prodding look, his silent urging to answer his inquiries.

"There's no need to worry," I said. "It's only a minor headache. I'm more tired than anything."

"And yet you're outside rather than in bed?" He gave me one of the crooked smiles I loved so well.

"The cold air often helps alleviate the pain," I said.

"So you've had these headaches enough to know how to treat them. I'm sorry to hear that."

Despite his sweet sentiment, I almost sighed. Why were we talking of such trivial things? These sorts of topics had only existed between us for the first few days after I'd found his mirror. Had we regressed that much? Or perhaps discussing my headache was a safer topic than the ones that remained unresolved between us.

When I didn't answer, Drake paused and searched my gaze, as if looking for something he was desperate to find. He hesitated before enfolding my hands in his. "Your hands are cold."

He began to rub warmth into them. Each touch was both beautiful and agonizing, made even more so when he stopped rubbing my hands and began to stroke them—tracing each finger, each knuckle, and then along my palm, his look concentrated. My heart pounded almost painfully in my chest.

"I can't tell you how many hours I spent while trapped wondering what your hands felt like. Sometimes when you held the mirror, I could almost feel them. They're just as soft as I imagined, more so, in fact." He raised his gaze to mine, his full of hope. "You're not pulling away. Does this mean you've had enough distance?"

I swallowed. "I don't know." Distance was undoubtedly best, what with my impending engagement, but I wasn't sure I was strong enough to continue keeping Drake at arm's length, just as it wasn't strong enough to allow him back in.

He was so near—I could see the flecks of gold filling his deep brown eyes, count each of his eyelashes. He began stroking my hands again, each touch causing a heated shudder to trickle over me. The sensations were too much. I slowly pulled my hands from his and stepped back, feeling both more at ease putting distance between us and more lost. While he looked disappointed, he made no move to stop me.

"I'm sorry if I'm moving too quickly," he said. "Does this mean you still need more time?"

I wasn't sure what the answer was. My fear at leaving my

heart vulnerable to him made me need all the time in the world, while the other part of me missed Drake and yearned to forgive him and have him back in my life.

"Rhea?" His voice was soft with understanding.

"I'm not sure what I want. I feel...confused. You've been so kind these past several days." I wanted to believe that I could allow myself to not only trust him once more, but to open my heart again.

"Because I care for you, Rhea," he whispered.

My heart lifted and tears filled my eyes, his words both beautiful and painful, all at once. "Do you mean that?"

He gently cupped my chin, his gaze incredibly tender. "I don't say things I don't mean." His expression crumpled. "You don't believe I'm sincere, do you?"

"I *want* to." After all, he had no reason to trick me now that he was out of the mirror. "But I'm still afraid." Despite this fear, I took a tentative step forward, needing to be closer to him.

"You have every right to be," he said gently. "I promise I will never betray you again. But what good are my words if I don't have your trust? I would give anything to earn it back. I don't want you to be afraid." He looked so...*lost*, and because I still cared for him, I ached to comfort him.

"You've earned more trust back than you think," I said. "Hence I'm walking with you now."

"Although we're not doing much walking, are we?" He gave me my favorite crooked smile that caused my stomach to flip before he looked out over the grounds. "This is the first time I've been in these gardens since being free."

"But you've been free for several days," I said. "Why haven't you explored them?"

He gave me a wistful look. "I wanted to experience them for the first time with you, and now I finally have my wish. Where should we go first? The orchard?"

I stiffened and his brow furrowed at my response. "No," I said. "Not there. The orchard is ruined."

He flinched and fierce remorse filled his expression, knowing without my saying anything that he was the reason I hated my old sanctuary. "I didn't mean to ruin it for you. I didn't mean for any of this to happen. Please believe me."

If only I'd learned of his betrayal anywhere else. Then perhaps my sanctuary wouldn't be poisoned with the memory of the man I loved breaking my heart. Now I'd likely always remember his deception whenever I smelled the orchard's apple blossoms or walked within its trees.

An awkward silence settled over us, broken by Drake when he offered his arm once more. "Shall we limit our stroll to the gardens?"

I hesitated a moment before looping my arm through his, curling my fingers around his elbow. It still felt strange to touch him, to see and interact with him as a real person rather than a reflection.

Drake grinned down at where my hand rested. "I can't tell you how pleased I am to finally be out of that mirror, if for no other reason than this."

"What do you love most about your freedom?"

He began walking, taking random pathways. "So many things. Where to start?" He tipped his head back to look at the sky, tinged with ruby and orange as the sun hugged the horizon. "It's amazing being able to see everything rather than having my perspective limited to whichever angle the mirror was pointed towards. And feeling the breeze and the warmth of the sun...smelling the crispness of the air...I feel as if I've come alive. There are so many details I never noticed and properly appreciated before I was trapped."

"And you've clearly enjoyed all your meals from the eager way I've seen you eating these past several days." I blushed as I realized the admission I was making.

His grin widened. "So I'm not the only one paying attention to the other?"

My cheeks warmed further and I lowered my gaze. He gave my hand resting on his arm a soft squeeze.

"Yes, it's been nice eating again. And sleeping. I've enjoyed everything...while also not enjoying any of it, considering you and I have been estranged." He paused to turn towards me, his eyes serious. "Being with you is definitely my favorite part of being free, Rhea."

Could that really be true? As I searched his dark gaze, I realized that I believed him.

A comfortable silence settled over us as we walked the dying grounds. I kept casting him covert glances, marveling at the wonder that I was *walking with Drake* through the gardens. I noticed so many new things about him now that he was free: the way the sunlight glistened against his black hair, the firm muscles of his arm where my hand rested, the sound of his footsteps against the cobblestones.

He was *here.* With me. Despite the wonder of the moment, I realized that if anyone caught us, surely they'd disapprove, especially the Queen of Malvagaria. Which reminded me...

"Forgive my asking, but I couldn't help but notice things seem tense between you and your mother." I would have thought she'd have been happy to finally have her son's curse broken, but the opposite seemed to be true...although I kept this observation to myself.

He smiled wryly. "So you've noticed how well we get along? The contention between us is nothing new, and the underlying reason for it hasn't changed, even if the particulars have—she wants something from me and I'm unwilling to do my filial duty in appeasing her."

"What does she want from you?"

He sighed. "I can tell you if you'd like, but I'd prefer to

talk of happier things. This is the first real conversation we've been able to have since I left that mirror, and I want to take advantage of it." He rested his hand over mine, warm despite the evening chill. He slowly grinned. "I can't help but remember the last time I was in these gardens—inside your satchel as I tagged along on your walk with Briar." His mouth twisted around his brother's name.

"I remember that day well—you risked discovery with your frequent interruptions giving your snarky commentary."

"I wasn't afraid of discovery, considering Briar knew of my curse," he said. "And I couldn't resist my comments. I was jealous." He tightened his jaw. "I think that's when I started realizing my feelings for you were becoming real, which made me fully comprehend the extent of my predicament—I wanted to leave the mirror so I could not only spend time with you, but show you what a true courtship could be like. But I knew enough of your heart to know if you broke the curse and found out I'd initially used you, I'd hurt you." He sighed. "And I have. I'd give anything to go back and prevent it. But it wouldn't change our circumstances—I have no hope of courting you."

"You never had the opportunity," I said breathlessly. "From the moment we met, there's been an understanding between Briar and me."

"But when you freed me, you were determined to break it off with him. What has changed?"

So many things had…yet I realized now, as we walked together, that at the same time, *nothing* had. This was still Drake, and I loved him. Could I set aside my fears and not only forgive him, but forge the relationship I desperately wanted with him?

Drake's touch caressed my cheek, compelling me to meet his dark eyes. "If there was no arrangement with Briar, if there had never been a curse trapping me inside that mirror, if I'd never hurt you...would you have allowed me to court you?"

My heart pounded furiously. "I—" My mouth had gone dry. "I don't know." Even though I did. The answer terrified me, especially if I couldn't act on it.

"Until you do know—or even if you decide we can't be together—can't we at least be friends? Because now that I've met you, I can't bear not having you in my life, at least in some way. Please allow me to spend the rest of our friend-ship proving that I'm worthy of your trust."

My pulse was deafening. He was so near. I ached to nestle against him, to feel his arms around me, to be friends with him once more. But now I was afraid of a new pain; the closer we became, the more difficult it'd be to be around him when I was married to his brother.

Before I could answer him, as if thinking of my intended had been a summons, I heard footsteps. I turned to see Briar approaching. Too late I realized how close Drake and I had been standing and hastily stepped away.

Briar paused several feet away, arms folded and his expression serious. "Have you decided not to retire for the evening after all?" he asked me, his tone not accusing but his eyes laced with disappointment and disapproval.

"I wanted a walk before bed, and then Drake..." Shame over my actions closed my throat so I couldn't even finish. Briar turned his frown on his brother.

"So I see. I warned you to leave Rheanna alone. Your actions are only hurting her."

"I'm not hurting her," Drake protested.

"I beg to disagree." Briar came up to me and wrapped his arm around my waist to gently pull me away from Drake. As if allowing it would atone for the brief affair of my heart, I reluctantly let him. "Since you obviously fail to understand

295

the situation, let me make it perfectly clear: you hurt Rheanna, who is soon to become engaged to me, and I won't stand for any more of your interference. You've already done enough damage."

Drake stiffened. "You two are soon to be engaged? Really? It was hard to tell, considering how attentive you always are towards her."

"And you're overly attentive," Briar said stiffly. "It was a mistake for me not to interfere the moment I realized Rheanna had your mirror. I should have taken it from her and given it to one of her sisters."

"Why, so you could more easily win the prize that you're only fighting for out of duty?" Drake turned to me, his expression desperate. "He's only going through the motions, just like you are. Don't you want something more, Rhea? Something *real*?"

I winced. Briar's arm tightened around me. "Stop it, Drake, I'm warning you," he said with chilling calmness. "You're hurting Rheanna. You need to leave her alone."

Drake's hardened expression immediately softened. His gaze snapped to my teary eyes and remorse filled his own. "Rhea, I'm sorry. I didn't mean—"

He reached a hand out to dry my tears, but Briar stepped in front of me and advanced on his brother with clenched fists. "I mean it, Drake. Stop it. Don't allow your selfishness to overcome your senses. Continuing to involve yourself with her will only bring her pain. If you care for her at all, you'll leave her alone."

Drake froze before he dropped his hand and lowered his eyes. Briar glared at him.

"I liked it better when you were still trapped in that mirror." He turned a softer look towards me. "How is your headache?"

"Better," I said. "The fresh air helped."

"Would you like to finish your stroll with me? We likely have a few more minutes before darkness settles." And he held out his arm.

I stared, first at it, then at Drake's crestfallen expression. My heart pounded as I looked back and forth between the brothers, my emotions overwhelming me. I couldn't do this. I wasn't ready to say goodbye to Drake—my best friend and confidant, the man who not only truly saw me, but helped me see myself.

This is for the best, I reminded myself as I slowly backed away from both princes before turning and returning inside alone. I couldn't allow Drake to hold my heart, not when it was meant to be given to Briar.

But I don't want Briar to have my heart. The truth of these words settled over me, illuminating the path I was desperate to take. And in that moment I realized I could, for although I was a princess who had certain duties expected of me, I was also a woman in charge of her own heart. It was up to me alone to decide whom to give it to.

CHAPTER 24

I spent the entire night thinking about my time with Drake the evening before, as well as dreaming of a future I hadn't allowed myself to fully imagine: a future where I married Drake and experienced the joy that came from being loved and cherished every day. I daydreamed about having and raising children with him, of growing old together, and of enjoying daily moments similar to the one we'd experienced last evening during our stroll. The more I opened my heart up to the possibility of such a beautiful future with Drake, the more I wanted it.

Liam had told me that duty took many forms and not to underestimate the duty to one's heart. It was only now that I understood what he'd meant. Failing to follow my heart—especially due to fear—would not only hurt me, but I couldn't be a good wife to Briar if I was pining for his brother, nor could I be an adequate queen when my heart wasn't in serving the people of Malvagaria. But if I married Drake, a man who loved me and helped me be my best self, I could be the best Princess Rheanna I could be.

Dawn finally caressed the horizon. My mind made up, I

rose and quickly dressed before hurrying towards Father's study, eager to speak with him. On the way I nearly careened into Drake near the stairs, whose surprise at seeing me so early quickly softened into my favorite crooked smile.

"Good morning, Rhea. Did you sleep well?"

While I'd slept very little, considering I'd spent more of the night daydreaming about *him*, it had been a lovely night nonetheless. "Very much." I searched his dark eyes and smiled when I found what I was looking for—the tender feelings that matched my own, feelings which confirmed this morning's decision.

"May I inquire what you're doing up so early?" he asked.

I reached for his hand and laced our fingers together. "I'm going to speak with my father."

"Are you?" His grin grew. "What are you going to speak to him about?"

I ached to share the decision I'd made to choose him, but I knew that, unlike the first time, I had to follow the proper order of things. I gave him a sly smile.

"I'll tell you later."

Hope lit his expression. He raised our clasped hands to press a soft kiss along my knuckles. "I look forward to hearing all about it."

I stood on tiptoe to kiss his cheek. "I'll see you soon."

After a lingering parting glance, I lifted my skirts and practically ran to Father's study, where I knocked and shifted restlessly on the balls of my feet until he invited me in.

Father—already dressed and working, despite the early hour—looked up from his papers. "Good morning, Rhea. To what do I owe this unexpected pleasure?"

He motioned for me to sit, but I remained standing. I took a steadying breath in an attempt to calm my pounding heart. Was I strong enough to do this? *Yes, you are.* I could choose the path that was best for me.

"At the beginning of the Malvagarian royal family's visit, you and Mother promised that if I found that Briar and I didn't suit, I wouldn't be forced into an engagement. Correct?"

Father was silent for a long moment before he sighed. "It didn't work out, did it?"

"I'm afraid not."

"I didn't think so. While I can see you two have gotten closer and are both making a valiant effort, it doesn't feel right. Still, I'd admittedly hoped…you really don't think it'll work?"

"I don't."

He frowned, clearly disappointed. "And you're not rejecting him due to fear of being an inadequate queen?"

I shook my head. How freeing it was to choose another path not out of fear but out of love.

Father was silent another moment more, deep in thought. Was he upset? I anxiously searched his expression. While it was grave, the emotion didn't reach his eyes, giving me hope that he wasn't angry. As if sensing my apprehension, he gave me a tired smile and motioned for me to sit. This time I accepted his invitation, perching on the edge of my seat.

He leaned back in his own seat, in that moment looking less like a king and more like my father. "The last time we spoke, you were determined to go through with the match regardless of your personal feelings. Can you please explain what changed your mind?"

"I remembered a conversation I had with Liam shortly before he fell ill," I said. Father raised his eyebrows and I continued. "He spoke about different types of duty—a duty to one's kingdom, to one's family, and to oneself. While Briar and I are becoming good friends and I have no doubt we'd have an amiable match, I've realized going through with it would require sacrifices that I'm unable to make."

Father nodded. "Liam's counsel is wise, and I agree." He leaned back further, stroking his chin as he studied me. "I trust you've carefully weighed this decision? That you're not blindly choosing which duty to uphold over another without considerable thought?"

I lifted my chin. "I have."

He studied me a moment more before smiling softly. "Then I accept your decision. You've grown into a remarkable and wise woman, Rheanna. I trust your judgement. Allow me to speak to your mother and the Queen of Malvagaria before you tell Prince Briar."

My heart lifted. "Thank you, Father." I stood and hugged him. He stroked my hair before pressing a soft kiss on my brow.

"I just want you to be happy, Rhea."

"Thank you. I am happy." I gave him one last squeeze and started to pull away, but he didn't let me go so easily. He tugged me back, his eyes twinkling as he looked down at me.

"So, who's the young man?"

My cheeks burned. "What do you mean?" I stuttered.

He chuckled. "Come now, Rhea, I wasn't born yesterday. You've been so stubborn about going through with this arrangement until now, even though it was obvious to your mother and me that your heart wasn't in it. Something must have changed your mind...or rather, *someone*. Now who is he? I must meet him to ensure he's worthy of you."

I merely grinned girlishly. "Perhaps there is someone."

Father tipped his head back and laughed heartily. "I thought so. The moment this is all resolved, I want to meet him." He cupped my chin and kissed my brow. "Thank you for coming to speak with me. I'll take care of everything."

I kissed his cheek and practically skipped out of the study, feeling lighter than I had in weeks. I couldn't wait to tell Drake, but there was still one other person I had to speak to first.

~

THAT EVENING, my stomach was a flutter of nerves and excitement as I entered the parlor and searched for Briar. My gaze froze when it settled on Drake, who turned from his conversation the moment I entered the room to look me up and down with wide eyes and an even wider grin.

My cheeks warmed that he'd noticed the care I'd put into my appearance. I hid my shy smile as I smoothed out my favorite lilac silk gown, which I knew looked particularly flattering on me, especially with the delicate beading that laced the bodice. While Drake had seen me wear it before, this was the first time I'd done so after he'd been freed from the mirror. By his soft, appreciative look, I could tell the full effect was clearly more pleasing.

Even though I needed to speak to Briar, my heart over-ruled my sense and I headed towards him. He immediately broke away from Aveline and Elodie and met me halfway, his eyes aglow as he bent over my hand.

"You look particularly lovely this evening, Rhea."

"Thank you." But before I could say any more, Briar appeared at my elbow.

"Good evening, Rheanna." He kissed my other hand. "That dress looks beautiful on you." Despite his words clearly being addressed to me, he was looking at his brother, his expression hard...and he wasn't the only one. Father noticed the interaction and winked, while the Queen of Malvagaria also stood nearby, her eyes narrowed and her disapproval emanating from her.

Her heels clicking against the marble floor announced her arrival. "Drake," she said with her usual sickly sweet smile. "You should escort Princess Elodie to dinner tonight and sit with her."

My stomach jolted and Drake wrinkled his nose. "Princess Elodie?" He glanced towards her, and to my horror, she was watching him with a rather flirtatious look. *Oh dear.*

"Of course. She's such a sweet girl and would make a fine dinner companion. It would be prudent for you to focus your attentions on one who is actually able to receive them." She gave me a pointed look that clearly said, *and that's not you.*

Hot, fierce jealousy washed over me. Did Her Majesty intend to match her second son with my *sister*? As if she sensed my revulsion, she gave me a sidelong glance that was accompanied by a smirk.

Drake glanced back and forth between Elodie and me. "But Mother, I—"

"Rheanna is soon to be betrothed to your brother," the queen said. "As a prince you must not only be honorable, but look to your own future." She tipped her head once more towards Elodie with a challenging glare that dared him to disobey.

"Mother is right, Drake," Briar said. "Elodie would make a fine match for you."

Drake was still hesitating, clearly not keen on leaving my side. The queen's smirk vanished and her eyes narrowed dangerously.

"Go, Drake. I won't tell you again."

After a lingering look at me, he gave her a defiant scowl before practically stomping to Elodie's side. She blossomed when he arrived. The queen gave me one more dark look, a silent order to stay away from her second son, before walking to the other end of the parlor; the fading sound of her heels had never sounded so sweet.

"Finally he's gone," Briar muttered. When I didn't answer,

his look softened in sympathy. "I'm sorry you had to witness that."

I forced a smile. "It's quite alright. It was just...startling."

He frowned at the Queen of Malvagaria's back as she conversed with my parents, her usual mask firmly back in place. "It's Mother's way to be subtle in some instances and not in others. But in this, I wish she had been more discreet and less harsh towards you. Other than her interference, how has the rest of your day been? I've missed seeing you."

I scarcely heard the question; my attention was riveted on Drake, now engaged in a conversation with Elodie, who was chattering away. I suddenly became quite aware of how lovely, sweet, and charming she was; the reminder sent a sharp pang through me. Should they make a match, she would likely make Drake a wonderful wife. The thought made me ill.

"Rheanna?" Briar's impatient tone compelled me to turn back towards him. His usual patience had vanished, replaced with an expression tight with suppressed annoyance.

"I'm sorry." I offered no other explanation, even though one was desperately needed. Although Father had cautioned me to wait, Briar deserved to know I was going to refuse our match.

He sighed. "I know this is difficult for you. It is for me as well." He lightly stroked the rose he constantly wore. "But please, I don't want to lose the progress we've managed to make." So many unspoken requests filled his words, the primary one being: *You need to let Drake go if we're to have any hope of making our relationship work.*

Although I had no intention of letting Drake go, I didn't want to ruin my friendship with Briar. Which meant I needed to tell him the truth at the soonest possible moment.

Until then, I turned my back on Drake and Elodie and made a conscious effort to focus all my attention on Briar, doing my best to tune out Elodie's grating laughter. It was a relief when it was finally time for dinner, for I was desperate for a distraction. I accepted Briar's arm and allowed him to escort me into the dining room.

As he helped me with my seat, I instinctively glanced towards Drake as he helped Elodie with her own chair. As if also drawn to me despite our best intentions, he met my gaze before we both hastily looked away.

Don't look at him, I repeatedly scolded myself throughout the meal, forcing myself to keep my attention on Briar. *Not until you've formally broken things off with Briar.*

But the sound of Elodie's chatter and Drake's deep voice responding was impossible to ignore, as was the Queen of Malvagaria's smug approval as she watched them.

Ignore them.

Elodie gave another loud, flirtatious giggle, causing my hand to tighten around my fork. This wasn't working.

Briar noticed my tension and paused in our conversation to look down the table at the couple with a sigh. "He's fighting to resist looking at you just as much as you're fighting not to look at him."

"Who?" I squeaked, even though we both knew whom he meant.

"Yet despite both of your best intentions, neither of you can seem to stay away from the other." His tone wasn't accusing, more...wistful.

Guilt squeezed my chest. I was being so unfair to him; I couldn't delay the inevitable any longer. "Briar, there's something I need to tell you."

He nodded slowly, his expression resigned, as if he knew the words I hadn't yet spoken. "I expected you'd soon request a conversation. Would you like to meet privately after dinner?"

I released a shuddering breath I hadn't realized I'd been holding. "Are you upset?"

He shook his head. "It's not your fault; you feel what you feel." He sighed. "If only the original arrangement had occurred as planned."

"What do you mean?" I asked.

"Aveline or Elodie was supposed to find Drake's mirror rather than you, but because they didn't, it's making everything all the more complicated."

My stomach jolted. "Wait, are you telling me that it was part of some sort of *plan* for Elodie or Aveline to break Drake's curse?" It was so obvious. I should have made the connection earlier—of course that was the plan all along.

Briar stiffened. He cast a frantic glance towards the Queen of Malvagaria and visibly relaxed when he saw her focus was still on Drake and Elodie, her insincere smile caressing her lips.

"Forgive me, I've spoken too much." He rested his hand over mine. "We'll talk later and work everything out."

After a reassuring squeeze, he returned to his food, leaving my mind swirling. I wanted to further examine this revelation, but it was impossible to do it with the distraction that came from the envy burning through me at Elodie's shameless flirting. It became more exaggerated as the meal progressed, and Drake's polite expression didn't discourage it.

This was the worst kind of torture. Suddenly, the memory of all of Drake's sullen moods during my own courtship with Briar came flooding back. Was this what it had been like for him? It only confirmed what my heart had always known: Drake truly did care for me.

The moment the meal ended, I turned to Briar with an expectant look. He nodded and offered me his arm, but before he could escort me to our private conversation—

"A word please, Rheanna dear?"

The Queen of Malvagaria was suddenly behind me. Foreboding knotted my stomach as she looped her arm through mine and tugged me away from Briar. I instinctively glanced back at his and Drake's worry-filled expressions. Drake stepped forward as if to intervene.

"Wait, Mother, don't—"

The queen's piercing look brought him up short. "This conversation will be between Rheanna and me." Her fierce tone forbade any further argument.

Drake hesitated, but at my reassuring nod he stepped back with a sigh. The queen dug her nails into my arm, her silent urging for me to follow her.

The moment we were alone in the adjoining antechamber, she spun on me. "Just what do you think you're doing?"

"Nothing," I stuttered as I shook off her arm.

"Don't lie. You're practically engaged to my son and yet you're pining for my other one, who will soon make a match with Elodie."

Her prediction was rather premature, given the two had only shared a single meal together. But then I remembered what Briar had accidentally revealed: Elodie had been one of Drake's original targets. But why?

The queen leaned closer, surveying me with a cold look. "I admit I'm a bit surprised you're resisting this so fiercely. When I first met you, you seemed a weak-willed girl who'd be easier to manipulate, but you're proving more conniving than I initially gave you credit for. Despite this surprising twist, I refuse to allow you or my sons to ruin my carefully laid plans."

"I don't see how I'm ruining anything," I said. "All you've wanted was an alliance between our two kingdoms, so there's no difference between Drake and me making a match and him making a match with one of my sisters."

Her lips curled. "You're wrong; there's a huge difference, but I wouldn't expect you to understand what it is."

I tightened my jaw and didn't answer.

"Now, I refuse to allow your silly feelings to interfere with all my hard work," she continued. "You'd be a fool to toss aside the opportunity to be queen, especially considering how unfit you are—you're weak and *pathetic*."

Each of her words attacked my heart, but rather than penetrating it like they used to, it was as if I'd developed a shield protecting it. *I'm not any of those things; I'm so much more.*

"If you believe I'm so weak," I said, my voice shaking despite the confidence in my statement, "then you're the fool for matching me with Briar and choosing me as Malvagaria's future queen."

She smirked darkly, looking like a hunter who'd just cornered her prey, and my heart pounded wildly. "I know exactly what I'm doing, but if you choose not to believe me and interfere with this arrangement, then you'll be forced to suffer the consequences. And trust me, that is something you'll regret. Best to forget all about Drake; Briar is the real prize as he'll be king. You'd be wise to focus on making that match work. Should you not...I'd hate to see anything happen to Drake."

My heart lurched. "You can't! He's your son. You wouldn't—"

She raised a dark eyebrow. "My dear, you'd be surprised by what I could do and would do to *anyone* who stands in my way. Being trapped in a mirror would seem like child's play compared to what *could* happen to Drake...and to you."

My breath caught. Was she saying...was *she* the one who'd trapped Drake inside the mirror? The possibility was too horrifying to believe, yet by the darkness filling her eyes, I realized it was true.

Just who was this horrible woman I found myself entangled with?

She took a menacing step closer and seized my arm in her iron grip. "You'd best not try me, little princess, because if you do, I promise that you will lose. Don't gamble away the opportunity I've given you. Have I made myself clear?"

My arm was starting to throb from her sharp hold. I tried to tug away but her fingers only tightened, her fingernails biting into my skin. "Let me go."

"Have I made myself clear?" she repeated, her eyes flashing another warning. I swallowed, trying to still the panic clawing at my pounding heart.

Her nails were digging into my flesh like claws. I winced. "Yes."

She gave my arm one more menacing squeeze before releasing me and striding from the room, slamming the door behind her. I stared at it for a long moment before slowly sinking to the floor.

I tugged up my sleeve and examined the nail marks she'd left. She'd cut my skin but I wasn't bleeding, as if my body was rebelling against her abuse by refusing to give her the satisfaction of having hurt me. But nothing could stop the panic now squeezing my chest. I took several long, deep breaths.

The Queen of Malvagaria had always been rude and critical, but now she was openly threatening me. Either she didn't find me capable of doing anything about it, or else she was confident enough in her outcome to take the risk.

Or she realizes your weakness. Drake had become my weakness. The thought that she'd do something to him to get me to comply with her demands knotted my stomach. I couldn't allow that to happen.

But I was also terrified of moving forward with her calculated plan by marrying Briar. But what would happen to me if I didn't obey? What would happen to Drake? The thought of the queen doing something to him was more frightening than any thought of what she'd do to me.

Is this what true love is?

I wrapped my arms around my middle, trying to still my shaking and quench my silent sobs, but they came anyway. It was in this position that Briar found me. He knocked on the door and entered even before I could invite him to do so.

"Rheanna?"

I hastily wiped my cheeks. "What is it?"

Briar was immediately at my side to help me to my feet, his gaze taking in my bloodshot eyes. "Are you alright? What happened?" He rested his hands on my arms, his fingers grazing where the queen had gripped me. I bit the inside of my lip to muffle the sharp hiss of pain aching to escape.

How much should I tell him? I took a wavering breath. "Your mother is threatening me into marrying you."

His eyes widened but he was clearly skeptical. "But I thought you were going to break our arrangement off."

"I was, and based on her threats, your mother is clearly opposed to my decision." It frustrated me that I still didn't know *why*. It had to be for a very big reason. Why couldn't I find the missing piece?

Briar frowned. "Was she threatening you? Or was she encouraging you into a match she feels is agreeable for the both of us?"

I scoffed. "Do you truly think I don't know the difference?"

"It's not that I think that," he said carefully. "I know Mother can be heavy handed, but she wouldn't—"

I rolled my eyes. "Fine, if you don't want to hear what happened then we have nothing further to discuss." I shoved myself past him and headed for the door. Before my hand could even graze the knob, he grabbed my wrist to stop me.

"Wait, Rheanna, I'm sorry. It's not that I don't believe you, it's just—"

I spun back around to face him. "It's just *what?*"

He bit his lip. "It's just…your words contradict what I've been led to believe. I know Mother has been a bit critical, but she likes you very much and repeatedly reminds me why she finds us well suited and why you'll make a wonderful queen."

I snorted. "That sounds like something your mother would do—tell us conflicting things."

He frowned and stepped closer. "What exactly did she say to you?"

"She threatened me, and not just in words." I lifted my sleeve to show him the marks her nails had embedded into my arm. His breath hooked. For a moment he stared at them, lightly tracing them with his fingertip.

"She did this to you?"

I nodded. "She made it very clear that I'm to marry you; if I don't go through with our engagement, she's threatened to harm Drake." A tremor rippled over me and Briar embraced me.

"I'm so sorry, Rheanna."

I nestled against him, feeling safe in his arms, just as I always did. Throughout our courtship he'd become a wonderful friend, but friendship was all I felt. It was time I finally told him.

I slowly pulled away. "I've tried so hard to make it work with you, but although we've become good friends…" I paused, and Briar waited with a solemn expression. I took a wavering breath. "I'm not in love with you. I'm in love with your brother. I'm so sorry."

He didn't speak for several moments before he sighed. "I know you are. I knew the moment I saw him out of the mirror."

I gaped at him. "You did? Then why didn't you say anything?"

"Because not only were you hurt, but this was a decision you needed to make without any influence from me." He didn't look angry or even disappointed, merely resigned.

"I'm so sorry," I whispered. "I never wanted to hurt you."

"I know you didn't, Rheanna." He lowered his gaze back to my arm and his thumb carefully stroked the marks from the queen. "But now I realize there's more going on besides us and our feelings." He raised his gaze, his eyes resolved. "We need to discuss this with Drake. Tell him how you feel and what happened with my mother this evening, and I'll see if I can figure out a way to break off the arrangement. We'll meet tomorrow morning." He gently brushed away the moisture clinging to my eyelids. "Don't worry, we'll figure something out."

I sniffled and nodded. I ached to believe his assurances. I tried to push aside the fear which had been pressing against my chest ever since my confrontation with the queen. Surely between the three of us we could figure out a way out of this tangled web. But if my earlier hunch was correct in that the queen had been the one who'd trapped Drake inside that mirror, that would prove quite difficult, for it'd mean she was not only capable of dark things, but would stop at nothing to get her way.

CHAPTER 25

*M*y mind raced and my body shook as I quietly slipped out of the palace, only one destination in mind. I'd made one detour to retrieve Drake's old mirror from my room. I clutched it, finding solace in it even though it was cold, absent of my favorite companion. The queen's threats made our being together feel impossible, but we would find a way. After all, I'd chosen him.

I reached the orchard, where I collapsed beneath my favorite tree to anxiously wait for Drake. It didn't take long before the sound of footsteps approached on the crackling leaves covering the orchard floor. "Rhea?"

I whirled around. The light from the setting sun shone around him, bathing his concerned expression in ruby-gold. I leapt to my feet with a strangled sob and flung my arms around him. Taken aback, it took a moment for Drake to respond before he wrapped me in a tight embrace. We didn't say a word as he held me close. I snuggled closer, burrowing my nose against his throat. I wasn't sure whether the alluring apple scent overwhelming my senses came from him or the surrounding apple-laden trees, but it was intoxicating all the same.

I broke the peaceful stillness first. "I hoped you'd know where to find me."

"Well, this is your special place," he answered with a shrug, his eyes bright. "You being here leads me to believe that it's no longer ruined for you." He reached a hesitant hand out to stroke my cheek, his caress growing more confident when I didn't pull away. "Are you alright, Rhea? Briar told me you needed to speak with me." Hope and fear warred in his tone.

I cradled his face. "I do. There is so much I want to tell you. But first…" I stood on tiptoe and gently kissed him. He immediately responded, his lips urgent and his hand pressing against the base of my back to bring me closer.

When we broke the kiss, Drake stared down at me in wonder. "Does that kiss mean what I hope it means?"

I smiled. "It means I love you, and although things will be more complicated than I thought, I want to be with you…if you'll have me."

"Oh Rhea…" He dipped down and kissed me again. "Of course I'll have you. I love you, too."

I smiled, but it faltered as the memory of my encounter with the queen returned, reminding me that too much still stood between us. Concern filled Drake's eyes as he noticed my change in mood.

He rested his hand over mine. "What is it?"

The words tumbled out. I told him everything. Halfway through the recitation, he stiffened and pulled back to stare at me, his somber expression hardening the more he listened.

A thick, heavy silence settled over us when I'd finished, broken only by my sob. "I can't bear the thought of anything happening to you." I hugged him tightly. "What are we going to do?"

He bit his lip. "I'm not sure, but don't worry, we'll think of something. Perhaps if we have all the pieces, we can better see the entire picture."

"But would that even help?" I asked. "You know your mother better than I do; would she really follow through with her threats?"

He tightened his jaw. "She will, I'm certain of it." He sighed. "I've kept a lot of secrets from you, a fact that I deeply regret. But you deserve to know what's going on…as much as I know, anyway."

My heart hammered in anticipation as we settled on the lawn for our conversation. He reached for my hands and held them between his, his dark eyes serious.

"Mother has been talking about a union with Draceria for as long as I can remember. She was originally planning a union between my younger sister, Reve, and Liam, but when your brother Kian died and Liam inherited the betrothal with Princess Lavena, those plans were dashed. So then she talked of uniting you and Briar. But when you became engaged to Prince Deidric, she set her sights on Aveline for Briar and Elodie for me."

I wrinkled my brow. "That's a lot of planning, but for what purpose? Why is she so interested in a match that involves two princes of Malvagaria and two princesses of my kingdom?" I frowned as I considered the puzzle. "While Draceria is a wonderful kingdom, it's not particularly special in terms of its resources. Both Sortileya and Bytamia are wealthier kingdoms, and although Aiden is already married and Princess Seren is betrothed, three of the Bytamian princes remain unattached, as does Crown Prince Nolan of Lyceria, which leaves several potential matches for your sisters."

Drake shrugged. "My only guess is it's because Draceria borders our own kingdom. And while Sortileya does have more in terms of natural resources and Bytamia is the wealthiest kingdom with all its trade, Draceria has more land and a slightly larger population, not to mention the land used to belong to Malvagaria hundreds of years ago."

I frowned. "If the queen believes it should still belong to your kingdom, that would explain her interest in an alliance."

"True, but..." He frowned. "I'm beginning to wonder if her ambitions extend further than a mere alliance. You need to be careful, Rhea. I'd hate to see you hurt."

At this point, that would happen only if I lost him, which at the moment seemed inevitable. "So you're supposed to marry Elodie?" I tried not to sound bitter, but it crept into my voice anyway.

Drake smiled wryly. "Ah yes, that *was* the plan, but I've never had any interest in marrying her. I wasn't ready to settle down, and when I did, I wanted to do it on my own terms and with a bride of my choosing. I told Mother so." He sighed. "It...didn't go well. We fought, and—"

He paused for a full minute before continuing.

"After I found myself in the mirror, Mother told me that in order to get out, I'd have to have a princess fall in love with me. When she placed me in the palace tower, she told me the curse's magic would draw the right princess to me. However, rather than one of your sisters finding me like she undoubtedly wanted, *you* did. It gives me great pleasure to know that her plans were thwarted in that regard."

He managed a smile.

"At the time I didn't care who found me; I just wanted to be free, both from my confinement and her plans. So when you discovered me, I decided to trick you into falling in love with me. Obviously, things turned out differently when my feelings became real."

He squeezed my hands.

Despite his sweet words, I frowned. He'd skipped over a

huge portion of his story...namely *how* he'd become trapped in the mirror and *who* had done it, though the implication was clear.

"Drake," I asked slowly. "How were you cursed? Who did it?"

He avoided my eyes and didn't answer. Horror tightened my chest. His silence only confirmed my earlier suspicions.

"Drake," I asked carefully, "is your mother the one who trapped you in the mirror?"

He squeezed his eyes shut, his expression laced with pain. "It was an accident. I'm sure she didn't *mean* to trap me in that mirror."

I knew deep in my heart that he was wrong. Frustrated with her stubborn son, the Queen of Malvagaria had trapped him in a mirror for *years* with a curse that would only be broken if a princess fell in love with him, ensuring Drake's cooperation in creating a coveted alliance with my kingdom.

"Drake," I said gently, hooking my fingers beneath his chin so he met my eyes. "Are you sure it was an accident?"

He hesitated. "No." He said nothing more, but agony filled his eyes, his acknowledgement of the truth. My heart wrenched to see it.

"I thought so. That queen is evil."

He still didn't answer. Instead he looked unseeing out across the orchard, still laden with fruit despite it being nearly winter. I wrapped my arm around him for a side embrace, and he melted against me. We sat in this position for several minutes.

"There's something I still don't understand," I finally said.

"Only one thing?" His lips quirked up, but his attempted humor didn't quite reach his eyes.

"I don't understand why she's so insistent on your making a match with a *Dracerian* princess—from before she trapped you in that mirror to now pairing you with Elodie. Am I right to assume that she's the one who stole your mirror from my room and planted it in Elodie's?"

He nodded.

I'd thought so. "But why is she doing this? Why has she not tried to arrange a marriage between you and Princess Seren, or you and Princess Lavena? It would make more sense for her to align herself with multiple kingdoms rather than creating a double alliance with just one."

"I agree, that would be the logical thing for her to do, and Mother is usually quite logical. She must have a very good reason, one we're not seeing."

He scrunched his forehead, his gaze faraway and pensive. Despite examining all the pieces before us, we were still missing something. What was it? And how would we discover it?

I sighed. "Unfortunately, not understanding her plot doesn't free us from it. We're both still trapped—me in an engagement to your brother, and you in an inevitable arrangement with my sister."

He wrinkled his nose. "I'm not going to court your sister."

"But tonight you—"

"Forgive me for having to temporarily go along with my mother's scheme; she caught me off guard, and at the time, I couldn't see how to wriggle out of it without causing a scene. I'm sorry if my actions brought you pain."

"You have no need to apologize," I said. "We both need to do what we must until we can find a way to be together." Which now felt more impossible.

He sighed. "I just hope we can, but if Mother follows through on her threats...I will undoubtedly have to make a political match." His expression twisted at the thought. "But even if I'm forced to do so, it won't be with either of your sisters. I know how it feels to watch the one you love with your sibling—it's *torture*. I promise I'll never do that to you;

I've already hurt you too much to put you through any more pain."

Hope warred with heartache. "Your mother will never allow that."

He smiled wryly. "She won't be happy, but I'll think of something, as well as accept any consequence for my refusal —even if I have to become trapped in another mirror."

"I don't want that," I said. "Especially after all the work I expended in order to free you."

"I'm still not sure I'm happy being free; the cost was too high." He nestled back against my hair. "I'm so sorry I hurt you."

"I know," I whispered. "I forgive you. Thank you for telling me the truth."

"I should have told you from the beginning."

We fell silent. Around us the light was fading as twilight melted into night, lighting the sky with pinpricks of stars. Despite the chill that settled over the orchard, I wasn't at all cold, not while nestled against Drake, his arm wound around me and his apple-scented warmth enveloping me like an embrace. I knew we needed to go inside, but the last thing I wanted was to end this beautiful moment with the man I loved.

As the temperature continued to drop, I shivered in the brisk air. Drake rubbed my arm. "Are you cold?"

"Not enough to go back inside."

His hand moved to my back, which he began to rub soothingly. I closed my eyes, basking in his touch, trying to memorize every detail. "But if we linger too long, not only will you catch a cold, but we're likely going to get caught."

"Still so mothering," I teased, but I reluctantly allowed him to untangle us from our embrace and help me to my feet.

He wove his fingers through mine and playfully swung

our arms as we strolled through the orchard, weaving around the trees, whose fruit glowed from the branches.

Drake glanced down at the mirror I held. "You still have that?"

"I want to keep it; it makes you feel close…unless you want it back?" I prayed he didn't.

He smiled. "You can keep it as a memento of how our relationship began."

I lifted it so I could stare into it. Even though Drake had been free for nearly a week, it was still strange seeing my reflection looking back at me rather than his image. "I can't believe you used to be inside this."

"Neither can I."

I ran my thumb along the frame, the way I used to do when he was still trapped inside. He closed his eyes, as if he could feel my touch, even now.

"Are you still connected to the mirror?" I asked.

"Sometimes. I can often feel you when you touch the mirror, and occasionally I can catch glimpses from other mirrors in the palace, the way I used to before my freedom."

He paused at the edge of the orchard and wrapped his arms around me, tugging me behind one of the trees to keep us hidden from view should anyone come looking for us. There he gently cradled my face, stroking my cheeks with his thumbs.

"Don't worry. I know it feels impossible now, but we'll find a way to be together." He leaned down to kiss me, sealing his promise, one I knew would give me strength as we tried to find a way out of the queen's threats. And we would, for now that I knew his heart was mine, there was no way I was letting him go.

CHAPTER 26

The following morning I met with my father to see whether he'd had a chance to talk with the Queen of Malvagaria about breaking off my engagement. Due to his many duties he hadn't been able to, but promised to by that evening. In the meantime, I met with Drake and Briar in the sanctuary of the library, where we discussed our dilemma.

Briar listened with horror as Drake told him that unlike what Briar had been led to believe, his being put in the mirror had been deliberate.

He slowly shook his head. "I had no idea that Mother's curse wasn't an accident."

"Surprised?" Drake asked. "Especially when we both know yours wasn't an accident either—nor were our sisters'."

Briar drummed his fingers on the table, his brows knit together in thought. "If she did it before, she wouldn't hesitate to curse you again, and not just you." His concerned gaze flickered towards me. "I still can't figure out why she's so insistent that Rheanna make a match with me rather than you, but this situation is rapidly spiraling out of our control.

Perhaps we should discuss the situation with Rheanna's parents and seek their advice."

A sense of foreboding settled over me; after the queen's recent threat, I was afraid of involving them. But this was a problem that was too big for us to handle alone.

I glanced at Drake, who'd looked up at Briar's suggestion. He nodded and my unease melted away. "You're right," I agreed. "This is too important to remain silent about. I'll speak to them after tea."

"Meanwhile, I'll approach Mother with my own request to break off our engagement; I'm hoping if the decision comes from me, she'll take it better." But by the solemn look in Briar's eyes, I could tell he considered this possibility unlikely.

Later that afternoon, we sat at tea with my family and the Queen of Malvagaria. My gaze was repeatedly drawn to Drake, who sat across from me. We exchanged several reassuring smiles. Halfway through tea, I caught the Queen of Malvagaria giving me a dark, almost murderous look. It quickly transformed into a triumphant smirk, as if she still considered herself the victor in whatever strange game we were playing.

Her gaze flickered towards Elodie, sitting on my opposite side. "Why Elodie, that's a very becoming comb you're wearing. It goes splendidly with your blonde hair."

I turned to look. Elodie wore a silver comb I'd never seen before. An ornate orchard design ornamented the top, with small, bright red rubies forming the apples accenting the branches laden with diamond leaves. I'd never seen such a beautiful design, so similar to the mirror I loved in the Hall of Mirrors.

Elodie smiled brightly. "Isn't it beautiful?"

"It's stunning," I said. "Where did you get it?"

She leaned closer, her eyes bright. "Drake gave it to me.

Isn't that the most romantic gesture? I just knew he was interested."

My heart skittered to a stop. I tried to speak but my mouth had gone dry, making it impossible to form the words. Surely I'd misheard her. *"Drake* gave it to you?"

"He did. I'll tell you everything following tea."

She pulled away and returned to her plate of fruit and sandwiches. I gaped at her a moment before slowly turning to face Drake, who was watching me with concern. *What's wrong?* he mouthed.

I averted my gaze, unable to answer. I tried to return to my food but I'd lost my appetite. I quickly gave up trying to eat and instead focused on fighting the tears burning my eyes as my jealousy festered in my heart like poison.

It's a misunderstanding, I tried to reassure myself. *It* has *to be.* But I'd no sooner thought that than my mind forced me to consider the terrifying possibility: *But what if it isn't?*

No, Drake was undoubtedly only going along with the queen's plan to pursue Elodie in order to protect me. But if he wasn't...

I immediately regretted the disloyal thought, but the doubt remained as my insecurities returned to attack with a renewed vengeance.

The moment tea ended, I seized Elodie's wrist and practically dragged her from the room, ignoring Drake, who looked like he wanted to speak with me. I couldn't hear anything he had to say until I got Elodie's version of the story.

I spun on her the moment the door closed behind us in the abandoned amber sitting room, my breaths coming up short and fast. "Drake gave you that comb?"

"He did!" She clasped her hands, aglow in her happiness and utterly oblivious of the attack her excitement made on my heart. "It's admittedly a rather forward gesture so soon into our relationship, but it's so romantic that I can forgive him for it."

My stomach tightened as the same girlish grin she always wore whenever she fancied herself in love with someone filled her face.

"*Drake* gave you that comb?" I asked again. "Are you sure?"

"Of course I'm sure." She gave a nauseatingly lovesick sigh. "He's so charming and handsome, isn't he? And he says the most amusing things that make me laugh. It must be love."

"No, it's most definitely not love," I snapped. "You two barely know one another."

She shrugged. "For now. But he's been paying particular attention to me of late. Perhaps he's desirous for a match? Then I could move to Malvagaria with you. Wouldn't that be splendid?"

"No."

Her bright expression faltered. "Why do you sound so cross? Aren't you happy for me?"

I struggled to maintain my composure. "There must be some mistake. That comb can't be from Drake."

"But it is. He even left a note. See?" She pulled it out from where it had been tucked into her bodice and handed it to me. I read it with shaking hands.

Might this be a sign of my devotion and my wishes to court you. Now that I've found you, I can't imagine life without you.

Your Drake

I stared and stared and stared at it, the betrayal washing over me, burning. There had to be a mistake. Not only was the note uncharacteristically flowery for Drake, but he was interested in *me*, not *Elodie*...wasn't he? Or after this morning when we'd discussed the Queen of Malvagaria, had he realized that our union was impossible and decided to move on?

Elodie cried in alarm when I crumpled the note. "Rhea! Don't ruin my love note." She tried to extract it from my fist, but I yanked away. There was only one way to resolve this. After glaring at the beautiful comb in her hair, I stomped from the room—

—and ran right into Drake, exactly the man I wanted to see. He caught me before I could fall. "There you are. I've been looking everywhere for you. Why did you run off so quickly?" He scanned my face and his eyes filled with worry. "What is it? Has something happened?"

I severed our touch, unable to bear it until I'd resolved this. I smoothed out the note and held it up. "Did you write this?"

To my horror, he grinned and nodded. "Yes, I did."

I stared at him in disbelief. "How could you?" I knew he didn't love Elodie, at least not yet, and was undoubtedly paying her special attention only at his mother's insistence. But giving Elodie a lavish gift that set an expectation for courtship? That was too far.

His eyes widened as he took in the tears already streaking my cheeks. "I don't understand. What happened?" As he spoke, he caught one of my tears on his finger.

I jerked away. "What are you doing? Is this some sort of game?"

"I—no, of course not, I—" At that moment, Elodie emerged from the room and lit up when she saw Drake.

"Hello." She batted her eyes. He glanced at her and his face paled as he pointed to the comb in her hair. "Where did you get that?" he asked in a horrified whisper.

"From you, silly." She fluttered her eyes again. "You left it and the beautiful love note in my sitting room." She glared at me. "But Rhea destroyed it. Will you write me another?"

"*Love note?*" Drake's gaze snapped back to mine, full of understanding, remorse, and horror. "Oh…*oh*." He burrowed his hands in his hair, looking like he very much wanted to yank it out. "This is a disaster." He gently took my hand, his gentle touch softening my hurt. "There's been a misunderstanding. Let me explain, Rhea. Please."

He looked so earnest that I found myself nodding. He released a breath of relief and, still softly holding my hand, turned to Elodie.

"I'd like to speak to Rhea in private, please."

Although she looked more than a little bewildered, she nodded and left. Drake tugged me back into the sitting room, turning to me the moment he'd closed the door behind us.

"Please listen to me, Rhea." His eyes were wild in his desperation. "I know what this looks like, but I promise it's not what you think."

"Isn't it?" Tears burned my eyes, replacing my anger. "I know your mother put you up to this, but even though we haven't had a chance to work things out yet, I'd hoped you would ignore her wishes considering you and I have an understanding. Instead you went along with her scheme, toying with both Elodie's and my feelings in the process."

"But I didn't, at least not intentionally. That comb was meant for you, *not* Elodie. I designed it myself and had the silversmith make it."

For a moment I stilled, my heart flaring. Could that be true? I searched his glassy eyes, wide with earnestness.

"Really?" I asked, desperate to believe him.

"Of course. Is your trust really so fragile that you don't believe me?"

I winced at his words, even as the lock I used to keep my negative thoughts broke, inviting them back in. *Even if he's telling the truth, perhaps you're too broken to make him happy.* Was this an example of what to expect from a future together —my sensitivity and overreacting and failing to ever fully give him my trust? Because if so, that wasn't fair to him.

Drake must have realized his words had been too harsh, for he gently squeezed my hand. "I'm sorry, I didn't mean that the way it sounded. With what this looks like, you have every reason to be upset."

"I'm sorry, too."

His fingers lightly caressed my wrist, each soft touch causing the walls I'd built back up around my heart to falter. "That comb was meant for you. The orchard is our special place. You must know I couldn't possibly give that comb to anybody but you. Please, you must believe me."

His eyes were so sincere and his words calmed my heart. I believed him. "Then how did Elodie end up with it?"

He shrugged helplessly. "I don't know." But even as he spoke, I realized *exactly* how Elodie had ended up with the comb. The memory of the Queen of Malvagaria's triumphant smirk at tea returned.

"Your mother," I whispered.

Drake's eyes widened. "My mother did this?" But by his resigned tone, I knew he realized the truth.

My heart pounded furiously. While her trick with the comb seemed harmless enough, I understood the message behind it: it was a reminder that she was behind the scenes, manipulating everything according to her desires, and whenever I did anything to ruin her plans, she'd always have a countermove, which she wouldn't hesitate to implement until she'd gotten her way. The comb was only the beginning. Would the next thing she did be just as harmless...or would it be far more sinister with more dastardly consequences?

"Rhea?" Drake took a step closer and, after a moment's hesitation, caressed my cheek. "Is everything alright?"

"Your mother did this," I said again. "It's a reminder— she'll stop at nothing until she gets her way."

Drake frowned, his expression grave. "You think this is a warning?"

I slowly nodded. "A harmless one, but who's to say the next one will be the same? Someone who would curse her own son will go to any lengths to achieve her ends."

I lightly traced where the queen had dug her fingernails into my arm yesterday, marks which were covered by my gown. Drake's gaze lowered to my fingers before looking up questioningly. I sighed and lifted my sleeve to reveal the five red and jagged marks.

His breath hooked as he lightly traced over them, his touch feathery. "Did my mother do this to you?" he demanded.

"Yes, when she threatened me. She clearly really wants the match between Briar and me."

"That's no excuse to hurt you." He gritted his teeth as he severed his gaze from my arm, as if he couldn't bear to look at it. "We can't let her get away with this. Who's to say her threats will stop once she gets what she wants?"

"It seems a safer bet than to wait and see what means she'll employ to achieve her ultimate goal, whatever that may be."

Drake jerked my sleeve down and rested his hands on my shoulders. "You can't be suggesting we let her win, can you?"

I bit my lip. I wasn't sure *what* I was suggesting. The elation I'd felt after choosing Drake had now been eclipsed by fear and uncertainty. I didn't know how to navigate the deep waters in which I found myself; I felt I was drowning.

"I need to talk to my parents," I said.

We'd no sooner left the sitting room than familiar foot-steps sounded at the end of the corridor...I tensed as they paused behind us. After exchanging looks of apprehension, we slowly turned to face the Queen of Malvagaria.

She stared at us, her expression hard, before scowling at our connected hands. Too late I dropped Drake's hand; the damage was already done. She lifted her cold gaze.

"I see that despite everything I've said and done, you've both failed to grasp the seriousness of my message. Perhaps I need to make myself more clear."

She took a sinister step closer, and Drake pulled me behind him protectively with a warning glare to his mother. She laughed.

"A rather valiant gesture, Son, but you'd be wise not to interfere unless you want to find yourself trapped in another mirror. This is between Rheanna and me." Her gaze snapped back to mine. "I received a very interesting visit from Briar just before tea. It appears he's suddenly no longer interested in a match with you. I have no doubt that's *your* doing, Rheanna, because you've deluded yourself into believing an arrangement with my younger son is preferable to one with Malvagaria's crown prince."

"I don't understand why it would be objectionable," I said. "My marriage to Drake would forge an alliance between our two kingdoms and leave Briar free to marry a woman you'd better approve of as Malvagaria's queen."

She smirked as she peered darkly into my eyes. "I suppose that does seem like a reasonable compromise...except for one thing. Unfortunately, you still fail to see the bigger picture. You think much too small, Rheanna, as do my sons. I have my reasons for wanting the match between you and Briar. You would be wise to stop this foolishness with Drake." She turned her icy gaze on him. "After all, it would be awful for another curse to befall him."

Drake lifted his chin. "I'm not afraid of your threats. I will be with Rhea, no matter what it takes. For once you aren't going to get what you want."

The queen glared at her son. "Brave words from such a weakling. While it appears you don't fear threats against you, what about against...her kingdom?"

My heart beat wildly against my ribs. "You wouldn't dare."

"Oh, but I would. Might I remind you that Draceria borders Malvagaria and that our army is much more powerful than yours. For the sake of your people, it would be in your best interest to cooperate." Her lip curled. "And then there's your dear, sweet sister Elodie. Such a charming girl, so young and innocent, with such a bright future ahead of her. It would be a tragedy if anything should happen to her… or to Aveline."

Horror filled my breast. *No.*

"You wouldn't harm Rhea's sisters." But Drake's voice wavered, revealing his own fear, the same fear which left me paralyzed.

"Wouldn't I? Need I remind you about what happened to your own sisters, Drake?" The queen smirked triumphantly and lifted my chin with her finger. "I hope I've finally made my point perfectly clear so there's no more *misunderstanding* between us. You will marry Briar, and Drake will make a match with Elodie. Stop interfering and all will be well."

I glanced at Drake, whose gaze was pleading. Although I loved him and wanted nothing more than to be with him, I now realized that this decision wasn't just about me anymore; there were dangers as well as other players involved. This choice was also about what was best for my family, my kingdom, and my people. Could I be so selfish as to choose to live a fairy tale with the man I loved rather than do my duty by marrying a man who'd become a good friend?

No, I couldn't, for I wasn't that kind of person.

"I see," I said after several strained moments. The path had become clear, even if I ached to turn away from it. But I was a princess; this was what I'd been born to do. I would do my duty; I was strong enough.

"Rhea." Drake grazed my fingers with his own. "Please, Rhea."

I slowly turned towards him and my heart broke at the devastation filling his eyes; without my saying anything, he knew my decision. "I'm sorry," I whispered.

"Please, Rhea. We'll figure something out. We'll—"

I pulled my hand away from his soft touch and, with a steadying breath, turned to the queen. "Very well. I will accept Briar's betrothal." The words were poison on my tongue, but they needed to be spoken in order to protect those I loved. There was no reason to speak to my parents anymore; I knew what I had to do.

Drake stiffened beside me and my chest squeezed, but I ignored the pain as I turned and walked away before I could change my mind, feeling as if my heart was shattering all over again.

How many pieces could one heart break into?

CHAPTER 27

*T*hat evening, the Queen of Malvagaria stood up at the dinner table to make her horrible announcement. "Princess Rheanna has accepted Briar's proposal. We should formally announce their betrothal tomorrow."

I stiffened at the queen's words, words that would officially take me away from what I cherished most. From further down the table, Drake's gaze snapped up and immediately met mine, his own full of anguish. Seeing it was too painful. I hastily looked away.

Father gave me a perplexed look. I hadn't had a chance to inform him that I'd chosen to fulfill my political duty after all. I nodded rigidly, but still he hesitated before turning to the Queen of Malvagaria. "If Rheanna is in agreement, I see no reason to delay."

The queen ran her finger along the rim of her goblet and smiled widely, showing all of her glistening white teeth. "Since dear Rheanna has accepted the suit, we should draw up the final contract tonight and have the signing ceremony first thing tomorrow morning. We've delayed long enough. Is that acceptable to you, Briar?"

He hesitated and glanced sideways at me with a look that clearly asked whether I was certain it was *him* I wanted to marry. We'd already discussed our arrangement and had come to the same conclusion: no, I wasn't certain, but I knew we had no other option, not when we were all caught in the queen's snare. When he didn't answer, the queen gave him a rather dark, threatening look, but he remained unruffled, his attention riveted to me as he sought my approval.

I rested my hand over his, my wordless assurance, and his fingers slowly wrapped around mine in a clammy, awkward hold. He turned to his mother. "Yes, that is acceptable."

Drake slumped. I tried not to notice...but of course I noticed anyway. The queen's smile widened, almost unnaturally.

"Wonderful. As soon as it's official, we can begin planning the wedding. Is holding it a week from today acceptable?"

My heart jolted, whereas Mother nearly choked on her drink. "A *week*? So soon? That doesn't give us enough time to—"

"Indeed." The queen pursed her lips, as if to suppress her triumphant smirk. "Briar and I have been away from Malvagaria far too long and must return to our duties and my ailing husband. Besides, a hasty wedding would be wise considering the state of your crown prince. I'd hate for him to miss such a joyous occasion. I understand he's taken a turn for the worst the last few days." She shook her head somberly.

I sank a few inches in my seat. Liam's worsening illness, losing the man I loved...it was all I could do to maintain my composure in front of my parents. Once more my gaze met Drake's; his attention had never wavered throughout the conversation.

My heart swelled. I wanted *him*. But he was slipping away from me. He'd never been within my grasp—first because he was trapped in a mirror, then because I pushed him away, and now because his horrible mother would go to any length to keep us apart. She'd been the victor of this battle from the moment it began…it was only now that I fully realized it.

But until Briar and I were officially engaged, couldn't I have just one more moment with Drake before I lost him forever? A moment where I could briefly experience the future that had almost been mine—one where I could know the joy of having a relationship filled with love?

It might not be proper, but I would give myself that…and then I'd say goodbye.

The rest of the meal passed in a blur. Around the table the wedding planning was already underway as my parents and the queen discussed what needed to be done in order to host a royal wedding on such short notice.

The first priority was the guest list so that the invitations could be sent out immediately and the royalty from the surrounding kingdoms could arrive in time. The Bytamian royal family wouldn't be able to make it, but the Queen of Malvagaria seemed to think that was "a worthy sacrifice for uniting dear Rheanna with my son as soon as possible." I almost gagged at the insincerity behind her words, an insincerity I'd never be able to escape once I married Briar and became her daughter-in-law.

What a horrendous thought. It was all I could do to endure the remainder of dinner.

I left the table at the earliest opportunity, pausing only long enough to give Drake a *look* that I hoped silently conveyed the words I couldn't speak. I waited several corridors away, staring unseeing out the window that overlooked the orchard shrouded in the crisp autumn evening.

He arrived quickly. Without turning around, I reached my hand behind me, waiting for him to fill it. He did, weaving his fingers seamlessly with mine. His touch was both soft and firm, sending heated shudders over me.

I said nothing as I silently led him through the hallways outside to our orchard, the most natural destination for us. Once we'd safely been swallowed up by the apple-laden trees, I spun around and melted in his arms. He held me close, nestling against my hair while I burrowed against his chest. He was so warm and steady, and his arms felt so secure around me. How often had I dreamed of being held by him in such a tender way? Now that I'd experienced it, how could I be strong enough to let him go?

"Rhea?" Drake pulled away just enough to cup my chin and tilt my gaze up. It was only then I realized I'd been crying against his shirt. I didn't answer as I reburied myself back against his chest. His arms tightened around me. "I can't bear the thought that I'm about to lose you."

"You haven't lost me, not even when the marriage goes through; you'll always have my heart. The only thing we've lost is more moments like this."

He leaned down and softly kissed my tears away. "I hate feeling so helpless as you're forced to make a decision that's hurting you. I wish I could save you." His expression twisted in despair. "You just can't marry Briar. You deserve more. There has to be a way out of this."

"I'm a princess, and as such I have a duty to my kingdom and my family." It didn't make my duty any easier. I sighed and nestled myself closer. "I'm sorry I wasn't strong enough to choose you."

He stroked my hair. "You did what you felt was best." He was silent a moment, so that the only sound was the wind rustling the branches above us and his steady heartbeat against my ear. "What was it that made your decision?"

"Your mother's threats of your kingdom coming to war against ours. How could I sacrifice the welfare of my people for my own happiness? Or risk your mother harming my sisters? I could never forgive myself if anything happened to my family. Accepting the match with Briar is the only way to protect all that I hold dear."

Drake sighed. "I wish I could assure you that my mother didn't mean her threats, but I have no doubt she's serious, as I'm sure you realize. You're such a brave and selfless person, Rhea."

I didn't *feel* brave or selfless, not only because my heart ached for his but because I'd never been so terrified of a decision in my life.

"I know he doesn't love me, but will Briar—" I couldn't even finish, but Drake sensed what I hadn't said in the way only he could. He sighed as his arms tightened around me.

"Briar and I have our differences, but he's a good man and will do his best to be a good husband."

"How do you know?" I whispered.

"I know my brother—not to mention he said as much when I threatened him earlier after you made your decision. He promised to care for you." While he seemed relieved over that fact, I still heard the heartbreak in each of his words.

"Do you think he could ever love me?"

"I do," Drake said. "You're incredibly easy to love. And while he may not love you in that way yet, I know he cares for you and considers you a good friend. You'll win him over in the end, because while my brother is many things, he's no fool."

So it would likely be an arrangement like my parents had —one where love had grown in time. I hoped I could learn to love him in return…if I could ever let go of the feelings I felt for Drake. I'd need to in order to embrace my inevitable future and make it bearable for all of us.

"I will strive to be a good wife for him," I whispered.

Drake flinched. "I know you will." He took a steadying

breath. "I don't want to speak of him anymore. I want to enjoy this last moment with you before everything else is taken from us forever." He caressed my cheek. "I wish Mother had chosen one of your sisters instead of you. Then I could marry you."

I smiled. "You want to marry me?"

"I'm sorry, I probably shouldn't admit such a thing. It'll make it so much harder."

"I still want to hear the words all the same. Please, Drake."

He managed a soft, crooked smile. I tried to memorize both it and the tender look in his dark eyes, so that I could always remember this moment and draw strength from it in the years to come.

"If you were free...it would be my greatest honor to marry you, my Rhea."

My heart both swelled and broke further at his words, but I didn't regret hearing them. I cradled his face. "If I were free...I'd gladly accept your hand."

Despite this not being a real proposal, his grin was joyful as he rested his forehead against mine. "Thank you, Rhea." But the pain in his eyes marred his smile.

Was I strong enough to go through with this? I met his gaze, full of fierce, unquenchable longing for what we couldn't have. He was so near, mere inches away, yet he was as far out of my reach as if he were within the mirror again. I longed to bridge that distance, to kiss him one last time, but I was certain that doing so would make it impossible to let him go.

I forced myself to pull away. The moment I left his arms, I felt naked without them wrapped tenderly around me and yearned to return to his embrace. To distract myself, I glanced up at the tree, whose fruit-laden branches looked perfect for climbing.

"We made plans to climb these trees when you were free from the mirror. Do you remember?"

Despite the sadness still filling his expression, he managed a smile. "I thought princesses didn't climb trees."

"Perhaps not, but future queens do."

His grin became mischievous. "I warned you I'm an expert tree climber. I bet I can climb higher than you."

"Even though I'm in a dress, that's a challenge you're going to lose."

He chuckled and stooped down, cupping his hands. "I'll give you a leg up."

"Confident in your success enough to help me?" I stepped into his hand and allowed him to lift me until I reached the lowest branch. I pulled myself into the tree and climbed a few feet higher before I glanced down. Drake had already pulled himself up and was climbing rapidly. I gave a soft shriek and scrambled higher before being forced to pause when the branches caught in my hair.

"I'm right behind you," Drake said playfully.

I made the mistake of risking another glance down at him and nearly swayed. The height was dizzying; I'd climbed higher than I'd thought. I squeezed my eyes shut and pressed my forehead to the branch I held.

Drake paused a few branches above me. "Are you alright, Rhea?"

"It's higher than I remember. Perhaps I was braver when I was younger."

"I disagree. You're braver now, although it's a different kind of bravery." Drake started to climb lower so our eyes were level. "Do you want to climb down?"

"I don't want to leave." Not yet. For despite the height, it was almost exhilarating being up here, doing something rebellious.

He grinned. "See? You're a brave girl. If you can climb trees, you can do anything."

Including marry Briar.

I inched a few branches down and Drake followed. We settled on the same level. The confining space forced us to sit close together so our legs touched, but I made no move to pull away and neither did he.

The surrounding branches cradled us in a cocoon. The thick branches masked not only the ground below but also the sky, making us separate from the real world, just for this moment.

"It's like we're in our own world up here."

"Then perhaps we can stay here; we have enough provisions to do so." As he spoke, Drake plucked an apple and began to toss it from hand to hand.

"Eloping to an apple tree, what a romantic thought." If only we could really do that. I leaned my head back against a branch to stare up at the cloud-shrouded sky that poked through the twisted canopy above us. "I'll miss this orchard when I leave. What's Malvagaria like?"

"Unlike the other kingdoms whose geography is primarily one type of landscape, it's quite diverse, covered in mountains, forests, and meadows. You'll like it."

"And are the gardens of the palace really enchanted?"

Drake slowly grinned. "Yes. They're mischievous, but I think they'll like you."

I raised an eyebrow. "They don't like everyone?"

Drake chuckled. "I'm afraid not. They don't like me much. Well, some of the plants do, but others..." He trailed off. I ached to hear more, to know all about Drake's time in the gardens where he'd grown up. There was still so much I didn't know about him, so many stories that, due to our circumstances, would forever remain untold. "They'll like you," he said again, as if he'd misinterpreted my frown and was trying to reassure me.

As lovely as my new home sounded, I knew I'd like it a lot more if I could live there with him instead. But I forced myself to push the thought away before it could take root. It wouldn't do to focus on what I couldn't have; instead I needed to focus on the beautiful present while it lasted.

Drake removed a knife from his boot to slice the apple he still held in half. His hand brushed mine as he handed me a portion. "You didn't eat much at dinner after the betrothal announcement."

I accepted the apple half gratefully. "You were paying me a lot of attention."

"Always." He started to withdraw, but I seized hold of his hand and rested it in my lap so I could slowly stroke each of his fingers. His breath hitched but he made no move to pull away.

"I still can't get over the fact that you're real and I can now touch you." At least for now. The thought was torturous.

"I can't tell you how long I wanted you to touch me." His fingers began caressing my hand, stroking all along my palm and causing me to shiver. "It didn't take long to see how remarkable you are, to want you because of who you are rather than what you could do for me."

My smile grew, as did the assurance from his words—I was worth caring about.

He reached out to lightly trace my smile. "I hope you have many reasons to smile in the future. If only I could be the one to bring them to your face."

"You are right now." I took a bite of the apple. Its sweet, crispy flavor danced on my tongue. "Or perhaps it's this apple making me smile. It's delicious. Are you still curious what an enchanted apple tastes like?"

He grinned rakishly in an endearing way that caused my stomach to flutter. "Perhaps I should see for myself."

And before I could register his actions, he scooted closer, cradled my face, and brushed his lips against mine. I didn't respond at first, paralyzed by the sensations his light kiss caused me to feel.

"Please Rhea," he murmured as he pressed his lips against the corner of my mouth. "Please choose me, even if it's just for this single moment."

I responded immediately. This time I was the one to pull him into the kiss, a kiss that was filled with all the yearnings I felt for him. The apple half slipped from my hand as I wound my arms around his neck and burrowed my fingers in his hair, while his heated touch pressed against my back, bringing me even closer.

The kiss was so tender, so sweet, filled with Drake's love. In this kiss I felt him put the broken pieces of my heart back together. It was such a beautiful feeling, made even more so by how safe and cherished I felt in his arms. I longed to stay here forever.

But it wasn't meant to be. Even so, I was grateful for this moment, one I would look back on as one where I fully experienced true love, no matter how fleeting.

We broke our kiss and for a beautiful moment we merely stared at one another. He stirred first, releasing a long sigh as he nestled against my hair. "I don't want to let you go."

"Neither do I. But we must."

Yet I made no motion to pull out of his embrace. Instead I lightly traced his face, running my fingers along his jawline before lingering around his dark eyes. I leaned in and lightly kissed him again, both needing another one and wanting to delay our inevitable parting. He returned it earnestly, so much so I feared saying goodbye would be utterly impossible. How could I lose this? It was too special.

But I was a princess with a duty. This time, when our kiss finally broke I knew I wouldn't be getting another one. By the emotion in his eyes, he knew it, too. He released me with obvious reluctance and together we climbed out of the tree, Drake frequently pausing to help me over tricky areas. He hopped down first and reached up to lower me to the ground, not releasing me even after I found my footing. There he stared into my eyes with such a smoldering look I felt dizzy. I clutched his arms for support and, overwhelmed, I looked away.

My gaze settled on the tree we stood beside, and I realized it was the tree where I'd carved my name. I reached out to stroke *Rheanna* with my fingertip, then the heart surrounding it.

Drake's jaw tightened. "Are you going to carve Briar's name in there?"

I hesitated. "Perhaps one day." When our marriage came to mean something.

He sighed and wrapped his arms back around me, pulling me against his chest and resting his forehead against mine. "Oh, Rhea. How can I let you go?"

His plea was making it so much harder for me to do the right thing, and I *needed* to. "You must," I said. "After my engagement tomorrow, it'll be inappropriate for us to be together in this way."

"I know." He sighed, sounding so defeated. He straightened to caress my cheek. "Will you be alright?"

I nodded.

"And you know that no matter what happens, I'll always care for you?"

My throat choked with tears and I managed another nod, unable to form the words to make the same promise.

"And"—he swallowed—"I'll find a way to leave Malvagaria. It'll be easier for you if I'm not around."

My eyes burned. I didn't want him to leave, but I knew it was for the best. I started to pull away but he seized my hand.

"Wait, one more thing."

"What is it?" I asked breathlessly, my hold instinctively tightening around his.

"I want you to know I believe in you."

My breath caught and the tears I'd been fighting finally escaped.

"You're an amazing woman. Despite all you've been through, you've developed a quiet confidence in yourself that will see you through anything. Please never forget that."

His words warmed me and I realized that I not only believed them, but I now believed in myself. While I couldn't deny I was frightened of marrying Briar and leaving my home to live in an unknown kingdom to become the Queen of Malvagaria, I was determined to face these fears bravely. And although I knew I couldn't have Drake, I would always cherish the memory of him and the beautiful knowledge that he loved me dearly, just as I loved him.

You're worth caring about. That truth would give me the strength for what was to come.

"Thank you, Drake. I'll never forget you."

"Nor I you."

We didn't say goodbye. He tenderly kissed my brow and then he released me. I kept hold of his hand until the last possible moment, feeling an immediate sense of loss the moment I let him go. After one final look into his soft, dark eyes, I turned and left the orchard.

Everything was going to be different tomorrow. I prayed that when that moment came, I'd be ready to face it.

CHAPTER 28

"*I* can't breathe! It's too tight." I gasped for air as I slumped against the vanity, my breaths short and quick as my maid tied up my corset.

"I'm so sorry, Your Highness, your corset is as tight as it usually is. Should I loosen it?"

"Please, and hurry."

I struggled for breath as the maid quickly loosened the corset, but it did little to ease the tightening in my chest. *I'm having a panic attack.* All the emotions of the last few days flooded my mind—my imminent engagement within the hour, the fear of what the queen would do if I went against her wishes, and my heartbreaking farewell with Drake last evening in the orchard. It was all too much.

The maid watched my continued breathlessness with wide, fear-filled eyes. "You're quite pale, Your Highness. Shall I fetch the physician?"

I shook my head. "I'll be alright. I just need a moment." *Get ahold of yourself, Rhea. This path may not be of my choosing, but I can make this work...I will make this work. Be brave.*

With each of my assurances, my breathing gradually

calmed—to my maid's fierce relief. I straightened and nodded, permission for her to finish helping me dress.

A soft knock sounded on the door just as she finished arranging my hair. Elodie peeked her head into the room. "Is this a bad time?"

"Not at all, I just finished getting ready."

Elodie approached, smiling as she took in my appearance. "You look lovely. Except..." She tilted her head from side to side, studying my coiffure. "Hmm, it's not quite right. May I?" She stepped forward and fiddled with my hair with exaggerated concentration; something was clearly on her mind.

Sure enough, the moment the maid left and we found ourselves alone, she made a show of looking around before leaning close and lowering her voice to a whisper.

"How long have you and Drake...?"

I stiffened. I'd been determinedly trying not to think of him ever since we'd said goodbye last evening, which meant I'd thought of nothing but him, both during my restless night and this morning as I prepared for my betrothal.

"Whatever do you mean?" I asked shakily.

Elodie put her hands on her hips and gave me a *look*. "Don't lie; you know exactly what I'm referring to: you and Drake have a *tendre* for one another."

I stared at her. Considering she'd been doing nothing but flirt with him since his arrival, she was taking this revelation quite well. If I didn't know better, I'd say she genuinely seemed happy for me. I scrunched my brow. But *why*?

She bounced on the balls of her feet. "Do give me all the details. How did it happen? *When* did it happen? For you two have practically ignored one another since his arrival." She brightened. "Oh! Was it love at first sight and you only *pretended* to be at odds with one another in order to keep your secret, when in reality you've been engaging in clandestine meetings?"

I continued to stare. "How did you find out about us?"

Her look became mischievous. "As the youngest, I've had many opportunities over the years to develop the talent of spying and eavesdropping in order to find out my elder siblings' secrets, and this was no exception."

I fidgeted impatiently. "And...?" I prompted.

She smirked. "Last evening I fancied watching the sunset, so I took a stroll through the grounds. As I was enjoying the lovely autumn weather and the apple-scented breeze of the orchard—"

The *orchard*? My heart sank as I saw exactly where this tale was going.

"—an apple suddenly fell from one of the trees." Her eyes widened dramatically. "I was quite shocked, to say the least. Apples don't merely fall from enchanted trees, and it wasn't just *any* apple." She leaned closer. "It was an apple half with a bite taken out of it, meaning it had been dropped by someone. So I crept closer and peered up into the boughs in order to investigate...and discovered my elder sister who's soon to be engaged *kissing* her future betrothed's younger brother."

I groaned and buried my face in my hands, as if I could bury myself and my shame alive.

"Can you imagine my delight at this juicy turn of events?" Elodie, oblivious to my discomfort, gushed. "It's like a twist found in a romantic novel—a princess kisses her future brother-in-law on the eve of her engagement."

My cheeks burned as remorse grew, and too late I realized just how wrong my behavior had been. How could I have done such a thing? I'd been so desperate for one final taste of true love that I'd betrayed the man I was soon to marry, rationalizing my actions as being alright because we weren't yet betrothed and he knew of my feelings for his brother. But it *wasn't* alright. Guilt tightened my chest.

"Rhea?" Elodie rested a light hand on my shoulder. "Are you alright?"

I didn't answer.

"I was just teasing you. I'd never tell."

"Even if you keep silent, it doesn't change the fact that that's exactly what I did." Which meant I had to confess and apologize to Briar. He not only deserved to know—although I doubted he'd be surprised—but I needed to do all I could for our marriage to start off on as firm a foundation as possible.

I looked up with a sigh to find Elodie watching me with concern. "What's going on between you and Drake?" she asked. "Kissing indicates you two have quite the history."

"Nothing is going on," I said stiffly. "Not anymore."

"Do you love him?" Elodie asked quietly.

I tightened my jaw. *Don't say the words.* "It doesn't matter, I'm not *supposed* to feel anything for him."

"Why not?" she asked. "You feel what you feel. If you love him, can't you two be together?"

Why was she trying to sway me from my chosen course? It would only make doing the right thing more difficult. "No, we can't. Our relationship is complicated and impossible, so we've said goodbye."

I didn't want to talk about this. Besides, the clock on the mantle revealed I was due in the throne room for the official signing of my engagement contract. I glanced into the mirror for one final check of my appearance. I wore a gown of dark blue silk, with sapphires donning my neck and ears, and my diamond tiara atop my elegant updo. I truly looked like a future queen.

I nodded to myself and turned away. It was time. I headed for the door, both eager to get away from Elodie and her romantic ideas and wanting to get the inevitable over with as soon as possible. But my hand had no sooner grazed the knob than Elodie seized my wrist, compelling me to stop.

"Your relationship isn't impossible," she said. "Love never is. Drake is a fine match. Marrying him will provide an alliance with Malvagaria, just as marrying Briar would. There's no difference."

"It's more complicated than that." I didn't have the time or strength to share the reasons.

She nibbled her lip anxiously, but she wasn't so easily dissuaded. "No, it's not. You must tell our parents you're in love with another prince. They only want you to be happy."

"I know they do, but there's more going on than you realize. This isn't just about Drake and me." I squeezed her hand. "I appreciate your concern, but you have to trust me when I say that I have to do this."

Elodie lowered her eyes in defeat. For a moment she said nothing, then all at once she spun around, her skirts swaying as she left my room. I gaped at the door but barely had time to wonder at her sudden departure before she returned, holding...

My breath hitched. In her hands was the comb from Drake. She handed it to me with a sad smile. "It was meant for you this entire time, wasn't it?"

My throat clogged with tears as I nodded.

"I'm sorry I flirted with him," Elodie said. "I didn't mean—"

"You didn't know." I cradled it in my hand, tracing my thumb across the ruby apples embedded into the comb's orchard design.

"You should keep it," Elodie said. "To remember him."

I slowly raised my gaze to hers. "Regardless of who it was intended for, you ended up with it. I can't take it from you." I started to hand it back to her, but she closed my hand around it.

"It's yours," she said. "Besides, I want my own token of love, not one stolen from another."

I lifted my eyebrow. "You're not upset Drake doesn't love you?"

She dismissed my words with a wave of her hand. "There are other princes and even more noblemen. The Duke of Eldenwood's son is quite handsome, isn't he? As is the Viscount of Brookshire. I'll find my own match in a few years; surely I'm too young to marry now, and I couldn't possibly marry before Aveline." She smiled sweetly and I realized she harbored no resentment towards me. Remarkable.

I embraced her. "Thank you."

She nodded, and after one final reassuring squeeze, she left me alone. Even though I knew I was due downstairs, I lingered, holding the comb close. Despite it being nothing but a painful reminder, I went to my jewelry box and locked it away, both to keep it hidden and to keep it close. As I turned away, my gaze settled on Drake's mirror resting nearby. That would be another token I'd always keep to remember this time from my life—a time when Drake had helped me see my worth, a sweet memory too precious to ever forget.

A knock sounded on the door, tearing me from my reverie. I opened it to reveal Mother. While her eyes were sad, she had a smile for me. She took my hands in hers as she looked me up and down. "You look beautiful, dear. What a wonderful woman you've become. I'm so proud of you."

"Thank you," I managed.

"Are you sure you're ready for this?" she asked. "It's rather rushed, and I'm concerned you don't really want to go through with this, considering you recently rejected the proposal and told us you're in love with another. Are you certain—"

"I am. Briar is my friend." Not to mention Drake had assured me he was a good man who would do his best to care for me. It would be enough.

Mother searched my eyes, desperately seeking my sincerity.

"I can do this." Especially since this was the course my own parents had chosen years ago. "I'm ready to." Delaying it any longer would only make it worse. I'd chosen my path; now I needed to walk it.

She nodded, giving my hands a gentle squeeze. "I'm proud of you, as is your father, and…Liam. I just came from visiting him."

My heart tightened. With my preparations this morning, I'd missed my morning visit, and I'd been desperate to hear his thoughts about the situation.

She saw the regret in my face and smiled reassuringly. "He understands why you couldn't come, so he told me to tell you he supports your decision and wishes you all the best. Isn't that sweet of him?" She forced a smile that didn't quite reach her eyes.

I was almost afraid to ask my next question, but nowhere near as desperate as I was to hear the answer. "How much longer?" Although if his condition was as it'd been when I'd seen him yesterday, I already knew the answer.

Mother's tears escaped. "Not much longer, I'm afraid. I'm just trying to enjoy as many moments as we have left, while giving him and Anwen space. The poor dears have only been married for a few months—"

Her words were swallowed by a sob. She hastily wiped her wet eyes while I bit my lip to keep my own tears at bay. I couldn't cry. I had to get through the betrothal announcement with poise and dignity befitting my station.

She squeezed my hands again. "Are you ready?"

I took a fortifying breath and nodded. *I can do this*. Even though at the moment the task looming ahead of me felt impossible, I knew I possessed the inner strength to move forward. I walked out of my bedroom and into the future with my head held high.

∾

I WATCHED as Briar looked over our engagement contract that dictated the details of the alliance between Draceria and Malvagaria our marriage would bring. I studied his expression as he read—the concentration lining his brow and the serious set of his mouth. He wasn't unattractive by any means, but he was so stoic, as if he felt it his duty to keep his emotions masked. But over the course of our courtship, I'd come to appreciate his steadiness and quiet kindness.

I searched my heart. Could I let go of my feelings for Drake and learn to love this man? I knew it wasn't a question of *if* but *how*, for I was determined to be a good wife to him. As my friend, he deserved nothing less.

After what must have been Briar's third perusal, he finally poised the tip over the signature line, pausing only to give me one last searching glance. Was I certain? I nodded. He nodded back and signed the contract, his expression blank, and handed me the quill. I shakily took it and approached the desk where the contract that would change my life forever lay.

I'd read it several times in the past few days, but it no longer matter what it said; I had no choice but to sign it. I felt the heat of everyone's gazes upon me, particularly *his*— Drake's—one that was both sorrowful and caressing. The feel of it made it impossible to move my hand. I needed to let him go, for the moment I signed my name to this agreement, everything would change.

My heart hammered as I rested the tip of the quill on the

parchment. *You're doing the right thing. This is the only way to protect your family and your kingdom.*

With a shaky hand I signed my name; the dagger in my heart twisted with each stroke of the pen. The moment I finished, two overwhelming and conflicting feelings washed over me: triumph that I'd faced something difficult and pushed forward, and…emptiness.

I dropped the quill. It was done.

Father stood next to the smirking Queen of Malvagaria. "We are pleased to announce the official betrothal of His Royal Highness Crown Prince Briar of Malvagaria to Her Royal Highness Princess Rheanna of Draceria. May their union bring peace and prosperity to both our kingdoms."

Briar extended his arm and I wove mine through his so that together we could face the crowd of our family and the nobility that had joined us. I smiled and nodded graciously at their applause, all while doing everything I could to avoid Drake's gaze.

Be strong, Rhea.

My smile tightened as we were surrounded by well-wishers who extended their congratulations in cheerful tones that didn't match the despair filling my heart. My cheeks quickly began to hurt as I kept my fake smile plastered in place.

Briar said very little. He merely nodded to those who greeted us with his usual stoic expression, but whenever he glanced at me, his gaze would soften. This small reassurance gave me the strength to be brave. Though this marriage was not of our choosing, together we'd get through it.

But my courage faltered the moment it was Drake's turn to extend his congratulations, forcing me to stop avoiding his eyes and look at him. The moment I did, my heart constricted.

Although he tried to *appear* indifferent, I knew him well

enough to see the devastation in his features as he looked at me as if he'd lost something precious. The thought both warmed my heart and crushed it.

Briar's eyes narrowed in warning. Drake attempted to school his expression as he bowed over my hand. A pleasant shudder rippled over me that became almost unbearable when he brushed a kiss along my knuckles.

"Congratulations, Rhea. I wish you all the happiness that you deserve." His tone was hollow, his eyes filled with pain as he stared longingly at me for a long moment. I returned his look, hoping he could see how much I cared for him. In that moment I ached to remember all the tender emotions we'd shared together one final time, but all I felt was a sense of loss.

He finally severed his gaze and glared at Briar. "You better be good to her or you'll answer to me." It was impossible to mistake the threat in his words. Even now he was determined to look after me.

Briar's expression, if possible, became even more serious. "I will."

Drake squeezed my fingers—a reminder that he cared and to be strong—before he let me go. I yearned to snatch his hand back but forced myself to resist the impulse. After one final look of longing, Drake quickly bowed and left. My heart tightened with each step he took away from me and the future we might have had together.

Come back. This was so much worse than yesterday's goodbyes; this was torture. My chest tightened and my breaths came up short. I felt moments away from losing it.

Briar must have sensed this, for he expertly led us away from our well-wishers to an alcove that masked us from the view of the crowd. "Are you alright, Rheanna?"

No, I wasn't. How could I be? Seeing Drake had nearly undone me completely. My eyes burned; I was near tears.

353

"I'm sorry," I said, pressing my hand to my heart as if the gesture could help stave off the pain. "I'm sorry. I'm so—"

Briar wordlessly handed me his handkerchief so I could wipe my eyes. He examined my face, worry filling his dark eyes. "It's alright. I know you still love him."

I squeezed my eyes shut. This was humiliating. "I'll try to stop. I promise. I'll be a good wife for you." I tentatively stole a peek at his expression, as serious as ever. He gave a curt nod.

"I know you will, Rheanna. And it's my duty to be a good husband for you in return. You're a sweet and capable woman, and I feel we've become friends."

His tone was questioning, seeking confirmation, and my heart ached that due to my feelings for his brother, he even needed it. I knew this wasn't easy for him either, but I was so grateful for his willingness to sacrifice the possibility of finding his own love match in order to help me. I silently vowed to do my part to make our union a wonderful one.

At my nod, he relaxed and stepped closer, lowering his voice. "I know this isn't the arrangement you wanted, but I hope we can still make it work. I'll do all I can to treat you well and to protect you throughout our marriage. My mother won't hurt you."

Fear squeezed my throat, but I forced myself to take a wavering breath and nod. As terrifying as the conniving queen was, I knew I could rely on Briar.

He hesitated before whispering, "And I'll keep Drake away. It'll be easier for all of us."

My first impulse was to plead for him not to do that, but I knew I couldn't. *This is for the best.* I managed a nod. He pressed a kiss to my brow—at which I felt nothing—and we exchanged small smiles. It wasn't often I saw Briar smile, but I liked it, especially the crinkles it caused to appear around his eyes...crinkles similar to Drake's, but in this instance, the reminder wasn't painful. A sliver of hope budded within me. Maybe this could work after all.

I stood on tiptoe and brushed a kiss along his cheek in return. When I pulled away and looped my arm back through his, I caught sight of Drake watching us, all attempts to hide his distress vanished. My heart cracked. Briar reached for my hand and gave it a reassuring squeeze, a silent acknowledgement of my pain.

Despite my wrenching emotions, I forced myself to turn away from the man I loved. I'd do the right thing. But looking away caused me to notice the Queen of Malvagaria watching us from the other side of the room, her look triumphant. My blood chilled, killing the hope that had been planted there, and I knew that despite her having achieved the first step in whatever her ultimate plan was, this wasn't over.

CHAPTER 29

J paused with my hand on the knob of Liam's door. With all the hasty wedding preparations, it had been several days since I'd last visited with him, and I was terrified of the state I'd find him in.

But I had to see him. Mother had warned me this morning that Liam was fading quickly; the end was near. It was no longer a matter of *would* he die but *when*. After the wedding I'd leave for Malvagaria, making this possibly one of the few remaining moments I'd have with my dear brother. I wasn't ready to say goodbye.

I took a steadying breath and knocked, loud enough that he would hear it but quietly enough that it wouldn't disturb him should he be asleep.

"Come in."

Alarm filled me at Liam's voice, much weaker than it'd been during my last visit. I braced myself for the worst, but when I pushed the door open and entered the room, my heart constricted—he was far worse than I'd imagined.

I stared. I felt like I'd traveled back to the last time I'd seen Kian. Just like in my nightmare, Liam lay lifeless on the bed, pale and gaunt, a mere shadow of his former self. My eyes burned and I wanted nothing more than to run out of the room and cry, but I needed to be brave for Liam. Losing it wouldn't make this any easier for him, and I had so few remaining chances to do anything for my brother that I wasn't going to waste this one.

His eyes settled on me and he forced a smile that was only a fraction of his usual wide grin. "There's my favorite sister. I was hoping you'd visit me soon. Come tell me about your wedding plans."

He weakly motioned to the empty chair beside his bed. The other one was occupied by Anwen, who clutched his hand with a wide-eyed, glassy look, like she was permanently on the brink of tears.

I hesitated before sitting down. "Is this a bad time?"

She rigidly shook her head as her hold on Liam's hand tightened, as if she were afraid my arrival would force her to let him go.

"Not at all; things are pretty uneventful at the bedside of Crown Prince Invalid," Liam said, his tone weak but still containing his usual good humor. "It's likely a bad time for you, considering you're soon to be a married woman and will be too busy for your beloved brother."

"I always have time for you." I perched on the edge of the chair and took his other hand, which was cold and clammy. He squeezed mine weakly.

"Thank you for coming. Now, how are the wedding plans? Exciting? Or, as is more likely, dull?" His eyes widened dramatically. "Wait, I know what you're really up to: you're visiting me to escape the tedium, considering I'm such stimulating company." He winked.

I managed a smile. "The latter."

"Uh oh, I thought so. Do give me all the details."

I raised my eyebrow. "You want to hear about my

wedding plans? Is your sickness addling your good sense?" I tried to sound teasing but the effort fell flat. I was still rewarded with the corners of his mouth twitching up, a sign of his amusement even though he was too weak to smile any wider.

"I just want to know how things are going for you. Being ill really puts what's truly important into perspective. Now tell me. I'll undoubtedly have some incredible suggestions." Mischief filled his eyes and my heart swelled. Despite his deteriorating health, Liam was still *Liam*.

But I didn't want to speak about my unwanted wedding. I wanted to laugh and joke like we used to, exchange stories and memories, and, most importantly, receive his advice on the situation I found myself in. But as I looked at him now, I knew he couldn't handle the burden, not when he looked so weak that even the slightest worry would crush him.

As if sensing the change in my mood, his expression became more serious. "And how is your fiancé, Prince Boring?"

I gave him a scolding look. "*Briar* is fine. He's been rather sweet, actually."

Liam visibly relaxed. "I'm glad. I've been worried, you know. I have to look out for my favorite sister." He patted my hand.

"You're not the only one who's been worried." I searched his face. His eyes were bloodshot and his pupils were overly large; he'd lost a lot of weight, which caused him to look haggard; and he looked not only weak, but exhausted, as if it took all his energy to simply lie in bed doing nothing. In the silence, I could hear his breaths coming out sharp and shallow, each sounding as if it took him great effort. My heart wrenched.

The light faded from his eyes as he watched my perusal. "Do I look as bad as I feel?"

I released a strangled sob and held his hand close to my chest. "Oh Liam, please don't leave us."

He said nothing for a long moment before he heaved a weary sigh and closed his eyes. "I'm so sorry, I really thought I could beat this."

My heart lurched. In all the visits I'd had with Liam since he'd fallen ill, this was the first time he hadn't insisted my fears were unfounded or that he'd get well. "Liam?"

"What's the point of lying to you—or worse, myself—any longer?" he asked. "No more. I won't pretend this isn't going to end how I fear it will"—he took a ragged breath—"and I won't pretend I'm not scared; I've never been more terrified. I never imagined I'd die so young; there was always too much I wanted to do. But now—"

His eyes fluttered back open, but it wasn't me he looked at but Anwen. Tenderness and fierce regret filled his gaze. He extracted his hand from my hold to weakly brush her cheek. "Anwen…"

She pressed several kisses along his palm. "Please, Liam." Her voice choked on a sob.

"I'm so sorry," he whispered. "I'm not strong enough to win this fight."

Her tears escaped. "You can't leave me. I can't live without you. *Please, Liam.*"

"I don't want to leave you. I tried so hard…but this is one fight I cannot win. The thought of leaving you…it's torturous. I'd give anything—" He couldn't finish.

Anwen buried her face against his chest and broke into fierce, shuddering sobs. At her tears, Liam's brave mask faltered, revealing his raw devastation, his hopelessness, and his fear. I had never seen my brother look so defeated.

He nestled against his wife's hair and weakly stroked her back, murmuring soothingly. "I'm sorry, Anwen. I'm so sorry."

I watched the scene unfold with tears streaming down my cheeks, my agony so acute it felt like it was clenching my insides in ice.

Liam is going to die. The words played over and over in my mind, but no matter how many times I thought them, they didn't feel any more real, for I couldn't imagine life without my dear, invincible, and full-of-life brother, even though by the despair squeezing my heart, I knew that was a reality I would face very soon.

A knock penetrated my grief-stricken thoughts. I managed to shakily stand and open the door—Mother and Father stood before me. Their sorrowed gazes slid past me to settle on Liam, and Mother's expression crumpled at the sight of him trying to comfort his grieving wife.

"Oh…" She bustled over and took the seat I'd just abandoned, her gaze riveted hungrily to her son. Liam glanced at her wearily but still attempted a tight smile.

"I'm quite popular around here." He looked down at his sobbing wife and pressed a soft kiss on her brow. "Sweetheart, my parents are here. Should we visit with them?"

She said nothing, nor did she pull away from him. Liam continued to rub her back, his movements slow, as if each one were a struggle.

"I'm afraid we're not very cheerful company at the moment," Liam said. "Contemplating my mortality isn't exactly a bucket of laughs."

Mother squeezed her eyes shut, pained at his words. Father came over and rested his hand on her shoulder, his expression grave. "I've talked to another physician who will visit tomorrow with another treatment."

While Liam nodded, it was without hope. Mother stroked his damp brow. "How are you feeling, dear?"

Liam's arms wound more securely around his wife, as if trying to gather courage from her embrace. "I—"

He hesitated, as if unsure how to respond. I could almost see him trying to think of something humorous to say, but as he slowly took in our sorrowful expressions, he slumped, defeated.

"I feel terrible. I can't imagine feeling worse, and the longer it goes on for, the more awful it becomes. I don't think it's much longer...I hope it's almost over, while at the same time..."

His words only escalated my grief. Liam wasn't the kind to give up, especially when he had something to live for. Mother's lip trembled as she took his hand. "Are you in pain?"

He nodded. "My insides feel as if they're slowly being ripped apart only to be set on fire. I don't want to experience this anymore, but not at the cost of leaving." He glanced down at his wife. "I want to live, and not just for Anwen. Shall we tell them, darling?"

She managed a nod and slowly sat up, her eyes puffy and her face streaked with tears. Liam rested his hand on her stomach and gave us all a meaningful look.

"Anwen is—"

He didn't even finish before Mother gasped, her hands fluttering to her mouth. "Oh...*oh*." And then she was in tears. She seized Liam and pulled him into a hug that looked quite suffocating. The moment she released him, she hugged Anwen, crying onto her shoulder.

I could only stare. *Anwen is with child*. While the news was unexpected and joyous, it was hard to be happy when all I could think about was the fact that Liam was leaving behind not only his wife, but their baby, a child he would never get to meet.

I saw the pain from this realization not only in my parents' expressions, but in Anwen's and Liam's as well. Whatever courage Liam had been fighting to maintain seemed to vanish in an instant as he gave Mother the most heartbreaking look.

"I'm scared." He whispered the words, as if ashamed of the admission.

"Shh. I know, dear. I know." Mother's touch went to his hair, stroking it as if feebly trying to provide him some comfort, all while her tears silently fell down her cheeks.

"I've been thinking of Kian a lot," Liam said. "He faced death so bravely. I don't feel brave at all."

"You are brave, sweetheart," Mother said in a trembling voice. "So brave. We're so proud of you."

Liam nodded and cradled Anwen's face, his expression adoring as he stared at her. Anwen pressed his hand against her cheek. "Take care of Anwen and...the baby. Please."

Mother couldn't answer, so I answered for all of us. "Of course we will, Liam. We'll love and spoil both of them."

Liam sighed. "How I wish *I* could spoil them." His gaze hadn't left his wife's. "I'll miss you so much."

"Don't leave us," she pleaded. He said nothing, merely hooked his hand behind her neck to pull her into a soft kiss. When he broke it, they rested their foreheads against one another's and held each other close.

I sensed they wanted time alone, but I couldn't make myself move. How could I leave when the remaining moments I'd have with my brother were quickly slipping away?

It was with obvious difficulty that Liam looked away from Anwen, only to gather her back in his arms and weakly resume stroking her hair. She tucked her head beneath his chin.

As if he couldn't bear being somber for so long, he gave a rather mischievous Liam grin. "Perhaps I can return as a ghost. I'll recruit Kian and we can haunt all of you. He's really wasted the only good part about being dead."

We all flinched at the word and Anwen actually whimpered. Liam's expression immediately became remorseful.

"Was that too far? I'm sorry, darling."

"Don't joke about this. Please."

"Of course I won't." He paused to take a weary breath. "We'll spend our time together discussing more pleasant things." His breathing grew even heavier. "I'll treasure every moment, darling."

He kissed the top of her head before settling back against the pillows with a sigh, his eyes closing. He looked ready to sleep for a long time. A few moments later he did fall asleep, his shallow breathing the only indication he was still alive.

It was our cue to leave. We said goodbye to Anwen, who didn't even acknowledge us, her teary attention locked to Liam's face with a look like she was measuring his every breath.

The moment we left the room, Father turned to me, his expression grave. "I'm afraid it's not much longer. You must be prepared to become my new heir."

My stomach jolted. "But—" I'd known deep down it would come to this should Liam die. I'd always known it. But it wasn't until today that I realized that the event we'd been dreading was really going to happen…and I wasn't ready for it. "But…I *can't*. Upon my marriage to Briar, I'm in line to inherit the Malvagarian throne."

"The line of succession always passes to the eldest living child of the reigning king or current crown prince," he said. "It's tradition. Because Liam lived long enough to provide an heir, you'll only serve as regent until the child comes of age or you inherit the Malvagarian Crown, whichever comes first. At that time, Aveline will serve as regent until Liam's child is ready to ascend the throne."

I shook my head, the tears I'd fought so hard to keep back finally escaping. "I can't be the heir. That's Liam's role."

Father's expression crumpled. "Liam won't live to fulfill it."

Whatever bravery Mother had managed to cling to faltered and she burst into tears. Father held her close while keeping his own devastated gaze on me.

"I know this is a heavy burden I'm asking you to carry, but I have no doubt you can do it." He patted my shoulder before gently leading Mother away, leaving me staring after them, numb.

Me, the future acting Queen of Draceria? As if inheriting the Malvagarian throne wasn't terrifying enough. I pressed my back against the wall and slowly slid down to the floor.

How could this be happening?

My doubts returned, but these ones were different than the ones that had plagued me most of my life. I didn't doubt I could do what was expected of me, but I knew this wasn't right. Even midst the heartache of Kian's death, we'd all felt the succession pass naturally to Liam. But this...this was different. Something felt...off.

There was no doubt in my mind that *Liam* was the future King of Draceria, no one else. He'd grown into his role, gained the necessary abilities needed to rule, and developed the confidence needed to perform his future responsibilities. The people loved him, trusted him. To have all of that torn away...

He can't die. I couldn't bear it. But the truth of the matter was he *was* dying, and despite all the best efforts of the physicians there was nothing anyone could do to stop it.

My helplessness pressed against my chest, smothering me. My sob escaped and I buried my face in my pulled-up knees, crying for several minutes in that abandoned corridor with my dying brother on the other side of the wall, whom I could do nothing to help.

Footsteps approached. My breath hitched and, not

looking up, I waited, sensing *him*. I peeked up through my blurry tears to see Drake settle beside me. I wasn't surprised to see him; he'd been my quiet support ever since my engagement, silently offering me strength despite my having chosen the safer path. Even now that we couldn't be together, nothing had changed.

He lightly brushed my shoulder. "Are you alright, Rhea?"

Before I could stop myself, I fell into Drake's arms and buried my tear-streaked face against his chest. I knew I shouldn't let him hold me, but I was so grateful he didn't push me away, for I needed him—his friendship, his steadiness, his quiet caring. Even though I felt as if my world was crumbling all around me, in Drake's comforting arms I felt safe, even if it was only for this moment.

It was quite some time before my sobs stilled, and even after I stopped crying, I didn't want to move. Losing my brother was difficult enough without also losing this stolen moment with Drake.

Forbidden as it was, I needed him—his warm arms wound securely around me, his heart beating against my cheek, the assurance that he was here for me, even when I was drowning.

"How did you know I needed you?" I finally whispered.

"The mirror." Drake motioned with his chin to the gilded mirror that had decorated this corridor for so many years I never noticed it anymore. "My connection with the mirror hasn't entirely worn off yet. I was worried about you, so I checked all of them to find you. Like I feared, you were crying." He hesitated. "Is it Liam?"

I squeezed my eyes shut. "He's going to die, Drake."

His hold tightened. "I'm so sorry," he murmured.

I was getting *too* comfortable in his arms, so I managed to sit up enough to pull myself away. But I didn't move from his side. I couldn't. "I feel so helpless," I said. "The physicians are at a loss and no treatment is working, just like nothing worked for Kian…" My heart wrenched, even as it protested against Liam's impending death. "It feels so…wrong."

Drake was pensive a moment as he searched my expression. "Do you feel there's something you can do about it? Did you feel this way with Kian?"

"No," I said. "Kian's death, as devastating as it was, didn't feel as if it could have been prevented. But…something feels *off* with Liam." And it always had, even if I couldn't pinpoint why.

"You've said that from the beginning," Drake said. "It's as if you know something you can't put into words. What is it, Rhea?"

My mind raced frantically, desperate to uncover an explanation…but I was at a loss. I took a steadying breath to calm my pounding heart.

Focus. You can do this, Rhea. There's an explanation; you just have to see it. What is different about Liam's illness from Kian's?

I squeezed my eyes shut, trying to still my frantic thoughts enough to concentrate. Liam's illness had befallen him so suddenly, almost *too* suddenly, unlike Kian's. I went over every detail I could remember about the night he'd first begun to feel unwell. We'd been at dinner…he'd been jovial as usual…but the more he'd eaten, the more subdued he'd become, all while the queen had watched him with that calculated smirk, one I'd seen many times since then, whenever she was plotting my union with Briar…

A horrible possibility struck me, one I'd briefly considered before, but never seriously. I gasped sharply as my eyes snapped open. "His illness isn't natural. He's—*oh*." Icy fear tightened my chest and I felt sick.

"What is it, Rhea?" Drake asked.

I tried to form the word, but it was as if my tongue had turned to lead. I swallowed. "Poison."

Drake's eyes widened in alarm. *"What?"*

"Poison." My voice shook and my heart beat wildly. "Drake, that's it! What if he's being poisoned?"

He gaped at me. "Do you really think—"

"I'm not sure."

I revisited all the pieces and tried to assemble them in my mind to form any sort of picture. *Was* he being poisoned? And if so, *how?*

A possibility occurred to me. "Do you think…his herbal remedy is laced with poison? It would explain why the different remedies we've tried never worked and why I was ill for several hours the day I took a sip. We had attributed my sudden sickness to a bad combination of herbs, but what if the herbs had been laced with poison?" I furrowed my brow. "But how was the initial dose of poison administered? We all ate and drank the same thing at dinner that night."

There was no time to dwell on the *how*, for if he was being poisoned, there had to be an antidote, which meant I had to find it in order to save him. There was still time. For Liam was the true future ruler of Draceria, and I would do all in my power to ensure he lived to inherit his throne.

CHAPTER 30

I ran through the corridors, Drake at my heels. "Do you really think he's being *poisoned*?" he panted.

"As I said, something has felt off, but now I'm sure something sinister is going on." The more I thought about the situation and all its unusual pieces, the more certain I was.

"But *why*?" Drake asked. "Why would anyone want to poison Liam?"

My mind had been working over that puzzle. "Father reminded me that at Liam's passing, I'm next in line for the throne. Not only will I inherit the crown, but upon my marriage, so would—"

Drake's breath hitched. "Briar."

I bit my lip, almost afraid to voice my suspicions. "Your mother has been so insistent on a union between Briar and *me*, rather than matching Briar with one of my sisters. Until now we couldn't understand why, but if she's trying to get rid of Liam, she only benefits from his death if—"

"—if she unites the Crown Prince of Malvagaria with the Dracerian heir to the throne, which would allow her to

368

annex it for herself." Drake's entire manner hardened. "We can't let that happen."

"Which means we must uncover an antidote before it's too late. If Liam—" I swallowed that fear. *He's not going to die.* "I need to look through that book I found a few weeks ago so I can discover which poison is being used on Liam. The sooner we realize which poison we're up against, the sooner we can discover its antidote, and hopefully…"

But even if we found the antidote, would it be in time to save Liam? If only I'd acted on my suspicions the moment I'd had them rather than allowed my doubts and insecurities to—

No, Rhea, you can't think like that. You did your best. Just focus on finding the antidote.

The moment we reached the library, I went to the bookshelf where I'd first discovered the book of toxic plants, nearly tripping over my skirts in my haste to scramble up the ladder.

Drake gasped below me. "Careful, Rhea, don't fall. Please let me be the one to—"

"I have to do it; you don't know where it is." I reached the top and searched the shelves, running my fingertips along the books' spines…and froze when I reached where I remembered it being. My breath hooked. "It's missing, Drake." Where the book had been was now nothing more than an empty space.

"*What?*"

He scrambled up the ladder after me until he stood directly behind me, his feet one rung below mine. His firm torso pressed against my back as he leaned closer to search the shelf. I instinctively leaned against him; touching him helped quell my rising panic.

He swore. "Where is it?"

I slowly turned around, careful not to lose my footing on

the ladder. "Someone must have taken it. What are we going to do?"

He enfolded me in his arms. "We'll figure something out," he murmured against my hair. "It'll be alright, Rhea."

I nestled closer to his warm chest, wishing I could simply let him hold me and never pull away. But I couldn't. Not only was our relationship now forbidden, but we needed to find that book.

"If it's been taken, that only confirms that the information we need is inside it. We need to find it."

Drake nodded and kissed the top of my head before releasing me with obvious reluctance. "Let's keep looking. Maybe there's another book about poisonous plants somewhere."

We perused the library, shelf by shelf. I used to love our vast library, but now the sheer number of volumes it contained was overwhelming, and although we stumbled across many books about botany, we still didn't find what we were looking for.

"Have you found anything?" I called up to Drake two long hours of searching later. He stood at the top of the ladder searching the upper shelves while I investigated the lower ones.

He sighed. "Nothing, but we won't give up. We'll find something, Rhea." His fierce determination soothed my frantic heart, reminding me that I wasn't alone.

After another hour crawled by, we froze at the sound of the library door opening. We both held our breath and waited in anxious anticipation as footsteps approached, pausing at the end of the row of shelves we were scouring.

It was Briar. I released my pent-up breath. "Oh good, it's just you."

He approached, his brow furrowed as he took in the stack of books we'd already searched. "What's going on?"

"We're looking for a book that used to be in this library, but has since disappeared. It's imperative we find it."

Briar frowned. "What's the book?"

"*Dangerous Plants.*"

Recognition lit his eyes even as his brows squashed together. "*Dangerous Plants?*"

Drake's gaze snapped to his from his perch on the ladder. "Have you heard of it?"

Briar hesitated. "Yes." A long pause... "Why do you need it?"

"We need to find it in order to help Liam. We suspect..." I swallowed my words.

His frown deepened. "You don't think something in there is being used to harm him, do you?"

I stepped closer. "We suspect Liam is being poisoned. If we could figure out which poison is killing him, then perhaps—"

"—you can find the antidote," he finished. I nodded. He released a whooshing breath. "Poison." He shook his head in disbelief. "Could it be true?"

"We don't know for sure," I said. "But if there's any possibility that it is..."

He nodded his understanding and slowly raised his gaze. "You need that book."

I lightly touched his elbow. "Yes. Do you know where it is? Please, Briar, we're running out of time."

"I saw Mother with that book a few weeks ago," he said.

Drake snorted as he descended the ladder. "I should have known. Mother must have taken it to cover her tracks."

Briar considered that before his eyes widened. "You don't think *Mother* is the one—"

"Yes, that's exactly what we think, and if you consider the situation carefully, you'll realize it's true."

Briar slowly nodded. "I'll search Mother's room for it." He turned and hurried away.

I nibbled my lip worriedly as I watched him go. The fact that the queen had taken the book of poisonous plants confirmed my suspicions that her ultimate goal was to get rid of Liam, making me the new heir to the Dracerian throne. We had to find a way to stop her before it was too late.

We settled side by side to wait. I yearned to curl against Drake's comforting warmth and rest my head on his shoulder, but out of loyalty to Briar I forced myself to resist the impulse. His presence was still soothing and helped ease my restlessness as time passed and Briar still hadn't returned.

Eventually Drake broke the silence. "I've been thinking… you made the right choice in accepting Briar's hand."

I looked at him in surprise. Pain filled his eyes.

"This is bigger than I could have ever imagined. I knew Mother was ruthless, but to be *poisoning* a neighboring kingdom's crown prince?" He shook his head in disgust. "If you'd chosen me, she would have hurt you. Nothing is worth that, not even a future together. I'd rather spend my entire life without you than lose you to her schemes."

As painful as his words were, I was glad he'd spoken them. "I was afraid she'd hurt you, too. That's what helped me choose this path."

He met my eyes and offered a wry but sweet smile. Slowly, hesitantly, he rested his hand over mine. "Love is all about sacrifice, isn't it? I'd rather love you and give you up than never have fallen in love with you at all."

We fell into silence, which, while comfortable, was wrought with anticipation for Briar's return. Several minutes later, we heard the library door open again and Briar's rushing footsteps. We yanked our hands away just as he appeared, breathless, at the end of the row, but by the knowing look in his eyes, he knew what we'd been up to.

To my surprise, rather than confront us, he simply held up *Dangerous Plants* triumphantly. "I found it."

"Thank you, Briar." I accepted the book and kissed his cheek before easing it open.

We all hovered around it as I frantically turned the pages, pausing to read each entry carefully. Almost every chronicled plant caused one or two of Liam's symptoms, but never all of them. As we reached the end of the book, I'd begun to fear that this didn't contain the information we needed when I suddenly paused on an entry detailing a rare form of poison hemlock, only grown in Malvagaria.

Briar frowned at the illustration. "I've seen this plant before. It grows in one of our enchanted gardens."

I pulled the book closer. My breath caught as I read each symptom the plant caused its victims: *Nausea, shortness of breath, bloodshot eyes, dilated pupils, headache, dry mouth...*and others, each fitting Liam's illness. But one symptom in particular stood out to me: *a rash that resembles a cluster of hemlock that appears on the skin during the poison's final stage.*

My heart lurched as I stared at the accompanying illustration, which matched what I'd seen in real life mere days ago. "The rash."

"Does Liam have it?"

"It appeared on his back a few days ago; I was there when it was discovered. The physician was at a loss as to what caused it. It looks similar to this." I tapped the drawing. "This must be the plant poisoning Liam; it all fits together perfectly." My chest constricted at the realization of what this meant: if Liam had the rash now, that meant the poison was nearly finished claiming his life.

Drake seized the book and read over the hemlock's information. "Yes, I think you're right. What do you think, Briar?"

"The symptoms are an exact match." He flipped a page and continued reading. "Not to mention it fits the timeframe —it takes about a month of continuous administration before killing its victims, which is about how long Liam's illness has gone on. Such a slow poison makes sense; it would allow Liam's illness to look natural so no one would suspect foul play."

Drake read over his shoulder and pointed to a paragraph. "And look, it's ingested via a liquid. That would fit Rhea's theory that it's been put in Liam's remedy."

"Is there an antidote?" I seized the book and I skimmed frantically. "There is one. It's—" My heart sank. "Wow, it looks complicated, not to mention the ingredients are quite rare." I sat back with a sigh. "What are we going to do?"

Drake studied the illustrated bottle carefully. Suddenly, his breath hooked.

"What is it?" I asked.

"I've seen this bottle before."

"You have? Where?"

"When I used to travel to different mirrors. It makes sense...she'd have the antidote on hand just in case things didn't go as planned."

And then I understood. Foreboding knotted my stomach. "In your mother's room?"

He nodded solemnly. "In my mother's room."

"CAN YOU SEE ANYTHING?" I whispered.

Drake, Briar, and I hovered outside the guest quarters where the Queen of Malvagaria's bedroom was located. Drake squeezed his eyes shut, his forehead furrowed in concentration.

"I can't. My ability to remain connected to the palace

mirrors has been fading more every day and is almost completely gone."

"Please keep checking," I pleaded anxiously.

He scrunched his face with concentrated effort while Briar watched, fascinated. "Can you really see through the palace mirrors? How ironic that Mother's own curse would come back to haunt her."

Drake nodded. "But like I said, it's fading." He opened his eyes and slumped. "I can't see anything."

"Then what are we going to do?" I wrung my hands as my thoughts raced, desperate to uncover a solution. "If Liam were here, he'd tell us to storm the room."

"If we did that, we'd find ourselves cursed," Briar said wryly. "We need to be stealthy. If all else fails, I'll pretend I need her for something and persuade her to leave, allowing you to sneak in." Drake raised a skeptical brow. Briar shrugged. "Do you have a better idea?"

It seemed to be our only option. I turned to Drake, expecting him to agree, and found him once more closing his eyes, his expression taut with concentration. "Wait! I think... yes, I've connected to her bedroom mirror."

"Is she inside?"

He didn't answer immediately as he searched. We waited with bated breath. Finally, he opened his eyes with a wide grin. "The coast is clear."

"Excellent." I clasped my hands. "I'll go in while you two stand guard and—"

"Oh no, you're not going in her room," Drake said fiercely. "One of us should go instead. If Mother discovers us we'd at least have a reason to be there, whereas you wouldn't."

"But—"

"I agree with Drake. It's too dangerous," Briar said. "If Mother has no qualms about poisoning Liam, she'll undoubtedly harm you if she catches you trying to thwart her carefully laid plans."

They were right, but even though I knew the risks, they wouldn't dissuade me. "Nothing, not even the two of you, can stop me. Liam needs this antidote and I want to be the one to help him. But if you're worried, one or both of you can come with me."

"We shouldn't *all* go," Briar said. "One of us needs to act as lookout."

"That can be your job while Drake and I sneak into her bedroom."

Briar frowned darkly. My cheeks warmed.

"It has to be Drake; he's the only one who can check the mirrors to ensure the coast is clear."

He looked back and forth between us before sighing in acquiescence. "You're right, he's the most logical choice. Very well, I'll stay out here and distract Mother should she come. Now hurry." He made a shooing motion and we tiptoed to the queen's room and wriggled the knob. It was locked. Of course it was.

I sighed, but to my surprise, Drake grinned. "I knew we'd encounter such an obstacle."

He pulled out a strange instrument from his pocket and knelt in front of the door, inserting the lock-picking tool. His brow furrowed in concentration as he worked, and I had the strangest impulse to smooth out the lines of his forehead.

The click of the door unlocking echoed through the empty corridor. Drake gave me a triumphant smirk. "Success."

"Where did you learn that trick?" I asked.

"My father taught me."

I shook my head in wonder. "Remind me not to leave any of my locked secrets around you."

He wriggled his eyebrows roguishly as he straightened and pushed the door open with a bow. "After you, my lady."

I slipped inside and looked around while Drake relocked the door behind him. The spacious room was impeccably neat, thankfully leaving very few places to hide anything. We split up, each taking a side of the room.

What if it's not here? I wondered as I opened the desk drawers and carefully searched their contents in a way that the queen wouldn't know anything was out of place. *What will we do if we can't find it?*

"Where was the antidote when you saw it?" I asked as I closed one drawer and moved on to another at ground level.

Drake didn't look up from rummaging through the night-stand. "She was actually holding it."

I sat back on my heels and gaped at him. "She was *holding* it?"

"No, more like…fiddling with it while we talked."

My gaze drifted to the vanity where this conversation would have taken place; it was laden with several bottles of cosmetics and perfumes. *Could it be in such an obvious location?* "Am I right to assume she was talking to you at the vanity and you were in the vanity mirror?"

He nodded. "Of course! I should have looked there first."

I'd just stood to approach the vanity when the queen's familiar heels sounded outside the door. I froze, my heart flaring as I exchanged a horrified look with Drake, who wasted no time. He took my hand and led me to the bed.

"We have to hide in case Briar can't hold her off. Scoot beneath the bed."

I obeyed, sliding underneath. It was a tight squeeze but I fit without too much trouble. Drake slid in after me and gathered me close. I burrowed myself against his chest and tried to still my rapid breaths.

Moments later, the lock jiggled and the door opened. "Not now, Briar," the queen snapped impatiently.

"But—" His protest was cut short as the queen slammed the door in a disgruntled mutter. I stiffened. Drake felt me tense and rubbed my back soothingly.

Her footsteps clicked as she moved around the room, rummaging through things, either looking for something or ensuring everything was in its proper place. Then she settled on the bed. It scrunched down, nearly crushing us, before she adjusted and her movements stilled. She was taking a brief rest, and we were trapped until she left.

What terrible luck.

Time stretched on. I wasn't sure how long we waited—it was likely at least an hour—keeping our breaths as quiet as possible. I took comfort in Drake's secure hold and his heart gently beating against my cheek. I nuzzled my nose against his throat, awash with his apple scent. Although fear cloaked me and our hiding place was cramped, I'd never been so cozy or felt so safe. What would it be like to spend the rest of my life being able to enjoy Drake holding me in this way?

I love him. If we could thwart the queen and were allowed to be together, nothing would keep me from him. If I could have him, I'd never let him go again.

A knock sounded at the door. I held my breath as the queen stood and yanked the door open with a muttered curse.

She gasped sharply when she saw who stood on the threshold. "Get in here before someone sees you." She stepped aside to allow someone to enter the room, a footman judging by the pant legs of his uniform. She slammed the door shut. "I told you never to come here," she hissed. "It's imperative we're never seen together."

"Forgive me, Your Majesty." The servant's shaking voice was unfamiliar. "I have something to report."

"Be quick about it."

The servant took a wavering breath. "I saw Prince Drake and Princess Rheanna scouring the library. I'm concerned they're after that book you had me steal."

The queen gave a chilling laugh. "You risked discovery to come tell me such a trivial thing? Your concern is ridiculous. Those two are too foolish to realize anything is amiss."

The servant nervously shifted his weight from foot to foot. "Forgive me, Your Majesty, but if they do discover that book and realize what's been occurring...we should have waited until after the wedding as was the original plan."

"And risk that meddling prince convincing his spineless sister not to go through with the arrangement I've been planning ever since her engagement to the Sortileyan Crown Prince fell through? I think not. The moment he tried to interfere, everything changed."

"But Your Majesty, I could be sent to the gallows for sneaking into the kitchens and repeatedly lacing—"

"*Silence*," the queen hissed. "I told you to never speak of the plan out loud. Now leave, and never come to my private quarters again. You know the consequences should you disobey me again."

The servant tripped over his feet in his haste to leave the room. When the door clicked shut, the queen walked to the vanity, where we heard the clink of several bottles as she rummaged through them. After a moment she left, the sound of her footsteps growing fainter until they faded completely.

We both released our pent-up breath but didn't stir. After several minutes, Drake closed his eyes to check the vanity mirror.

"She's really gone, and she's not in the corridor either. But Briar is, frantically pacing with a look like he expects Mother murdered us and stowed our bodies away in her wardrobe."

Despite the anxiety still clenching my chest, I managed a breathless chuckle. "That was terrifying."

"We're safe for the moment, and we now know she had an accomplice. Let's find the antidote and get out of here." He scooted from under the bed and I reluctantly followed, not ready to end this time with Drake, as tense as it had been. He helped me to my feet and rubbed my arms soothingly. "Are you alright?"

"Yes, but we wasted too much time. We need to find that antidote."

It was time to see whether my idea had any merit. I went to the vanity and rummaged amongst the bottles. My heart lifted. Resting beside a gold hand mirror accented with onyx was the antidote bottle, which matched the illustration in *Dangerous Plants*.

I turned to Drake with a grin. "Where do you hide a bottle of antidote? How about in plain sight?" I lifted the bottle triumphantly.

Drake beamed. "That's my clever Rhea." He took it and examined it. "I remember some of the ingredients the book listed. Some, like mint, have a distinct scent, so we should be able to ensure this is the right…" The moment he uncorked it his face paled.

"What is it?"

He looked up. "It's empty."

"*What?*" I seized the bottle and peered inside. Sure enough, it was. My heart lurched. "How can it be empty?"

"Knowing Mother, it's a red herring…or a warning that we can't outsmart her. She's thought of everything."

I released a frustrated sigh. "What are we going to do now?"

Just then, someone knocked on the door. We stilled before I hastily hid the antidote bottle.

"Drake, Rheanna, are you in there?" It was Briar,

sounding rather frantic. Drake opened the door to glare at his brother.

"You made an excellent lookout; we were nearly caught."

"I tried to stall her, but you know Mother isn't one who's easily swayed." He glanced at both our hands and frowned when he saw they were empty. "Haven't you found it?"

I pulled it from my bodice. "We found it, but it's empty." We stepped into the hallway and locked the door behind us. "But we can't discuss this here; your mother or that footman working for her could return at any moment."

"Then what should we do?"

I nibbled my lip as my mind swirled frantically, but I felt as if I were trapped in a dark maze with no way out. I grasped upon the first slippery idea I stumbled upon. "We should take the bottle to the apothecary and have him examine it. Perhaps he'll recognize it and know how to prepare the antidote."

Neither Drake nor Briar had any objections, so we headed down to the entrance hall. We froze halfway down the stairs when we saw the Queen of Malvagaria coming up.

She paused with a suspicious frown at seeing all three of us together. I hastily enclosed the empty antidote bottle within my palm to hide it from view. Anxiety knotted my stomach as she slowly ascended the steps one by one, drawing ever closer.

Be brave. I lifted my chin, urging myself to display a confidence I didn't at all feel.

She paused directly in front of us and glared at me through narrowed eyes before glancing between me and her two sons flanking me. "What's going on? I would certainly hope you three aren't planning something amiss, especially with the wedding fast approaching."

My fingers grazed Drake's hand to get his attention.

Although he didn't so much as glance at me, his pinky stroked my hand in response.

Briar wrapped his arm around my waist and pulled me close. "There's nothing to worry about, Mother. The wedding is still happening, just as you want."

"Splendid." Although she gave a tight smile, her eyes flashed darkly, and I suddenly wished I were confronting Her Majesty anywhere but on the long staircase.

I subtly used my thumb to push the bottle hidden in my hand into Drake's. I felt his fingers encircle it before he tucked it out of view. The queen didn't notice the exchange, nor did she give Drake a second glance as he descended the stairs to go to the apothecary without us; she was too busy searching my eyes, as if she could detect any sign of rebellion within them. I stared steadily back.

"Your concerns are unfounded," I said evenly. "I'll do whatever it takes to protect those I love."

"I should hope so," she said coolly. "For I'd hate to see a curse befall you after you join our family."

Briar stepped forward. "Rheanna will soon be my wife, and I'll not stand by while you threaten her."

The queen turned her icy gaze towards him and he narrowed his eyes in warning. She smiled sweetly. "Why Briar, I'd never dream of hurting your dear bride, not after all the work I did to ensure this coveted match. As long as you both continue to acquiesce to my wishes, I see no reason for things to get…messy."

And with that, she ascended the stairs, leaving us staring after her. I glanced in the direction Drake had gone. I ached to follow him, anxious to interview the apothecary and discover if there was any hope for a remedy. But before I could take a single step, Briar gently turned me around and led me back up the stairs.

"But—" I protested.

He leaned towards my ear. "We can't go with him in case Mother follows us and discovers what we're up to."

I knew he was right, but it frustrated me all the same; I hated feeling so helpless. I allowed him to escort me to the study in order to speak to Father and finally tell him what was going on, but the attending footman informed me that the king and queen were away for a few hours. With a heavy heart we trudged to the library instead, where we waited by the crackling hearth for Drake's return.

He arrived an hour later, and by his grim expression, I knew his visit hadn't gone well. He sank wearily into an armchair.

"The apothecary recognized the label on the bottle. The poison it counteracts is particularly powerful and potent, though rather slow moving. The only known antidote is derived from a rare flower that's only grown in Malvagaria. Even if he had access to the flower—which he does not—he said it's a complicated recipe that would require at least a week to prepare."

I slumped at this terrible news and buried my face in my hands. "What are we going to do? Liam needs that antidote now, and there's no way to get one made up in time." Which meant he was going to die. My heart constricted at the thought.

Drake looked as helpless as I felt, but when I turned to Briar, I found him staring unseeing into the crackling flames.

"Briar?"

He blinked rapidly and glanced at me, his expression resolved. "I have an idea."

Hope pierced the suffocating despair filling my chest. I leaned closer. "You do? What is it?"

He took a wavering breath and cradled the rose he always wore. "I'll give Liam my rose. Because it's enchanted and comes from the same garden the poison came from, I have no doubt it'll heal him."

I seized his hand. "You'd give up your rose for him?" I didn't fully understand its significance, only that it was special.

He nodded, but Drake frowned. "Briar, that's really risky for you. There has to be another way."

"There's not." He sighed, sounding weary but determined. He flipped his hand over beneath mine and stroked my palm once. "I want to do this for you, Rhea, and for Liam."

My heart gave a strange flutter as Briar used my nickname for the first time, and in that moment, I felt closer to him than I ever had before.

"Are you sure, Briar?" Drake asked. "Once you give it up, you won't be able to take it back, and you won't have much time before—"

He nodded firmly, his expression resolved. "If the poison came from our kingdom, it's our duty to provide the antidote; it's the honorable thing to do." He smiled at me. "Besides, it'll make you happy."

I flung my arms around him. "Thank you," I whispered.

Even though I didn't understand why Briar always wore that rose, I could see from both his and Drake's expressions that giving it up was a great sacrifice.

You're worth caring about.

And more importantly we would save Liam.

CHAPTER 31

*S*kirts lifted, I ran through the corridors to Liam's quarters, Drake and Briar close behind. My heart pounded wildly with each step. *Please say I'm not too late to save my brother.*

When we arrived, I wasted no time knocking or waiting for the attending guards to open the door before I burst, panting, into the room, the Malvagarian princes at my heels.

"Poison." I hunched over and clutched my knees as I took one shaky breath after another. "*Poison.*"

My parents and Anwen sat around Liam's bed, gaping at me, while Liam lay sickly pale and lifeless, as if he were already dead.

"What are you talking about, Rhea?" Mother asked in a deathly whisper. "Poison? What—"

"Liam is being poisoned."

Anwen pressed her hand to her mouth to smother her breathless sob while Liam stirred from his pillows and wearily opened his eyes.

"*Poison*, Rhea?" he said in a raspy voice. "Do I have an

unknown enemy? Quite impressive of me to have someone try to assassinate me before I even take the throne."

He tried to laugh, but it came out as a sickly cough. Anwen helped him drink a glass of water, which he gulped down before weakly resting his head back against the pillows with a heavy sigh, his eyes fluttering closed once more. Anwen fretted beside him, stroking his damp brow, staring desperately first at him then at me.

"Are you certain it's poison?"

I nodded. Father frowned, his expression grave. "Poison is something we've never considered seriously, for Draceria is peaceful and prosperous, with no known enemies. I see no reason why anyone would want to usurp Liam after he's proven himself worthy to inherit the throne. Are you sure, Rheanna?"

I lifted my chin and nodded again. "I researched Liam's symptoms in the library." I opened *Dangerous Plants* to the entry I'd bookmarked. "We found a rare plant that only grows in Malvagarian soil, whose slow-moving effects match Liam's illness."

At the mention of Malvagaria, Father frowned gravely but said nothing. Anwen and Mother continued staring at me in disbelief. "But—who would want to poison dear Liam?" Mother asked shakily.

I swallowed my accusation. Now was not the time to make it. Instead, I continued. "This book outlines a detailed explanation of how this particular poison works; it exactly matches Liam's symptoms and how his illness unfolded— down to the telltale rash that appeared a few days ago. According to this, the time he has remaining is…not long at all, mere days unless we administer an antidote."

"Is there an antidote?" Anwen's gaze was pleading as she held Liam's hand close to her heart.

"There is. Unfortunately, the bottle we found was empty."

Anwen squeezed her eyes shut at the news and a tear trickled down her cheek.

"However, Briar has a solution." I turned to him and he stepped forward, his hand hovering over his rose as if trying to draw strength from it for however long he had left.

"The plants growing at the main Malvagarian palace are enchanted," he said, "each one with a different type of magic. There is a particular rose that sustains life, just the thing to counter the enchanted poisoned hemlock."

Drake stood by his side, holding his arm to steady him. With a shaking hand, Briar removed the rose he wore and held it out on his palm.

Mother stared at it before slowly raising her gaze to Briar's. "Your rose?"

He nodded, his eyes almost fearful as he offered it. "Steep each petal into a tea, and it should act as an antidote."

Anwen leapt to her feet so quickly she knocked her chair over. She seized the rose from Briar, who immediately slumped as if suddenly exhausted. Drake hooked his arm around his brother's waist to keep him from falling over and helped him into a chair.

Anwen tore a petal off the rose—causing Briar to wince—and, foregoing Liam's usual goblet, put it in a clean cup. As she began preparing the tea, I knelt in front of Briar, frowning at his pasty skin.

"Are you alright?"

He took a shuddering breath. "I should be fine."

Drake rested a steadying hand on his shoulder and worriedly eyed his brother's paling face. "You need to return to Malvagaria. Immediately."

Briar wearily shook his head. "I'll be fine for a few days."

"But it's a three-day journey. In your current state, you can't risk any delay else you won't make it in time before you—"

Briar waved aside his concern. "I'll be fine."

Drake didn't look convinced, but we were distracted from Briar's condition when Anwen returned to Liam's bedside, a cup of the rose tea in her hands.

"Can you sit up, dear?" she asked, winding her arm around Liam's shoulders to help him scoot into a half-sitting position. She turned to us. "How much should I give him?"

I retrieved the book and scanned it. "Start with a spoonful every half hour so his body can gradually wash out the poison."

If we weren't too late. He'd been ill nearly an entire month, the time it usually took for this particular poison to kill its victims. What if there was too much poison in his body to wash it out in time? My stomach clenched at the thought. If we failed to save him when we were so close…I'd never forgive myself for doubting my earlier suspicions.

Liam opened his mouth and allowed Anwen to administer a spoonful of the antidote. He swallowed and leaned back against his pillows. We all watched with bated breath for signs of it working.

Nothing happened.

I nibbled my lip. "Perhaps it takes awhile."

No one answered, everyone's attention riveted to Liam, especially Anwen's, who stared so intently she rarely blinked.

"If it's really poison"—Mother's voice was strangled —"who would do such a thing? And how? It can't be from his food, considering he and Anwen have been sharing their meals."

Father looked away from Liam first, his expression grave. "She's right, it would be quite the feat to administer poison so regularly without our noticing. Do you have a theory for how this was accomplished, Rheanna?"

I pointed to Liam's teapot. "The remedy. Not only is Liam the only one drinking it, but he always seems to grow worse after doing so. I took a sip once and it made me sick for several hours."

Rather than the baffled looks I expected to receive, Father's expression became thoughtful. "That sounds like a plausible method. I'll have the tea tested immediately in order to discern whether—"

Liam interrupted with a sickening retching. Anwen acted quickly, seizing the basin on his nightstand in time for him to be ill into it. When he finished, he looked up. To my astonishment, his usual pallor had improved slightly.

Anwen stroked his brow. "Liam dear? Are you alright?"

He actually smiled. "I…feel a lot better." He straightened by himself and with a shaking breath glanced around us. "Not great, but…*a lot* better. See, I told all of you I'd beat this. You shouldn't have doubted me."

Tears trickled down Anwen's cheeks as she looked back and forth between Liam and the basin he'd just been ill in. "You haven't thrown up before."

"Perhaps his body is trying to get rid of the poison," I suggested.

Anwen's teary gaze met mine, dazed, before she wrapped her arms around Liam and hugged him close. "Oh Liam, I was so scared we were going to lose you."

"Please don't cry, darling. I'll be alright. After all, I have tea made from an enchanted rose."

She said nothing, only held him tighter.

"It will take some time for the antidote to enter his bloodstream and fully disperse throughout his entire body," Briar said weakly. "But it should move quicker because the rose is enchanted."

Father turned to me, expression serious. "The fact that the antidote is already working proves he *was* being poisoned. Do you have any idea who's responsible?"

I took a deep breath. "The Queen of Malvagaria."

His eyes widened and Mother gasped, covering her mouth in disbelief. Father got over his surprise first and glanced warily at the Malvagarian princes sitting nearby.

"They knew nothing about it," I said hastily. "Save for assistance from one of her servants, to my knowledge Her Majesty acted alone."

His jaw tightened. "Please explain."

"She wants to murder Liam so I'm next in line for the Dracerian throne," I said. "If I inherit the throne while married to Briar, he would be acting regent. Because he's to inherit the Malvagarian throne, the queen could peacefully annex Draceria—a land that centuries ago belonged to Malvagaria—and make it one kingdom."

Which meant I'd been nothing more than a pawn. Despite having known it for a while, my chest still tightened. As if sensing my discomfort, Drake subtly gave my hand a reassuring squeeze.

His comfort gave me the strength to plunge into the entire story—the queen's harsh words and sinister threats, the conversation I'd overheard between her and her servant, Aiden's own suspicions and the letter he'd sent...everything. My parents listened, eyes wide with shock.

Briar and Drake supplemented my recitation with all the information they knew. When Drake mentioned how the queen had cursed him to remain in a mirror until one of the Dracerian princesses fell in love with him, Mother interrupted.

"You were trapped in a *mirror*?"

Drake nodded. She gaped in disbelief while Liam chuckled from the bed, looking and sounding far more cheerful than he had in weeks. "That is quite the epic story. I'm sorry I missed out on such an adventure."

Mother shook her head. "And one of my daughters broke

your curse by falling in love with you? Which one? Was it Elodie?"

I almost snorted in disgust. Drake actually blushed and exchanged a searing glance with me before we both hastily looked away. Mother raised her eyebrows and Father's expression became solemn.

"I see. This is the young man you told me about, isn't it, Rhea? The one you harbor feelings for?"

My cheeks burned and I lowered my eyes.

"Is there any reason you didn't tell us about your feelings for Prince Drake? Or, more importantly, that the Queen of Malvagaria has been threatening you into making a match with Prince Briar?" His regal manner faltered, revealing his heartache and fierce disappointment.

"There's nothing you could have done to stop her," I said. "The queen is too formidable of a foe—with the ability to curse, a huge army behind her, and no qualms about poisoning another kingdom's crown prince. Telling you would have been too dangerous. I was trying to protect our kingdom and our family. You might have done something rash to protect me, and my happiness was of little conse-quence compared to the safety of our people."

Father managed a tight smile. "Even though I'm still upset you kept this from me, I understand and am proud of you, Rheanna. This has been a heavy burden for you to have borne alone. You'll make a remarkable queen." He sighed wearily, looking rather helpless. "If only I could have protected you and Liam. I've failed you both."

"You haven't," I said. "The queen hasn't won yet." And we'd do all in our power to ensure that she never would.

As if to affirm my words, Liam made another choking noise and was ill again, proving the antidote was thwarting Her Majesty's poison. Anwen rubbed his back until he'd finished retching and straightened with another wide grin.

"That also felt really good." His weak voice did nothing to mar his cheerful tone. "Wow, I survived a poisoning. I haven't even taken the throne and already my story will go down in history—*The King Who Prevented His Own Assassination.* Just imagine: I was slowly wasting away as my enemy tried to kill me in order to steal the crown that wasn't even on my head yet."

His goofy grin faded as he caught sight of Anwen's distraught expression. He cradled her cheek.

"No worries, darling, I've been snatched from death at the very last moment and thus am going to be fine. I'm afraid that my ghost haunting days will have to wait for many more years."

Her lips trembled. "Oh, Liam." She let out a choked sob and kissed him. Although he kissed her back, he tried to wriggle away.

"Darling, you probably don't want to be kissing me right now considering I was just—"

"Just kiss me, you wonderful man."

He made no complaints. When they ended their kiss, she pressed several more across his damp face. "You're going to be alright?" she stuttered between each one.

"You can't get rid of me that easily."

She embraced him, burrowing against his shoulder, and he stroked her back as he turned to Briar.

"Thank you for the rose."

Briar briefly raised his head and managed a weak nod.

Liam's gaze met mine, full of a brightness that had been absent for weeks as he'd slowly faded away. "And thank you for solving the mystery, my clever Rhea. You're now officially my favorite sister."

I laughed and hugged him. "I assure you, I did all this for purely selfish reasons—I can't imagine not having you around to tease me."

He glanced over my shoulder to where Drake stood next to Briar, whose head was buried in his hands, as if he was not only exhausted, but nursing a headache. "So this is the famous cursed man? You fell in love with a mirror, Rhea?"

I grinned. "I certainly did. It couldn't be helped; he was a rather charming mirror. You've never done something quite so unusual, have you?"

"I did something better—I survived a poisoning attempt." He gave my earlobe a playful tug before he turned to receive a hug from our parents. "Should we proclaim my achievement for everyone who's been worried?"

"Yes, of course." Mother brushed her lingering tears from her eyes as she pulled away from Liam, but Father shook his head, his expression serious.

"Your recovery must be kept a secret. Should the queen learn her attempts to secretly murder you have failed, I fear she'll do something more drastic. As such, you should pretend to still be gravely ill so as not to arouse her suspicions until we figure out how to deal with her."

Liam grinned widely, a grin that was so familiar and charming, but which had been absent throughout his illness. "Excellent, feigning a slow and agonizing death. Sounds like an adventure." He turned to Anwen. "Are you up for grieving a bit longer, sweetheart?"

She stared at him with glassy eyes before all her pent-up emotions escaped, as if she couldn't bear their burden any longer. She burst into tears and buried herself against Liam's chest. He held her tenderly, nestling against her hair as he rubbed her back.

"Oh Anwen, I know this has been terribly difficult for you, but it's over, so please don't cry. I'm really going to be alright. I've been saved at death's door, thanks to my clever sister, Prince Briar and his antidote, and undoubtedly that lucky goblet of mine. It'll be an epic story we can recount to our children."

She only continued to cry.

"I'm not sure I'd classify your goblet as *lucky*," I told him. "I suspect that's where the queen initially put the poison the night you fell ill. Your goblet is not only distinctive, but is used exclusively by you. It would have been very easy to taint it or your drink."

Liam gaped at me, looking almost more astonished at this revelation than the fact he'd been poisoned in the first place. But in typical Liam fashion, he recovered quickly. "Yes, but without that goblet, I'm sure I'd have succumbed to the poison sooner."

"Even so, we're not out of danger yet," Father said gravely. Liam raised an eyebrow in question. "It's imperative that no one learn of Anwen's pregnancy until the threat to our kingdom has passed. If the queen will go so far as to try to murder our crown prince, then she'll undoubtedly have no qualms of hurting the next in line: the future heir Anwen is carrying who will inherit over Rhea. We can't risk harm befalling her or the baby."

Anwen's hand instinctively lowered to her stomach while Liam looked murderous. He tried to get out of bed, as if determined to stop the queen right then and there, but Anwen gently pushed him back down.

"We can't just sit here," he said fiercely. "We have to stop her immediately."

That was easier said than done. We discussed ideas for several minutes until Liam's eyes began to droop, a symptom of his lingering illness that the antidote hadn't yet overcome. We all took our leave, Drake and me each taking one of Briar's arms to help him from the room.

Once in the corridor, Father rested his hand on my shoulder. "Well done, Rhea. I'm so proud of you. Can I trust you to help us uncover a way to stop the Queen of Malvagaria's sinister plot?"

I lifted my chin. "Of course."

He nodded, and with a fatherly smile he left with Mother to give the apothecary the tainted remedy Liam had been drinking in order to test it, leaving me with the two princes of Malvagaria. I turned to them. Despite my determination and having successfully uncovered many of the answers to the intrigue surrounding us, I felt so...lost.

Now what?

CHAPTER 32

"$\mathscr{H}$ow are we going to stop your mother?"

Drake, Briar, and I huddled in a secluded section of the library, engaged in yet another discussion on what to do, having stayed up all hours of the night exchanging ideas and now up early the following morning to continue. It had only been one day since giving Liam the antidote, and between that and discontinuing the poison-laced remedy, his health had already remarkably improved… while Briar's faded rapidly.

I watched him worriedly as he slumped in his seat before forcing himself to straighten. "I'm fine," he assured us for the dozenth time.

Drake frowned. "No, you're not."

He sighed wearily, conceding that point. "You're right, but we have to persevere, for we're running out of time. Not only can I not avoid Mother forever"—for the moment she saw him without his rose, she'd realize what we'd done and know that Liam was being healed—"but the wedding is tomorrow. If we don't stop her by then…"

I placed my hand on his arm. "I know we're running out of time, but please don't strain yourself."

He rested his hand over mine and squeezed it gently. "Thank you, Rhea. I appreciate your concern, but I assure you I can hold on awhile longer."

We exchanged small smiles, and when I turned away I noticed Drake was determinedly avoiding looking at us, as if doing so pained him. My heart wrenched in guilt at the heartache I was causing him.

"The wedding does put us on a much stricter deadline," Drake said. "Not to mention that Mother is bound to realize sooner or later that Liam's no longer being poisoned."

That was true. The more Liam's health improved, the more fantastic he found the idea he'd nearly been poisoned to death and the more fun he had pretending to still be deathly ill when anyone outside the family visited him. But while his performance was convincing, our joy was much more difficult to hide. Even if Liam continued acting ill indefinitely, the queen would quickly realize he was outliving the estimated time it took for her poison to work. Would she then choose another method of killing him?

"We have to stop her in such a way that she can't choose another means of accomplishing her plot," Briar said slowly. "As long as she's around, she'll find a way to annex Draceria, even if it takes her the rest of her life."

"It won't take that long," Drake said grimly. "Once the wedding takes place, she'll be closer to her end goal. What's then to stop her from murdering both Rhea and Liam?"

"It would be foolish for her to harm Rhea until we've secured the succession with the birth of an heir," Briar said. "Not to mention it'd be messier, which would harm our relations with the other kingdoms."

"Mother won't care about that," Drake argued. "Not when our already large and powerful army will be doubled in size after annexing Draceria. Malvagaria will be too great a force for her to care that the other kingdoms won't take too kindly to her taking land that doesn't belong to her."

Briar's expression grew more solemn. "And what's to stop her at just acquiring Draceria? She'll undoubtedly set her sights on the other kingdoms next, especially with two unwed daughters to marry into other royal families. In fact, I wouldn't be surprised if that's been her plan all along." He leaned his head back with a sigh. "This is going to be a disaster. If only we hadn't signed that engagement contract. She'll never agree to our breaking it."

I never would have imagined I'd one day end up in the same predicament Liam had found himself in with his own political arrangement—desperate for a loophole. But I knew there was no way out of mine so long as the queen remained a threat.

Which put us back at the original problem. "We don't have enough concrete evidence against your mother to stop her with the law, which means we have to find another way."

Drake frowned. "And I doubt we can do it before tomorrow's ceremony."

Briar reached for my hand. "I promise to be a good husband to you, Rhea, and to not only treat you like a queen, but to not allow Mother to hurt you."

I squeezed his hand and we exchanged another smile, all while I tried to ignore the miserable look filling Drake's expression. I hated hurting him, but unless we found a solution within the next twenty-four hours, this path was unavoidable. All that remained was navigating it as best as we could.

"Since our marriage is, at this point, likely inevitable, the best we can do is figure out how to keep Mother from annexing Draceria or hurting Rheanna," Briar said. "Liam is getting better, but we need to ensure she doesn't do anything else to get him out of the way."

"But we're powerless to stop that," Drake said. "Just as we were powerless to stop her when she cursed every one of her children."

"It seems to me," said a familiar voice, "that the best way to solve a problem such as this is to come up with an unconventional solution."

We spun around to see Aiden leaning against the bookshelves with a thoughtful expression. He stepped out of the shadows and bowed in greeting.

"Aiden! What are you doing here?" I asked.

He raised his eyebrows. "I'm here for your wedding, of course."

"You know that's not what I meant." I stood and hugged him. "Thank you for coming, and for your recent letters."

"Did they help?" he asked as he settled at our table.

"They did, but now we have a new dilemma." We quickly summarized the situation. Aiden whistled when we finished.

"That's quite a story, not to mention a rather large predicament."

"Do you have any ideas?" I asked. "We've thought this through for hours and can't see a way out of it."

He leaned back in his seat with a thoughtful frown. "Situations like this are precarious, for we're not just dealing with rulers but also the people under their protection. A monarch who cares for nothing but power and has the ability to curse others is a force to be reckoned with, and thus must be handled with extreme caution…and, like I mentioned earlier, unconventional means."

"What do you mean?"

"I mean: an opponent with as much power and ruthlessness as the Queen of Malvagaria can only be defeated when confronted with one equal to her in might, someone who can beat her at her own game."

Which wasn't us…or was it? I frowned, considering the puzzle from all angles. *An unconventional method…one equal in might…beating her at her own game.* As I thought, my gaze drifted around the library, settling on the gilded mirror hanging on the opposite wall. As I stared at it, the beginnings of a rash and strange idea formed in my mind.

I gasped, straightening with a jolt. The others all turned to me. "What is it, Rhea?" Drake asked.

My mind was whirling. "Drake, can you tell the story again about how you were cursed?"

His forehead furrowed in confusion but he humored me. "We were arguing about my needing to do my duty to our kingdom and woo Princess Elodie so we could have a double alliance with Draceria. I wasn't ready to settle down yet, and she got upset and cursed me."

"Can you tell me about the actual curse itself?" I asked. "How did she do it?"

Drake considered. "I could, but I'm not sure how helpful it'll be; I don't pretend to know much about magic or how Mother's powers work."

"I've done a bit of study in magic," Aiden said. "Shortly after my marriage, my wife's best friend created a love potion, and I became rather obsessed with the study of spells to see if there was a way to reverse it."

I smiled. Liam had told me *that* story many times. "What did you learn?"

"An individual's magical powers are usually limited to one source," he explained. "The Sortileyan Forest, for example, can only shift its pathways; Rosie's magic was limited to an enchanted recipe book of baked goods. I imagine the Queen of Malvagaria's is the same."

We turned to Drake and Briar for hopes of elaboration.

Briar was rubbing his temples—trying to ward off the headache that he'd had ever since sacrificing his rose so that he could focus—but Drake was thinking hard, his brow furrowed. His eyes suddenly widened.

"Of course...every one of Mother's spells share a key element." He leaned closer. "All her spells *trap*."

I wrinkled my nose. "*Trap?*"

"Yes. Gemma is in a tower, Reve is trapped inside her head...in a sense, I was in a mirror, and Briar—" He cut off his words at his brother's glare and cleared his throat. "Yes, well, Briar...is trapped as well." He said nothing more.

Briar was trapped too? *How?* I gave my fiancé an imploring look, silently begging him to divulge the details, and he sighed.

"Should our wedding go through tomorrow, I promise to tell you all about it, but until then, I'd like to keep it a secret." His hand instinctively went to where his rose used to be and he seemed frustrated that it wasn't there.

Although I was more curious than ever, the mystery of Briar's curse wasn't important now—stopping the queen was. And with Drake's information, I was confident my idea would work.

"There likely won't be a wedding tomorrow, for I think I know how we can stop the queen."

"I'm not so sure this is a good idea." Drake had been voicing his concern as we made our way towards the Hall of Mirrors where, after much searching the palace mirrors, he had found the Queen of Malvagaria.

"This is going to work," I said firmly. "It's as Aiden said —the only way to beat the queen at her own game is to play by her rules." Despite my outward confidence, I was rather nervous; anxiety tightened my chest with every step I took.

"That's not exactly how I said it," Aiden said as he kept pace with us, while Briar lagged behind.

"Well, that's how I interpreted it in order to come up with my rather ingenious plan."

"Yes, it is quite brilliant, but it's still risky. I can't bear the thought of her hurting you." If Drake hadn't looked so worried, I'd have been annoyed at his lack of faith in me. I paused in order to face him.

"I can do this, Drake; I *have* to do this." A quiet confidence I'd never quite experienced before filled my heart. After all I'd been through and overcome, I now knew I was strong and capable, enough to stop even the evil queen herself.

Drake's gaze seeped into mine before he stroked my cheek. "I know you can, Rhea, but I still worry for you."

"I know you care," I said. "But I'll be alright. I promise, so don't doubt me."

"Never." His gaze smoldered with his belief in me, one that only fueled my own.

We reached the Hall of Mirrors, where I would continue alone. My fingers had no sooner grazed the knob than Drake's feathery touch caressed my wrist, compelling me to turn to him. Despite the worry still filling his face, the tender way he looked at me was filled with complete faith.

"I wish I could go in with you."

"I know. But this is a battle I must face alone."

He stepped closer, his hand cradling my cheek, which he stroked with his thumb. "If the worst does happen, I'm sure the countercurse will be similar to what it was before. I'll free you, just as you freed me."

He started to lean down…but paused inches from my lips when Briar cleared his throat in warning.

Drake sighed and glanced at his brother imploringly.

"Please? I know your engagement isn't broken yet, but since you promised you'll do it once Mother is taken care of…"

Briar looked at us sternly for a moment before rolling his eyes good-naturedly. "Do what you will; soldiers always deserve a kiss before going into battle." He winked at me.

That was all Drake needed to hear. He closed the distance between us and kissed me softly and sweetly. I kissed him back, and wanted to keep kissing him forever, but in order to grant that wish, I would have to do what it took to claim him.

He broke the kiss and rested his forehead on mine. "I love you, Rhea."

"And I love you. We'll be together soon. After all, this will work."

"It will." Confidence filled his eyes. "I believe in you."

"I believe in me, too." That was what gave me my strength.

He kissed me one more time, as if he couldn't help himself, and then he released me. After a wavering breath, I entered the Hall of Mirrors.

THE QUEEN STOOD ALONE and poised, her gaze riveted to one of the gilded mirrors as she admired her reflection. At my entrance she slowly turned with an expectant look. With a flick of her wrist she dismissed her guard. The moment he closed the door behind him, she gave me her usual sickly sweet smile.

"Hello, Rheanna. To what do I owe this pleasure? Are you excited for your wedding tomorrow? As you know, I myself am *very* pleased."

My heart pounded, and for the first time since coming up with this plan I felt fear. But I forced myself to push it away. *You can do this, Rhea.*

"There isn't going to be a wedding tomorrow," I said. "I'd be a fool to align myself with a prince who's being controlled by a conniving puppet master. I refuse to risk the wellbeing of my kingdom."

The queen's eyes widened. "Such harsh words, Rheanna. Whatever did I do to deserve them?"

"Do you want a list?" I asked. "For I have one. You've been poisoning Liam in order to ensure I inherit the crown. You'll use my union with Briar as the claim you need to annex Draceria without bloodshed, after which there will be nothing stopping you from using your larger army to conquer the surrounding kingdoms, which has been your master plan since the beginning."

Her eyes widened and for a moment she seemed stunned into silence. Then her calculating eyes narrowed.

"So, you've figured it out, have you? Then I see no need to pretend any longer. You're right, I *am* poisoning Liam. It was the least messy way to get what I want. I'd hoped I would only need to commit one murder, but your knowledge of my plans has now put you in grave danger."

"I was already in grave danger," I said. "Do you think I'm naive enough to believe that you'll let me live after you've stolen my kingdom from me? I have no doubt you would poison me next. You've never liked me."

She smirked darkly. "Yes, I did think you were naive enough to believe that. And you're correct: after peacefully taking over Draceria, I'll have no further use for you— you're a weak, pathetic girl who would make a terrible queen."

My newfound confidence acted as a shield against her sharp words. "I'm not weak, and I'd make a fine queen. But that's not my destiny. Liam will be the next King of Draceria and I will marry Drake, for Briar and I are breaking our engagement."

The queen sneered. "You can't break your agreement. The contract—"

"Briar has agreed to terminate the contract," I said. "Now that he knows what you're up to, he'll no longer let you control him. With the King of Malvagaria currently unable to rule, Crown Prince Briar is the true regent, not you. As acting king, he has decided to null our engagement. You won't be able to steal my kingdom for your own selfish gains. Don't you see? You've lost."

"*Lost?* I never lose." Her smile became cruel as she took a sinister step closer. "You think you've won? Then you don't know what I'm capable of. Since you refuse to cooperate, I have no further use for you. I'll get rid of you and, after a bit of *persuasion*, I'll force Briar to unite with Aveline, a princess who knows how to do her duty and not put up a fuss. I should have chosen her from the beginning, but I thought it would look suspicious if I killed two royal children. Now I see I should have gone with my initial plan."

She advanced and I took a step back. "You can't kill me." My voice shook. "You just said it yourself: murder is so messy, not to mention suspicious. I'm not the only one who knows what you've been doing to Liam; harming me will only create more evidence against yourself. It's too risky."

"Yes, but having you *disappear* isn't." She raised her hand, palm up, and it began to glow red, just as Drake had described.

I widened my eyes in mock fear, although I wasn't at all afraid. "Wait, what are doing? You're…not going to trap me inside a mirror, are you?"

She grinned wickedly. "Hmm, that's not a bad idea. After all, there are so many in this room to choose from."

"You can't." I forced panic into my voice. "*Please.* Alright, you win. I'll go along with your scheme. Just don't—"

Her cold laugh cut me off. "I knew your newfound

bravery was all an act. You're pathetic. Do you really think I'll let you go so easily after you confronted me?"

I took another step back. "But if you trap me, Drake will only break the curse and—"

"Not if I trap him, too. He's proven a rather disappointing son. He only had one task to perform and he failed." She smirked. "But I'm not completely coldhearted. If you want to be with him so badly, perhaps I can trap you in the same mirror."

I backed up urgently. She laughed again, a chilling sound.

"Pathetic and weak, that's what you've always been. Your puny attempts are nothing compared to my power, as you'll soon see." She lifted her glowing hand. "Goodbye, Rheanna."

I braced myself as she twisted her wrist several times. After muttering a brief spell, she flung the curse, her blazing red magic directed straight for my heart, all as Drake had warned me about.

I acted immediately, whipping the hand mirror out from its hiding place within the folds of my dress and holding it up against my chest. It felt as if time slowed as the red stream of light reflected and bounced off the hundreds of mirrors in the room, creating the illusion that the magic was ricocheting, until it slammed against the mirror I held like a shield in front of my heart. The mirror vibrated roughly in my hand, and then it became searing hot, the heat and power intense; I almost dropped it, but I forced myself to hold on to it.

And then it was still. For a split second I feared it hadn't worked. But then the red magic vanished at the same instant the queen did, and an angry, defeated screech emanated from the now icy mirror. I stared at the back of the onyx-encrusted gold mirror I'd stolen from the queen's room before flipping it over to see her horrified expression staring back at me from within the glass. Relief and triumph washed over me.

"What did you *do?*" the queen shrieked.

"*I* didn't do anything," I said. "Your own curse trapped you—within your own mirror."

"Get me out this instant," she commanded.

"You got exactly what you deserved and have no one to blame for your circumstances but yourself. Surely after everything you've done, you'll understand why neither I nor anyone else will be keen on showing you any mercy." I headed for the door but paused to give the queen one final confident look. "One more thing: I'm not weak. I'm strong, and I'll never allow you or anyone else to tell me otherwise ever again."

At my words, she faded from the mirror.

I stepped out into the corridor, where not only Drake, Briar, and Aiden were waiting, but also my parents. They all looked at me anxiously and I held up the mirror with a grin.

"The problem of the scheming queen has been taken care of."

While Mother looked relieved, she wrung her hands. "Although I understand the severity of the situation, I'm worried for the repercussions of trapping another head of state."

"Even a monarch can't escape the consequences of their crimes," Father said gravely. "Especially considering she attempted to murder our crown prince. Trapping her not only serves justice but will protect the other kingdoms from her." He smiled proudly at me. "Well done, Rhea."

But his reaction, as sweet as it was, was nothing compared to Drake's. With a whoop, he seized me in a tight embrace, spinning me in his joy.

I smiled when he gently set me down. "I'm afraid your mother had to leave unexpectedly and will miss our wedding. Forgive me for failing to give my regrets over this turn of events."

He chuckled as his arms looped around my waist, tugging me closer. "Snarky, Rhea. You surprise me. So long as I get to marry you, I don't care who's at our wedding."

I rested my hands on his shoulders and stared adoringly up at him. "I'm so happy that you're now my groom. From now on, I'll always choose you, every day for the rest of our lives." And I stood on tiptoe to seal the promise with a kiss.

"*A*re you ready to slip away, Rhea darling?"

I glanced at my new husband, whose adoring gaze was filled with mischief. I tried to look stern. "You're no longer in a mirror, dear, and thus can't get away with your usual poor mirror etiquette."

He chuckled and squeezed my hand, which he held beneath the banquet table. "Considering it's our wedding and we're the guests of honor, I'm sure our faux pas will be forgiven."

I smiled. It was my wedding, the same wedding I'd planned with Briar, only the groom wasn't him but instead the man I loved.

Briar had wasted no time as the acting ruler of his kingdom in terminating our engagement contract and drawing up a new one: an alliance between Draceria and Malvagaria made possible by my marriage to the younger prince. He'd explained to my parents that although I was a lovely woman who'd make a fine queen, he couldn't in good conscience go through with a union that had been part of the

Queen of Malvagaria's scheme to annex our kingdom, especially when his fiancée was in love with his brother.

"You're really in love with Drake?" Mother had asked me, her eyes bright as she took in our entwined hands.

I looked at Drake and marveled at the tenderness seeping from his expression. "I am. He makes me a better person." For he helped me see my worth so I could believe in myself. As Liam had once told me, such a man was the best match of all.

The ceremony had taken place this morning and now we were enjoying a splendid wedding breakfast. Briar left immediately following the ceremony to return to Malvagaria —taking the mirror with his mother inside—and had assured me that he would be well once he returned to his enchanted gardens. Down the table, Liam—still recovering but continuously growing healthier and stronger with each administration of the antidote—sat with Anwen, telling everyone who would listen about his near poisoning.

"I was almost The King Who Never Was," he told Aiden brightly. "I bet *you* haven't survived a poisoning." His expression was rather smug.

Aiden grinned. "I'm afraid I haven't. I'll leave that adventure exclusively to you."

Liam's own grin widened as his arm tightened around Anwen, who couldn't stop smiling and looking adoringly at her husband. "It was quite the adventure. I was drinking several pots of poisoned tea every day. If it weren't for my strong will to live and my lucky goblet, I may have succumbed sooner. I'll undoubtedly have a long, prosperous reign. I bet I outlive you."

Aiden raised an eyebrow. "Is that a challenge?"

"It certainly is."

He and Aiden laughed good-naturedly, while Anwen and Eileen gave one another fond, indulgent looks.

Drake chuckled beside me. "That story won't be good for Malvagaria's foreign relations."

"Likely not, not to mention it's one I have a feeling we'll be hearing many times over the years."

We exchanged amused smiles before Drake's gaze settled on Eileen, who held her son on her lap. He leaned towards my ear.

"Is that the common girl who won Deidric's Princess Competition? I'll have to personally thank her for breaking up your engagement so I could marry you myself." He continued studying her. "Well, I'm afraid seeing her confirms one thing: Deidric is an idiot, although in this instance, I'm grateful for his lapse of judgement." He gave my hand another squeeze.

I slapped his arm playfully. "Be nice, she's a lovely girl."

"You're superior, darling." He kissed my temple.

At that moment, Aiden looked away from Liam and glanced towards me. We shared a friendly smile before he turned back to his wife and son.

Drake's expression became solemn as he watched the exchange. "Are you still upset about your broken engagement?"

"Not at all," I said. "We're better off as friends. Besides, I wasn't a good fit with either of my past fiancés, and ending things with them allowed me to find my true match. Just think: if Briar hadn't come to court me, I may never have been led to your enchanted mirror."

Drake grinned crookedly. "That's not true. I'd have found you, somehow, even if I had to lure you all the way to Malvagaria. If your union with either Deidric or Briar had gone through, things would have gotten quite messy when I stole you from them."

I rolled my eyes, but I was smiling. "More poor mirror etiquette, dear? Although I admit it would have been amusing to watch an army led by a mirror. Tell the story to Liam; he'll love it."

"Maybe later; I'd rather have my attention eclipsed by you." Drake swept a kiss across my cheek. "My initial invitation stands. I won't apologize for my poor mirror etiquette, especially if you allow me to indulge in it now so I can steal you away."

"From our own reception?" I asked teasingly.

He grinned, stood, and held out his hand. I accepted it, allowing him to help me from my seat and tuck my arm through his.

Mother and Father looked up with frowns of disapproval. "You can't be leaving already?"

"I'm afraid I must insist on it, Your Majesty," Drake said. "Having spent most of our relationship either with me trapped in a mirror or having Rhea engaged to someone else, now that she's my wife I'm feeling rather selfish."

Mother looked as if she was about to protest, but Father chuckled and waved us off. "Go on, you two."

Drake unhooked our arms to lace his hand with mine and lead me outside into the gardens, awash in the colors of autumn and the last blossoms before winter arrived.

I lifted my wedding gown so I could more easily keep up with Drake's brisk pace. "Where are we going?"

He flashed a mischievous smile. "You'll see."

Of course it turned out to be the orchard. Nearly all the leaves had fallen, creating a multicolored carpet on the ground, but the enchanted apples still hung from the branches. Drake slowed and, still holding my hand, led me through the trees.

"I love it here," I said reverently.

"As do I. It's our special place—where we became friends and fell in love, I tried to sabotage your relationship with Briar, we shared our first kiss, nearly ran away together..."

He paused beneath my favorite tree, where my name was carved into the trunk. He pulled out a small dagger from his boot and handed it to me.

I grinned as I took it and carefully carved Drake's name in the bark beneath mine. When I finished, I straightened and admired the effect of having my name enclosed in a heart with Drake's. His arms looped around me from behind.

"I love the way that looks."

"We'll have to carve our names on a tree at our new home in Malvagaria," I said. "After we plant an orchard, of course."

"Of course. It'll be a new tradition, one I hope will allow you to feel at home there." He turned me in his arms and I stood on tiptoe to lightly kiss him. He glanced above us with a mischievous grin as we pulled away. "I fancy an apple. I'll race you to get it."

He released me and jumped up to grab the lowest branch in order to hoist himself up.

"Drake, I can't climb after you in my *wedding dress*."

He peered down with a rather wicked grin. "Of course you can, my tree-climbing princess. But as one of your wedding gifts, I'll forgo mirror etiquette and be a proper gentleman by giving you a head start."

I pulled myself into the tree and carefully maneuvered my way through the branches until I climbed past Drake. He allowed me to before following close behind. We settled cozily in the tree and I plucked an apple from the branch to bite into it, allowing its tart sweetness to envelop me.

"Would you like some?"

He accepted the apple, but rather than taking a bite, he crawled closer, a purposeful glint in his eyes. He pulled me into a sweet kiss, one full of such love and desire. I grinned against his lips.

I am loved.

We didn't pull away for a very long time, and when we

finally did we pressed our foreheads together, both breathless. He smiled softly and caressed my cheek. "I'm going to love being married to you."

"Things have turned out quite wonderfully so far," I said.

"And they'll only get better." He kissed me again, this time on my brow. "I can't wait to show you off in Malvagaria. The gardens at the older palace aren't enchanted like they are at the main palace, which I know will disappoint you considering Briar nearly wooed you with them."

I wrapped my arms around his neck. "Then you know I must really love you if I want you even without those fabulous gardens."

"We'll plant an orchard," he said again, as if thinking I needed a reminder.

"You sure know how to please your wife." I lifted the apple. "To celebrate, shall we finish this off?" I'd no sooner taken a bite than I pulled him into another kiss, one which he enthusiastically returned.

Love had never tasted so sweet.

ALSO BY CAMILLE PETERS

Pathways

Inspired by "The Princess and the Pea" and "Rumpelstiltskin"

Spelled

Inspired by "The Frog Prince"

Identity

Inspired by "The Goose Girl"

THANK YOU

Thank you for allowing me to share one of my beloved stories with you! If you'd like to be informed of new releases, please visit me at my website www.camillepeters.com to sign up for my newsletter, see my release plans, and read deleted scenes—as well as a scene written from Drake's POV.

I love to connect with readers! You can find me on Goodreads, Instagram, or on my Facebook Page.

If you loved my story, I'd be honored if you'd share your thoughts with me and others by leaving a review on Amazon or Goodreads. Your support is invaluable. Thank you.

Coming Soon:

Prince Briar's story, *Thorns*, inspired by *Beauty and the Beast*.

ACKNOWLEDGMENTS

I'm so incredibly grateful for all the wonderful people who've supported me throughout my writing adventures.

First, to my incredible mother, who's worn many hats over the years: from teaching me to read as a toddler; to recognizing my love and talent for writing and supporting it through boundless encouragement and hours of driving me back and forth to classes to help nourish my budding skills; to now being my muse, brainstorm buddy, beta-reader, editor, and my biggest cheerleader and believer of my dreams. I truly wouldn't be where I am without her and am so grateful for God's tender mercy in giving me such a mother.

Second, to my family: my father, twin brother Cliff, and darling sister Stephanie. Your love, belief in me, and your eager willingness to read my rough drafts and help me develop my stories has been invaluable. Words cannot express how much your support has meant to me.

Third, to my publishing team: my incredible editor, Jana Miller, whose talent, insights, and edits have helped my stories blossom into their potential; and Karri Klawiter, whose talented designs not only continue to amaze me, but who was willing to return to make changes to this cover long after it was completed.

Fourth, to my wonderful beta readers: my dear Grandma, Charla Stewart, Alesha Adamson, Mary Davis, and Emma Miller. I'm so grateful for your wonderful insights and suggestions that gave my story the last bit of polish in order to make it the best it can be. In addition, I'd like to thank all my ARC readers, who were so willing to give my book a chance and share their impressions. Thank you.

Fifth, to my Grandparents, whose invaluable support over the years has helped my dreams become a reality.

Last but not least, I'd like to thank my beloved Heavenly Father, who has not only given me my dreams, talent, and the opportunities to achieve them, but who loves me unconditionally, always provides inspiration whenever I turn to Him for help, gives me strength to push through whatever obstacles I face, and has sanctified all my efforts to make them better than my own.

ABOUT THE AUTHOR

Camille Peters was born and raised in Salt Lake City, Utah where she grew up surrounded by books. As a child, she spent every spare moment reading and writing her own stories on every scrap of paper she could find. Becoming an author was always more than a childhood dream; it was a certainty.

Her love of writing grew alongside her as she took local writing classes in her teens, spent a year studying Creative Writing at the English University of Northampton, and graduated from the University of Utah with a degree in English and History. She's now blessed to be a full-time author.

When she's not writing she's thinking about writing, and when's she's not thinking about writing she's...alright, she's always thinking about writing, but she can also be found reading, playing board games with her family and friends, or taking long, bare-foot walks as she lives inside her imagination and brainstorms more tales.

Made in the USA
Middletown, DE
01 January 2022

57435053R00253